PATHS OF FORTUNE

PATHS
OF FORTUNE

Susan Moore

St. Martin's Press
New York

Library of Congress Cataloging in Publication Data

Moore, Susan, 1944–
 Paths of fortune.

 I. Title.
PR6063.O644P3   1985   823'.914   85-11816
ISBN 0-312-59799-1

First published in Great Britain by William Collins Sons & Co. Ltd.

First U.S. Edition

10 9 8 7 6 5 4 3 2 1

Chapter One

That day, as it dawned, seemed more like a beginning than an end.

The village and the downs behind were caught within a web of light in which everything was still. Though the dawn chorus had dwindled, it was too early yet for the first breeze of the day. The dim masses of the elms in the fields were as motionless as the cattle asleep beneath them. Throughout the Vale only the shallow streams were moving, twinkling so gently that on their bed a moorhen's footprint might stay unchanged from night till noon. In Cannings Fitzpayne there was no smoke from any chimney, and the surface of the village pond lay unbroken by the swallows beginning to twitter in barns and outhouse roofs. Soon the first field labourers would be about – many of the women carrying babies, the men bow-legged from working since childhood knee-deep in mud. But now the rutted high road through the village was empty, and in nearby farms there was scarcely the sound of a dog growling in his sleep.

Down the Vale lay a different scene. Hitherto no one in Wiltshire had even imagined such a thing. Below the white horse carved on the down a thousand years before to mark King Alfred's victory against the Danes, a larger army now advanced. Water meadows and orchards were overlaid by a spill of dirty tents, turf shanties, and shelters made from canvas, branches, bales of straw, loose barrel-staves, piles of bricks or bits of wattle fencing. Along the line of the new canal, the earth was laid open to show layers of chalk, or clay, cobalt blue when sliced bare and later turning brown. A cottage, its outhouse smashed in half, stood above a cutting as though lifted by a wave of the sea. Farther on an unfinished embankment, its flanks streaming spoil, ran its head toward a rise, for all the world as if one hill were charging at another.

The place was a virtual city; and by daybreak every

5

inhabitant was out of doors. The sun struck brightness from a thousand surfaces – random pits of water; picks and shovels noisily at work; the wheels of wagons squealing along a wooden railway; the harness of the horses pulling them; and whiffs of steam from makeshift forges. A stream, diverted, had flooded around a temporary brickworks, whose smoke mingled with that of cooking fires and hung over half the plain. Whatever might stand in the way of the canal, its progress seemed irresistible.

Lawyer Byford's house stood in Cannings Fitzpayne, amid newly planted grounds beside the high road. In the attics and stables none of the servants were awake. But behind the windows where the Miss Byfords slept, someone was.

Sophy could wait no longer for the day to start. Though the world outside was damp and pale, already it was too warm to stay in bed. Everyone would have to get up early anyway, to see papa off on his journey. Not wanting to wait until the maid was due, she dressed by herself, leaving her heavy baby-blonde hair tumbled loose to her waist. At one of the windows to her room she turned back the shutter. Beyond the lawn and shrubberies was the garden wall and a lane; beyond that, the tussocks and hawthorn thickets of Cannings Fitzpayne Common. In the brightening air every shape was flat and faint. The most distant thing in sight was the church spire above the market square at Upstowe, two miles beyond the trees of Lord Fitzpayne's deerpark.

Now she was up, how could she pass the time? What time was it, anyway? Sophy had scurried out of bed two, maybe three hours early to taste the prospect of a new summer day. And now she had no idea what to do with it. Would anyone else in the house ever be awake again?

Wrapping herself in a shawl she paused as always before the marvellous creature, sweetly disarrayed, that looked at her from the mirror. She slipped out onto the landing and tiptoed past the rooms where her parents, brother and elder sister slept.

At the tall window in the stairwell she paused ...

Three men were coming out of the trees on the common. The early light made them insubstantial, and only by looking hard did Sophy understand why they looked so strange. One of them, supported by the others, could hardly walk.

It was the wrong time of day to see a man dead drunk. With his feet half dragging on the ground, he looked like a drowned man carried upright by an underwater current. Sophy watched them pass out of sight into the lane. And reappear – through the side gate in the garden wall. Two of them, including the man being helped along, looked like navvies from the new waterway beyond Upstowe. Both were as muddy as plough horses. She stared again at the man, whose companions were half carrying him toward the house – then saw his clothes darkened with blood.

She ran – and, breathless, opened the scullery door as the other man with them was about to knock. Like the injured navvy, he was almost a boy. His thick fair hair and good clothes were plastered with filth. It took a moment for Sophy to recognize him.

'Mr Fraser!'

He looked at Sophy without acknowledging her. 'The doctor's been sent for. I need something to use as bandages until he arrives.' They made their way past her into the kitchen. 'Put him on the big table,' he told the other man.

'No one's out of bed,' said Sophy, meaning whoever of the servants should surely cope with this. Taking another look she added hurriedly, 'But I can help.' Close to, the injured youth appeared even worse. His dirty velvet waistcoat and torn breeches were heavy with blood. Though his eyes were tightly shut, she could see he was near to spilling tears of fright. Fraser undid the boy's shirt and turned it back. The wound was more ugly than menacing. It made a wet red hole, already brown about the rim, above his collarbone.

Sophy tugged the bell for the housekeeper's room and ran on next door to where she thought the laundry might be stored. She had almost no idea how things were arranged in this part of the house. Throwing open every cupboard door, she pulled out their contents until the stone floor was deep in crumpled sheaves of fresh linen. What could she best tear up? Finding some of her brother's satin neckwear she thought of his hunting stocks. Hadn't George said – hinting at his bravado in the field – that they could always serve as a bandage or sling? She rummaged further, casting a heap of clean shirts into a corner of the floor, and found what she was looking for.

Fraser was sluicing his hands clean at the scullery pump. 'Is this what you need?' she asked. Taking it without a word, he started tearing up poor George's stock. Sophy watched as he set about making a bandage. She'd never met him before to speak to, and was surprised to guess he couldn't be more than two or three years older than herself. It seemed strange that at twenty or so he should have charge of several hundred navvies.

'Where's the other man who came with you?' she asked.

'Gone to see the doctor finds us.'

'How did this man suffer such a terrible accident? – Oh!' She gasped as he seized her by the arm and motioned her to silence.

'He's not so badly hurt,' he said, speaking partly for the injured man's benefit. ' ... And this,' he added in a contained voice, 'was not an accident.'

Sophy looked at him. She'd taken his manner to mean nothing more than urgency. But now she realized he was breathless with anger.

'It can't have been!' she exclaimed, round-eyed. 'Did you see who did it?'

'One of Lord Fitzpayne's men – No, I didn't. But we wouldn't have been surveying by night if we weren't on disputed land. It's my fault this happened – I should have taken more men. We'd have been a match for them then.'

Sophy was silent, turning over the thought of pitched battle beyond her papa's new shrubbery.

'Miss Sophia!'

It was Mrs Cudlipp, the housekeeper. She wore curl-papers and a look of injury. Apparently it was Sophy's

8

fault her scrubbed kitchen table bore a wounded man, dirty enough to have been dug out of a grave.

'Miss Sophy!' she exclaimed from beyond the doorway. Sophy hurried up to her. 'Who are those men?'

'Mrs Cudlipp, you know perfectly well who Mr Fraser is.'

'I don't mean you to tell me who they are. What I want to know is, why are they in my kitchen?'

'Surely you don't expect me to answer such a question!'

'But think of your father!'

'Whatever for?'

Fraser, tying the bandage, looked up in Sophy's direction. 'Do you want to go for your father,' he said, 'or shall I? One of us will have to ask him to settle all this,' motioning at the housekeeper.

Mrs Cudlipp turned purple and retreated. Sophy followed and found her in murmured conference on the stairs with Mrs Byford.

'Sophy! Sophy!' Her mother signalled from the landing in a stage whisper as Mrs Cudlipp made a conspicuous exit. 'Sophy! Your father's a lawyer! He can't have men bleeding here!'

'Why ever not, mama?'

'Now you're not to ask things like that. Besides, you ought to have sent for your father or I, since he's the man in this establishment. And letting navvies in! Don't you know they're all heathens who sleep with their boots on?'

Thomas Byford appeared, half dressed. 'What's this, then?' He was a robust, handsome man who bore himself, among womenfolk, with authority.

His wife, after her fashion, explained.

'But Dr Brown should be sent for!'

'He has, papa.'

Byford was irked that he had not been there to show mastery of the situation from the start. 'Are you sure? Who told you he had?'

'Mr Fraser has sent a man.'

'Fraser the engine-wright is here,' Mrs Byford broke in, 'and by all accounts he looks as if he's just walked right through Bassett Brook.'

9

'Is he now? – the girl had better be right about the doctor – Young Fraser, is it? Well, good God – I'm a shareholder in his company, am I not? Can't you show him some kind of acknowledgement? With what I've got invested, I'm damn nearly his main employer.'

'You mean have him offered something to eat in the kitchen?'

'In the parlour, woman!'

'Thomas, do you think we should? If he's waited on with us, the servants could find it very confusing.'

'Nonsense! He's a rising man. He goes astride better horseflesh than I do.'

'I know he's been away. But people here still remember. From when he couldn't even read, you know.'

The doctor's arrival put an end to this dilemma. The injured navvy was pronounced not too badly hurt to be conveyed back to his lodging in Upstowe; and Thomas was able to show he was in charge after all, by insisting that the lad was taken there in the Byfords' own carriage.

Fraser stayed only long enough to discuss the doctor's fee. It was Thomas, however, who insisted on paying. He was not acting entirely from self-importance – behind his bluster there really did dwell a generous spirit. 'The poor fellow got his injury – not a dangerous wound, I grant you – I agree, not dangerous, but an injury for all that – he got his hurt pursuing my own interest as a major shareholder.'

In the breakfast room with his family, Thomas continued to savour his good deed. 'And I can tell you,' looking from under his brows as he paused in carving, 'if it was one of Lord Fitzpayne's keepers that winged him, he can't look to the law for recompense.' As usual he addressed young George, as the other man of the house. 'Fair or not,' for emphasis pointing at George with the knife, 'that's a sound piece of legal information I'm giving you.' Thomas liked an audience, and his voice rang out all the more confidently for the room being full – even though the butler, the manservant and the two parlourmaids were supposed to act as though they weren't there.

They were at table early, on account of his departure. He was to go post into Gloucestershire, to the seat of a wealthy client, before returning to do business together with his cousin in a neighbouring town. It was something of an occasion for him to be travelling to another county; and the prospect had Mrs Byford a little downcast. She was distressed, too, that her husband had yet another scheme for investment. In recent years he had speculated in roadmaking, in the wagon trade, in tin, in spirits, in corndealing and – with particular enthusiasm, and less success than ever – in horseflesh. Now, with the approach of the canal and cheap transport, he planned to borrow from his cousin and augment his income by trading in timber imported from Virginia. Mrs Byford frowned across the new inlaid mahogany table, on which every shining piece of ware looked both heavy and fragile. 'I cannot understand why your cousin won't conduct your joint affairs for you.' Even at this hour she looked neat, in the way very busy people mostly do. Few might have guessed, though, that she was once as pretty – no, as striking – as her daughters, both of whom – dark Kate as well as Sophy – had a grace and slenderness that suggested formidable strength. By comparison her husband was almost youthful; but then the disappointments of their marriage had nearly all been suffered by her. His most recent adultery ... the girl had died a few months later. Of a fever of the brain, so the lie had been given out ... And worse than that, she had been of respectable family: the daughter of a corn-factor from Upstowe. For days after the scandal of that death, few people had dared address Thomas to his face. Had his abominable rage been from guilt, or grief; a grudge against the girl for getting with child and then showing him up – or from mere embarrassment at the rumours surrounding the hussy's last disgusting hours of life?

'Uncle Norton isn't free, mama,' Sophy replied. 'He has to do committee work and help save the new canal.'

'Look you here, miss,' Thomas said. 'There'll be no talk of saving anything. We can't afford uncertainty among the other investors.'

'Sophy means, papa, he has to help advance its progress,' said Kate. By contrast with her sister, she was a patient, subtle creature whose mild manner and serene disposition made everything she said or did carry authority. Even as a little girl she had humoured her elders – and now that she was nineteen not even Thomas – did he but know it – cared to contradict her. It was in Sophy that one sensed motion and change – though toward what, who might tell at this stage of her life, any more than one can guess the strength of a current by the lights shooting from its surface?

'Papa, will a timber yard help to make us so very rich?' Sophy asked.

'Shush, dear, and don't harass your father,' said Mrs Byford.

Sophy frowned – in someone with her infant softness of feature and diamond-bright health even this was delightful – but she couldn't have said whether her mother protested from feminine delicacy at talk of business, or from distrust of her husband's commercial judgement. Privately none of Thomas's family shared his high opinion of himself: not bookish Kate; nor Sophy, heedlessly clever; not even George, as yet hardly grown enough to promise good looks. As for Mrs Byford, from various signs, as a dog can tell his owners are about to go away, she had guessed what even the servants knew for certain. Thomas's legal practice had almost no clients among the local gentry. And among the professional men and tradespeople of Upstowe it was solid enough only for the present.

'But if the canal is halted?' Sophy continued, impatient of her mother. 'Could you still trade by road, papa? And what about the money from Mr Fraser's contractors? Wouldn't it take a lot of timber, just to help build his part of the waterway?'

George, wolfing boiled ham with motions of his entire body, paused and looked up. 'Old Fitzpayne would never let the canal company into his park. And no wonder he won't do business with Fraser anyway, when the fellow's grandson to his own housekeeper!'

'And even if Lord Fitzpayne died,' Sophy broke in, 'I

12

know for certain that that land would never be inherited by anyone who'd sell it.'

'And don't we all wonder how you know that?' leered George. To no one in particular, 'Sophy's been talking with swell Rawley Fitzpayne again,' he confided.

Sophy turned pink. She knew she should have said nothing; but the temptation to make *some* reference to his lordship's heir – to hear the subject spoken of by somebody, if only herself – was too great.

'Sophy, you haven't, have you now?' Mrs Byford tried to avoid her husband's look as she spoke.

'Of course I have, mama.' Sophy's tone rose all the steadier for the sight of Thomas's swelling rage. Of them all, only she was unafraid of him. 'But you must not think –'

'Yes?' shouted her father, in a voice that could be heard all the way to the kitchens.

'– that either Mr Fitzpayne or I have been mixing –'

'*Yes?*'

'– with someone of unsuitable rank!' Sophy's eyes glinted as she spoke, elated with anger. She felt a yard taller than anyone else in the room.

Thomas drew back his hand, as if about to send a ringing blow against the side of his daughter's head. One of the maids, changing plates, hesitated rather than step too close.

'Thomas, you're going away today!' pleaded Mrs Byford.

He turned to glower at his luckless wife, but heeded her nonetheless.

Sophy, though, would not be put down. 'Not everyone in Cannings Fitzpayne,' in a lower voice, 'is too obscure or tedious for him to know.'

'Harriet!' bawled Thomas. Having missed his cue to assert himself as a parent, he rounded on his wife. 'By God, you will see these damned children behave themselves while I'm away or – by God, I don't know what I'll do! You, miss – and you too – you, yes – Harriet, if ever I hear that one of these wretched girls is making eyes at anyone above her place – or if I find that one of them is flirting with that damned young fornicator –'

'Oh, now Thomas!' protested Mrs Byford, at his language rather than his hypocrisy.

'Yes, goddammit, with that fornicating young dog – they can count themselves damned fortunate if I allow them out across the way to church.'

'I think, sir,' said Kate, 'Sophy only meant to mention George's acquaintance with Mr Fitzpayne.'

'Yes, yes, of course,' exclaimed their mother, avoiding Sophy's eyes. 'That's what she meant. And she knows as well as anyone that hunting together doesn't make George his intimate. That's what she really meant to say.'

Rather than show disdain for his wife, Thomas was silent. He knew that regardless of everything his family was fond of him; and he wanted to part with them on cheerful terms.

The breakfast parlour was left to be cleared; and soon afterward the wheels of Thomas's hired chaise were heard in the drive. While Kate took it on herself to direct the menservants with the luggage, the rest of the family loitered in the big drawing room. Against the sunlight on the wet lawns and tidy gravel walks outside, this side of the house was still cool and dim. Above one of the three tall windows, sparrows were chattering and a wood pigeon could be heard. Across the common, and in the fields and park beyond, fainter, and then fainter still with distance, sounded the day's new birdsong.

It felt strange to be confronted with anything so unfamiliar as a leavetaking.

'Poor mama,' said Sophy, seeing her mother so much less brisk than usual. 'We shall have to make a great fuss of you now, you know.'

Mrs Byford submitted with a blush of gratitude to her daughter's embrace. Kate, with her quiet ways and sly sense of humour, had the more sense. But ever since Sophy had reached her fourteenth year or so, it was her younger daughter to whom she had begun to defer.

All was made ready, and the family gathered round Thomas Byford, flustered and sad, to say goodbye.

'Now, young George, you're to be kind to your mother and sisters.'

George turned red and moved his feet around and felt melancholy at the thought of spending time in a house full of women.

'Goodbye, my two lovely girls,' Thomas said, embracing them with mingled vanity and affection.

Mrs Byford clung to her husband, past resentments dulled by regret at his going. 'You silly lady, don't cry,' he said, and kissed her on the head before hurrying – for the sun would soon be well up – under the portico and into the high draughty privacy of the yellow post-chaise. The door slammed; the post-boy, astride the nearside horse, whipped up his nags; and they heaved into motion. For a moment longer his family were all visible, Sophy with an arm about her mother. Then the chaise turned through the gates onto the high road, and Thomas was borne away, toward fresh schemes, and new prospects for his family.

It was not the only departure from Lawyer Byford's house that day. In the evening, his family had an engagement. The Byford girls were apt to grumble at how few people they knew; and certainly since they'd come home from boarding school in the county town their lives had been dreary rather than tranquil. In the Vale, where they lived, for days on end the nearest thing to violent motion might be the sailing of clouds in a summer sky. In Cannings Fitzpayne itself, apart from their father, only the parson and his curate read a newspaper, shared between the three of them, to follow the course of the war with Bonaparte. And throughout the village, every day mothers put out babies and young children to play in the dirt of the high road, confident that nothing more terrible or astonishing than a dung cart was likely to pass that way.

But the family did live in enough style to dine with a few others of the same rank throughout the district. So, before the heat of that day had quite gone, Mrs Byford and her children could be seen stepping up into the carriage in evening clothes: George not looking old

15

enough for what he wore, and the girls slight and gauzy with jewels in their hair.

They were bound for a select party in an establishment a short way beyond Upstowe. Their road took them through the village, a scatter of overcrowded thatched cottages built from timber frames and brick nogging. Across a scrubby green where geese grazed were the almshouses, the gift of a former Lord Fitzpayne. In a niche on their low brick front stood the statues of two Quakerish charity children, and a plaque declaring that they had been built to sustain eight old men of the parish, eight old women and six orphans. Mrs Byford looked the other way as they were driven past. What mightn't her unfaithful husband have done to help fill that place?

The village ended with a tithe barn the size of a cathedral. Next to it stood the church, a solid Norman building with a short square tower and a massive semi-circular south door whose carvings were ancient enough to look almost pagan. And one fierce, tiny female figure was notorious throughout several parishes for being very obscene indeed. The churchyard lay within the park of Cannings Fitzpayne Hall, so that the little church stood overtopped in a landscape of oaks and English elms. Beneath the boughs of the great trees, where the deer had reached up and browsed to the height of a man's head, the foliage appeared perfectly horizontal; and at one point under this upside-down leafy horizon, the Hall itself could be glimpsed.

It represented well the fortunes of its successive owners. Over six centuries, by bloodshed or guile, the Fitzpaynes had risen in the world. As they did so the land within the moat had been built on by stages, until by Jacobean times the walls rose sheer from the water on every side. The Great Hall, the even loftier kitchens, and the little barrel-roofed chapel dated from an era of the Middle Ages when London was a village. The east front, where the draw-bridge stood, was Elizabethan, a fantastical terracotta whim under a skyline of monstrous chimneys in sculptured brick. It was climaxed by a deliberately old-fashioned gatehouse with pepperpot towers.

But the house stood as a mere detail within the deer-park itself. An avenue of bushy-trunked limes, planted in the seventeenth century by a Fitzpayne ennobled for betraying James II, led a mile to the family's Baroque mausoleum beneath a knoll on the summit of the downs. The newest thing in sight, made two generations back by Capability Brown, was the lake. This lay some way from the house beneath a steep hangar of beech trees. Placed to look like a bend in a mighty river, it formed a slender crook of water nearly a mile long.

For much of the way to Upstowe the road was shadowed by trees overhanging the eight-foot wall around the park. As the Byfords' carriage passed Park End Wood and came into open country the coachman could be heard shouting a greeting to someone up ahead. They overtook a cart laden with brushwood and barrels of tar: fuel for the lookout's signal, standing, as in the wait in 1588 for the Armada, up on Hychpen Beacon. It was some years since the war in Europe had first threatened an invasion, and there had been successive scares, as fleets were assembled for the purpose across the Channel at Boulogne. Notices had been nailed up in the church porch describing arrangements for the south coast to be evacuated if the French should finally attack. For fifteen miles inland crops would be burned and cattle driven north; and plans had been read from every pulpit for moving women and children without blocking the roads to southbound troops.

From racketing along before a cloud of dust the carriage was forced almost to a halt. Several dozen swine lolloped around it, driven on their way toward new stubbles by a barefoot girl who whistled at them and urged them on with a switch of hazel.

The sight of her cast Mrs Byford into confusion and dismay – for an instant she had had the illusion of seeing one of her own children in rags. Kate, was it? Sophy?

In any place as small as Cannings Fitzpayne, a cheated wife was apt to imagine likenesses where none existed . . . So Mrs Byford told herself, as she was driven on into Upstowe's broad main street. Certainly the girl had given her an instant's surprise. And without a doubt it had been young Charity Michaelmas. She had been surnamed after the day the almshouse-keeper's wife had found her, a baby a few hours old, wrapped in rags and nearly dead. According to one rumour, the infant's weakening cries had been ignored by two or three respectable women passers-by, for fear that they themselves should be suspected of having borne her.

But then why, Mrs Byford thought, should she be put in mind of either of her daughters? The girl's body, so delicately formed for someone raised for menial work, the graceful set of the dark head as though a burden were balanced on it – none of this was extraordinary in any of ten thousand girls lucky enough to spend part of her life looking like some kind of miracle. No; it was simply that in thinking of her husband she fancied evidence of his betrayals everywhere.

Beyond Upstowe, the road, its hedges white with dust, held westward toward Bradford-on-Avon. On either side of the Vale rode grassy, whale-like downs, marked by the shadows of clouds. Here and there, like a cloud fallen to earth, grazed a flock of sheep. In the Vale itself wheatfields lay between elms darkened by weeks of summer heat. Lines of harvest workers moved in ragged unison, leaving a pattern of cone-shaped stooks of corn. Across this warm quiet expanse the loudest sound was that of human voices, rising in a murmur out of every other field.

A short way from their destination Mrs Byford began to fidget. 'Sophy, you will remember, won't you, who should have precedence into the dining room? And, George –'

'What's that infernal stink?' said George.

Kate had noticed it too. 'It smells like a city! Out here?'

The sudden stench of over-used latrines was like the casting of a vile enchantment. But then, over another little summit, and there were the workings. Miles of them.

And here, too, was their neighbours' house. It had been built, not many years before, with a view over several miles of country. Its gardens, planted with the latest fashion in trees, were halfway to maturity. Scots pine and hollies screened the kitchens and the stable block, and the

18

lawn was dotted with acacias. Beside the pretty conservatory a weeping willow stood nearly as high as the house.

But a dozen paces from the carriage entrance to the house lay the bed of the canal. From out of a great gulf of dirt a line of wooden barrow-runs reared up like pieces of siege machinery into the wreckage of a rose garden. Beyond, hedgerows and copses had been trampled and stripped for firewood; and for more than a mile not a nettle was to be seen – all gone for food. Where before, Sophy remembered a thatched summer house, there stood a mass of scaffolding, within which was hatching a half-built bridge. The carriage slowed to go around this thing, lurching across the rutted course of the canal. The Byford family stared across a landscape in which hodsmen, brickmakers, carters, blacksmiths, carpenters and navvies swarmed in accord with some incomprehensible masterplan.

The other guests were already in the drawing room, talking in lower tones than usual. The ladies, in particular, seemed not to know whether they should acknowledge their hosts' beleaguered condition out loud. They were all there at the invitation of Mr Leggatt, a prosperous wholesale grocer, who was also the town's principal carrier. The guests included one of his best customers, Thomas Byford's cousin Norton, owner of a large woollen mill in Bradford-on-Avon. Also present was Dr Brown, who at Fraser's demand had attended the Byford house that morning. Together with their wives they made up a convenient party – not too crowded for a little private music and not too small to contrive a table for whist.

Normally there would be no talk of business in the ladies' hearing. But there was no avoiding the topic of the canal. Besides, its approach to the town was likely to affect the fortunes of nearly everyone present.

'I think it's altogether thrilling,' Sarah Norton told Mrs Leggatt over dinner, in a determined attempt to make the best of things. Sarah was a fashionable, socially ambitious woman, with a faultlessly disorded chignon of curls and a gown of flowing figured silk. 'I feel as if we were repasting from a picnic hamper while the cavalry charge each other for our entertainment.'

Their hostess scarcely heard her. Mrs Leggatt could still have been attractive herself. But any advantage her looks might have given her were cancelled by the closeness with which she habitually watched her husband's every move. And, predictably, tonight most of Leggatt's attention was taken up with Lawyer Byford's nubile daughters.

'Speaking of battlefields, Dr Brown,' said Norton, a youngish man heavy about the face and girth, 'I hear you had dealings today with another of the wounded.'

'Another – why, is Mr Fraser careless with the lives of his men?' Kate asked.

'But he can't be, can he, uncle?' said Sophy. 'He was ever so angry with Lord Fitzpayne this morning, wasn't he?' turning to the doctor.

'Possibly,' Dr Brown said. 'If James Fraser *was* angry, though, it was probably from self-reproach.' His manner suggested that the subject, as a professional one from his own point of view, was at an end.

But Sophy was not silenced. 'And if he did sacrifice others' lives so readily, he wouldn't have offered to pay all that money, would he?'

'My dear!' Mrs Byford exclaimed from across the table. Charles Norton, with an awkward smile, told Sophy, 'I think the question of a fee is best discussed only between doctor and client.'

Leggatt looked up, his ruddy face solemn from too much good wine. 'With respect, sir, the question of the good doctor's fee is the concern of all sorts of people.'

'You mean of the canal company?' said Norton, embarrassed but not knowing how to turn the subject.

'Of the company, sir. The very same! They can't afford their section engineers to set a precedent for subsidizing these people every time one of them steps on a man-trap or falls down a barrow-run. Goddammit – with your pardon, ladies – *we* cannot afford it! Show me a man here who's not got shares in the waterway – and if he hasn't he can't know his own interests! You have,' pointing at Norton, 'and you, sir,' indicating the doctor. 'And so has

Byford,' with a sweep of his arm toward Kate and Sophy. 'You're doing well enough,' addressing Norton, 'you've got your water transport now – you've got it all the way to Bristol. But *we* can't afford to see our investments frittered on incidentals – with due respect, doctor.'

'At least,' said Norton cautiously, 'a low rate of deaths – of accidents, I mean –' with a quick look at the ladies '– will keep the men from tramping off to other works.'

'Now there you have it,' Dr Brown put in, seeing Leggatt about to speak. 'In wartime even horses aren't more scarce than good men.'

Leggatt wasn't listening. 'And these people – the navigators – they don't want doctors. They have their own way of dealing with things. These people – when they're sick they have more independence than that. On that point I can assure you. The salt of the earth, the good ones – the good ones, mind.'

'Is it true,' Sophy asked her aunt, across Leggatt, 'that men from the lower ranks, such as Mr Fraser, usually make very cruel employers?'

For answer, Sarah Norton appealed by look to her husband.

'Generally –' he responded.

'And who was this Scot fellow, anyway,' Leggatt broke in, 'before he came back here? The man's a foreigner – he's three hundred miles from where he belongs. His father was a mason from Renfrewshire.'

He was interrupted by the party reorganizing itself as the port was brought in. It was time for the ladies to go to the drawing room and walk about, or merely pretend to sit, until they knew how the men would place themselves when they in turn came in. In a corner of the room Sarah Norton saw fit to resume the subject of the canal and its maker. 'I do not think,' she murmured to Sophy, 'that it would look well – or that it would please your father – if you were to speak too readily of the engine-wright – of Mr Fraser.'

Sophy guessed her aunt's full meaning. To cover her confusion – her indignation too at being misunderstood – she said, 'But papa speaks highly of him.'

21

'To speak too readily of him at all – that is, for a member of our sex – might be taken by some persons to mean that you consider him an equal. Indeed, as something more intimate.'

Poor Sophy blushed. Distinctions of rank had been more important in her education than anything else. 'Papa said he was to be asked into the parlour.'

'I dare say that was because Dr Brown was expected. It might have been difficult to entertain both men separately. Besides, among men only, these things can be done a little differently, you know.'

'He does speak very nearly like a gentleman,' Sophy protested, more for her own sake than Fraser's.

'Not altogether. I think, Sophy, if you were to hear such a person speak for long enough, you would notice he does use some words in dialect. Just like the ordinary people hereabout, in fact.'

They were half overheard by Dr Brown's wife, a no-nonsense little woman suspected by her neighbours of especially Low Church origins. 'Ah, now, if you speak of people who have ceased to be ordinary, you must mean the young man whose people have almost levelled this establishment.'

Sarah Norton suspected she was about to be contradicted. 'I was on the point of telling Sophy,' she said in a firm voice, 'that Mr Fraser, when he lived nearby as a child, was employed to lead the plough horses. My husband says, at twopence a day.'

Mrs Brown failed to catch her disapproval. 'You must admire these people when they set out to improve themselves. But I do wish they could do it without disrupting the whole town.'

'My husband informs me,' Sarah persisted, 'that before last year the man in question could not write his own name.'

'Dear me! Then he needn't hope for gentility, to be sure. I suppose he must dictate all his correspondence. Still, no one reckons it the mark of a gentleman to write legibly ... Shall we change the subject, before the men come in and start talking waterways all over again?'

And meaning to make the conversation more interesting for young Sophy she set about asking after George's prospects when he should shortly have gone up to Cambridge. Meanwhile the girl was left feeling that, though the canal was interesting to anyone merely as the only thing that had ever happened in Upstowe, it and Fraser were undoubtedly the foremost topics among their neighbours – and the most forbidden.

Thomas Byford was returning from Gloucestershire in low spirits and, as he saw it now, at high expense. His latest fees, from the great house where as a form of upper servant he had just spent several days in and out of the steward's parlour, now looked to be even less than he'd feared. For the twentieth time that afternoon he wondered, firstly, if the law had really been right for him and, secondly, if he shouldn't have economized and taken the stage. Meanwhile the post-chaise was seventeen shillings for every change of horse – and all for being dashed about at a hand-gallop and rattled half to death.

It was a relief to be making the final part of the day's journey by water; he was due to travel up as far as Bradford-on-Avon in the comparative comfort of a barge owned by his cousin Norton's business. On their arrival at last in Bath, the post-boy – in fact a grizzled, jockey-like man of uncertain age – came to the window, his short, brightly coloured jacket and beaver hat covered in dust; and Thomas, steeling himself to look indifferent to the price, paid him off. Groggily he clambered down into the innyard and followed his luggage toward the waterfront.

The quayside at Bath gave a good idea of the changes the new canal might bring further up its course. On the wharf stood factories, stables, sheds, weigh-houses, offices and cranes. There were piles of paving stone from the Marlborough Downs, Welsh anthracite, Bath building stone, timber, lime and gravel; and warehouses for grain, flour, cheese, wool, wines and spirits, and copper for the local brassworks. On the water lay wherries, lighters, and flat-bottomed West Country barges. The whole was overlaid by the smell of droppings from nearly a hundred draught horses, mingled with the odour from three hundred tons more of the stuff, being shipped through in a train of barges to Claverton.

In the Navigation Inn, formerly the Pack Horse, Thomas met Jenkins the cost-bearer, as the captain of his barge was known, who showed him aboard.

'This ain't your gentry's packet-boat, sir,' said Jenkins, a thick-set, weatherbeaten man whose rolling walk had been got not as a sailor but as a Wiltshire field-hand. To Byford, though, as the barge slid from its moorings at five miles an hour, it seemed like taking wing after the rigours of travelling by road.

The waterway bent south through the wooded valley leading up to Limpley Stoke. Byford marvelled to see their vessel carried over roads and streams. 'Does the water run?'

'Indeed it does, sir. You'll see that right enough when we take her through them locks. Up or down, it only takes two men and that half-loon wet-nosed boy –' and along with Jenkins' bargehand Thomas noticed a pale furtive child of eight or nine – 'but there's four horses to take us up, and coming back down, now, we'd be needing just the one.'

'Are all these goods the property of Norton's mill?' Thomas asked, looking along the humped, tarpaulin-covered barge.

'Most of this is Norton's, sir. And some of this here space is rented. Going down, there's always wool from Norton's, bound for Staffordshire; and this way there's gunpowder, for blasting the canal further up, and coals and groceries this time, all bound for Bradford. If we make haste and there's a moon, we can be safely moored by midnight, sir.'

Joseph Lee was riding hard. Behind him the sky's last light was palest green. The close little hills above the River Avon had lost all colour, and the trunks of the roadside trees shone faintly lighter on their twilit side. He was bound for Bradford-on-Avon, where at eight next morning he was due to do business with the man Byford.

24

There was no need to make haste; he was spurring his hired nag in a bad light simply because travelling at a hand-gallop was what he preferred. He was a young man whose whole life was carried on in the same spirit – why, he even troubled to go on making money for the sole reason that doing so gave him pleasure. Joseph wasn't greedy, or avaricious – neither did he have a special liking for his trade. He was someone who, by trying only a little harder than others, had met success in everything he tried – and as occupations went, he had to confess, succeeding in itself was agreeable.

Certainly, there were easy takings now for his firm's Bristol warehouse. The war with Bonaparte had over-turned the European timber trade, and made it, for America, a lottery in which no one could lose. At twenty-five Joseph had already made a fortune. Not four years before, his clever, self-defeating father, having gambled his last cent, had died, leaving the family's trading empire in ruins. At first Joseph had hated giving up his education in Europe to go home to Virginia and support his mother and sisters. Later, with his father's example in mind, he was glad. A life of idleness would have ruined him, too.

Joseph slowed his horse to a canter as the highway, pale now in the moonlight, led up toward the hillside village of Hanscombe. Another road joined it, across a bridge span-ning a lock where the canal climbed a further thirty feet toward the distant pin-prick lights of Bradford-on-Avon. At this hour the only moving thing in sight was a tarpaulin-covered barge working its way up eastward behind a team of four horses. Joseph reined in his hack to watch as the boat's traces were cast off and it drifted through the first pair of gates into the lock chamber. He marvelled, the more for understanding how it was done, that so many tons of water could be poised within the lock, or moved about, by no more force than the bare hands of a bargee's wife.

Something was wrong. There was shouting on the barge, a man running, howls of urgency, of a desperation you might hear, throughout that choir of silence, a full mile away. Joseph caught his breath, watching hard. Over the

25

snorting of his mare he heard the word that made him rear the squealing beast around and gallop hard, her belly bloodied beneath his spurs. Not toward the lock, but away.

It was the boy. At first even Jenkins, jealous as a jilted woman for his vessel's welfare, had noticed nothing. Then the boy, crouched aft against a bulwark, had begun to whimper out loud.

'Now stop that, boy,' said Jenkins, staring over him toward the approaching lock. 'Unless you say right smartly what it is you want.'

Ahead the lock-keeper was opening the gates.

The boy lifted his voice and wailed, a despairing sound with an edge of terror. Jenkins raised his first.

'Done something wicked, sir,' squeaked the child, almost inaudible. His fear, if not his meaning, took hold of the cost-bearer. Jenkins, not deliberately cruel, crouched over him and said, thick-voiced, 'You poorhouse scum, I'll break your back if you don't answer me.'

The gates were closed behind them and chamber sluices opened at the other end. Water surged in between high streaming walls.

'I didn't mean it, I didn't mean it, I'll say I'm sorry!' screamed the boy above the waters' roar. 'I stuck the candle in that barrel –'

'Where? Where? Where?' Jenkins bellowed, visionless with rage and dread.

Under a shrunken sky the boat was still almost at the chamber's floor. There was no chance to run for it.

The boy pointed.

However much in character Thomas Byford's weaknesses had been, no one could doubt his nerve when he was threatened physically. He it was, while the bargemaster stood struck half-dead with self-reproach, who stumbled, shouting to the men above, toward wherever the infant poltroon had stuck a lighted candle upright in the gunpowder.

The flash was almost invisibly brilliant. The exclamation

of sound that followed could be felt in the gut even more painfully than you could hear it. A fifty-foot edifice of earth and water stood an instant, then lapsed. Above the village Joseph reined in his horse and stared, not perceiving what he saw. There was no bridge.

There was no bridge, nor was there a flight of locks. Joseph's mare skittered like a terrified cat, her ears laid flat to her skull. For some moments there was silence. Down among the houses an infant wailed, a few seconds later a woman started shrieking. Within moments shouts of dismay and astonishment rang out, over the crying of children woken to find the village half blown apart. A line of hedgerow trees lay like spilt needles where the blast had stripped them and knocked them down. Nearby, a barn stood broken-backed, smashed asunder by an uprooted elm. One stone-built cottage had been taken clean in half like a mouse's nest, to show God knew how many human shadows running to and fro among the rubble in their nightclothes. A rickyard was on fire; by the hellish light Joseph could see three rows of round pointed stacks, the sum of that year's work for everyone in sight, spattered with flocking sparks. Over one big-voiced man's pleading for a line of water-buckets to be formed, the confusion voiced one fear: the French had landed, and Bonaparte, the bedtime ogre used so carelessly to threaten every naughty child, was here.

Of the real cause there was nothing to be seen. Where the bridge and lock had stood some seconds earlier, was now a masonry-strewn rapid above a spreading pool a quarter of a mile across. No one but Joseph was there to say they'd seen the barge, its passenger or any of its crew. And no one else, nor any wreckage, survived as witness that such a vessel, or such people, had ever existed.

Chapter Two

An unknown horseman in Cannings Fitzpayne was itself enough to have the populace agog. This traveller, though, had not just ridden through the village at a careful pace and vanished. He had entered at a gallop that had the gleaners in the hot roadside fields straightening up and staring until well after the dust of his passing had disappeared. When Sophy and her mother heard him slacken, then ride up the drive, there had been a face – a ludicrous effect, had anybody witnessed it – at every door in the village street. Sophy ran out under the portico into the sunlight, before even the manservant could open the front door, to find her uncle there. He got down from a steed that steamed and shivered with exhaustion, and made his way stiffly past her without a word, toward Mrs Byford's astonished and terrified greeting. 'What? Why? Tell me – Tell me what it can be?'

For an instant Sophy was appalled, not at what she guessed, but at what she found herself thinking of her mother: '*Mama doesn't look undignified at all, now that something dreadful is going to happen.*' Then ran toward them both with a shriek as her uncle began to speak, and her mother fell senseless to the floor.

Thus had the terrible news been brought. For several days the village watched the house of mourning for any sight of its inhabitants. The parson called; but nothing could be learned of what took place at that encounter. Mr Norton also came and went, looking harassed as he now struggled to deal with the lawyers – and with what was described in the alehouse and the bakery shop as a formidable array of creditors. Comment on the family's tragedy grew louder when Sunday came and not a soul among them was seen in church. Meanwhile the congregation waited, rapt, to hear what would be said about the accident from the pulpit; and Parson Beddowes did not disappoint them.

He was an appointee of Lord Fitzpayne, at whose form, slumbering in the big box-pew, his every word was aimed each Sunday – not excepting, folk said, the prayers themselves. The little cleric's grovelling was almost redeemed, however, by its sincerity. In cheerful moments he would even joke at Lord Fitzpayne's expense, as other men, red-faced and meek, might venture a jibe against their own politics or a despotic mistress.

So now that he had an opportunity as spokesman for his lordship's opposition to the new canal, the parson spared nothing in describing the further disasters it might bring.

'And I stood upon the sand of the sea, and saw a beast rise up out of the sea, having seven heads and ten horns, and upon his horns ten crowns, and upon his head the name of blasphemy.' From this text he explained for two hours how hardship and danger would be the only consequence of the new waterway for anyone in Cannings Fitzpayne. He denounced the paltry compensation paid to owners of local watermills, farmland and pheasant-coverts, and went on to thrill his listeners with the menace of several hundred heathen navigators bringing this abomination, at so many yards a day, right up to their own fields and hearths. 'It ought not to be – nay it must not be –' straining from the pulpit toward his hearers like a ship's figurehead, 'that the purity of your maidens and young matrons should be made to suffer a single blush at the grossness and foul depravity reported from among these wild and savage men, drawn from the uttermost ends of the country.' In conclusion he drew attention to the awful warning they had all received that very week. The same catastrophe would doubtless happen yet again, when quantities of armaments and whole trains of powder-boats would travel past their village – would pass them every day – aye, even on the Sabbath, too. 'Go not lightly hence, my brethren. The shadow of the wings of the angel of death hath but recently passed over every one of ye; and the melancholy event hath meaning for ye all.'

For once Parson Beddowes' flock had attended to every word. Never had they been so eager to repeat his precepts among themselves. From the Byford house they could be heard streaming out onto the high road and making their way home through the noontide, as talkative as ten-year-olds. Outside the railings of the front lawn and drive the voices of the women, as they passed, sank; and every face turned to peer through at the upstairs windows.

Within the house, meanwhile, who was there who could help the family wrestle with their grief? Mr Norton had been first numbed, then horrified, his own financial loss cast clean out of mind, when called away to carry the news to them. Now he felt helpless, even cowed, at the storm of wretchedness that had broken around him, as for several days and nights the family were astounded at the bitterness of their own sorrow.

How reluctantly, then, did he ride slowly back to their mourning household from Upstowe one still warm evening that week. The whisperings in the village had turned out to be right in one respect: Thomas's finances were simply too dismaying to be complicated. The need to tell the widow and her family bore down on Charles Norton as though he, rather than poor feckless Thomas, should be blamed for their future life of hardship.

In the silent hallway he paused. Listening, he took stock of the house, like a doctor surveying the face of someone desperately ill. George, as the family's new head, should be told the news as soon as possible. Mr Norton went in search of the boy. The drawing room was empty – deserted enough to feel like a forbidden place. Passing Kate's chamber, Norton hesitated, feeling ineffectual, at the sound of the girl's choking sobs. He started, as the door opened and Sophy, with face turned away and drowned eyes, hurried by. She was clearly too distressed to acknowledge him; even so, he felt embarrassed at seeming to eavesdrop.

George was not in his mother's room, either, where he and his sisters sat by turns at Mrs Byford's bedside throughout their waking hours. Their mother had lain, conscious but nearly corpse-like, in a darkened room, ever since the moment when the sight of her cousin's face had made her swoon away. Strangely, and somehow worse to bear than poor Kate's suffocating grief, she had showed no other outward distress – no protest nor complaints – though her unfaithful husband had been more a part of her than she'd been ready to admit. Instead she lay quite still, night and day mostly awake. Her voice never rose above a whisper; but otherwise she conversed with her stoic, tear-stained younger daughter in the most ordinary way. Poor Sophy! She could have faced her mother's usual overstatements far more easily than the calm murmur in which she was addressed now, as Mrs Byford asked if the maids knew how to brew the vinegar unsupervised, or whether they had hired a new boy yet to help the gardener.

George was in his own room; and Norton, hearing voices, knocked and went in. He quickly made an excuse and retreated, however. George was sitting on the edge of the bed, his back to the door, while beside him Sophy alternately paused to dab her own eyes and murmur some attempted comfort at him. The gap in their ages looked far greater than a year; for the lad's bent head and shaking shoulders made it plain to Norton that no one could have any other kind of conversation with him for the time.

In the end it was his nieces who heard from Charles Norton about the family's affairs. While George, ashamed to be seen so overcome, stayed out of sight, it fell most of all to Sophy to try to hide her tears and comfort the others. Kate, meanwhile, was calm enough that evening to resume an appearance of her usual mild efficiency, and take up the running of the house, going about pale-faced with a haste that no task properly required. After supper, Norton found himself alone in the drawing room with Sophy. She was working, dry-eyed and mindless, on a piece of ornamental sewing that had no point but the effort it took to do it. As he came in there was an awkward silence. To break it, rather than from real anxiety, she asked, 'Uncle Norton, do you know how much of papa's income is secure?'

'Well,' he said, looking away from her, 'it may be just as well that you asked.' For once he wished she was less fearless in everything she did – even if her self-confidence might spring from nothing more than innocence. It would have helped him to feel more avuncular and in command.

'We shan't have to make economies, shall we? Papa did always encourage us to spend whatever we wished.'

'I know. But his assets ... well, there are some debts, if the truth be told.'

'But they can be paid off, can't they?'

'Oh, yes, yes – you need not trouble yourself on that account.'

'But should we find ways to economize?' asked Kate, who had come in after him.

'Well – Kate – yes; since you ask, I would say yes; you should.'

'How much?' Sophy asked.

Norton paused. He had the look of a man who didn't quite know the answer, and must consider. Outside in the hall, the quiet of the house was broken by the big grandfather clock striking the half-hour. In the sunlit road beyond the garden a wagon-load of sheaves lurched past, followed by three labourers and a pack of mongrel dogs. As it passed, the roadside trees became snagged with straw. The girls looked at their uncle. Neither of them suspected how reluctant he was to be asked about the money.

'I think for the present at least, you should persuade your mother to keep no more than one servant. And I consider too,' he went on, speaking quickly, 'that you might sell what furniture you think you might not need, and take a lease on somewhere more modest. But – and I am sure you need not feel your situation will be altogether bad – you must remember that you do all have a friend in me. Two or three months from now – no more than three, I'm sure – I'm confident that George can take a post in our new London warehouse. I know his position there might not be very grand at first; but he must not let himself become impatient on that account. And there's no doubt at all that your aunt and I can surely do something very substantial for Kate and yourself. A sum of money, perhaps – or some introductions, now. We must make haste now to get you both husbands, you know; I'm sure that if you came to stay with us awhile we could get you both some fine introductions in the best society.'

There was silence as they took this in. Kate was the first to speak. Her doubting, sceptical nature made it easier for her than for Sophy to believe the worst of what their uncle might know. 'Uncle, does this mean we shall have, for example, upwards of five hundred pounds a year?'

'No – no; not quite as much as that, I fear.'

'Four hundred pounds?' said Sophy. Even as she spoke, she was astonished to hear herself name such a limited sum.

'Well, no, not three hundred either, in all probability. I would say –'

'Can we expect a hundred pounds a year?' said Kate.

'No, I –'

'*Fifty*, then?'

'– I was about to say, indeed, that in all likelihood, that is roughly what you can hope to receive, yes.'

Sophy, too bold ever to have doubted her own good fortune, was speechless. Though she had scant idea what even important things such as music lessons and saddle horses might cost, still she could guess – perhaps – what such an income might mean.

Sensible Kate was the first to make any show of fortitude. 'Then there is only one thing I can do; I must find work, as well as George.'

'Oh, now I'm sure it needn't come to that,' said her uncle, without conviction.

'I must find a position as a governess, or go away to teach somewhere in a school, or do whatever thousands of women in my circumstances generally do.' It was anxiety rather than courage that made Kate speak out. 'It is very kind of you to say you'll help us – but I think that I should also try to help myself. Even if Sophy can stay at home, she can't make mama comfortable on one income.'

Unlike her sister, Sophy had only ever known how to say the first thing that came into her mind. Confronted by the first misfortunes of her life, she could make no brave speeches; silence was her only hope of not shaming herself. Nonetheless her first impulse was to meet their new-found poverty with resolution rather than bitterness – to fight, not just endure. For the sake of doing, she went into the kitchen and relieved the maid of the tray being laid ready for her mother's supper. Upstairs in the fusty bedroom she persuaded Mrs Byford to have the curtains at last pulled back a little. There were tears in her eyes as she leaned down and whispered to her mother to try and eat. Not from self-pity, however, but for poor mama, now, in their new life, to be more helpless than any of them. The summer evening seemed to gleam brighter as it died. Sophy sat, turning her head to miss the level sunlight, while her mother let her feed her a few spoonfuls of warm bread-and-milk, like a wounded bird unnaturally nourished by its own fledgling young.

The next morning brought another, expected caller. The family had agreed to accept his visit of condolence; but they were not looking forward to meeting him. Kate was in their mother's room when one of the maids came and whispered that a gentleman below wished to pay his compliments to Mrs Byford.

'I'll receive him,' Kate said.

She walked downstairs slowly. It was, she told herself, only a formality. The man was calling on them more as a connexion of her uncle than of poor papa. And but for one thing he would have sent his condolences by letter.

In the drawing room with Mr Norton was a slim young man with light-brown curly hair and a good-humoured face. It amused Kate to see how obviously he had been expecting a middle-aged woman to come through the door. Without knowing what he did, he shot a glance at her uncle, to share his own surprise at her looks. Kate's face was drained of colour, and she wore her plainest gown – it seemed more fitting to mourn by being shabby than in her splendid only black dress. Even so, she bloomed with something more than mere perfection.

Mr Norton introduced Joseph Lee and excused himself. If young Lee was not embarrassed at a social duty like this, he was.

Their visitor showed no unease, however. He was too busy trying not to look as though Kate attracted him. Also, being kind-hearted, he was genuinely sorry for her – and would have been even if she hadn't been pretty.

'I hope you don't feel obliged to tell me anything about

the accident,' she said. 'It's not that I'm ungrateful to you for calling. I know you wouldn't have troubled to do so if you hadn't been a witness.'

Her forthrightness appealed to him, too. 'I'm glad to hear you say so,' he replied, trying not to look at her too much. 'I shouldn't have much to tell you in any case.'

They were silent for a moment. Then he added, 'I hope losing income from business with me won't be too much of a hardship.'

'It begins to look as though papa ran up debts anyway, whenever he thought money would be coming in. And he speculated, too.' Kate had not meant to be so frank. But the sympathy in his steady gaze had caught her unprepared. In her countrified experience young men of her own class were without exception overdressed and self-conscious. 'We think now he can't have been very good at that kind of thing. In fact I don't believe he can ever have been clever with money.' Her eyes filled with tears. 'Poor papa! He was always fond of us. And he was such a fool. He was always a braggart – and he was always ineffectual, too. It seems a crowning touch of incompetence, that he should get himself killed – should perish so thoroughly – like that, even though I'm sure he couldn't help it.'

Joseph, a romantic man, felt his heart swell at the sight of this touching creature whose melancholy became her so well. He fancied that, if he might, he could have put his arms around her without the smallest thought of lust.

'I'm sorry,' he said, in the gentlest tone. 'And I'm sorry, too, that you think you might be poor.' He really meant it. After all, he had been poor himself. But he had been trained up to inherit a business in which only an utter wastrel like his father could fail. He had no idea how a household of a boy and three women might prosper here in England, starting from nothing.

'Most of us will be able to take on some kind of work,' said Kate.

'Will your brother not go into your father's business?'

'George knows nothing of the law. Papa intended him to go to Cambridge – he'd never been a university man himself. He meant George for the Church. I think he saw him as a future bishop or archdeacon.' She smiled. 'I can't imagine how.'

Her smile made him want to know everything about her, down to who ironed her handkerchiefs. 'At least your brother can still take his degree?'

'Oh, no. My uncle says we can never afford that now. But – who knows – if George goes into some other sort of work, it may be for the best.'

Joseph was more than ready to agree about the benefit of having no degree. It counted for nothing that he himself had attended the University of Virginia and the Sorbonne. Anything must be true, spoken by a girl whose beauty only emphasized her intelligence.

He had already stayed longer than intended, when Kate's uncle came to say that he was going out on business to Upstowe. Mr Norton also brought a letter, delivered from the parsonage-house and addressed to himself, as the family's executor. Joseph felt this was his cue to go. Without much conviction, he said so.

'Oh, no – won't you stay? Please do!' Kate's plea was entirely artless. She would have spoken so to anyone who gave her the same sympathy. Not that her feelings weren't soothed by the interest of a fine-looking man with agreeable manners.

He was persuaded. As Kate was looking at the letter, Sophy came in and was introduced.

'It's from Parson Beddowes,' Kate told her, seeing her glance in the direction of the letter. 'A relative of his – let me see – yes – has a smaller house where we can live.'

'Oh, where?' Sophy exclaimed. The thought of hardship was still a novelty to her, and she was eager to be doing.

Kate finished reading and looked glum. 'It's very kind of him,' she said in a guarded voice. 'I've always thought him a well-meaning man.'

'Yes, but where is it?'

'It's Drove Cottage.'

'It can't be! I mean – are you sure you can read his hand?'

For confirmation, Kate passed her the letter. 'I think we

should do as he suggests, and look at it. There's nothing lost if we can still afford another house.'

'Is it nearby? Could you go there today?' said Joseph. The girls' lack of enthusiasm had escaped him; and he himself was only anxious to show himself useful to Kate. 'It's in the village,' she told him.

Mr Norton, in haste to take his leave, paused in the doorway. 'I think,' he told Sophy, 'you might do well to consider what Mr Beddowes has said.' Sophy, trying to hide her bewilderment at his advice, said nothing. 'I know in the past you may have thought him someone to be laughed at. But you shouldn't ignore the fact that he's making you what is now a very valuable offer.'

'If Uncle Norton believes we're desperate,' said Sophy as they were walking to the cottage, 'why cannot *he* do something for us?'

Kate had no answer. She wished that Joseph had not accompanied them. The cottage was offered for a nominal rent, so that they would almost certainly have to take it; and she was embarrassed that he should see her there. Worse, she was ashamed of her embarrassment.

Drove Cottage stood at the entrance of the straight, marshy trackway from which it took its name. Both cottage and droveway were overshadowed by thickets of elm saplings. The rank garden blossomed with giant hogweeds, and in any other season the area would be full of rushes. Behind the cottage were the signs of a household that had lived half the year out of doors. The wreckage of a dresser stood by the door, still carrying some broken pots full of stagnant rain water. Nearby was a bare patch of ground where cooking fires had been lit. The billows of the thatched roof were crusted with moss and shredded thin at one place.

'It looks like a dungheap with windows,' said Sophy.

'I know the people who lived here before were very poor,' Kate replied. She didn't mention that when they were children, one of the two families living here had been James Fraser and his widowed mother.

'It looks sound,' she said, when they had spent two or

three minutes peering about inside. 'We shall have to replace the oilcloth with glass in those upstairs windows.'

'But the rooms are so mean!' From having been shocked into silence, Sophy was at least recovered enough to protest. 'Even living on a ship must be better than this.'

Joseph regretted having come with them. Whatever he'd expected, it hadn't been this humble place. He could see that these two gently reared young women would far rather have surveyed the decline in their fortunes without a witness to make them self-conscious.

Back at the house – how grand it seemed now – Joseph said goodbye to Kate alone at the front door. 'That little house couldn't even hold a pianoforte. I hope very much – for your sake – that you think your future worse than it is.'

'If we start out as lowly as possible, we can only rise in the world.' Kate spoke briskly, abashed at how openly he admired her.

Her seeming coolness put him off not at all. What courage! he thought, as he rode away. And with such a face! A girl like that could say or do anything and it would look right.

In most ways Joseph was the most practical man alive. But where women were concerned he was too sentimental to judge aright. Before he'd ridden far, he'd ceased to think of the Byfords' future poverty as distressing. A few miles more, and he could see it only as a picturesque background to bring out everything in Kate that was most splendid.

It was agreed they would take Drove Cottage, at the end of the quarter, when their own lease ran out. Meanwhile the dreary days passed, though nobody believed each one would. The summer dwindled, until one too-clear morning the wind in the great walnut tree in front of the house was strong enough to turn up the underside of its leaves; the season of warmth was over, and by noon the rain had set in. As the autumn saw whole weeks go by, the Byford family became, not reconciled to their loss, but at least able to face each mealtime without fearing to see their own grief looking at them from across the table.

Mr Norton did find a prospective post in London for George. His own work as executor complete, he rode away home. He had continued full of descriptions of intended generosity toward Kate and Sophy, though neither could properly believe him. Mrs Byford meanwhile began to mend. She slept deeply, took toast with her gruel, and began to leave her room for several hours a day to sit, wrapped in a blanket by the fire while Sophy read to her. The benefit of letting life pass them by awhile was never so well shown as when Mrs Byford recovered enough to become trivial again. What would their neighbours say, she asked one day, now up and fully dressed, since there was no proper grave? 'It makes us look miserly, you know, just to put up a tablet in the church. Besides, if we do purchase a tablet, people will expect it to announce all sorts of things – who the deceased's parents were, and where they came from, too. You mustn't let this go beyond this house, but your father's parents weren't carriage folk at all. Just between us, they attended chapel, rather than a proper church like normal people.'

At length it was time for another change. Before Kate's own efforts had found her any work, she received a letter, from Bradford-on-Avon. The thought of paying two whole shillings for it cast Mrs Byford into agonies of indecision. 'My husband has died recently, you see,' she said, having come to the door to see the post-boy herself. 'If he were here I'm sure he could tell you if we ought to pay for it.'

'Mama,' said Sophy, 'if it comes from uncle Norton, very likely it will be to our advantage. We should pay for it; indeed, we must.'

Its news was reasonably good. A place had been found for Kate as a governess, not two miles from home. She was to be engaged in fact with the Leggatts, at the new house they had taken this side of Upstowe to avoid the canal workings. Formerly Mrs Byford would have been all huffiness to see her daughter go virtually into service at an establishment where they had been used to visit. Her family's loss of income, however, had impressed itself upon her enough for her to see the offer with relief.

There was little good cheer though, on the day set for Kate to leave. Mrs Byford made no effort to conceal her tears as the Leggatts' manservant, dressed rather more lavishly than Kate herself, stowed her things inside the carriage that had been sent for her. 'Now, Kate, you will write to your aunt and uncle and show proper gratitude, will you not? I'm sure they've taken ever so much trouble in finding you this post.'

'I'll do my best to please them,' said Kate, dropping her air of calm resignation just long enough to exchange a satirical look with Sophy.

'It didn't cost them any money, did it?' Sophy said.

'Sophy, it's not nice to say such things. They've acted very handsomely by Kate and George. Who knows what large emoluments your brother may be destined for if he's prepared to work, and isn't too impatient?'

Sophy said nothing as she embraced Kate in farewell. He'll be middle-aged before that, she thought. And then he won't be able to stop my life from being dull in any case.

'I see no reason why Miss Byford should wish for brandy.'

'Of course she does! How else can we drink to her arrival?'

'She has not said she wishes for it.'

'I'm certain Miss Byford agrees that she should drink,' said Mr Leggatt. 'Do you not, Miss Byford?' turning to Kate with a look of gallantry.

Kate assented uneasily. Mrs Leggatt, ignored by her husband and stiff with humiliation, signalled to the maid who was waiting on them at supper to bring glasses.

'You see. Of course Miss Byford would like to drink with us.' And he sought Kate's approval with a comradely smile in which there lurked a flash of mischief.

'You'll have to make allowances for our style of living,' he said, looking Kate over as if he hadn't done so already. 'I'm sure most of your school friends at the Academy came from grander establishments than this.' The Byford girls' school had been the most expensive for young ladies that the county could offer.

'It wasn't always possible to know,' said Kate, as an afterthought adding 'sir' in an effort to keep her distance.

'And such a modest girl! Come, Miss Byford, if there were young ladies of rank at the Academy, you must have known them for who they were.'

'I suppose so. But there was nothing to make them conspicuous.'

'Well, that would be your quality for you!' said Leggatt with relish. 'And were you a guest at any of their houses?'

'Only once, when my sister and I stayed a month with Miss Gresham.'

'I knew it! From the first moment I saw you introduced into company I told myself: this is a young lady who belongs in the highest social sphere.'

It was clear that Kate was the latest in a series of expensive domestic purchases. Leggatt was accordingly determined to flatter himself at anything she might say. The conversation turned to their surroundings. His big new house and grounds had Leggatt as vain and anxious as a young girl dressed up in company for the first time. It was decided that of course Miss Byford should want to see round the place. No matter that the night was upon them; she could guess at the look of things from a description. So Kate was called upon to walk about beside him and stare through a wavering sphere of candlelight at suites of new Egyptian-style furniture, or peer up against the window into the darkness outside, where lay seedling shrubberies and freshly made walks.

It was like a hateful parody of being a bride carried across the threshold. With the dark for a pretext, Mr Leggatt gave her his arm, his fingers intertwined with hers, so that she shouldn't stumble. Mrs Leggatt followed one and a half paces behind, in a trance of hatred.

'Well now! What did you think, Miss Byford?' he asked at length. 'Don't spare me your honest opinion.'

He still held on tightly to her hand. Kate nearly started with disbelief. Almost within sight of his wife he was paddling and scratching his horny fingertips in her palm.

'I think it's very fine,' she said miserably, wresting herself free with as little show of violence as possible. Remembering that Leggatt and her father had had an unspoken social rivalry, she added, 'I know papa always had a desire to live in a house like this.'

'Ah!' said Leggatt. 'Ah, yes! But answer me this. Did he ever aspire to want his children reared by a fine young lady like you? You mustn't think I lack respect for his memory – I wouldn't be guilty of a thing like that. But – secretly, now – don't you ever wonder if some other man in your father's position might not have been a little more ambitious?'

Kate looked away without answering him. For discretion's sake she tried to hide her anger by changing the subject; and asked if she might see whichever room was to be her own.

'Oh, but on that, you must advise *us*,' said Leggatt. 'I think the south-east room, do you not?' appealing to his wife.

'I thought the girls were both to go on using that as their schoolroom,' she answered, looking hard at Kate.

'Good Lord, no. I didn't mean one of the attics! Miss Byford is to have a corner room on the first floor. We can't possibly offer anything less,' turning to Kate, 'to someone who has been a visitor in the houses of the quality.'

'The south-east room is for guests,' Mrs Leggatt replied.

'Oh, no, no; they can use other rooms,' he said soothingly, to Kate rather than to her.

'It is due to be re-papered,' his wife told him with an upward hitch in her voice. 'This week.'

'Yes, yes, yes – well ... never mind that,' still smiling at Kate. 'I dare say we can make some suitable arrangement – perhaps tomorrow – can we not?'

The room felt damp, and its air was tainted and vinegary. Beneath a sloping roof within which the odd starling or something shuffled and bumped, the narrow bed took up almost one wall. The evening over, Kate edged in round the door and into a beam of moonlight that shone through the dormer window as if down from the opening of a tunnel.

Leggatt might talk of keeping her in luxury, but to her this room looked altogether permanent. She took off her heavy dark blue silk travelling dress with its tiny ruched trim on bodice and sleeves and hung it from the hook on the door. Tired as she was, she felt restless. Thank God, she thought, unhooking her petticoats, she wasn't such a fool as to take her new employer at his own value. But – oh, how his advances depressed her! By comparison, being ignored would be bliss. She sighed up at the window and the night beyond, and started going to bed, trying not to think about the hopes that everyone dearest to her had now lost.

A few days after Kate's departure from her home, Cannings Fitzpayne saw what was, apart from church-going, one of the year's only excitements. After a summer of fierce, blissful heat, the closed-in weather made the Vale so dank that one might imagine the real out-of-doors was away somewhere else. The wind and rain gave a fillip, though, to the junketings that followed harvest home, as the bailiff of the Fitzpayne estate contemplated a four-acre yard set, like another village street, with newly thatched ricks of wheat. In the tithe barn, stacked to the roof with sacks of grain, hoarded mutton-fat candles had been set in place, the rafters had been garlanded with green branches, and a space was cleared for a night of fiddle music and carousing by a company wild with relief at getting in the harvest.

The Byford females would not, of course, be attending such a party, with raucous dancing on a dirt floor, and goings-on beyond the murky globe of candlelight. They were to stay at home, joined by the parson's wife, who would take turns with Sophy to read aloud by a working candle while the others sewed beside the fire.

But George, armed with the social advantages of a man, was hell-bent on joining the evening's sport. As he scampered across the water-filled ruts of the home farmyard the lights and music in the barn confirmed his determination to commit any folly if it would only bring a little more excitement than usual.

The great barn filled up, as a premature dusk came down. Whole families were there, the younger children drowsing in their mothers' arms. As they noisily trooped in, the open doors of the barn made an entrance for them bigger than a city gate. At the end where in church the altar would be, a platform supported four fiddlers, who were sweating heavily and already several parts drunk.

George gawped around him in hopeful curiosity, for all the world as if among strange faces. Having satisfied himself that the village girls were as he remembered from lusting after them in church last Sunday, he felt free to start in on a barrel of gut-rot cider, together with the parson's eldest son, the under-butler from the Hall, and two young tenant farmers from the other side of the estate. As bachelors they drank with purpose rather than cheerfulness, making the odd remark sideways as they stared about them, each in a private trance of sexual hope or desperation.

In the centre of the floor the dancers whooped and swooped in two long lines, sending up clouds of chaff and dust. Among them George's eye lighted on Charity Michaelmas. In recent weeks she'd no longer come to church in clothing washed to rags. Instead she wore neat pattens and a dress which, if patched, at least had been repaired discreetly. She had become apprenticed to the Fitzpayne household as an undercook. Each Sunday morning George would see her sitting in church in one of two mute rows of housemaids, all with hands and feet and eyes aligned out of mischief's way. And each time, as he focused for a couple of hours on the bewitching back of her neck, he would wonder why her type of face and body made her more disturbing than any other pretty girl he knew.

As the evening prospered, the drudges from the Hall stamped ever more vigorously about the dancing floor, even the twelve- and thirteen-year-olds screeching like witches. George was still half-a-gallon clear of falling down speechless when, an hour from midnight, he forced

himself to prance about, hands across from Charity. In
this state he could still marvel at the change from her
everyday appearance, as she twirled and laughed and
gasped out loud in a rage of delight at all the noise and
motion.

The dancing made him nearly sober, and her drunk. He
would never have harassed himself into speaking to her
otherwise, as they trickled away from the dance together.
She wasn't impressed, of course, to hear him confirm her
own opinion of the weather. But he showed such a
mixture of timidity and headlong exultation in her
company that she was bound to look solemn and not meet
his eye. She took it for granted that George was finer-
looking – or soon would be – than almost any man in the
Vale; or indeed in whatever places might lie beyond.

At his panic-stricken hint they wandered out, past
scenes of shadowy embracing into the cool, now clear-
skied night. Still capping one another's commonplaces
they crossed the yard, with a casualness that deceived no
one but themselves. In truth, Charity admired George
more than he could guess. She was too diffident – too
strong-willed, perhaps – to tell him so. But even he had
begun to divine a little of what a splendid figure he cut in
her eyes, and it made her irresistible.

'Gentlemen are likely to grow taller, so Cook says,' she
told him. 'I've heard, since I've begun up there at the Hall,
that folk like you might get to eat a dish of meat, why, ten
times in a week. No wonder you all look so strange beside
the rest of us, when what we mostly get is skim milk and
potatoes.'

George gazed at her, concentrating more on Charity
herself than on anything she said. Unlike him, she'd
finished growing. She stood at that moment of repose that
sometimes follows childhood, before the briskness many
women show in the face of adult hardship. Mantled in
blushing calm, she never thought to trick him, like other
girls, into pining for her even more. All the orphanage had
taught her to expect from life was hard work and sparse
food. Pleasure was a word, rather than something she'd
ever thought to understand.

Now, though, she had an inkling of what it was to feel desire. Under the fierce stars, and almost out of hearing of the shouts and music in the barn, her senses felt at once confused and clarified. George was talking about his departure for London – it didn't interest him at that moment, but nor did any other subject he could find. And all the while it seemed to Charity that every sound throughout the Vale was magnified, much as the lightest human footstep must be to the earthworm beneath its thunder. As they loitered through an empty curing house toward a range of lofts and pens, two farm dogs at the foot of Hychpen Beacon, then a badger in a neighbouring copse, barked loud enough to make an echo. In the nearby undergrowth it seemed that every snail and harvest mouse was moving in the dark with clumsy tread. She shivered; and on this excuse George, fumbling with her shawl while privately cursing his unforwardness, suggested they sit inside one of the barns. There, beside her on a slithery pile of hay, he leaned suddenly closer, almost in despair at what she might say. His shifting made her roll against him, with a laugh of fear. Instantly his near-despondency changed to desperation. Big and wretched, he leaned across the girl and kissed her, well-nigh slaughtered by the sudden massiveness of his cock. No one had ever done such a thing – or as she found some moments later, such things – to Charity before. As they squirmed like stranded fish, ache to ache and astonished by delight, she swooned, seething, into the first embrace of her life. Not just as someone come to womanhood, but as everyone she'd ever been: the flailing infant, still blind as a kitten due for drowning; the wary child who never cried; the girl who shouldered each day's loneliness with unmoved resolution.

He flurried his way between her warm thighs like a sleepwalker; and lived the falling dream as he thrust on the endless voyage into her opened body like a man dealing his own death-stroke.

Chapter Three

From a distance the unfinished canal looked even more formidable. By November it had advanced east of Upstowe, and its trail of pulped-up acres was visible from the Iron Age fort on Cannings Hill, above the village. Its shanty settlements, with their scurrying inhabitants and the smoke of hundreds of cooking fires, stretched back for miles. Sophy strove to ignore this view as she half ran, one frosty sunrise, up Hychpen Bottom toward the summit of the down. There was an edge of unease to her satisfaction at escaping briefly before the day's chores: was this countryside now dangerous? It seemed one of Mrs Byford's fears was justified at last: the navvies from the canal, close to, looked every bit as menacing as their reputation. Sophy had seen a group of them a few days back, walking through the village in pursuit of work. She could believe what the parson's wife had said – that they were permanently drunk, and took off their iron-shod boots only when the soles fell off.

The sound of hoofbeats, though, held no apprehension for her. When, frowning into the sun, she saw James Fraser coming along the trackway on his dark-coloured grey, she merely felt cheated that he hadn't been Rawley Fitzpayne.

Fraser hadn't encountered her since the shooting. But the solitude of the place made it necessary for them to speak. He reined in his horse and dismounted. 'An unlikely hour to find you here, Miss Sophia.'

'I like this time of morning.' She wanted to complain about the household duties she had now that they only kept one servant. But pride of both kinds, good and bad, prevented her. 'I have to keep mama company a good deal for the rest of the day. Her health is still not better.'

'Your life must be quiet down there.'

Sophy had indeed found herself shockingly lonely since her family had become poor. To hear her own thoughts spoken so readily was almost too good to be true. 'Have you ever been so bored that you can't understand how you go on breathing?' Without waiting for an answer she went on, 'Is it true what our neighbours say – that you've travelled? To Dublin and Oxford – and to London several times?'

'I expect my Oxford and my London are different from the places you've heard described. I've seen nothing of Christchurch Hall or Mayfair.'

'Have you been to Salisbury? Kate and I went to school there.'

Sophy had not been a model pupil. But her regret for those hopeful times was strong enough, now, to bring her up the hill just so that she could gaze toward where she knew the city was. 'Parson Beddowes says it's the finest place this side of London. And you can even see it from here, he says, if it's about to rain.'

'Ah, for that you must look through my spyglass,' he said, putting one hand in his greatcoat pocket. 'Here –' as the big gelding plunged about – 'You'd best hold his head.'

Fraser focused the telescope, and Sophy resolutely hung onto the snaffle as the horse's bony head, big as a human trunk, clattered the bridle and jerked her arms about.

'This adjustment, now, will show you the farther distances.'

'How far is that?' she asked, taking the glass to sneak a look at what she hoped were private apartments at the Hall.

'Thirty miles.'

'A half a day from here! Good heavens!' She looked again. The day was too fine for anyone to see far with the naked eye. In Hychpen Bottom a deep shadow was creeping round as the sun came up, one edge rimmed with white where the frost was not yet melted. The brilliant winter sky was tinged with grey-brown above its horizon, and the Vale's frozen water meadows bloomed with a thin mist.

But the glass changed things more than she'd thought. On the south side of the Vale another valley breached the downs. Between a series of steep grassy promontories the Wiltshire Avon flowed away, past orchards and villages, each visible as a cluster of trees and a church tower. Every detail seemed new made.

'But I still can't see a city,' Sophy said. 'I can't even see a big town.'

'The houses are behind a hill. What you can see is the cathedral, beyond them.'

She tried once more, and saw what she was looking for. Between the downs the slender spire soared, the loftiest building in the kingdom and six hundred years old. 'Oh yes; oh yes; I see it now. Oh, just think of that! To think that you can see a place as well as that, and maybe never get there all your life. Oh! Oh, I wish you'd never shown me. And yet I'm so glad you have!'

Fraser was looking at her, curious. He had never known a woman of her class to speak to. 'How long were you at the school in Salisbury?'

'Oh the –' She checked herself from saying 'the usual number of years', remembering that he was said to be nearly illiterate. 'Since I was thirteen. We had a governess before that.'

'You studied everything that was taught there?'

His tone made Sophy look at him, confused. 'Oh yes,' she said, wondering why he should be so interested.

'So you've read Euclid and Aristarchus and Leibnitz?'

'Why – no .... Though I did look into George's copy of ... that one you mentioned first.'

'Then which mathematics did you study?' frowning at her.

'Well ... we had to learn all the names of the ancient Greek philosophers. Some of those were mathematicians, weren't they?'

He said nothing. His look unnerved her; he seemed as intent as if trying to stare right through her to something else. 'And,' she added, 'we learned history – I mean of course all the principal rulers and their dates – and geography: the countries of the world and their most important features. And we were taught the natural sciences, too –'

'Indeed?'

'Yes – we had to memorize the names of all the metals. And we had guessing games, as part of our study of astronomy. We each chose the name of a planet and the other girls had to find out which it was.'

She realized – though without any idea why – that he didn't want to hear any of this ... Perhaps it would be polite to ask him the same sort of questions. 'Do you know about astronomy?' she ventured.

'No, I don't.' He sounded as though her question had nothing to do with him. Was there anything she could say, she wondered, without showing up his lack of education?

Fraser was bewildered at Sophy's account of her expensive accomplishments. By perseverance, in recent years he had gained, not scholarship, but at least a good idea of his own ignorance. Yet nothing she described included the knowledge he was set upon. 'Your sister is paid as a teacher, is she not? What subjects has she studied?'

'Oh, all the same ones that I have. She teaches most of them too. Of course the Leggatt children are too young to learn French or Italian properly.'

His face had changed. 'Your sister – both of you – can read French and Italian?'

'Of course – I mean, yes.'

'How long did it take? How long would it take me?'

He looked at her again. How much of her gentility was due merely to her beauty rather than an education? Her figure – it was impossible to ignore such facts – was slender yet voluptuous, and her face had an originality that made every sight of her seem like a first glimpse. He couldn't imagine looks like hers in a fieldwoman. Was it only freedom from toil, then, that had made her different from him?

' ... I found them easier to read than to speak,' she was saying.

'I don't need to speak them. But there are books I intend to read. About the work of Fournier and several others.'

'Who is he?'

'He was an engineer. None of the best histories of engi-

50

neering have been translated.' His face changed again. 'Could I pay you to teach me?'

His earnestness left her taken aback. He was looking at her in a way that made his request more like a demand. If she could earn some money to help set up their horrible new home – Sophy and her mother had moved house last week – then dare she refuse? But were they really that poor? Wouldn't it be even more humbling to give lessons for a fee to a labouring man – since that was how Fraser appeared to everyone *she* knew? If he'd been poorer, there would have been no difficulty. She could have taught him for nothing, as an act of charity.

He noticed her indecision. 'You've no need to question my grounding. I don't write fluently; an idiot could tell you that. But that counts for little in a matter like this. Mr Price's night school taught me enough for what I want.'

The mention of the night school lessened Sophy's waverings. It was not so bad for Kate to give lessons. However galling that the Leggatts had once been their equals, she did so as part of a respectable household. But to put oneself on the same level as Mr Price, the saddler and Dissenting preacher from Upstowe!

'Would you?' he persisted, without taking his eyes off her. She retreated a few steps, all her normal fearlessness replaced by uncertainty. His horse was trying to graze as they talked, but he heaved the creature after him without seeming to notice it.

'Oh ... no,' she said, 'I couldn't do that.'

She was doubtful enough to look anxious. 'Are you sure?' he asked, with a searching look.

'Quite,' Sophy replied, trying hard to look matter-of-fact.

'Is there some particular reason?'

'No – no. Only ... '

'Yes?'

'I do not think mama would let me,' blundered Sophy – she who had never readily obeyed anyone in her life.

He was mystified. 'Unlike your sister?'

She could find nothing to say.

'If it's because you think you don't know enough –'

51

She was embarrassed enough to say, 'Oh, no –'

At last he began to guess what was in her mind. She returned his hardening look, resolute but blushing, and he understood. 'Then be damned to you,' he said; and getting on his horse he rode away.

Sophy let herself feel no regrets about Fraser. But only because she couldn't bear to. It wasn't so much that she had refused him – no one from her past life would have expected her to humble herself so. It was ... what? She guessed – rightly enough – that she hadn't hurt his feelings. He didn't look as though anyone could do that. But – oh, how could she have spoken so clumsily? It was she who'd been made to feel a fool.

She tried everything to comfort herself. In the end she made herself believe – more or less – that it was actually Fraser's fault for being presumptuous. He should have known how to behave toward someone of her rank.

A few days later, though, something happened to make her see herself more as others now did.

It was her job one late afternoon to go to the village bakery and fetch the supper home. Hannah, the maid, had taken it to be cooked, but could not now be spared. Sophy hated this chore more than anything. It was a sign to all the village that they could hardly spare money even for fuel of their own. She had been astonished, then angered, at how promptly their neighbours had adapted to her family's altered income. A half-dozen households in Upstowe had started forgetting to ask them to dine. And twice now Sophy had been cut by people who had been frequent guests at her father's own table.

Yet, having fallen from one class of society, the Byfords had no chance of being made welcome in another. The ambiguity of her situation had begun to be reflected in Sophy's appearance. She had been comforted at first by continuing to wear the elaborate bonnets and perfect gloves her father had always encouraged her to buy in such number. Soon, though, she had noticed that while showy dress did nothing to improve her lot, it did make the villagers whisper that she had got above herself. Besides, good clothes had to be spared now.

So today she picked her way through the mud in pattens and went bareheaded, in her plainest pelisse. She carried a basket, and looked less like a lady than someone in well-bred hand-me-downs. As she walked along the high road the light was fading from a cold sky as clear as glass. Turning through a private gate she took a path down the side of a little orchard, whose fruit hung from naked boughs above a mulch of blackening leaves. At the end of the path she knocked at a cottage door and went through a parlour to the bakery. The pie was returned, and Sophy made a point of covering it with the cloth as clumsily as possible, to show how unused she was to such a task. The woman who worked as the village baker meanwhile watched in silence without offering to help.

Back in the road she found herself staring at a passer-by without, at first, knowing why. It was Charity Michaelmas. The other girl was coming toward her in that half-darkness when only things in silhouette against the western sky are visible. Then Sophy understood: Charity carried a basket – she too was on some errand – and her mudstained hem and bare neck were only the least similarity with how she herself looked. Sophy had noticed the likeness between their clothes even before she'd known it.

A couple of turnings on, she was reluctantly turning this over in her mind, when she heard two horsemen coming up behind. As though her wish had made it come true, it was Rawley Fitzpayne, followed by a groom. Their horses, walked at a stiff pace, were gaining on her. She stepped aside and turned to look up and greet him.

But he hadn't stopped! 'Mr Fitzpayne!'

He glanced down at her without slowing his glossy seventeen-hand bay. It was hard to tell whose well-being was more carefully tended – the beast's or the young man's. Sophy quickened her pace. Her head was not quite as high as the saddle. 'Mr Fitzpayne?'

He reined in his horse so suddenly that it danced backward several steps, the whites of its eyes flashing. 'It would suit your own convenience to call me sir.'

'*What?*'

'Miss Sophia! Well I'm damned!' He laughed heartily at his own mistake. 'By God, I disgraced myself there, did I not?'

'Who did you think I was?' She couldn't help smiling back at him, even though an instant before she'd been chilled by his tone. No one could dream of not responding when he made a point of laughing.

'Damned if *I* know! And how is it with you? Still better worth stopping for than most, I see!' Self-parody, he found, was the way to woo them. The more sophisticated they were, the less they understood that he meant every word.

'If you say so!' She sounded as easy as he did. In fact she was aware only of being fired up to meet the challenge of his interest.

'And the devil take you otherwise, woman; you'd be a fool if *you* didn't think so too.' Females of her class were always the easiest. They had enough ambition to be dazzled by rank; yet their families were too obscure to make trouble afterward. 'Anyone can see you and I are the best-looking pair in the county.'

Sophy met his conspiratorial smile full in the face. 'I know.' She felt as though flying must be like this. It left you even lighter-headed than being furious or sobbing your lungs out. And answering him came so naturally!

His reply was to go on grinning at her over his shoulder as he rode on. For effect, he put his horse from a walk straight into a canter – he could ride as though he were a centaur. The groom splashed after, knowing he would never keep his job if he spoiled everything by lagging behind.

Sophy's elation lasted only a little way home. Then a sense of anticlimax swept over her. She should have taken pains to keep him talking longer. Nothing else interesting was likely to happen for as long as she could foresee. How should she have handled him differently? And, oh – if only she'd felt free to spare her best clothes for walking out in all this mud! What did his good humour really signify? Was he more serious than he cared to show in public? But – perhaps he didn't know they were poor now. And when he found out he would disappear, like so many of their other, closer, acquaintance.

She was still reviewing each word of their exchange when someone else passed her on the road. The Michaelmas girl again. Sophy scrutinized Charity's back with distaste, knowing now that she herself might not look much more genteel.

A new thought occurred to her. Its implications were so shaming that Sophy stopped dead. Looking up at the kindling stars, she gave a soft gasp of horror. She had been mistaken by Rawley Fitzpayne for *her*! Michaelmas, from the kitchens at the Hall! He had taken her for a kitchen maid!

All her life Sophy had been encouraged to see herself only through the eyes of other people in respectable society. She was to have been dainty and vain, not for her own pleasure in herself, but as a duty, to do her family credit. To glance aside at the condition of people who were *not* respectable – to guess at what their lives were like – was next to blasphemy. And it had been inconceivable that she should come to this. That she should be mistaken for a drudge!

It said much for the stronger, new-born Sophy – the one not chivvied into vanity at her expensive school – that she felt no resentment at how others saw her, now. She was still angry, certainly. But only with herself. There must have been something she could do to lessen their poverty. 'Of course there must. Of course there must,' she said out loud, if only to hold at bay the unwelcome thoughts that crowded her. Tears of humiliation sprang to her eyes; but she would have none of them. Instead, head erect, she walked faster, blushing even in the flaying winter cold, as she tried to scold herself out of wretchedness. 'I am not helpless! I'm not – No! No!'

Did Rawley Fitzpayne look ever so little scornful, as he rode away? Now that Sophy's notion of herself was jolted, she no longer knew what anybody might think of her. She was ready, in her confusion, to read the harshest thoughts in every face she saw. Did everyone consider her as pitiable as she did herself? ... Was that part of the reason for James Fraser's disdain, too?

She had to be doing *something*. It was hardly possible to run after Rawley Fitzpayne and explain ... what, anyway? Perhaps ... perhaps ... if she could make even Fraser think better of her, that at least would lessen the sum of the world's disapproval. His good opinion might not count for much. All the same, if *he* could think well of her, then surely anybody would. She would say she was sorry – that was what she would do. And she would make him take lessons from her, too – to show he really did forgive her. To make some money, as well. Her elders had said much about the horror of being on a footing with persons of low birth. But they hadn't told her – well, had they? – that being poor oneself was far, far worse.

So – she would act. She wasn't going to sit the years out, and grow down and die, in maidenly submission to the fates. No matter what became of her, she would do something.

Fraser was a good deal less concerned than Sophy with what he thought of her. Currently he had even more than usual to occupy him. Most pressing was a meeting of the executive committee for the Wiltshire part of the canal. This was the stretch for which he had responsibility, as resident engineer. It was also, for reasons some years old, the last and most difficult section of this great trunk route, planned to link Bristol's Atlantic trade with the Thames and London.

The meeting was in a private dining room of the New Inn at Upstowe. There, a number of respectable local citizens were digesting their boiled fowl, their loin of mutton and their gooseberry pie and cheesecakes as the cloth was cleared and business commenced. In the chair was the district's principal shareholder, the Earl of Pomeroy. He was a bland, red-faced old man who now sat before the annual minute-book like an expressionless avenging angel. At present the greatest source of strife within the committee was Lord Fitzpayne's claim.

Not for the first time, Mr Royal, a local lawyer and the

company's secretary, in charge of raising funds, proposed that the canal take a different course. 'A deviation – no, a straighter line, indeed – would take us past Cannings Fitzpayne entirely on the land of shareholders and their tenants. I think anyone here can see the reason in that.' He was a handsome little man who fancied himself forceful, in a way that would have suited an actor better than a solicitor.

'No. That won't serve. There's only the one route that will.' Fraser spoke in the tone of someone going through a formality. 'I agree there is another way, even in geological terms. But that would take you over more of Fitzpayne's land.'

Mr Deniff, the treasurer, spoke up. 'Could we not solicit a new Act of Parliament, to take the waterway across the lower slope of the sheep run?' He glanced about him to see if this frugal suggestion provoked any sarcasm. His own position was nothing if not compromised. As the town's principal banker he had already refused the canal company's request for further working capital.

'No,' Fraser said. 'All that hillside's chalk; it's too porous to hold the surface water we'd need to fill the waterway. Even in winter the locks wouldn't pass traffic clear of their sills.'

'So what concerns you is the possibility of drought? Yes? *That* is what you think your difficulty is. Is it not?' To show his superior wisdom, Royal fixed Fraser with the stare of a fair-minded man who never shrank from being hard.

Fraser took the trouble to look back at Royal until the man had spoken. For answer he ignored him and addressed the chair. 'My lord, a higher route would cost you less to purchase. But it would cost you thousands more to build and operate. You'd be asking for a cutting in bedrock, along a hillside four miles long. And when you've paid fifteen hundred men to move all that, you'd need to buy extra land to clamp the spoil. There'd be no banking works you could use it on.'

The noble earl made the smallest acknowledgement. He at least knew he had little to contribute beyond the calls on his shares. Fraser turned again to Royal. 'And as I don't doubt you know' – it always angered Royal to be given precise information in an argument – 'the sum of made banks should always equal the sum of the area taken by the excavation's section.'

To hide how slow he was to master this, Royal held Fraser's look and persisted. 'You're concerned about drought. Very well. Then we must take a southerly route, along the valley bottom.' His expression announced, answer that if you can.

'Would that not flood?' asked another leading shareholder.

Fraser regarded the man for a moment. 'Exactly.'

'The answer in that case is quite simple,' said Royal. 'The southerly route must still be taken, and banked up. I know that would cost money; I appreciate that. But can *you* give this meeting an argument to the contrary?' leaning forward at Fraser as if to project his case by physical force.

If Fraser had any youthful folly, it was a reluctance to humour his elders. He should have answered the company secretary in kind, and bristled at him. Instead, hands in pockets, he remained tactlessly at ease. 'I think not.'

'You think not! Do you mean you don't know?'

'Gentlemen' – Fraser found it hard to speak to Royal directly; his own disdain embarrassed him – 'the same disadvantages meet you if you detour to the south. Even without a risk of drought, you'd need pumping equipment to keep a banked-up pound filled with water. And crossing that marshland would cost you extra on any terms. There's no spoil close at hand for banking. And the contractors' men will charge you by the distance – yard for yard – as well as by the volume, for transporting it.'

'If one route, at least, would leave extra spoil,' someone else said, 'could we not raise money by selling what remains? Surely some of it has value?'

'I fear not,' said Fraser. He found it hard not to sound as if reciting a lesson. The facts were so much more familiar to him than to anyone else. 'There's no coal for stripping; no brick earth; no proper building stone; and no gravel this far beyond the eastern section. *I* can't make your money for you; I can only take the cheapest route that will let you keep down the cost of maintenance. Fitzpayne's land will cost you nothing compared to moving water uphill with steam pumps, or building extra reservoirs above the highest stretch of the waterway. And that's if you could buy the water rights to do it.'

'Now look here,' Royal said. 'You tell us you're concerned to save money. Yet in the past you have several times told this committee that extra expense must be incurred, when not every member has thought you justified. Not every member, by any means.'

'If you mean I opposed using stone quarried on site, I do remember that you disagreed.' Several of the committee smiled at this. Where it had already been used, the local oolite was found to be perished, and several lock-chambers had had to be rebuilt.

'But you do admit that you yourself are liable for expenditure beyond our budget?' In debate it was not Royal's tactic to stick to his guns. He preferred to muddle his opponent by changing ground. 'You are liable, are you not? Right?'

Fraser could hardly ignore this particular condition. It applied to any post of resident engineer as a matter of course. In the event of serious mishap on the workings, he would be answerable for a sum many times greater than his income. And once that happened, only a fool looked to the company that employed him in the hope of sympathy or help.

'You are liable?' repeated Royal. 'You do admit that?'

'Mr Royal,' said the chairman, 'you are, I trust, arguing to the position?' It was what he usually said when anyone talked too long. These meetings bored him so much. And any income on his shares seemed as many years off as ever.

'My lord, I think we owe it to Mr Fraser to point out that if we take the route he proposes, we shall have to make representation against Lord Fitzpayne. If every appeal to law then fails, we shall have suffered God knows what delay – which will bring further expense. And undue expense, Mr Fraser, may not break the company. But it could well break you, sir.'

'For this reason if no other,' said Fraser, impatient of the glare in which Royal tried to hold him, 'I must recommend the route through Cannings Fitzpayne park. It's no use to ask me for other economies. This is the cheapest expedient you can have. You're free to examine the accounts – and every survey that's been done. But there's no point in talking further on how the money's spent. Only on how it's to be got.'

There was a pause, broken by Deniff. 'I'm for Mr Fraser's proposal. Given due consideration of the details, of course.'

'Do you speak, sir,' said the chairman, 'as treasurer of this company, or as head of your own concern?'

Deniff ignored the impolite smiles of his fellow members. 'I see no conflict of interest, my lord. As treasurer I consider that time spent contesting this claim will allow income from shares to catch up with expenditure on construction. And as a man with responsibility to the customers of Deniff's Bank, I shall then feel at liberty to make this company a further advance.'

As the meeting was breaking up, 'A pleasure to see the right man carry the day,' said Deniff to Fraser.

'Good.' Fraser responded coolly, with the combined righteousness of youth and superior knowledge. He didn't know whether to be impressed more by the banker's stinginess or by his hypocrisy. Still, however dear the terms, it was true that a victory had been gained – for the present.

The questions discussed at the meeting made up perhaps a quarter of the problems in Fraser's mind. A contractor, hired for the navvies he could bring with him from another navigation in the Midlands, looked set to put up faulty masonry. Then there had been disagreement on the committee over contractors' rates of pay. It had taken persistence to arrange payment according to the cubic, rather than lengthwise, yards of spoil their men were to shift – and so keep any of them fit to hire. Then, too, the

60

banks in the district had difficulty finding coin to pay so much labour. Tokens were one answer – but with the result that profiteering was all too common in the few shops and public houses that would take such tender. Only that week the landlord of the Golden Fleece in Upstowe had provoked near-riot by demanding four times the usual rate for ale.

Such things left little room in Fraser's mind for Sophy. So he felt a nudge of surprise one morning when, riding up the trackway on Cannings Hill, he saw her. She was sitting on the ground, staring beyond the Vale with the patience of a shipwrecked sailor. He had actually forgotten her rejection of him at their last meeting.

She, though, had had leisure to think of nothing else. At his approach she stood up, eyes downcast. Six days of coming here in vain had sharpened her self-reproach so that she couldn't bear to look him in the face.

He reined in his horse and waited for her to speak. Though what more could she have to say?

'I've been waiting for you,' she managed.

Fraser wasn't a grudge-bearing man. He was as unlikely to suffer wounded pride as he was to care about it in others. 'Why?'

Only self-respect made her stand her ground. 'To say I'm sorry.'

'For what?'

His bluntness was not unkindly meant. But it angered Sophy. It fired her with enough resentment not to care what he might say. Because she was rehearsed, however, she plunged on with the words she'd originally planned, merely looking at him harder than she otherwise might. 'I'm sorry I disobliged you when last we met. I should be glad if I could make amends.' She seemed daring him to show scorn.

He dismounted and came closer. 'I can't say you disobliged me. Or if you did, it didn't matter.' His inquisitive look made her feel like a mechanical oddity he was forcing himself to understand. 'But you did show me disrespect.'

She had the sensation of jumping blindfold off a roof.
'I'm sorry I showed you disrespect –'
'Then I'll think no more of it.'
'– and I wish to know if I can make amends.'
'Does that mean you'll give me lessons?'
'Why – yes.'
'Good. Tell me what I must pay.'
'Oh –' Sophy had never shared a commercial transaction before. Only now did it occur to her: suppose he thinks I've apologized because of the money. 'Oh, no –' she blurted. 'No, I should prefer it if you'd accept the lessons as a gift.'

'There's no question of that.' Confident of having said everything needful, he was turning away, ready to take hold of his stirrup.

To hinder him, she seized the horse by its bridle, so fiercely that the grey backed a step. 'No! That's not why I just said what I did!'

'I never thought it was.'

Sophy still held onto the bridle. From facing him, she turned her back. She felt lost. Was that all he could answer?

Fraser himself had little idea what he should say. With a man – of any class – he might have been more abrupt. Watching her, he said, 'We must both take each other on trust, then. *I'd* prefer it if you'd accept whatever payment is usual.'

She made no move.

'You can do it to show you believe me.'

'Believe you?' looking round at him.

'That I don't accept your apology just to suit my own convenience.'

'Oh ...' Sophy looked away again, to hide her face. She was astonished at the suddenness of her relief. He waited. To his own surprise, he too was slightly ill at ease.

'Yes.' She tried to smile. 'Of course. When should you like to call?'

Both were too embarrassed to prolong the encounter. They shook hands, each glancing furtively at the other, and parted.

Sophy might have looked serious enough as Fraser rode out of sight. Once alone, however, she sighed, then stretched and gave a yawn of relief; then by degrees she brightened until she found herself smiling. On the way down the long shallow path by Hychpen Bottom, she ran. It didn't match with notions of genteel behaviour, but Sophy didn't care. It excited her, more than any feeling she knew, to stand, arms wide, on the crest of the old rampart, and lean forward till her own weight pulled her into the grassy ditch below; then, through momentum, up the further slope and, poising again, down the outer rampart, running faster all the way. She couldn't help herself or slow down or stop until she reached the bottom of the combe, her hair blown free behind her like a starburst, her limbs trembling, and she herself laughing out loud fit to cry, for all the world as if someone else were there whose sensations were as blissful as her own.

Chapter Four

Fraser may not have given much thought to the younger Miss Byford; not so Rawley Fitzpayne.

The marvel, Rawley told himself, was that when doomed to waste whole months down in Wiltshire, as a dutiful heir dancing attendance on his uncle – the marvel was that he didn't ravish her in his imagination even more.

It was in winter that he most resented his banishment from town. Then, the rain all but closed the roads to other people's carriages; and getting through an evening at the Hall without company usually felt worse than being lost at sea. Dinner was the most tedious part – for then he and his aunt and uncle were obliged to sit all together in one room. And if, on wild nights, the Hall felt like a dismasted ship, then the apartment where they ate together seemed as isolated as if it were a mile beneath the waves.

It was one such evening now. They were all the same; and each one felt worse, as the cutlery clinked deafeningly against the third-best dinner service and the five footmen tried to will themselves back to the noisy servants' hall several seconds earlier than usual. The port came in and Lady Fitzpayne had to withdraw; and Rawley was left with the nightly dilemma of whether his uncle wanted conversation. Nothing he could find to say ever had the old cove hopping up and down in sympathetic glee. Yet some form of chat was probably required. If only, Rawley told himself, because he'd never actually seen the goddamned will that everyone said – they only said, mark you – declared him heir to three estates. Not to mention the London mansion in St James's Square.

After what seemed like half the night the butler withdrew the coffee things, and they all fled each other to their own sitting rooms.

This won't do, thought Rawley, once the candles had been lit. He contemplated, tetchily, the thought of the Byford girl. Then, ringing for a lantern, he went the quarter mile out to the stable block to look at a favourite hunter with a swollen hock.

Beyond the ancient drawbridge and its new gravelled drive, he thought he saw someone moving as though they were an intruder. He walked faster, toward the grove of young holm oaks around the stables. The figure's pace quickened. He felt a moment's disbelief that anyone hoping to be ignored should scurry down a cul-de-sac. Yet that was what this stranger did. He followed, through the archway to the stables and, by now convinced that the stranger knew the way, over to the coach-house door.

Inside, she turned – he hadn't guessed it was a woman – to face his light. Charity Michaelmas, the undercook. By sight he knew her, of course – he'd even lusted after her.

She looked tearful. God Almighty, how he hated weeping women, whether or not they sought a private corner for their snivelling. He failed to realize his dislike of this one was due to frustrated lechery. Putting down the light by the door, he walked, as if by an agreed appointment, up close to her.

She stopped crying at his approach, uncertain what he could want to say. He put his hands against the wall on

64

either side of her – and then she remembered his distasteful reputation.

'Look at me then.'

'I only came out for a moment's quiet, sir.' His nearness made her oppressed rather than fearful. 'They'll be wanting me downstairs, to give out their supper.'

He seemed unconscious of anything she might say. 'Why won't you look at me?' he said, in a voice trying to sound insinuatingly soft. 'Why? Tell me; why? Why won't you look at me? Go on; tell me why. Why won't you?'

'Oh sir, I can't stay here. Honestly I can't.'

'Why won't you look at me? I only want to see you look at me, truly I do. That's all I want. It is, truly. Why won't you look at me? Tell me; go on. Why won't you?'

In a clammy voice like this, she thought, the serpent in the third chapter of the Good Book must have wheedled Eve.

'I just want you to look me in the face,' he said. His tone now very slightly indicated thwarted authority. 'Now that's all I want. You do appreciate that, now, don't you? That's all I'm asking of you. That's all I want.'

She glanced up at him, calculating her chances of escape. In the darkness his eyes were unreadable. All she could see in detail was the odd curl of auburn hair silhouetted in the lantern's light.

'I have to go back, sir. I only came out for a –' As he squeezed her breast, she cringed not from pain but from sexual nausea. Lately her breasts had become so sore that even snagging their wounded nerve-ends on a garment distressed her.

'Why are you so tense?' he murmured, in a voice as soft as putrefaction. He was leaning against her; she could feel him stiffen in his breeches. 'Why do you go like that? Mm? Why are you tense? Why is that? Why do you go tense when I touch you? Why do you do that?' All the while he was gathering up her skirt with one hand as if somehow she wouldn't notice.

'I don't want you to touch me,' she said in a hard dry voice.

'Yes you do,' he whispered. 'Yes you do. Yes you do

want me to touch you. You do. Yes. Yes. You do. You want me to. You do. You know you do. You know that's what you want. You want me to touch you there –'

She made a movement of resistance, and his voice changed. 'Now – now; don't do that; don't be silly.'

'I don't want –'

'Now don't be silly. Just don't be foolish. Will you? Will you?'

As she tried to dodge away, he seized her. She glimpsed his face in the faint light; his eyes were almost expressionless. 'You'll make me cross,' he said. 'You know you wouldn't like that.' He held her down hard and went on fumbling at her. 'You've got to let me touch you here – or here. Which do you want? You've got to tell me; here – or here?'

Charity's good sense told her she should do as he said. But some other, unanswerable instinct also moved her. She lifted her head; paused; and spat all over his mouth and chin and beautifully hand-laundered stock.

Teeth bared in calculated revenge, he seized her by the hair and wrested her to the floor. Though she was too terrified even to scream, a calm corner of her mind persisted in the thought that he wasn't nearly as angry as she would have been, had someone just spat at her. He didn't even hate her; he was just implacable in collecting what he thought of as his due.

'Right –'

'No –'

'Right.'

'No – no –'

'You know what you've done now, don't you?'

'No, no, please; no, please; please don't; no, please!'

'You know what whores like you want, don't you? You are a whore, aren't you? Aren't you? Go on, say it! Tell me you're a whore!'

'No, no, no, no,' she cried out senselessly, through tears of rage and shame.

'Tell me you're a whore!'

'Oh no; oh no!'

'Tell me you're a whore!'

66

'Oh no, please God!'

'This is what you whores all want, isn't it?'

Charity raised her voice and wept, louder than she thought she'd dare. She did so more at the menace in him than at the meaty, horrible blind eye he held on its stalk of gristle – or even at the pain as he intruded it into her body, already, to her terror, made bloated and tender by George Byford's fertile seed.

Bad as the roads were in February, early that month the Hall was pitched into sudden activity by Lord Fitzpayne's decision to go to London on business. Such a journey, for a man in his position, was like a small tribal migration. The stables, the servants' hall and the upper servants' offices were scenes of anxious to-and-fro for days beforehand. The butler and a party of menservants left in advance, to open up the house in town and see the plate and linen safely transported. My lord's carriage was made ready for him and for Master Rawley, together with a chaise for further services of china and a coach for those servants not due to travel as an outrider or driver.

Lady Fitzpayne would not be going up to town. Nor, as relations with her husband had darkened over the years, had she done so since most of the household could remember. His absence always gave relief, sure enough. Yet she still ached for London, with a zest unmatched by any half-grown girl. As a place of youthful fashion the city itself had little further use for her. But she still held it dear, remembering grand nights spent dancing in the pleasure-grounds of Ranelagh till the sun came up and made the river smoke with mist. She had been set, at forward sixteen, to try and snare the eligible new young King. It had been a ridiculous exercise, involving dressing as a shepherdess, only in silk, and wielding a hayrake with pretty ineptitude beside the byway where he rode each day. Still, as she recalled with bittersweet pleasure, in the months that followed their encounter all London said she pleased him better than any of the other panting fillies in the field.

But now, a respite from her husband's moods and freezing looks was the best her life could offer.

So it was a ménage without womenfolk that set out in the darkness of one early morning. The first change would be at Marlborough, where the horses were to be sent back and eighteen hired nags harnessed or saddled in their place. Meanwhile the liberated, bachelor feeling of the journey touched everyone. The sun came up, and grew from a presence in a white fog to a pale shape, then surprised them as they thrashed up the slimy chalk highway, like a narrow watercourse, that took them onto the downs. Once on high ground, the servants who'd got down to spare the horses resumed their places; and where the road allowed, they travelled at the trot, not just with consequence, but with much cheerful noise. The hooves of their orderly herd of horses thudded, the wheels hummed, the harnesses clinked, and the door handles rattled. To all this, while they rose out of the fog as if from the sea, was added a mysterious jingling of bells, as a great tarpaulined wagon crawled toward them through the brightening obscurity. They passed the local mail coach, too, the Paragon, its name on each varnished door – not, as one might expect, clattering along to the excitement of passers-by; instead, it dawdled, to raucous singing from driver, guard and a roof full of rowdy young men with muzzle-loaders to hand and four brace of new-killed partridge.

At Marlborough they provoked a satisfying to-do down the broad main street; and at the Golden Lion the innkeeper himself came out into the yard to smile and bow at Lord Fitzpayne, as a regular long-distance customer, while the horsekeeper vied in obsequiousness by shouting extra loudly at the stable-boys running out with the new horses.

The bright cold weather lasted. Two mornings later saw them near the capital, on a road still held passable by heavy frost. London made its nearness felt long before they drove onto the stones and were clanging down a properly cobbled street. From a dozen miles out the villages were full of box-like, elegant mansions, with high garden walls and plantations of young trees. The fields, from empty ploughland amid woods or thick hedgerows, became a lake-like expanse of market gardens, with glass-houses and other outbuildings for ships upon its surface, and the tall trees of walled parks for islands. Where the Middlesex fields were not set to feed London's inhabitants they made huge stretches of frost-blackened pasture for the thousands of horses in the metropolis. Soon the Fitzpayne entourage became hindered by other traffic – barouches or curricles from smart country houses one change of horse out of town; ponderous wagons harnessed to eight Clydesdales each; local carts and gigs; a herd of Hereford bullocks bound for Smithfield market and a flock of geese continually changing its shape across the roadway ahead like a mirage. Further in came an area of brickfields set with stumpy kilns. Here, the whole melee was held up amidst the lowing of cattle and the shouts and whistles of drovers, by an oncoming pack of stag-hounds fresh from a kill somewhere in Kensington.

The elms of Hyde Park rose over the nearby fields, and the city could be said to begin. Rawley surveyed the press of carriages and people by Green Park with hopeful impatience. From forcing himself on snivelling kitchenmaids, and rat-catching with yokels and their dogs in the estate barns, he could now, within a quarter mile, fall in with any number of acquaintance, and meet his carnal desires in the glittering stews of Covent Garden and the Strand.

That evening, he was out to see if time really had stood still since last he'd been dead drunk in splendid company at his club. Rounding the corner from St James's Square, he felt an angry stab of fear at being jostled. His readiness to hand out mortal injury turned to guffaws of satisfaction, though, when he found he was being pinioned, and his kidneys buffeted, by none other than Sir Jack Boone and Frederick Nordaby. One was the young squire of a neighbouring estate in Wiltshire. The other, Rawley had known since a caper at Harrow when a mock marriage ceremony had featured Nordaby's pet ape. Rawley's left hand was still scarred where the creature had bitten him to the bone, shrieking at the blasphemous union's consummation.

'Good God, man, you can't piss the night away in there,' said Nordaby on the steps of Rawley's club. 'You're coming to Emmett's with us.'

So to Emmett's rooms, off St Martin's Lane, they bent their way for the odd draught of alcohol and a large plain meal of oysters and mutton pie. On their progress arm-in-arm up Piccadilly and through Leicester Square their number increased. Boone's cousin Walter, like him an agricultural-looking man with red face and pale eyebrows, pitched up against them in the light from a hatter's above the Haymarket. With him was a discreet-looking junior colleague from the Inns of Court named Kilpatrick. And opposite the yard leading to Emmett's itself they were hailed across the street by two other long-lost cronies from out of town, Dobson and Underwood. Both were wont to hunt with one private pack or other almost daily when down in Wiltshire – and indeed both had the pigeon-toed lollop more common to post-boys or jockeys. With them was another fellow who had occasionally led the field, with more dash than expertise: George Byford.

They bellowed and stamped their way under the entrance to the yard and up the wooden steps beneath the loft-house entrance to Emmett's fashionable rooms. Their glee at falling in together was loudest in Rawley, feeling like a discharged conscript, and in George, to whom this evening looked to be the only good thing that had happened since he'd first come to London to be lonely and dull. For him the coincidence of their all meeting up seemed almost too happy to be true; and before many pints of porter had been drunk George was ready to believe everyone present was an excellent fellow, and destined to prove a lifelong friend.

From Emmett's they made their way to Covent Garden Theatre, to see what faces they could recognize among the audience. Out in the oil-lit lanes of the city, every age and mood of human voice rose up through the dark as though crowded inside one vast room. From the theatre gallery the racket was even louder. It had never occurred to George that so many people could afford four shillings for one evening's entertainment. Nor that such a well-dressed company could be so restive – for the box-keeper, a formally dressed, meaty figure, had stationed several bruisers about the auditorium as a matter of routine.

He also saw with envy that his companions were on speaking – or shouting – terms with nearly half the theatre. They had of course been schooled with each other's cousins, or gamed or hunted with them up at university. It was becoming apparent to George, educated by the curate, and the grammar school ten miles from home, that once of age, someone such as Nordaby or Rawley might expect never to shake hands with a stranger for the rest of their lives.

Their acquaintance evidently included several ladies in the most expensive seats. George was straining for a better look at one ochre-haired young lady, when, to his surprise, he recognized her. At a chance meeting with Underwood at a pastry-cook's in the Strand, he had been introduced – though for reasons he had not understood at the time he had only been told her Christian name. Only now did George suffer the shock of understanding exactly how it was Miss Lucy got her living. For she was quite unchaperoned; of that there was not the smallest doubt. Besides, she wore her tall ostrich-feathers, her yards of white satin and her diamond-sparkling acreage of decolletage with an air that had nothing to do with the politeness of the marriage market.

In the interval all eight young men scampered, tittering, round to Lucy's box. Her maid let them in, to take turns at hanging over the edge and hailing their acquaintance from beside the splendour of Miss Lucy's arms and breasts. Normally young George would have striven to be as forward as the worst. But four pints of porter and a half-bottle of cheap champagne were not enough to put down his embarrassment at a former conversation with the lady. He had believed her when told, with a smile whose glint of naughtiness he hadn't noticed, that she lived on an allowance from an uncle out of town. She, however, seeing George in well-heeled company, was careful to say not one word about their encounter. Instead, she took pains to flatter him, showing the familiarity coloured by respect

71

that he might hope for as an intimate friend. She had of course no notion that he wasn't rich ...

'You buffoon!' Dobson's prematurely weatherbeaten features were working violently from the emphatic stage of drunkenness. 'Byford! Why did you not tell us Lucy would be here, you cockroach dropping?'

'But I didn't – I didn't expect to find her here – upon my word I did not,' stammered George, as if meeting Lucy in her working clothes had made him responsible for her being a harlot. 'Did I?' he appealed, turning to her. The next moment he blushed, furious at having shamed both himself and her by asking something so inept. Someone behind him sniggered, and Dobson and Walter Boone laughed out loud. Even the discreet little Kilpatrick, with his polite smile of sympathy at the general merriment, was probably brimful of contempt. Lucy herself sat perfectly collected, looking down at her opened fan with the faintest lilt of mirth about the corners of her mouth. George sought to stumble upright, with a thought of threatening whoever was nearest.

'Won't you be the one to sit by me?' said Lucy, putting her slender hand on his sleeve. 'No, Jacko, I don't want you beside me, you oaf. I'd rather be leered at from a distance by the likes of you – Won't you, George?'

The use of his name, spoken with the most private of smiles, made George her creature. Still blushing, he sat down. She proceeded to murmur at him, pointedly excluding the others, while he stared down into the dim noisy theatre and occasionally glanced at her when he thought he might not meet her eyes. After a minute or so Dobson remarked: 'Damn me if Lucy hasn't got the cackiest little box in the place,' and led the others across to where another fallen acquaintance, attended by a huge bewigged black footman in scarlet and gold, was flaunting herself.

The play ran its course; and Shakespeare's Prince Troilus, mouthing vengeance, left the stage, garbed in riding boots, and to show that this was ancient Troy, a breastplate and monstrous feathered helmet. After the curtain, Lucy, passing her hand through the crook of

George's arm, said: 'You won't desert me later tonight, will you?' With a look both earnest and naughty, she gave him a card bearing a printed address and whispered an hour of rendezvous. 'I cannot stay – I have to go,' she murmured with nicely judged melancholy; and kissing her gloved fingers to him, she hastened away, followed by her maid as by a drab shadow.

Among the crush of people waiting inside the theatre entrance for their carriages George re-found his companions, still on the prowl.

'Never seen such a pocky choice,' muttered Rawley, looking about him.

'What, no jolly times tonight?' Dobson leered, seeing George alone.

The feeling was that the evening owed them more. So to the nearby Crown Street hop they went, another resort of fashion, up an alley leading to a rope-maker's. There, against a noise of voices that made the theatre gallery seem inhibited, half a hundred well-dressed whores paraded or sat, or danced the hay quadrille, with gentlemen admitted for their social standing, plus a fee.

Some brandy-and-water was sent for; and, soon enough, some more, followed by a quantity of rum punch. George looked on, appalled and envious, as Underwood and Kilpatrick went upstairs with a remarkably pretty girl of fifteen or so, and having serviced her, returned simultaneously. Opposite him, Dobson and Jack Boone were disputing the establishment's merits with those of a rival bawdyhouse across the Strand. 'Damn your eyes, Dobson, I don't want to mince about with these mares. I want a good show, where the trollops do the job properly – where they do their job, they do – where they do it properly, and dance about without any damn clothes on, and twinkle their fannies at you first, just like they should. If we were at Mother Higgins' by midnight we could see the damn nuns in her abbey perform their South Sea fertility whatsit-called. They could show us – I'm telling you, now – they could show us a gross of virgins – real virgins, sir – being decently defiled. On the very stroke of midnight. On the stroke!'

'They aren't virgins!' said George, trying not to sound surprised.

'They are – I tell you they are, sir. You see –' indicating George to the rest of the company. 'Here's one fellow at least who wants to go to Mother Higgins'.'

'They wouldn't let him in,' muttered Dobson. 'Even if he could afford to pay.'

Lacking any preference stronger than Sir Jack's, that was where they set out for. Meanwhile the drink had quite obscured George's awareness of past or future. He might have forgotten Lucy's invitation, had not the cold out in the alley brought him to.

'Must go home,' he mumbled, as they passed the street named on her card.

'Where's he going?' asked Jack Boone. 'Hey, Byford, where're you going?'

'He's going home.'

'Dammit, man, you're not going home. You're coming with us!'

'Let him be,' murmured Underwood. 'They'll only turn him away at the door.'

'If they think he's not a gentleman,' guffawed Dobson, staggering against a wall as he was literally knocked sideways by his own wit.

'Damn you to hell, Byford,' roared Sir Jack. 'You can't go home now!'

'I know where he's going,' someone else said.

'Where's he going? Where's he going?' Dobson asked.

'To hell with him,' mumbled Sir Jack. 'In God's name, we're wasting our time, standing here.'

'He's going to Lucy's.'

'The devil he is!'

'Our Lucy's!'

'No, he's not going there. He ... haw, haw ... he can't ...' gasped Dobson, buckling from laughter while the others looked on indifferently, 'he can't afford *her*, either.'

George was too drunk to wonder for long why Lucy should invite him to her apartment. Or indeed why he was

74

favoured above his companions, whose annual debts to their glovemakers alone might come to hundreds.

'Oh, I knew you'd come,' breathed Lucy as she locked the door behind him. Even in an artificial light it seemed that she was blushing.

The apartment was mainly one large room. It was discreetly lit with the best wax candles and a fire of sea-coals burned in the grate. Everything was glossily new – the smart wallpaper, the rosewood bed beneath a canopy of crimson velvet – even the two white angora cats, each with a red ribbon in its tail. On the walls were framed some very pretty scenes of rape and bestiality from classical antiquity. Lucy herself was tricked out in a wine-coloured silk *deshabille* that combined the lines of a medieval Madonna with hints of nakedness.

She watched his glance run from the smooth swells and shadows of her body, slyly half-revealed to the waist, to the room, which spoke so clearly of her trade. 'I wanted you to see me like this.'

Gallantry left George tongue-tied.

'With any other man, I could have gone on pretending. But not you. You do understand that, don't you?'

He looked back at her impersonation of grave earnestness. Already he was confused – what could she still have pretended?

'You were angry with me this evening, weren't you?'

'No – no.'

'You were – you are still. I know you are. Oh, don't try to be forbearing. I know what you really think of me.'

'No, truly!'

'It wasn't me you came here to find, was it? You came here tonight to find the woman you thought you saw in me back at the theatre. Did you not?'

'No, I did not,' he protested tactlessly. 'And I'm not being forbearing,' he added, as firmly as he could.

'The woman who hardens her heart and laughs out loud, and holds her head up high in front of ... all those people. But perhaps you think my true place is on display before the multitude.'

'No – no – I'm not like that, upon my word.'

'And I do it well, do I not? Let them all say what they will; I do know how to play the – dear God, I can hardly say it, even now – the fallen woman, as though I gloried in it. Do I not know how to perform the part of a strumpet?'

'I don't think ill of you, I swear I don't,' he said with difficulty. 'I'm sure I never meant you any harm.'

'Oh George! What can you say to make me believe you? How can I be certain that you're more capable of delicate feelings than those others? – No; no, don't touch me,' she whispered, moving toward him in order to keep him at arm's length. 'Not you. No. Not you.'

'I'm sorry – if ever I said anything to make you feel I'd slighted you – or not thought well of you. I'm sorry, indeed I am,' he mumbled, aching amidst a haze of lust.

'If you didn't truly believe in the real feelings of my heart, I couldn't bear it. Can you understand what it means to say that?' looking up at him with wide-eyed seriousness.

He nodded dumbly. His hands felt moist enough to leave a stain on anything he touched.

'You don't belong among those people you were with tonight, do you? Any more than I do, if the truth were told. Even now I still think, sometimes, of the village where I was born.'

Her eyes dimmed as she invoked this innocent setting for her years of maidenhood. She was in fact the daughter of a paymaster from Chatham, and hoped soon to bring out two younger sisters into her own line of trade.

'But I've no business any more to talk of that,' she added with a brave, melancholy smile. 'You must know that though you see me humbled here,' indicating the room, with its huge disrupted bed, 'dressed like this,' and she held her arms wide, in shimmering disarray, and bowed her head, 'yet am I a stranger to any feeling of contrition. I may have regrets, but you may not look to me for apologies. If you will be my friend, you must accept me not as I may once have been, but just as I am now. I don't want your pity; no – that I would shrink from. Not your pity, George. What I ask is more than that. What I want of you is your regard!'

'Well, yes – yes, honestly I do. I do hold you in the – well, in the highest regard.' Strands of her loose hair, haloed in the firelight, were stirred about her brow by the breath of each word he whispered. He found himself held silent in her gaze, excited and unhappy. A coal dropped from the fire and the staircase creaked outside from someone going past.

'What can I say?' he pleaded. 'What can I do so that you'll understand me – what I think – so that you'll know what I think of you? Just tell me what I must do. Anything – you know I'll do anything. Please!'

She hid her face in her hands. 'Oh!' she gasped, looking back up at him. 'Oh! Oh, how could I have doubted you? Say you forgive me. Oh, please!'

'What for? Why? What have you done wrong?'

'Oh! To think that you should say that to a creature such as I have become! To me! Oh George, to me!'

And with shining eyes she met his terrified desire with what seemed to him a courageous gesture of purest modesty. With a movement of exquisite simplicity she bared her perfect breasts to him and let the robe drop about her feet.

Though no longer a virgin, he had never seen a woman's naked body. The sight of her moved him to a tender yearning to seize and ravish her, as a dog might sink its teeth into a hare. But lascivious though he was, George was far enough above the common ruck to feel awe as much as lechery. To his fuddled perceptions, her body stood like a still flame in a universe of chaos.

She reached her arms to him, every fingertip expressive.

'Byford! We know you're there!'

The door shook beneath a clamour of blows. There was a sound of stifled laughter.

'Byford! Stop it, whatever ... haw, haw ...' and the speaker paused, labouring feebly against his own mirth, 'whatever it is you think you're doing!'

'Don't do it, Lucy,' shouted someone else, faint from laughing. 'Don't do it! He's skint!'

'He's not a gentleman! He hasn't even got debts!'

Lucy thrust her robe on as a pugilist might take off his shirt to batter another man, and strode to wrench open the door.

Mother Higgins had failed to claim George's companions. On the dark landing they swayed and collided, ecstatic with derision.

'Lucky for you runts that I'm a lady,' snarled Lucy, 'or you'd have the bloody piss-pot emptied over you.'

Her abuse only made them laugh the more. 'Good God, Lucy,' someone shouted, 'if you've started peddling it to City clerks, I'm not coming here again!'

She would have treated them to stronger language, had not George hurled himself, speechless, upon them. For a minute or two he flailed about, choking on tears of rage and blundering against the wall. With unseen discretion, Lucy sneaked the door shut and locked it from inside.

'Damn you, Byford, that hurt.'

'Fellow can't take a joke, can he?'

'For God's sake, can't somebody stop him?'

'Get his arms, in God's name.'

He found himself, at length, held against a wall. They were all winded as well as drunk.

'I challenge you! I challenge you!' he gasped at all or any of them.

'By God, though, that was funny!'

'He kicked me! The sod kicked me!'

'God damn you, I challenge you to fight!' George raged, at the last person he thought had spoken.

'Lucy puts on a better entertainment than I thought!'

'Doesn't he know that no one's going to fight him over a whore?'

'I've got a stitch. Bugger me, I've got a stitch from laughing.'

'Aw, let him go.'

'What's that –? Hey, Fitzpayne; do it outside!' someone yelled down at Rawley, who was noisily relieving himself onto the marble floor of the hall.

George sat down on the topmost stair, suddenly feeling

clammy and cold. He wished the planes of darkness about the stairwell wouldn't keep sliding toward him like that.

'Bad luck, Byford.'

'The trollop would've fleeced you anyway.'

'I wager in his condition he couldn't even do it!'

Someone muttered an interrogative.

'The devil we should! He's all right.'

'What should we do now?'

'Damn me if I know ...'

'I'm going home.'

'You can't do that! Dammit, man, it's only one o'clock.'

Eyes shut, and bent double against his nausea, George only partly noticed their going. At length, shivering, he spewed, and having done so, fancied himself just able to find his way home. He remembered that he'd left his coat in Lucy's room ... It lay outside her locked door, a signal of rejection more final than violence itself.

He must have got downstairs unaided; for when he came to himself again, he was plumb across the gutter that ran down the middle of the street. He got up, cringing from the cold, his clothes soaked by loathsome week-old slops. All around, the church clocks were striking two in long-drawn-out succession, as he laboured up the five flights to his room, vowing never again to entertain a single thought of drink or fornication.

Chapter Five

Though the two elder Byford children had been launched in the world, the Nortons' patronage was not exhausted.

'This *is* handsome of them,' said Mrs Byford when her cousins' manservant rode over one day with a letter.

'What do they say?' Sophy demanded.

'Oh, I've only glanced at the letter; you mustn't think there's anything extraordinary in it. But how kind, to send their own man! I only hope he didn't think too ill of being entertained in our little kitchen. People's servants can be so critical about that sort of thing.'

'I'm sure our kitchen is big enough to satisfy him, if our little parlour is too grand for Mr Fraser.'

Sophy spoke in self-defence rather than from loyalty to Fraser. Her mother had protested on hearing that she intended giving him lessons; he was after all a person of whom no well-established family in Upstowe knew anything. The lessons were proceeding, however. Two or three evenings a week Sophy and Fraser would sit together at the table, for economy's sake sharing the light of a single candle, while Mrs Byford sewed by the fire, tight-mouthed with embarrassment. Knowing how badly they needed the money, she strove to be civil – with the result that she was merely awkward. It was not that, in order to see, the two young people had to sit with their heads almost touching. Nor that they talked together in low voices – they did that so that neither she nor the maidservant in the kitchen should be disturbed. What showed, in all her forced attempts to be agreeable, was that to her the man was out of place even here: the grandson of one of the Fitzpayne servants, and little more than a labourer himself. Sophy found her mother's manner excruciating – the more so for reflecting her own doubts and prejudice.

The letter was less uninteresting than Mrs Byford had suggested. In truth, the Nortons were conscious that they had not done as much as they might for their young relatives. So now they sought to meet their obligations once and for all by taking Sophy away with them – to Bath.

'To do them justice, I suppose it is kind of them really,' said Mrs Byford. 'But Sophy, do you think you should go? You can't spare your good clothes that readily; and you would have to be seen in company with your aunt Norton. And her dress allowance – in confidence, now, I know this for a fact – has always been better than we could afford to give you.'

Sophy didn't even hear. To get to an actual watering place, she would have walked all the way barefoot, and presented herself in rags.

So it was, one February morning, that the Nortons' carriage was seen at the gate of Drove Cottage, its coachman's head on a level with the upstairs windows and all the village agog. Even as Sophy danced down the path to where the footman held the door for her, Mrs Byford was unreconciled to her going. 'If only you weren't travelling down the same road your poor father last took. And you don't know this, but he once saw an overturn on the way to Bradford, with two horses having to be shot, and Lord knows how many people killed. I hope your uncle Norton realizes it won't be fair to me if anything should happen to you.'

Sophy, all blissful smiles, was lost to every word. 'Of course, dearest mama. I'm sure he does.'

At Bradford-on-Avon Sophy was to spend the night with her uncle and aunt before their departure for Bath. The Nortons' house – more a mansion – was in a lane at the bottom of the steep little town, near the canal. Its fine Palladian façade bore fourteen sash windows and a fanlit door. Next to it, between stone pillars a storey high, stood the wrought-iron gates to the mill-yard. Norton's woolmill itself was older than the house; a tall, box-like structure with three rows of mullioned windows on each side and built, like the rest of the town, in honey-coloured limestone.

Sarah Norton was in the hallway to meet Sophy, clad in a gown that shimmered with the discreet richness of the best half-mourning to be had. The four children had been shut away with their nurse, because Thomas was still formally being grieved over and they were too young to act as downcast as they ought. Her husband was there too, clearing his throat a lot while looking at Sophy and offering politenesses she didn't need.

'You mustn't think,' said Sarah at dinner that evening, 'that this visit won't be a great social opportunity for any girl like you. Will it not, Charles?'

'Oh yes, yes indeed,' involuntarily casting an eye at Sophy.

His wife, too, was embarrassed to be staring at her so much. Her new poverty notwithstanding, the girl had a radiance that struck one anew at every glance. Sophy herself hardly noticed their looks. The thought of the morrow had her almost speechless with happiness. Their dinner itself! It seemed like a promise of eternal earthly bliss, to be restored to the propriety of finger bowls and a sideboard of extra cold meats. Passive with delight, she answered their remarks absent-mindedly and tried not to look greedy beside the elegance of her aunt. Sarah, for her part, while silver-forking in the odd morsel and covertly watching the parlourmaids' every move, looked at her niece with a satisfaction not entirely unselfish. While her own good looks kept her free of jealousy, she also knew the advantage of having such a creature at her side, to draw favourable attention in public.

She had another motive, too, for inviting Sophy. The Leggatts were to be in Bath, taking Kate with them. On hearing this, 'Charles, what do you think?' she had asked. 'Could the girl's – you know, position, in the Leggatt household – be embarrassing? I mean, to us?'

Her husband had been silent a while. 'Not,' he pondered at length, 'if her sister were there, and we made it plain that as one of our party *she* still has the standing of a gentlewoman.'

In the drawing room, Sarah continued to tell Sophy how grateful she should be. 'Of course, there's no saying exactly when the chance might arise for you to get yourself a husband ... that is, if you don't choose not to marry ... ' Sophy inwardly shuddered at this euphemism for spinsterhood and tried to look patient as her aunt went on. ' ... But in the meantime there will be no harm to your prospects if you are seen in good company. In the long term – and I'm sure your uncle agrees with me – it will certainly be more profitable in a material sense. I mean, than now, when your earnings come only from giving lessons to that young man.'

Sophy frowned steadily enough into the glowing landscapes within the drawing room fire. But she felt as though even her hands and feet could give away how much she was blushing. Did her aunt's implied criticism of Fraser make her angry for him or ashamed for herself?

'Is he a particularly low sort of person?' Charles Norton

asked ... And on seeing the agitated looks of the ladies, pretended that he hadn't spoken.

'Who's that? Good Lord, who can that be?'

'I beg your pardon?' Joseph Lee nearly said – and realized a couple nearby were talking to each other. On a whim, he had turned along the grand vista of the Royal Crescent one morning to survey the company alone.

'I never saw *her* before,' said the man. His wife, anxious to seem above jealousy, held up an eyeglass and exclaimed her own delight at the stranger's appearance. Joseph followed their stare fifty yards across the grand sweep of the pavement. Amid a party of promenaders a dark-haired girl was talking, partly turned away. She moved, and he felt a shock of satisfaction. It was Kate Byford.

She was worth remarking on. Though her clothes were still sombre she was dressed in expensive muslins (to her embarrassment, the gift of Mr Leggatt) that moved about her as fluently as if she were walking under water. Her employer had also wheedled her into changing her hair. Its luxuriance had always been suppressed, but now the most expensive hairdresser in the city – of course the only one acceptable to Leggatt – had trimmed it to release a garden of tendrils about her face as profligate as new-made leaves in May.

Joseph would have been delighted to see her in any circumstances. Several times he had debated whether to post all the way into Wiltshire just to visit her again. But the unexpectedness of discovering her here made her more wonderful than ever. Never self-conscious about his impulses toward women, he not only hastened to meet her – he ran. In front of Kate's party, a fashionable group, all lavender water and unwashed embroideries, broke up, bewildered by what they took for an emergency.

The Nortons and Sophy were there, as was Mr Leggatt. The other people present were also known to Joseph: Sir William and Lady Barrington, a pleasant, middle-aged couple whose prosperity made them two of Sarah Norton's most valued acquaintance. Sir William was likewise in the timber trade, and in doing business with him

Joseph had been a guest at their new country house near the city.

It has to be said that at this moment Joseph's manners, either in greeting established friends or being introduced, were not perfect. He was delighted to see every one of them – they were all splendid people to have made such an encounter possible – but in saying as much he looked at no one but Kate. She herself looked prettier than ever. The morning had begun well for her, with the arrival of her relatives and the presence of only one Leggatt, and now it lacked for nothing.

No one had more to say on the coincidence of the meeting than Sarah Norton. She had already identified Joseph as an excellent match for her niece, and was searching for the right way to say so. 'You cannot have expected to see either of my nieces here,' she remarked as they walked on. 'They are foreigners in this county, after all.'

'Why, yes,' said Lady Barrington. 'Your family are moonrakers, are they not?'

'But that story,' Leggatt broke in, 'concerned a very ordinary class of person.'

'They were felons, if that is what you mean,' said Sir William. 'In any case, Lee has encountered many more remarkable forms of mankind in his own country. Have you not, Lee? I mean, in Indian territory?'

'Why, sir, that depends. As a rule I'd say nothing could be more glum than Virginia west of the staging road.' He was in fact an observant man with an intensely curious mind, who had travelled widely, in his own country as well as Europe. At this moment, however, he wanted only to talk of what concerned the elder Miss Byford.

'The moonrakers, then,' said Lady Barrington, on being pressed. 'How did that story go, Sir William?'

'Oh, Kate,' Sophy exclaimed, 'you must be the one to tell Mr Lee!'

'But Sir William is the one who had it at first hand,' said Charles Norton.

'Why, yes; from Adams, my father's servant. He rose in

the world to become Adams the smuggler. They say he did so well for himself that he died quite respectable.'

'How shocking!' said Sarah Norton. Not at any felony, but at one of the poor getting above his station.

'It was a shock to the excisemen, certainly, when they found how he'd cheated them on one occasion. Adams came from Bishops Cannings, you know, in Pewsey Vale. One night they got word that he and his associates –'

'His accomplices, surely, Sir William,' said Sarah, interrupting in the hope of ingratiating herself.

'His accomplices, rather – had hidden several kegs of brandy in the village. The excisemen came; found nothing; departed – and doubled back.'

'To do your fellow justice,' Leggatt broke in, 'I recall he did show a degree of enterprise.' Even sober, he made a bad listener. 'His case reminds me –'

'What happened?' asked Joseph, genuinely interested.

'Why, when the excisemen had cantered back, they found half the village, with lanterns, by the duckpond – which to all appearances they were trying to scoop dry with hayrakes. But so low did they consider the intellect of Adams and his kind, that this sight surprised them hardly at all. "Why, you mun see, sir," Adams explained, "as folk be raikin' for to get that there cheese." And he pointed at the reflection of the full moon. "You fool," said one of the excisemen. "Why be you doing that? That's the moon, that is." "Ah, sir, you may laugh iffen as you will. But we know as that there b'ain't no moon." '

Everyone laughed, mainly at hearing Sir William render Wiltshire speech. (It was in fact how his father had talked.)

'And so,' said Lady Barrington, 'the excisemen were deceived; the brandy was recovered from the pond; the village was well-to-do for weeks thereafter; and Adams himself went into trade and had five sons who all style themselves Esquire.'

'I don't wish to outdo your tale of mercantile initiative, sir,' said Leggatt to Sir William – and tried to do precisely that. He had recently become a contractor to the new canal, and wanted to recount how he had ousted a

85

competitor. But his story was more braggart than amusing, and got no very lively response.

To make up for this and carry the day, in parting he proposed that several evenings thence they should all dine at his lodgings. 'I should warn you, though; it won't be a mean affair. But then, if it were,' with a knowing laugh, 'I should have invited someone else, should I not?'

'Would you do me an important favour?' Kate asked Sophy some days later.

Sophy was surprised to see her so solemn. The evening, spent dancing at the Upper Rooms, had so far been almost everything one could wish for. Joseph had been one of their party daily now for over a week; and in her sister's company he had looked more serious – in the cheerfulest sense – every time they met. Tonight, he and Kate had scandalized some, and delighted Sophy most of all, by sharing every dance; and as she should have become more tired, Kate had looked stronger and happier by the minute.

'Whatever is the matter?'

'Tomorrow, at dinner – you will try to ignore Mr Leggatt and his wife?'

'Oh – I know what you mean. He's idiotic, and she always looks maudlin. But they wouldn't provoke their own guests, would they?'

'I think you may be surprised when you see them for several hours at once ... I mean, when I'm there ... especially if aunt and uncle aren't close at hand.'

'Is *she* so unbearable? She lets you keep company more than she does herself, after all.'

'At her husband's demand. And to oblige uncle Norton, while he's here. Besides ... she contrives that I'm seen unchaperoned with her husband, so that people will talk and so feel sorry for her.'

Sophy was silent from dismay. 'Oh, Kate, I am sorry!' she exclaimed at length. To herself, she insisted, 'It can't be true!' If someone as dear to her and as superior to all the world as Kate could be made miserable, the same fate might befall herself. Kate had to be mistaken. It would be too unjust, otherwise. Sophy's notion of her own brilliant destiny was something in which no change had yet shaken her belief. Everything would be all right for both of them – it had to be.

Their time in Bath had indeed enabled Kate to guess how any evening with the Leggatts might be. When giving a dinner to which Kate's relatives were not invited, Mrs Leggatt would contrive things so that Kate could only put out the numbers. This meant the girl had to go down to the kitchen, where everyone was running around as if on a sinking ship, and challenge the cook for something she could eat in her little bedroom. She always had to wear something expensive, though. Two hours into the evening a bell would most likely be rung for her to go down to the drawing room, so that over coffee Leggatt could display her to the company.

Today, though she was to eat with the guests, she still had to wait until summoned. Leggatt liked to have a roomful of people present before introducing her, to make her entrance conspicuous.

' "And this," ' she mimicked into the spotty dimness of her bedroom mirror, ' "is my best new set of Chinese-Bristol china. A hundred and seventy-five guineas, not a penny less. And this, now, is Miss Byford!" '

The bell did go; and Kate went down. As she opened the doors to the drawing room, the lights, swaying in the draught, made her blink beneath their brightness. On Leggatt's instructions she wore her dove-coloured gown with the outer layer of white gauze, in which her least movement looked as if she was walking on air.

'Here she is,' said Leggatt. 'Here she is, now.'

Sophy, seated with her aunt and uncle at the other end of the room, felt for Kate with a mixture of triumph and indignation. She was glad they were a large party. Not only would Joseph see Kate outshine so many women more, but the horrid Leggatts would be less in evidence. One or two guests looked up in surprise as Kate entered, not expecting this silken creature, so evidently part of the household, to enter unannounced. Joseph, in lively conversation near the door, turned to see who she was. Sophy felt as if she could brim over with happiness for her sister as she watched his face change from ordinary cheerfulness to exultant calm.

To the company nearest him, Leggatt announced, 'Miss Byford is our latest acquisition.' His eyes were already brilliant from too much wine. 'My wife's companion,' he lied, anxious to raise Kate in the eyes of his guests.

'Miss Byford,' said his wife, 'has been hired to take care of the children.'

Seeing that Kate didn't look lowly enough for a nursemaid, several people stared, uneasy at her ambiguous status.

'Or alternatively,' Mrs Leggatt mumbled, not daring to raise her voice, 'one could indeed say Miss Byford has been good-natured enough to become my husband's latest acquisition.'

Joseph started forward as if he'd seen a viper at the hem of Kate's dress. 'I hope, madam, that one day Miss Byford *can* aspire to the company of her equals.' Despite Kate's obvious wretchedness, he found it hard not to look glad at such a chance of gallantry.

'Miss Byford! Miss Byford! What are you doing? Where are you going?' queried Leggatt.

'I am leaving, sir, so that you may be the one to answer Mrs Leggatt's innuendoes, since you yourself have done so much to provoke them.'

'What's she talking about? What are you talking about? What is all this, girl? Sit down, in God's name – sit down, now. Sit down, and let's hear you talk to us.'

Had dinner not been announced at that moment, Joseph would have spoken up yet louder, careless of any audience.

At table, even out of earshot Kate was not to be spared, as Sophy discovered. She found herself among people she knew little or not at all; Leggatt was fond of collecting the largest number of new acquaintance. Nearby, at the end of the table, sat Mrs Leggatt. As they were taking their seats one gentleman was querying Kate's place in the household.

'I don't wonder that you ask,' said Mrs Leggatt, wilfully misunderstanding what had been a perfectly polite question. 'The truth is, my husband having invited our governess's connexions, I had to ask the girl to eat with the guests for appearances' sake. I assure you she's not normally a member of our parties.'

Only determination not to disgrace Kate made Sophy hold her peace, sitting upright and bright-faced with anger throughout all six courses.

As always, dining well did nothing to make good company of Leggatt. In the drawing room, joining the ladies, he too was asked about Kate. Unlike his wife, he was all too happy to pursue the subject.

'How much do you pay for her?' said one of the men, a portly woman-hater whose wife was expecting her thirteenth child.

'Aha! That would be telling! One thing, though; she's wonderful cheap at the price. Are you not?' stabbing a finger at Kate. 'Go on, you tell them! Are you not damn good value? You are, you know!'

'I appreciate that, sir, only too well.'

'You see! You see! The girl says so herself. What I say to all of you is, it's a damned shame none of you can have a dependant like her. You'd have to wait until my brats are grown – but then, why not? She'd still be pretty. You would, you know,' turning to Kate. 'No – no; don't walk away, woman. We're talking about you, for God's sake.'

Joseph, coming in from the dining room, overheard the last of this, and hastened up to Kate as if he'd just galloped twenty miles for the purpose. Taking her by the arm, 'I know your uncle would like to speak to you,' he said in a confidential tone, 'as soon as can be.'

Merely the kindness in his voice proved him a liar. Kate, too furious to smile, could only just look her gratitude to Joseph as he shepherded her to the safety of fifty feet away.

In vain had Sophy, sitting with her aunt, striven to overhear. But what she had seen made her furious enough. There was just one consolation: the more Kate was humiliated, so much more Joseph must be smitten seeing her thus – an exiled princess feeding husks to swine.

'There *can't* be any doubt he's in love,' she whispered to her aunt as, the evening over, they crowded into the hall to wait for their carriage. 'So how long can he bear to go on not saying so?'

Sarah Norton, busy thinking the same thing, motioned Sophy to silence ... But a few moments later Sophy thought she heard Lady Barrington remark, from nearby, 'I defy you, though, to tell me that young man has doted so much before.'

'Yes, yes; as you say.' It seemed her husband, too, thought the subject should not be pursued.

'How he must wish he could play the rescuing knight in every particular,' Lady Barrington persisted.

Sophy heard no more. Did they really mean Joseph? It sounded like him, and yet unlike – surely he could never look at Kate as he did, and all the while have a motive for hanging back? Should she say something? If so, what – to whom – and how?

Another week went by. Whether at the theatre or a concert, dining, dancing, or driving out, Joseph acted as if in conspiracy with Kate to exclude every other creature from their company. The Nortons tried not to look tense and cheerful, and Leggatt was swollen with smugness to think of himself as owner of the future, prodigiously wealthy, Mrs Lee. Twice, too, some slight acquaintance had mistaken Joseph and Kate for a betrothed couple, and on each occasion Joseph had responded with a look of excited gratitude.

Sophy's visit had now reached the stage where it was hard not to count the days again – only this time in anticipation of returning, to the hopeless dullness of home. But in the meantime they were all to be present for an event that every soul in Bath spoke of with interest.

The king and queen were to pass that way, amid all the ceremonial to be expected from a city built in pursuit of pleasure. There were preparations in the streets, and leading citizens were looked at with new eyes as it became known who would stand nearest or speak most often to Their Majesties.

Meanwhile, a few days before the Nortons' planned departure with Sophy, they, the Leggatts and Kate were to attend a concert in the Upper Rooms. Now that Kate seemed virtually engaged, the Nortons were moved to show her particular generosity. Her wardrobe especially had been added to under her aunt's direction. This evening she wore a gown of pale grey silk embroidered about the hem of its train in silver thread, and with short puffed sleeves and a low-cut bodice that showed off her wild-rose complexion to every advantage. Seeing her in the full candlelight of the concert antechamber, the others faltered in the face of her beauty and looked, rather than spoke, their compliments. Sarah Norton even lost her self-possession to the point of becoming talkative. 'I know it's foolish to give credit for good looks,' she murmured to her husband, 'and yet how should one show indifference?'

Kate was favoured from another source. The king's arrival was to be marked by a public dinner and a ball in the Pump Room. Sir William and Lady Barrington were to go, in the same party with Joseph, and they had gained admission for Kate and Sophy. It was, thought Sophy, as though all their friends, seeing Kate and Joseph as lovers, were moved to pay court to her sister themselves.

As they waited for their number to be complete – Joseph was late – the Barringtons themselves also appeared. Their invitation was of course a topic.

'But with all deference to His Majesty,' Lady Barrington said, 'I wish the old gentleman had chosen this year instead to be mad.'

'What for?' Sophy asked.

'Why, then, he should have visited another time, when Sir William was not a member of the city corporation; and then we could both have stared at him for nothing. Instead, we must pay all these tailors' and dressmakers' bills so that we in turn are grand enough for royalty to ogle us. I declare if our new clothes were costed by the length of time Their Majesties are due to look us in the eye, we should each be garbed at fifty pounds a second.'

91

'Be grateful to me, Elizabeth,' her husband said, 'that I'm an upstart. Or it might be you who had the expense of royalty stepping across your own threshold for a month or more, as freely as they pleased.'

'Indeed, I am grateful. Who would want to entertain somebody one had never seen except in scurrilous cartoons?'

'I'm sure His Majesty cares as little for these junketings as any man alive. Can you imagine anything more absurd than that no-nonsensical infirm old man at a ball?'

'We two old folks will look moderately ridiculous ourselves,' replied his plump, dainty little wife.

Sarah Norton laughed disbelievingly. 'But Sir William, surely you will attend as an officer of the yeomanry?'

'Not I, thank heaven. It's some years since I became too old for that.'

'The local militia was not real soldiering in any case,' Lady Barrington said. 'Sir William and his men would have been derisible if pitched against Bonaparte.'

'Indeed we would. No one confessed it; but we were for show, like the Emperor of China's army. Not a man of us would have been mistaken for a warrior.'

'Why, yes,' Lady Barrington said. 'When you were a young lieutenant, how like toy soldiers you all looked, in those wondrous uniforms conceived by your commander's wife. Poor lady! She had no notion of the cost to most of you.'

'You were ready enough, I recall, to be seen alongside me.'

'Oh, I thought you were wonderful. You had more gold frogging than a ducal footman. I was so smitten, I didn't even mind that you carried an umbrella to protect it all.'

The orchestra was tuning up, and they could wait no longer for Joseph. Sophy wondered how Kate could look so calm throughout the half-hour of music that passed before he appeared. When he did finally hasten in, instead of taking the place reserved for him, he sat as if about to leave again, on the edge of the bench at the end of another row.

The interval came. He was evidently waiting to speak to

Kate alone. The others loitered while she went to greet him, shimmering with happiness. Sophy, peeping through the crowd that thronged about the high echoing room, expected to see the look on Kate's face reflected in his.

But instead she saw only an expression of harassment.

Everyone else saw it too, and tried the harder to pretend interest in something else. To keep in countenance, Sarah Norton started to talk of the morning before the royal reception, when from their lodging they were all to watch the king's arrival. 'I hope you will not be impatient, Charles, with all the waiting. *You* have seen the king before. But I dare say the rest of us are foolish enough to look forward to it. Even if the royal family is as frumpish as they say, the other onlookers may furnish a spectacle.'

'You may all wish to gawp like fish in a bowl,' her husband replied. 'But Leggatt and I might well prefer to entertain ourselves downstairs in peace.'

Across the room, Kate and Joseph were still talking. Sophy didn't understand. If he was so downcast, why did Kate not look so too?

'Oh no, my dear fellow,' Leggatt was saying. 'You and I must indulge the ladies and follow their example. Besides, if we were not to be there, the windows in that room might be let at twenty guineas each.'

'Aye. You'd think at the very least we were to see an executioner chop off the old fellow's head.'

Sarah Norton, unable to see the lovers without turning her head, was watching Sophy's face for signs of what was happening. Guessing at their approach, she composed a smile, ready to turn and greet them.

But if Kate appeared serious, Joseph looked as though he could hardly bear to speak.

'What's to do?' asked Charles Norton in surprise.

'I'm only here to apologize,' said Joseph, evidently too flustered to look anyone in the eye. 'I have to leave tonight for Bristol, to make ready for a longer absence.'

'But where? – I mean, where shall you be going?' Sarah Norton asked.

'Oh, not to Virginia for some time, I dare say' – though no one had even thought such a thing. 'But I have to go to

Liverpool; I don't know for how long. One of my agents there has written me urgently.'

Everyone exclaimed their regret at his going – all except Kate, who stood by in silence trying not to look self-conscious. He was to return, briefly, in a few days. Meanwhile, in taking his leave, he looked as gloomy as if being transported for life.

Normally, Kate was reticent about the things that touched her most. But everyone was so apt to talk about Joseph's absence that she could hardly avoid doing the same. 'There was nothing special about realizing we were in love,' she told Sophy, some mornings later, as they were strolling down the shadowy nave of the Abbey among the other well-dressed visitors. The day was wet, and the town was taking its exercise indoors. 'It's just that being apart has come to seem unnatural – not what things should be.'

'I hope you don't think well of him, too, because the Leggatts are horrid.' Sophy could be as tactless as a five-year-old. It was not crassness, though, that made her speak out now – just anxiety for Kate's happiness.

'It's not like that,' Kate replied in a matter-of-fact voice. They walked a little way in silence. 'You know, I'm past the point of looking forward to seeing him. I suppose at first even separation had its pleasures. It meant anticipating the next time we'd meet. But now it only makes me tired whenever I think, so many hours to wait, doing things that mean nothing.'

The week passed. On the eve of the king's arrival there was no news of Joseph's return. Sophy went to bed almost as impatient as Kate herself. So intent was she on sleeping, to get through the night, that she began to drowse only as the first blackbird spoke up from across the water meadows behind the great terrace where they were lodged.

When she awoke it was almost late enough for the day's visitors. About a dozen guests were to watch from the Nortons' windows while the king went by. As she entered the big first-floor drawing room almost everybody had arrived. The Norton children, joining the adults as a treat, ran about and squealed as excitedly as if they were out of doors. A little apart from the others, Kate was talking to her aunt Norton. She looked paler than usual, but as graceful as someone whose happiness was already complete.

Sarah Norton was trying to discuss Joseph while not mentioning his name. 'It's plain, in my opinion,' she was saying, 'that it matters nothing if certain people said your position in Mr Leggatt's household would not bring you every social opportunity. Your mother, I dare say, reckoned little enough of it at first ... Would you not agree that was what she thought?'

'I shouldn't like to say,' murmured Kate. She felt crosser than usual this morning at having to be grateful to her aunt.

'Oh, but I'm sure that in her letters at least ...'

Kate was spared further questioning by the approach of Sir William and her uncle.

'I'm almost certain I saw him down the street just now,' Sir William was saying.

'Why, not the king, Sir William?' asked Sarah – not that she believed it.

'No, ma'am, your absent guest.'

'Now, who can that be?' And looked about her as if she didn't know.

'Lee's the only fellow we lack now,' said Charles Norton.

'That's the man,' replied Sir William. 'Though I wasn't certain it was he.'

Outside there arose a murmur. It increased, as a tidal wave of sound suddenly cannoned up the street. Immediately the military band on a dais opposite the house broke into 'Rule Britannia'. 'The king! The king!' was the cry of the children in the room. They ran to look out of the three tall windows into the street, and the adults followed, trying not to appear every bit as inquisitive.

The street was packed with people, craning their heads in unison as the outriders of the royal party came into view. A strewn high tide of parasols, bonnets, hats and flags bobbed and shoved. On first-floor balconies down the length of the street, fashionable onlookers were clustered like roosting birds. The scarlet-clad musicians in the band sweated as they played on. Sophy noticed that on the facing balconies the men were taking off their hats. A heave of motion passed along the crowd below as the same gesture was repeated there – and suddenly the noise swelled again. The eldest Norton boy looked up at his mother and shouted something. Below, the royal carriage was passing up the street at a stately trot. But as it did, Kate became aware of something unexpected on the pavement opposite. Among the faces turning in an agitated mass to watch the king and queen pass, there was one that ignored them – that was turned upward, in her own direction. It was Joseph, unmoving and bareheaded. Had he been watching her, or had he glanced up at that moment?

In all the public excitement, she had been thinking of nothing but him. Yet what should she understand by the look he gave her? She'd raised her hand, smiling, to wave. He made no response beyond a nod, and continued to look in her direction for several seconds before turning away through the crowd.

This was not what she'd expected. It was true that the expectation of seeing Joseph again had felt too intense ever to be satisfied. But she had never imagined a response like that once they caught sight of each other. And why had he not come to the house? The evening seemed further away than ever; and Kate felt as if the whole world would run out of time before they were both in the same room. She strove not to torture herself by imagining how it would be. Perhaps the intentness with which he'd just looked at her would expand into the same ardent attention he'd shown before their last parting. At the worst, it must be impossible he should not make up for the way he had simply nodded and turned away.

With the other guests she made her way through a five-course lunch as if suffering an hallucination. Later, after the ladies had dawdled into their shawls and bonnets and gloves, they all walked in Sydney Gardens. The place felt as crowded as if the other people there were fleeing a natural disaster rather than looking for enjoyment. By the time she and Sophy had dressed for the evening, she was almost sick with disbelief that they would ever get to the ball. Lady Barrington, however, had evidently noticed what was in her mind, even before she and her husband had returned, dressed for the evening. As Kate descended with Sophy to greet her, in a gauzy white gown that had made the dressmaker herself sigh with pleasure, the older woman patted her on the arm and gave a smile of reassurance.

'Well,' said Sir William, as their carriage set out for the Pump Room, 'let's have this over with.' And he too took pains to smile at Kate.

Joseph was there, of course. It might be two hours before he could speak to them, for it appeared he was to dine with another party. But it was something to be certain he was there, even ten yards down the table. They hastened to their seats, for everyone had to be present before the king could enter. The heat from two hundred well-cared-for bodies was already filling the room. All unseeing, Kate gazed in turn at the half-ton chandelier glittering overhead, the towering pink ostrich feather in the turban of the fleshy woman opposite her, and a silver and rock-crystal table stand for something or other, whose pedestal, in the overblown modern fashion, was shaped like a dolphin.

Another military band, banked about by flowers, struck up. Everyone got to their feet, and the half-blind old king entered on the arm of his dumpy queen. Behind them came three of the royal princesses and a file of dignitaries. The national anthem finished; the company sat; and the first dish of the banquet was announced, with almost as much flourish as the king had been.

Kate felt they were eating as a punishment. The courses were innumerable, and each one far too beautifully wrought to look like proper food. The crayfish in aspic looked elaborate enough to wear on your head; the skewered larks and cocks' combs formed a piece of architecture two feet tall; and one of the three meat courses was presented in a pastry case sculpted to look like an oriental temple. Just as it seemed even the ginger ices and the *millefruit* might be followed by something else, the band burst into more brisk music to signify the end of the meal and the royal party left their table. Kate, noticing the fleshy woman looking at something behind her, turned, and saw Joseph.

He looked anxious to greet her, rather than pleased. So much so, he almost forgot to acknowledge Sophy and the Barringtons. Kate, rising, took his arm. Despite the heat, and the jumping of her heart, her hands and face felt cold.

Joseph hurried her, without speaking, toward a corner of the room. He stopped and frowned, searching for words. She wondered if he must have forgotten whatever it was he wanted to say. All around them the crowd shuffled and pressed as though something downright urgent were happening.

'I've been waiting twenty hours to speak to you privately,' he finally said. 'This isn't a private place, I know. But it will have to do. I owe you an apology,' he went on, speaking with determination.

'How? Why?' exclaimed Kate. Behind her, the Barringtons threw anxious glances, and Sophy looked as if she might be about to jump up and strike somebody.

'Say it how you will, I have behaved to you like a lover. And for that I have to ask if you will ever forgive me.'

A passing group of revellers, not seeing Kate's expression, murmured appreciatively at her appearance. To shield her, Joseph moved round so that she was facing away from the rest of the room. His hunted look told her almost everything. 'Of course I'm tied to someone else – of course I am,' he said, as vehemently as if she'd asked him out loud. 'I never thought it would come to this – upon my word I didn't!'

'Come to what?' After days of waiting, Kate found her release into anger was nearly a relief. If only for the moment, her rage made her feel strong enough for anything. She sounded almost calm.

'Oh God! I never meant to go past the point where I started to deceive you! I don't know what I intended. Maybe I started hoping she'd just cease to exist.'

'Is she here?' Kate asked in a low voice, almost without a tremor.

'Good God, no! She's in Richmond, three thousand miles from here.'

'Of course.' Kate could conceal her bitterness no longer, though she still spoke hardly above a whisper. Another group of people, some of whom seemed to know Joseph, went past. He pretended not to notice them.

'Her father ... he's my principal supplier ... at one remove he as good as owns me. He's in Liverpool now, and means to discuss the marriage contract. The ceremony can't be put off much longer ... In God's name! Don't just look at me! Can't you say something? I don't care what it is! What in damnation am I to tell you? I don't love her! I can't love her! I never can! I never did! I never did love her! I was merely infatuated, at a time when I was too young to know better –'

'So you expect to be wretched with this woman?'

'Of course I do!'

She gave a disdainful laugh. Joseph saw several people look round at her. 'I'm the one to blame!' she exclaimed, with a look he wished could slay him. 'I should have known what your intentions were, from the day you saw me in the crowd, and ran. You were so anxious to present yourself that you ran!' She spoke through clenched teeth, her voice vibrant with the effort of restraint. 'I should have known then what you were about. No man runs after a woman in that way just to pursue her. He only does so if he's fleeing someone else! You never loved me! You only came panting after me to show yourself how much you hated your future wife!'

She was dazed with rage. Joseph wondered if she was about to faint. 'I know I've no right to ask your forgiveness,' he said. 'So if there's anything you want to say to my face, say it now and let's be done.'

Kate stared back as if she hardly saw him. She wanted to crush him for ever. And yet even now she could not bear the wretchedness in his voice. 'I think,' she said at length, 'that you mistake me for someone who thinks of you as an equal.' She tried not to see how he looked at her. 'Why should *I* take the trouble to feel contempt for somebody like *you*?' And she turned and walked away, not trusting either of them with another word.

Lady Barrington, to her own consternation, could guess everything even more readily than Sophy. 'My dear,' she was meanwhile obliged to say. 'My dear, I'm so sorry; but we have to be presented to Their Majesties. Now ... I promise this will all be over in a very few moments. Then if you wish we can go home.'

She had the goodness not to say another word. They took their places to be presented to the crabbed, semi-formally attired old couple seated amid a bright blur of uniformed or bejewelled courtiers. Kate heard her own name boomed out and stepped forward. She looked at them both as she rose from her curtsey as from the bottom of the sea. Between them they had endured blindness, dementia, fifteen childbirths and sixteen years of war. And a loveless marriage. No wonder they looked so ordinary.

He was a kind-faced old man, Lady Barrington thought. Probably he would have looked even more benevolent, if instead of seeing a blur of light on darkness he'd known he was confronted with one of the most beautiful girls in the city. Someone's guardian angel should be thanked, meanwhile, that Kate's swimming eyes and flushed face could be mistaken for nothing worse than nervousness. Lady Barrington waited while Sophy, looking enraged, dropped a curtsey, and hastened through her own obeisance. Then without offering either sister an explanation, she hurried them away before Kate's torment became openly too much to bear.

At the hotel there was a letter for Sophy. It came from her mother, forwarded, with some delay, from Bradford-on-Avon. Most of it concerned the usual daily doings. But the postscript read differently.

I cannot think, Sophy, that if you knew how things were here you should have stayed away. Upon my soul, I do not. Here am I alone in the house – no, not even with Hannah to do the work of the place. She must stay away in Upstowe, because they say the fever has spread from the village and taken two of her sister's family. And if the Leggatts say Kate

100

cannot leave them, there is no help for that, I'm sure. But what am I to do if you are not here? I cannot countenance that you should be away from me at a time like this. What else can I do but pray you will be home?

Chapter Six

Sophy hadn't stopped to wonder if it might be folly to return. She was only too glad to be leaving Bath. Her aunt and uncle, too, after the defeat of their ambitions for Kate, were relieved to break up their party. Readily they gave her the money to travel alone, starting at sunrise by post.

It was on the road into Upstowe that she first saw something out of the ordinary. The chaise had been slowed to a walk, to avoid some obstacle. They were passing a row of frowsty thatched cottages behind a low stone wall covered with laundry spread to dry. The cottagers, mostly barefoot children, were staring at something in the road up ahead. One small boy was yowling at being punched and shouted at by his mother, who sounded more frightened than angry.

Under the hedge the man lay dead, right enough. His tongue protruded like a rotten stick and there was a fly on one of his eyeballs. He was a navvy, from the canal. Sophy looked as closely as she could while the post-boy clicked his tongue at the horses and spurred his nearside nag to a hand-gallop. She had seen a dead body before, of course. When she was six, she had watched two younger brothers sicken and die within a few days of each other. She could still remember being taken by the hand – far more frightened of her father's sternness than of disease or death – to see the germy little corpses, each decked out in hand-embroidered frills.

At least the man's face hadn't shown the disgusting eruptions of smallpox. Besides, if it were the pox itself that had broken out, even her mother would have sense enough to tell her.

On the canal workings there was no sign of anything extraordinary. Not three miles on from passing a man dead in the highway, Sophy found it startling to hear the bang and rumble of the spoil wagons still discharging down an embankment and see lines of men at work up and down the barrow-runs.

The last stretch of road seemed unreal in its familiarity, after weeks spent in a strange place. The chaise passed the almshouses, and a dozen stray heifers that no one seemed concerned to round up. An absurd thought flitted through Sophy's mind: suppose her mother were not there – was nowhere to be found?

Mrs Byford was there, of course. At the sound of the carriage wheels she appeared from the back of the cottage, teetering along the muddy path and blinking in the sunlight. 'Oh, Sophy,' she exclaimed, as Sophy sat down in their little dark parlour and untied her bonnet, 'at least I know you're safe!'

'Do other people have the fever? Is that why I saw a man dead on the way?'

'Oh, Sophy, you didn't, did you? Are you sure you didn't go too close?'

'Dearest mama, you haven't the smallest need to worry about me. But I would have been perfectly safe where I was.'

'I know. But now I can be certain where you are and what you're doing. And Hannah isn't here. They said it was camp fever, and only the navvies would have it; but she went to Upstowe on her afternoon off and her sister in St Peter's Alley fell sick.'

'So Hannah is in quarantine?'

'Well, yes, and if she has to stay away she must. But I take it hard that people should suspect we have a servant whose character can't be trusted. I know they all say it's only degenerates who would yield to an illness like that.'

'Yes, but now I'm here, mama, we can do very well on our own for a while.' Sophy looked around the room, with its little four-paned window and its feeling of a badly weatherproofed burrow. After the dismay she felt at the thought of Bath and people of fashion in general, she could face the dinginess of Drove Cottage almost with satisfaction. How glad she was not to have written too much of Kate in her letters home! She tried not to think about the horrible evening before, with Kate choking on tears of rage and furiously flinching from all shushings and embraces as she was driven back to the Leggatts' ... Being home, and having work to do, seemed a good deal less dreadful than it had done.

In any case her mother was probably exaggerating; Sophy knew how she enjoyed being anxious. 'Surely, mama, even in the navvies' camp there cannot be so much sickness? I saw men working, below Beacon Hill.'

'Now, isn't it just like those people not to care? Only last Sunday the parson told us, how can they be concerned for their own moral welfare, when they act so recklessly? If they aren't content with wanting to take away Lord Fitzpayne's park, they're building a tunnel now beyond Highcombe. And Parson Beddowes says there were three men killed because they tried to light a charge by blowing on the powder. He buried eleven of them not two days since. But then people said this would happen, when your poor father died.'

'Eleven men blown up?'

'Good heavens, no; that wasn't what I said. There were three men in the tunnel; the others died of the fever. They've started bringing them into this parish to be buried, now the workings have got so close. And sometimes there's been more than a hundred of them following the corpse, and what's more they get themselves intoxicated afterward and last week when it rained so much, one of them had the disrespect to fall down drunk into an open grave and drown himself there!'

Sophy was silent. So the danger was not only real, but worse than she'd guessed.

Part of her was too frightened to be sorry for anyone. Duty to her mother apart, she felt a fool for having returned so blithely – without even the credit of having got her courage up beforehand. But another part of her felt a pang of excitement – of fear lifted into careless aggression, as a sailor facing into a hurricane or a caval-

103

ryman borne along in a charge might become beside himself . . . 'Is anyone sick in the village?' she asked.

'Good heavens, I can't tell; not with everyone shutting up their doors, and not shaking hands when they meet, and sitting apart from each other in church with every pew smelling like an apothecary's shop. They buried a man from Preston's farm yesterday; I know that because I heard the man from the yard of the Red Lion saying so in the lane while I was sitting here not half an hour ago. And the curate has sent his wife and children away, to his cousin the miller in Salisbury; and Mrs Lovell's girl, who she trained up herself at the Hall, I heard them say she's deserted and run off; I don't know where she's gone, to be sure.'

'Why – did she fear Mr Fraser might bring the sickness into their house?' Mrs Lovell was Fraser's grandmother, and his last surviving relative.

'Oh, I know how people believe it is with typhoid; folk say anyone might carry it and not suffer on their own account. That's why they reckon you can't trust even your nearest in a time like this. But Mrs Beddowes says the best thing is port wine with brandy, which is why she sent us some of her own cellar, which is very kind of her, when you don't know if your own neighbour might not bring down a pestilence on your head.'

The news of Lord Fitzpayne's old housekeeper disquieted Sophy more than she cared to say. If there were sickness in the house, it was someone's duty to go there. The more she tried not to think of this, the more the fact oppressed her. In days gone by, when she and Kate had been admired every week of the year in drawing rooms as distant as Salisbury, Mrs Lovell had merely been someone to be nodded to. Since then, Sophy had learned to be humbled by gratitude for small kindnesses – a surplus cabbage or a clutch of eggs – from the old lady. There was nothing to be done but go to her cottage with an inquiry. Without waiting, Sophy tied on her bonnet again and made haste.

It didn't look like weather to seed fever in anybody's home. There was a brisk March wind, and the sunlight, clear as a bell, shone into the bottoms of leafless hedge-rows and made Cannings Hill appear half a mile nearer than it was. Every blade of grass cast a sharper shadow than it had for months. At Mrs Lovell's back gate Sophy looked across the poultry run for smoke from the kitchen chimney. Something mysterious was moving among the beaten dirt and islands of grass, where the fowls were shut up for the night. She went closer, and saw, blown to and fro, the stretched-out wing of one of Mrs Lovell's prized guinea-fowl. Every one lay, a swatch of dirty feathers, dead from thirst.

The back door, like most people's in fine weather, was wedged open. But dead leaves had sidled in across the brick floor of the scullery, and above the kitchen table a couple of early bluebottles spiralled over the remains of a meal. A young tortoiseshell cat came skipping in after Sophy, tail held high in greeting, and leaned into her skirts, purring. Sophy opened the door at the foot of the stairs and started up the bare wooden treads. Being an intruder made her unreasonably timid; and she tiptoed, trying not to make any noise. The sunlight, lancing through an open bedroom door, showed every grain of dust suspended in its path.

She stopped, listening. From the room ahead, she heard a mumbled conversation; now pausing, now continuing, but always in one level voice. Creeping to the door, she ducked under the lintel and looked inside.

The gloom was deepened by the springtime brilliance out of doors. She found it hard to distinguish the figure on the bed at all. Mrs Lovell, a thick-set, normally vigorous woman, was too feeble to speak out loud, and too delir-ious to know that anybody else was there. And what had happened to her face? Sophy shuddered – then reproached herself for a ninny. The mess, blackened and cracking, was something she should have expected, had she sense to remember the disease caused a nosebleed.

Was there time to fetch a doctor? Should Fraser be sent for – or warned away? She hesitated, hearing the woman's crazed whispers sound through the quiet house. The cat darted in, jumped onto the bed and off again, and rubbed an ear around the toes of Sophy's boots. Absurdly, the sight of mortal sickness left her more repelled than frightened.

But there was another sound – good God, what could that be? She started again as the cat mewed at her, drowning whatever it had been. Had she imagined it? She stood still, listening. There were the usual noises of an old house like this: sparrows chirping and thumping about in the thatch, and the timbers that framed the brickwork creaking as if they still grew . . .

There it was again – from the room next door. The cat turned her head, ears pricking to and fro, then skittered out of sight.

Silence again. Sophy, scowling from disdain at her own cowardice, crept across the passage and peered in.

On the workings no one had recognized the epidemic at first. It had been brought into the camp, Fraser realized, by a group of men trampling down from work on a navigation in Yorkshire. By any standard they had arrived in a desperate condition, since the country people on their way could hardly have welcomed them. One – he looked sixty but could have been thirty-five – had fallen asleep in the taproom of the Golden Fleece in Upstowe while being signed on by one of the gangers, and no one was much surprised when he was found to have died on the spot.

The four survivors were lodged at a cottage in the path of the new embankment. They had arrived on a monthly pay day – a time when the citizens of Upstowe had learned to stay at home and lock their doors. When, two days later, a couple of them failed to present themselves for work, it was assumed they were still blind and paralysed from drink. The following morning at six, one of the boys who led the horses of the spoil wagons was sent to order them onto the workings.

'They say as you don't want neither of them out here,' reported the child, a wizened eight-year-old as humourless as a hanging judge. 'They be a-dying. And I ain't carrying no more messages that way, neither.'

The men took some days to die, during which work

106

along the line of the canal went on as usual. Fraser knew there was no guessing how soon the disease might reappear. Once, as an assistant engineer of seventeen, he'd seen forty men perish from it without warning on a single day.

On the morning the men were buried, the fever was reported among two families in the temporary shelters of the camp itself. Fraser ordered Dr Brown to be sent for once more, as much as anything for reassurance' sake. The mass of people in the camp lived too hard to be careful for their own safety. But were a panic to set in, enough of the better-paid men – the masons or the blacksmiths and the gangers – might be ready to desert, leaving behind them a leaderless rabble.

The doctor, however, was delayed by a well-paid attendance at a country house near Bradford-on-Avon. He sent word that he should not be back for some hours. When he did return Fraser was waiting at his house. The young man, hat in hand, was stalking up and down the drawing room as if the house itself were in motion. In the hall Mrs Brown was shooing a brood of inquisitive children back from the door.

Without taking off his coat, the doctor came to the point. 'If that riff-raff of yours has brought an epidemic into the district, there's nothing I can be expected to do. And it's not that sixpence a week per man doesn't make up funds enough. Your people live too reckless and too dissolute to profit from professional help.'

'I've not come to be fobbed off with talk of will power and moral failings.' Fraser was not only angry but in haste. He had to ride ten miles within the next two hours, to attend a meeting of the section committee. They were due to appoint a contractor for part of the Long Pound, a fifteen-mile section without locks this side of the tunnel. If the committee insisted on giving Leggatt more work despite his inexperience, this was the stretch on which he would be least of a risk. Impatient, Fraser met the doctor's dogged professional look. 'Any fool can prescribe a quarter-pint of brandy and a session of prayer.'

Dr Brown was used to being heard out with respect –

107

and by well-regarded citizens older than he. 'And if they did so, they'd be passing on the best advice that you could get, sir. In the circumstances.'

'I'm not interested in your reasons for crying off,' said Fraser. 'If you don't feel competent to save any lives endangered thus far, I'd still be obliged if you'd show yourself unafraid in front of the men. Once they start to flee the camp, not only will work stop, but the danger could spread around the countryside.'

He knew he was being tactless. But it galled him to humour a man who demanded such respect – when the doctor's work, unlike his own, was bound to have such random results.

'I'll thank you to leave out any question of being afraid.' The doctor was rigid with forced politeness. 'I have been present – from choice – at such incidents before. Since that seems to be your idea of a qualification.'

'It isn't,' said Fraser, not bothering to see that a snub was meant. 'But I'm sorry if you think I meant to call you a coward.'

The doctor could see there was no persuading him to defer. To end the conversation he agreed to attend the camp later that day.

With no hope for their recovery, as it proved, the sick families were visited and packages of medicine sent. Four days on, there were fourteen more cases in the camp. And now, sure enough, beyond Upstowe the effects of the fever also began to show. Word came, that of those who had already run away, a young carpenter and the woman with him had been found dead of cold and hunger to leeward of a cornrick near Salisbury. And three navvies had carried the sickness to an upland hamlet from which in turn the local shepherds and their families had fled.

Ten days after the first deaths, Fraser rose to find himself suffering what he prayed with all his strength was no more than sleeplessness. There had been urgent paperwork to do the night before: negotiations for a woollen mill whose owner would otherwise charge several hundred pounds a year for water rights. He'd gone to bed two hours short of first light, and far too late for his exhausted brain to stop rehearsing the next day's events.

That morning, first thing, he was to make an inspection of the half-completed tunnel. It stood at the point where the canal was planned to leave the Vale, beneath a saddle in the downs at its head. To see such a piece of work under construction was both marvellous and appalling. First, ventilation shafts had been sunk to the depth of the canal bed. In this way some idea was gained of the soils to be moved. It was hoped, too, that this would show whether the men mining beneath the hill should fear any sudden inrush of water from an underground source. The tunnel was being dug outwards from the shafts with picks and shovels, by scores of men working naked in the chill waters that dripped or streamed past them. As they hewed, they were supported by a many-tiered scaffold across the blind face where the waterway was due to go. The chalky rock they had to shift was as bad for their purpose as could be; not only porous but brittle as burnt wood. There could be no listening, though, for any run of rubble that might signal a collapse. The thud or scrape of several score of digging tools, the rumble of barrows down their wooden runs from the scaffold, the shouts of the bricklayers' teams scrambling to and fro on their own huge framework as the tunnel was lined with masonry – all these combined, in such a narrow chamber, to make the noise atrocious. The work was illuminated by candles, so that each bulk of scaffolding was pricked about with lights like a distant town at night. Looking toward the skyward shafts, the view along the tunnel was blocked by a column of daylight tainted with smoke and dust.

The approach, where a gentle combe had been, was now a dusty, rock-strewn parting of the hills. Later it would be paved with a dark trail of puddling, as the canal got its lining of gravel and clay. It was hard to tell where the top of the cutting came, for as far as the eye could see, the surrounding pastures and hedgerows were floured over with dust so that they looked bled of colour even in broad day.

As Fraser rode up toward the tunnel mouth, Howchin,

the ganger in charge, came to meet him. With him were a number of the men. Unexpectedly, it seemed Fraser had been awaited.

'T'weren't I as held off the early shift,' was Howchin's greeting. 'There was every man accounted for after that stupid bugger O'Donnell blew himself up. So now what's *that* doing in there?' jerking his head in the direction of the tunnel.

From out of the darkness, just audible, came an uneven thread of sound. It was as if the earth itself were murmuring.

With a pain behind his eyes that half blinded him, Fraser was particularly impatient of humouring the men. 'Find a hurdle or what you will, to make a stretcher,' he said over his shoulder as he pushed past them.

'Nay, we've told ye: there's no one there.'

'Shut your mouth, Howchin, if you'll do nothing. It'll save you making excuses afterward.' And without waiting for an answer he went into the tunnel.

Even now he was astonished at the superstition of these men. They would kill themselves almost for sport – O'Donnell had blown on the gunpowder for a bet. Yet they were tyrannized by old wives' notions past belief. A couple of days since, a group of them had roasted a cat alive as a charm to keep the fever off. And now that a sick man, as it must be, had taken shelter in the excavations, it was not the fear of contagion that held them back, but the certainty of meeting a ghost.

No one could be blamed for finding melancholy associations with the place. Of the men who had died in the explosion, one had been horribly burned, and another had been caught under a fall of rock that had crushed his bowels out.

It was not far to the rockface. There was light enough there at least to make the darkness visible. The place stank like a city lane. Not just from the sourness of stale smoke, but from the cloying stench left by the men, who shat wherever they were labouring. Recently there had been an outbreak of dysentery among the gangs working on the tunnel. It came, of course, from drinking the water that ran down the surface of the rock. Yet the men seemed quite careless of their own distress – and certainly they did nothing to hinder it.

'And she'd see me here, she would!' a voice intoned in the darkness. 'I'd have told ye so.' Fraser followed the sound to where the man must be lying. He – or someone – had had diarrhoea. 'I could have told her, too. She knew, she did!' Fraser seized him by one arm and stooped to lift him across his shoulders.

As he carried him back toward the light the men were already tramping in and the boys were leading up the wagons for the next eight hours' work. In moving through the dusty air they cast broad shafts of darkness before them. They passed Fraser without a look, and with hardly a word among themselves. Smitten by the light of day, the sick man cried out. Even so, Howchin too was trying to behave as if nothing had happened. Whatever he'd said in front of his men – they knew they intimidated him – he'd had the sense meanwhile to send for a couple of hurdles and some sacking.

Fraser gave orders while his horse was being brought, for the doctor to be sent for, to attend at the man's lodging. Mounting up, he then set out without further loss of time. His first destination had not been here, but at the nearest vertical shaft of the tunnel. He'd been due to inspect it at half past six, with Peters, his superintendent of earthworks. Though he planned to ride more than fifteen miles that morning without a change of horse, he forced his steed to a canter up among the spills of chalk rubble around the mouth of the shaft.

Peters, a well-spoken lad a couple of years younger than Fraser, was already there. Together they climbed into the iron spoil bucket suspended above the shaft, and the man working the creaking wooden frame of the whim roped them down twenty fathoms into the tunnel. It was a necessary routine to question the ganger in charge of each face below, and to scrutinize every yard of exposed rock for signs of trouble, as closely as if they hoped to find diamonds. Back at length in the light of day, they hawked and spat dust and screwed up their eyes against a watery sun. Already they looked as if their gentlefolks' clothes, filthy and rucked, had been plundered from a rubbish heap.

Next, the further cutting had to be inspected, to check that the baulks of timber at its base would hold against any further spoil mouldering down under the weight of the springtime rains.

Some miles on, there was as yet no waterway a passer-by might recognize. Down the dry valley where the barges were to pass, a series of stakes had been planted. There was one every three paces, across little fields like outdoor rooms, with shaggy hedges as tall as a house. Fraser had memorized every yard of this section, as closely as a poacher knows where the best rabbit runs go. There was no guarantee the markers would be undisturbed, either by cattle or deliberate human interference. By now he had walked or ridden the four hours' journey east from Upstowe nearly two dozen times.

Across these meadows, a string of rubble heaps flow-ered. They were white on the high ground, and darker toward the lower part of the valley where a brook rose between alder trees and the soil changed from chalk to gravel. By every other stake, a shaft had been sunk to one yard beneath the bed of the future canal. By this means it was possible to tell how porous the sub-soil was, and how much waterproof puddling-stuff would be needed.

It was Peters' job here, as they rode, to give an account of how the work was progressing. To Fraser's relief, in the short time the lad had been employed he'd shown a mastery not only of the theory of his trade but of each unpredictable site. He'd been recommended by the Earl of Pomeroy, no less: his father was his lordship's land agent. So far as Fraser could guess what was taught in a grammar school, Peters' education seemed impossibly grand and utterly irrelevant. Who knew but that he was fool enough to have an embankment made up only to its final height, without allowance for settling? Or to think watering points for cattle could be as conveniently dug in one soil as another?

Fortunately the steward's son had proved fit for more

than just writing a good letter in a slapdash hand, or showing a knowledge of Greek. Lacking proper maps, he could compare the outline of a contour with the state of its crops, or observe the site of a hamlet in a valley, and predict as closely as a man of fifteen years' knowledge what problems the local geology would bring. East of the summit pound, they'd been plagued by the lock pits filling with spring water faster than the men could dig. And it was Peters, Fraser noted, who'd been the only other person to foresee such a thing.

Ten miles beyond the tunnel the eastern section of the canal was finished. It was planned that it should meet the western part at Cannings Fitzpayne. Here, in the hamlet of Nethercombe, there was already a large new coalyard; and from a distance the place now looked bigger than it was, from the smoke of the lime kilns sprouting around it now the waterway had reached this far. The north-south coaching road crossed the valley here, too; so the other feature of the hamlet was a large inn whose walls rose four storeys above the nearby hovels, as though dropped into these solitudes from the middle of a city.

It had been a bright, brittle morning with too much sun too early. While they were still a mile from shelter the weather turned foul. Behind, the horizon suddenly stood closer as the downs were blotted out by rain. The trees leaned away from them as promptly as if a door had let in a draught. Within a few minutes both men were wet through. The horses, miserable, put their ears back and shuffled along with heads and tails held low. The creatures' coats were dagged and runnelled with wet, and the reins were almost too slick to hold.

As they crossed the new humped bridge, 'I don't see his lordship's carriage in the yard, sir,' Peters remarked. Whereas he himself was due to have his horse baited at Nethercombe and return, Fraser was to attend a meeting there of the section committee. The settlement was remote; but it was often chosen for such gatherings because of its nearness to the Earl of Pomeroy's country seat.

There was no reply. Glancing at Fraser, Peters saw that

113

he was shivering and his face was ashen and pinched. 'Is aught amiss?'

Fraser, looking irked, shook his head.

Contagion in the camp or not, Peters found it hard to think of his chief as ailing. The possibility made him feel foolish and diffident; and he was glad to take his leave without the need for further conversation.

In a dining room of the Pomeroy Arms most of the committee already loitered, reading the newspapers or talking while they waited for their number to be complete. Fraser, furious with impatience at the chance that he might be ill, found himself drawn into a group that included Royal, the Company Secretary. They were discussing the hiring of Leggatt as a contractor on the canal.

'... Of course the man's services are an investment for us,' Royal was saying.

'As a future customer, perhaps,' ventured Deniff, the banker. 'But no one here knows how he'll show when it comes to any building work.'

'He'll have to use the waterway in any case,' someone else said. 'Once it's complete, no one in his line of whole-sale would have their wagoners pay road tolls.'

To Fraser, their voices somehow seemed both uncomfortably close at hand yet hard to follow. From being too shaken with cold to speak, he now felt basted in sweat... If he could see this meeting to its end, he would think about the day's other appointments only as they happened. He had to arrange with his superintendent of masonry for the siting of a brickworks as near the tunnel as the local shortage of clay would allow: its lining would need two million bricks. A landowner required a design of bridge never before achieved: it would have to cross the canal at an angle, so that his Grand Avenue could still run straight as a plumbline from the big house to a hilltop six miles away. Then arrangements had to be made for the main committee to view the canal along its western extent, by a specially appointed packet boat from Bath...

Deniff at least was still unpersuaded. 'I hope someone

knows their business in hiring Leggatt. We've had delays enough without making payments for them in advance.'

'Oh, to hell with that,' Royal said. For a lawyer, he was astonishingly apt to pass off carelessness as boldness of vision. 'The more of these sort of people we can put in our pocket with offers of work, the sooner they'll damn well pay the calls on their shares.'

Fraser sensed nausea moving in his gut. He felt as parched as if he'd tried to slake himself on sea water. It must have been like this to find oneself a traitor on the scaffold, as the executioner thrust his hand in among one's entrails ... Was Royal being more of a fool than ever, or was his own physical wretchedness making nonsense of what the man had to say? As if to fend off sickness by force of will, he went on surveying what he had to do that day ... *Then* he must settle a dispute over the cost of extra fencing on one stretch. And twenty miles further west a hillside needed drainage, where a layer of fuller's earth on a base of clay threatened to slip and block both the canal and the River Avon... If it really were the fever, would it not have seized him several days ago? He'd several times been as close to it as in the tunnel that morning ... When he reached the New Inn at Upstowe he must send for his assistant and dictate three hours' correspondence...

Fortunately, the meeting over, his horse knew it was homeward bound, and would have carried him back even without being directed. Some way short of Upstowe he realized firstly that he had no recollection of the last two miles, and secondly that he was too ill to care about anything. At the Red Lion in Cannings Fitzpayne he gave his horse over to the ostler and went to seek shelter at his grandmother's house.

It was there that Sophy found him next day. His delirium had been broken for a time by a horrible sleep whose dreams alternately menaced and worried him. The bedclothes were tangled into ropes, his hands twitched, and the flush of his fever was overlaid by grime from the

115

previous day's ride. Her entering had woken him, but he had not the least idea who she was.

Parson Beddowes, at Sophy's entreaty, had his stable boy mount up and ride off to Upstowe for the doctor. She herself hurried back down the lane to Mrs Lovell's cottage, nearly overbalancing as she jumped and slithered between one water-filled rut and another, her soaking skirts held carelessly high about her in her anxiety to make haste. Several neighbours, who still remembered her as a gentleman's daughter, stared to see her, bonnet fallen back and hair tumbled to her waist, splattering through the puddles as if in flight for her life.

'Oh, please be quick!' she murmured out loud, pumping water at the back door to take upstairs. She started scurrying through the most urgent chores as if her own haste would make the doctor appear sooner. As she finished lighting fires in the bedrooms and kitchen – a year ago she would not have dreamed of doing such a task – a servant, with a basket of food, arrived from the Parsonage to help her. But as the afternoon drew on, there was still no sign of Dr Brown. Fraser lapsed out of sleep into delirium again; and it was a heavy business either to do nothing or to carry on with everyday work while upstairs he was shouting nonsense out loud.

At length a horse was heard in the lane. It was the stable boy. Sophy ran out to the gate. 'Yes?' she breathed. 'Oh, please tell me what he said.'

'Who, miss?'

'The doctor!'

'I didn't see no doctor.'

'What?'

'He's gone from home –'

'Where? Tell me where *I* can find him, if no one else will.'

'– to that encampment place, miss.'

'But when will he be back? What has he said?'

'It's no good you asking that,' said the lad, as if the crisis were Sophy's fault – having ridden hard, he was ready to be irked by her insistence. 'There ain't none of them at his house that can answer you that.'

'But he must be found!' said Sophy, to herself as much as anyone. Back inside she cast on her outdoor clothes again, and, scarcely waiting to tell the maid where she was going, set off through the village for the Upstowe road.

However she was not bound for Upstowe itself, but for the camp. She had not the least idea what to do when she got there, but it was getting too late to worry about that. Already the sun was low enough to cast a radiance such that you had to shade your eyes to see. Soon it would be too dark to find the way home alone.

Half walking, half running beside the churned-up road, she came at length to the embankment, spilling itself along toward a newly deserted farmyard. At the foot of the first barrow-run she stopped, panting. The ganger in charge, seeing what his men were staring at, came up to her. Sophy was not only out of breath, but muddied up to the knees in the good travelling clothes given her by her uncle. The man looked curious, and a little cynical, to see a young woman in such a place, alone and dishevelled. Behind him, all up the embankment men had stopped work to stare, just as surprised but, since she was pretty, also grinning hilariously.

'Yes?' Sophy was asked. The man was frowning at her as though she had no business there. He clearly felt his dignity imperilled by having to speak to someone of her looks in front of his navvies.

'Dr Brown has come by here?'

'Are you asking, or telling me?' One of the men snickered. The ganger glanced aside but dared not turn right round.

'Why, what do you think!' exclaimed Sophy, contemptuous of the suppressed excitement she was causing. 'The doctor's needed in the village. Just tell me if he's passed this way!'

The man shrugged. 'There's been no one here. If you reckon that's what you're after.'

His implied insult left Sophy too angry to care what any of them might say or do. 'Where are the people here, then, who are sick?'

'You can find *them* all over.' He gave her another hard look. 'For all the use they'll be to one like you.'

Sophy met his eyes with furious coolness. 'I hope you'll be one of them too before long. Anybody as frightened of his own men as you are doesn't deserve to be in work.' And she turned and walked away, indifferent to how she had to lift her skirts before them to keep her balance in the mire. Her outburst surprised them; as she went, it was only the men who'd been out of earshot who jeered at their leader for the chance of talking to her.

The temporary way to the camp led beside the embankment. Slips of clayey slurry had deluged the path every few yards. The towering rampart of earth due to carry the canal was broken by a man-made valley. Through it passed a little stream, its banks scuffed quite bald. The gulf in the embankment was knitted up by a mass of scaffolding where an aqueduct was being built. The path forded the brook beside a series of foundations for the piers, each big enough to hold up a church. A wilderness of hewn stones surrounded them, as if the aqueduct had been completed, and worn back down into a ruin. Looking up at the sky above the earthwork it seemed not that the clouds moved but that the whole structure was slowly falling on one's head.

At the first shanty, Sophy asked an old woman with no nose where the doctor had last been seen.

'You want Botany Bay,' the woman told her, pointing out a mass of huts dug back into the bank of the stream.

There were fewer people about than she had expected. She stopped again to ask directions, at a turf shack with a sagging timber roof, in which a room as small as a ship's cabin held twenty bunks. No one was there but two starveling children beating a dog to tear a rabbit's head away from it. Another such building held neither beds nor furniture of any kind: just a mound of sawdust across the earth floor. A woman and two children were there alone. Sophy came to an open space where there was a fire big enough to burn a house down. Around it a few people stood or sat, looking into its depths as if it were a mirror. In vain she questioned a ragged girl her own age with two children and a baby. The girl, staring at Sophy as if she were a creature beyond her own comprehension, merely shook her head, looking solemn, and went on staring as Sophy walked away.

Meanwhile, 'He were there, not long since,' an old-looking man told her. Without removing his clay pipe he nodded in the direction of a group of shanties that appeared to have grown up out of the earth and then collapsed in on each other.

'Are you certain that's the place?' she asked, indicating an open door in one of them.

'Aye, aye; get on wi' ye; go on.'

'If there are people inside, why is there no smoke from their chimney?'

'Ye heard what I said, did ye not?'

'Yes, and I don't believe you.' But she went across nonetheless to look inside.

Returning, she said, 'The men in there are both dead.'

'Ah. T'were said there were little hope for them.'

It was becoming clear that there must be little more than a hundred people left in the camp. Apart from those gangs still at work, few remained except the helpless, the foolish or the sick. Angry with impatience she took out her purse. 'If I give you sixpence,' glaring at the man, 'then will you tell me where to look next? The doctor's needed for Mr Fraser without delay. You can't ask me to go on guessing where he might be.'

The man took the pipe from his mouth and looked at her properly for the first time. 'Eh, now, you should've told us that,' ignoring the money. 'It's no good just coming here and saying aught.'

'Good God – one man with the fever is the same as any other!'

'No, you can't say that.' Though reproachful, he showed not the least urgency. 'Where be the use, if you don't tell us what you be doing here? He be gone back to 'us home. I could've told you that straight out, iffen as I'd've known to.'

Sophy still wasn't certain she could believe what she was told. Back on the highway, in a panic of indecision, she turned around and around as if playing blind man's buff. Beneath the dusk she nearly missed the glow-worm light from the lamps of the doctor's gig. He was being tipped this way and that above the ruts of the highway as he drove away from her toward Cannings Fitzpayne.

He was going too slowly for her not to catch him up. 'Where are you going?' she cried, her voice cracked from breathlessness. 'You must come immediately to Parsonage Lane.'

'Must? I must be everywhere!'

'No – no,' Sophy exclaimed. It didn't occur to her that she was announcing two more cases among dozens in the village. 'They have the fever there, at Mrs Lovell's.'

He looked at her fur-trimmed merino plastered with filth. Her wild appearance surprised him more than he showed. 'I don't doubt you, or I wouldn't be on my way thither. But you may ride with me only to the almshouses, first. I've a case of poorhouse fever on my hands now, as well as camp fever.'

It was dark when they reached the cottage. They were let in by Mrs Beddowes, still in her bonnet and pelisse. She seemed more concerned at how Sophy looked than for the two patients. While the doctor was still upstairs she made her sit down and try to taste some hot milk and toast.

At length Dr Brown reappeared, backing down the narrow stairs as if their steepness were a deliberate affront to his dignity. In parting he prescribed medicines which as it turned out both patients were too ill to take; and indeed he seemed to think his time should not have been wasted by a call on someone as deeply unconscious as the old lady had become.

'I think, my dear,' said Mrs Beddowes as she in turn prepared to go back to her own home, 'I can arrange for your mother to be persuaded you should stay here.' She glanced anxiously at the girl, not knowing how frank she ought to be. 'I shall be here most of the time, as well as Mary.' She blushed. It was actually harder for her to discuss the propriety of Sophy staying here than to mention the fatal danger others might suffer if she were *not* quarantined. 'And I'm sure everything can be explained to her so that she won't worry more than she must... About your safety, I mean. Also I'm certain I can have her looked after... But I shan't tell her, you know, where you've been today.' The parson's wife was a good woman, and a brave one, too, who without a thought would carry food, medicine and kind words into pestilence-stricken hovels one wouldn't care to use as a chicken-run. Mention of the camp, on the other hand, affected her as though she'd never ventured anywhere less genteel than her own pantry.

As evening became night, Sophy wrapped herself in her outdoor clothes, loosed her hair, and sat down by Fraser's bed to wait out the hours. She was more tired than she could have imagined – and soon, despite the servant asleep downstairs, terribly lonely. The fire clicked in the grate, the silence outside was as great as if the house had fallen into a bottomless gulf, and the man beside her appeared sometimes to wake, only to start up and rant out loud without the least awareness of anybody else.

Several times, at the stage of thinking dawn must surely be near, she dozed off. Once, from dreaming she was sitting in that room, but unable to move, she found she'd been asleep while Fraser talked on in a voice that could have been heard throughout the house. At length he lapsed once more into a shallow sleep and Sophy felt her way through the dark to pass time by tending the fire that burnt in the tiny grate, like a breast-pocket set upside down, in Mrs Lovell's room.

Toward dawn the old lady died. Sophy was not quite sure when her breathing had faltered for the last time. At sunrise the maid from the Parsonage, tiptoeing up the stairs, found the body covered by a sheet, and Sophy fast asleep beside it in a chair.

Within minutes the house seemed full of neighbours. Mrs Beddowes came, prepared to supervise the laying out of the body with practised efficiency. 'I'm afraid, my dear, we cannot delay taking the poor thing downstairs to be washed. She won't stay pliable for long; and those stairs are far too steep to take a coffin.'

121

Sophy, heavy-eyed, only felt fatigue. Had it been safe, she would have fallen down on the dead woman's mattress without a thought that its lingering warmth had been held there beneath a corpse. Still dressed, she pulled a blanket over herself on the improvised bed made up in the parlour. 'Is mama all right?' she asked. And without waiting for a response she fell asleep.

Two mornings after the funeral Sophy went into Fraser's room to find him conscious. 'Were you here before?' he asked.

As he slept again and woke into faint-spoken languor, she found herself less at ease than before. While he had been incoherent and in danger for his life she had done what chores she had to without a thought. But now Sophy, who'd never been apprehensive of anyone in her life, was surprised to find herself becoming awkward. He looked so unfamiliar, lying there hollow-eyed, with his hair cropped close because of the illness. It was as embarrassing as if someone had presented himself at his own funeral. Now, whenever she was in the room, she became brisk and blushing, and made a point of not looking him in the face. Needlessly so, for at first he was too weak to care about anything.

But as the next sign of recovery, he too began to share her unease.

'Would you help me with some work?' he asked one day, as she was helping him to sit up ready to be fed. He'd started saving up things to say at just such moments as this. It was too absurd, otherwise, to pretend his arm wasn't around the neck of a girl in whose face every perfect curve was both inevitable and astonishing.

'Of course,' said Sophy, wondering for the hundredth time if he knew she'd helped Mrs Beddowes' servant to wash him and change his sheets.

He needed someone to whom he could dictate letters. It was a relief to both of them to share a task that didn't smack of intimacy. Writing things were got and Sophy sat down, looking tired, but open-faced with pleasure at doing something different after so many days indoors.

122

The doctor, on finding out later that week what was going on, was furious.

'God in heaven!' he exclaimed at Sophy when they were alone. 'Do you not know better? To let a man in his condition work ten hours at a stretch?'

'Oh, don't you shout at me!' said Sophy, keeping her own voice down with difficulty. 'It's not for me to make him do anything!'

Dr Brown, seeing her look bruised about the eyes from lack of rest, said nothing. He reflected it was as well she too would soon be out of danger.

Back upstairs, Sophy didn't return immediately to her makeshift writing desk. Instead she loitered, fidgeting and humming a tune, under the dormer that gave the only shaft of light in the room. Through the window she could see a square of blue sky, with wisps of warm-weather cloud all blurry about the edges like a watercolour made too wet. Part of an elm tree was visible too, the profile of its topmost twigs underlined by a wavy row of rooks' nests. Its branches had been bare, sheened over with faintest purple, when she'd first looked out at it. Now it was clouded with breaking leaves. For nearly a month she had been shut up in this little house, having to act distantly toward Fraser the more they were thrown together. Part of her yearned to be at liberty – and yet it was almost unbearable that she was about to return, maybe for ever, to Drove Cottage. How soon would it be, she wondered, before every garment she owned would have been unstitched and reassembled inside out, to make it last? And in a little while, when she was her mother's age, would she too be always short of breath and talk about her nerves?

'Do you wish to go on?' she asked Fraser, without looking at him.

'I can't stop work now!' Convalescence was making him snappish. He was really too tired to force himself to be idle.

With an abrupt movement Sophy sat down at the desk.

'I can send for one of my assistants soon, if you'd prefer it,' he said, noticing how uncheerful she looked. Anyone else he might have ignored as they worked on. But it was hard for him not to gaze at this girl, whose looks were only made more interesting by tiredness and disarray.

'No – oh, no! Besides, I doubt Mr Peters would be free to see you for at least five days, and the others are both deputizing for you – and who could you put in *their* places?'

On Sophy's part, it was more than a gesture of wanting to oblige. She had taken on the task of writing out Fraser's correspondence quite without wondering whether she would understand a word. Her own education had taught her to memorize rather than think. Only now did she begin to see that knowledge amounted to more than making lists. By a series of leaps, all of them unexpected, she was discovering how the parts of Fraser's work each acted on the others. The novelty of it made her as pleased as if she'd just thought of it all before anyone else. It gave her the exultant jolt of an explorer who finds the blanks on his map smaller than he thought.

Not that she became ashamed of her own mostly useless accomplishments. She was still too well conditioned into young ladyhood for that. The interest of what she was doing was only for the present, like being lent an unfamiliar book, or seeing something new made up for her to wear. She wasn't even conscious that it was changing her opinion of Fraser. While he could only work with her help, propped up on pillows, it was hard to think of him as more than an ailing boy.

And though in the circumstances they were bound to be intensely aware of one another, it never occurred to her that his own perception of her might be changing.

One morning that week he was dictating a memorandum to his superintendent of masonry. It was to do with quarrying stone for the aqueduct above Botany Bay. He paused, remembering something. 'It was you who went for the doctor, wasn't it?'

'For all the good that did! He would have got here just as soon.'

'I hope I haven't seemed ungrateful ... What an object

I must have been that day!' He grimaced cheerfully, stretching his arms above his head.

'Oh, you were horrible!' she exclaimed. Fraser was due to get up next day. The prospect of release from the sickroom had them both as expectant as brats about to burst out of school.

She's someone more worth noticing than I'd guessed, he thought. If I go on taking lessons in her home, will it look like paying court? Fraser was at that stage of pleasure in the girl's company that was all the more delightful because, as yet, not one word or look had committed either of them. Perhaps, he told himself, he would still go to Drove Cottage – and simply not think about her when she wasn't present.

Walking home through the village next day, Sophy sang to herself. Now that she had escaped into the open air from a place of death, she felt complacent just to be alive. A whole season seemed to have gone by – and now the birds were shouting from every branch, and gilded bumblebees were wafted through the sunshine, just to celebrate her own survival. She was bursting with good intentions. She would help her mother and Hannah do – oh, all sorts of useful things about the cottage. And then, since her mother was mending in health, she would look for a position. In a big town – maybe even London. Not all employers could be as disagreeable as Kate's. Besides, even if life beyond the world she knew were horrible, it still would not be something that had just happened to her. No – she would be living that way because *she* chose it so.

But Sophy was wrong to think she would be greeted at home with nothing but relief. As she embraced her mother, Mrs Byford said, 'Now, Sophy, I do so hope you'll be sensible. I'm sure *I* don't know what I think you should do. But this was brought for you, only this morning.'

It was a small parcel, exquisitely confected. The wrapping itself looked like something marvellous to wear. Inside was a box, upholstered in bright new leather.

Mrs Byford looked at it as if it might contain a scorpion. 'Sophy, I really don't think you can keep it. It was a man in livery who brought it, you know.'

The box was lined in satin and filled with tissue paper. Its contents could not have looked more cherished if they'd been a living creature. Amid the hardships of recent weeks Sophy had not cared to notice how her spirits had been worn down. Until, that is, she saw this token from a world of luxury she thought had forgotten her for ever. She was lost between laughing and crying as she pulled the tissue paper apart, like the petals of an unopened flower, and took out a pair of teardrop pearl earrings.

But what was this? Sophy's expression turned from pleasure to dismay and then to doubt, as she realized why her mother viewed the gift as something that might compromise her. With the jewels, short and formal, on heavy embossed paper, was a note, signed by Rawley Fitzpayne.

Chapter Seven

As the spring days expanded, the Vale underwent a change. On the farms, with lambing safely past, thousands of sheep were driven from the water meadows where they'd spent the winter, up onto the downs. In the bottoms, the grass, later to be cut for hay, was growing fast and the willows along the boggy streams were faintest silvery green. The ploughed fields around the farms, between the low ground and the downs, had been deserted by their winter flocks of redwings and fieldfares. Instead the coppices rang with the song of the chiff-chaff and the sound of the green woodpecker drumming against a hollow trunk with the urgency of courtship. In deep hedges beside each muddy lane, primroses flowered, and drifts of delicate violets. There was movement everywhere – in the bleating flocks driven with shouts and whistles up deep downland lanes; and in farmyards, where scraggy outhouse cats and the prize boar himself ventured out to lie and stretch in the sun. In the farmhouses, doors and windows were thrown open for the summer, so that passers-by might sometimes see right through a passage and the big kitchen behind to a patch of sunlit field or garden framed in a further doorway. Each hedgerow tree and blade of grass seemed to strain with the bursting upwards of its sap. It was as though with your ear to the ground or to the trunk of an elm swelling into leaf you could hear a cracking sound beneath the stress of all this growth. Every shade of green blossomed across the Vale, changing with the seeming swiftness of sunshine chasing shadow. Along narrow downland coppices, where the ground fell too steeply for grass to grow, dark yews stood out against the palest green of wayfaring trees and shimmering foliage, bright as an angel's wing, breaking from tall beeches. Down by the streams, where marsh marigolds shone bravely among soggy groves of alder trees, the cattle, taken out to graze, cantered about in undignified bliss before settling to feed. The grass already grew hock-high, its wettest places sprinkled with mauve lady's-smock. This was the time when farmyard dairies were busy amid the smell of whey, as the springtime yield of milk was made into huge cheeses or churned and patted into butter.

At Cannings Fitzpayne Hall, the annual rhythm of activity was as set as on any of the farms. Always, at this season, there were extra chores in the still-room; and in the walled kitchen gardens with their long lean-to glass-houses dozens of under-gardeners tended potted orange trees and melons and vineries. Above stairs there was also much to do; furniture in rooms of state had to be sheeted over and heavy curtains and shutters were closed for the rest of the summer. Though the epidemic had spent itself, in summer Lord Fitzpayne was unlikely ever to be in Wiltshire for long. Usually, April was when the mansion in town was opened up, for his lordship to pass several months there on whatever business, Parliamentary or purely social, the London Season might bring.

Lady Fitzpayne was to remain in Wiltshire meanwhile – though her presence was but little noted even by the servants. Her habits had become ever more restricted, and she no longer made work by receiving visitors, or calling on other county families, as formerly, with the pomp of six servants and a coach and four. Recently, too, she had become ill – mysteriously so, since the doctor brought from Salisbury to attend her had so far withheld any name for her painful, slow-growing malady. She kept to her bedchamber now, sometimes refusing food and light, and sometimes screeching with rage or whimpering, according to whether the servants' neglect was imaginary or real. Her ladyship's maid, Miss Hodgkiss, meanwhile grew surly from insecurity, as Lady Fitzpayne's own status at the Hall sank to little more than that of a family ghost.

'There wasn't the trace of a smile on your face yesterday when you went upstairs to her ladyship,' she said one breakfast in the great kitchen, whither she had gone to stand over the maid who took up Lady Fitzpayne's meals. 'Oh, you needn't think she doesn't notice you, my girl. I should watch out if I were you. And you –' swerving round to stab a finger at where Charity Michaelmas, looking ill, was dishing up Lady Fitzpayne's grilled bone. 'You – yes, you. You don't have to act as if I mean someone else. And you needn't look so miserable, neither, just because you're having to do a job of work.'

The covers went on the tray and it was hastened on its long journey to the upper regions of the Hall. Behind it came Miss Hodgkiss, though she was far too conscious of her status to help the maid by opening any doors.

Charity paused to ease her aching back. Every day now she felt increasingly swollen and soft all over. But the few terrible mornings were past when, to conceal her pregnancy, she had had to act as though every sickening piece of food didn't seem to have a slightly fuzzy edge, or the walls and floors themselves didn't look like something disgusting she was going to have to eat.

She had no plans. How, she reckoned, once the horror of her situation lost its novelty, could she? If anything except endurance could help her, would it not have helped the wretched woman, whoever she had been, from whose womb she herself had been thrust unwanted?

Someone was whispering. Almost out of sight. From

where Charity stood, serving up devilled kidneys for the steward's table, only odd words were audible. But fear of discovery made her certain of their meaning. She sneaked a glance, on the pretext of turning to load a tray – and caught Cook and Mrs Richards the housekeeper pretending not to look at her.

Oh, please don't let them speak to me, prayed Charity. Their tone was disapproving, yes; but in a melancholy way, as though in examining her shape beneath her mercifully loose, high-waisted dress they had found a victim rather than a wrong-doer. The thought of being offered sympathy in her hopeless state was more than she could bear.

Sure enough, amid the noise and activity of the kitchen and the servants' hall she was left nonetheless to nurse her growing sorrow in solitude. Until ... in one of the pantries she encountered two of the under-housemaids, Eastcot and Dace, both of them scrawny fourteen-year-old hags-to-be. They were giggling together, and daring one another to go up to her. Seeing Charity, one of them darted up and exclaimed in her face, 'Be you expecting, then?' and with shrieks of laughter they fled from her, in the doorway almost knocking down Mrs Richards.

'Oh, no, ma'am. I know what to do to take care of myself,' sobbed Charity a few minutes later beside the fire in the housekeeper's parlour. 'Honestly I do. I've got a friend in London who'd look after me. That's if I needed help from other folk.'

Mrs Richards, a dour-faced widow who at least meant as well as most, recognized the false hopefulness of desperation, and said nothing. She waited, while the girl poured forth all the anguish that for months she'd been keeping to herself. At length Charity, drawing a sigh that had a catch in it from weeping, fell silent.

'Now,' said Mrs Richards. 'Charity, you know I've always thought of you as a good girl. As a very good girl. For every kind of reason.'

'Yes, ma'am.'

'And I still do. It's very important that you should

129

understand that, now.' Charity nodded, tears leaking from her scorched eyes yet again.

'But you do also understand, do you not, why you must leave this establishment without delay?'

'I think so, ma'am.'

'It's not because the other girls will be hateful to you.'

'No, ma'am; I know it's not that.'

'But London, now! Is that really where you wish to go? Mm?'

'Yes, ma'am.'

'Are you sure, now, Charity?'

'Oh, yes,' said Charity, as firmly as her feeble state would let her, though in truth the idea, in the agitation of the moment, had only just formed itself.

'I hope you're right, you know. I've heard all conditions of people say it can be a terrible place.'

Charity said nothing, having no knowledge with which to answer.

'Yes ... well ... I only hope you'll think about it very carefully. But now I'm sorry to say there is one thing on which you absolutely must take my advice. If you leave here on the instant – even without a – well – a final destination – then Mr Freeman might not yet have heard the reason for your going, and we can still get your half-yearly wage for you after all. Now don't –'

'Oh, but I'm sure I don't need to go near him for money. I've got some saved.'

'– don't tell me you don't need the money. It's only natural that you should want to make light of your difficulties; but believe me, it's a very foolish way of doing so. Now I shall go to the steward's office and speak to Mr Freeman myself; you need not worry about seeing him. But I want you to promise me – quite solemnly, now, mm? – promise me – that you will take the money. If not for your own sake, then out of respect for me. I do know that if you are to get it, you will have to have your things bundled up within a very few minutes. But you will need it, now.'

And Mrs Richards hurried off, secretly relieved at having such an argument to help get the girl off her hands.

Charity's possessions were so scanty that even she could carry them without looking burdened. Mrs Richards, returning in almost no time, gave her two guineas from the steward, together with one of her own good handkerchiefs to tie them in, and found, as if from nowhere, a piece of oilcloth in which to wrap Charity's few things.

Thus did the manor house show Charity its kindliest face. As she was hastening, like a mouse running for cover, toward the servants' exit, she passed the maid who carried Lady Fitzpayne's food, bringing away her ladyship's untouched breakfast.

'Where be you going, Michaelmas? ... Michaelmas! You ain't been crying, have you? Where be you going with them things?'

Charity walked on, ignoring her. Never more, she told herself, could she afford to care what other people thought. Big-bellied already beneath her shabby cloak, she made her way under the shadows of the gatehouse arch and out across the windy, sunlit park to where, she knew, the high road lay.

'She b'ain't going to London!'
'She is!'

Below stairs at the Hall the news of Charity's dismissal was almost too exciting to be true. None of the younger housemaids had properly heard of the last time such a thing had happened.

'London! She never will!' whispered little Temperance Eastcot as a group of them sanded the vast kitchen floor, like labourers tilling a field.

'How'd she find her way there, then?'

'Michaelmas would know. And it's not like you had to go across the sea, now, is it?'

'Aye, Michaelmas knows. She told me once – she told me –'

'She's sharp, that Michaelmas. She don't say much –'

'If she be so clever, how come she got one in the oven, then?' Sally Dace exclaimed.

Cook, overhearing their stifled squawks of mirth,

glowered; and for the space of several seconds they all smirked privately, with downcast eyes.

'She don't say much. But she knows her letters –'

'She told me once –'

'Aye. She can write them, too, can Michaelmas!'

'She told me how you get to London, once, she did.'

'No! She b'ain't never been to London. How could she know that?'

'You can't just follow all them milestones down that road. The constables would have her, for a vagrant.'

'She said London were over where the sun come up.'

'That's no use, knowing that!'

'It is!'

'That's no use to anyone, that is!'

Kate's hopes, recently so high, now concerned themselves with nothing more than letters from home. While the Leggatts remained in Bath, Sophy's news, good or bad, was the only thing that breached her loneliness.

Her status had changed in recent weeks. Word of the epidemic had prompted the Leggatts to send for the children, and lengthen their own stay in the safety of Pulteney Street. Kate's holiday from her duties as governess was at an end – which was as well: she sorely needed the activity, to help fill up her thoughts. But she was also made to feel that in being discarded as the future Mrs Lee she had thwarted her employer's own social ambitions. And indeed, in his cups, Leggatt took pains to say so. 'You know, you've not turned out as I hoped. You know that, don't you? When I made you part of my establishment, I said to myself, there's a girl one might do well to know, given time. And I said as much to acquaintances of mine – I want you to know that. I didn't hesitate to say so to anyone in this city ... I don't know what you've done, to turn away my friend Joseph Lee. I shan't ask you what you did wrong. Maybe you said something to give offence; or maybe there was something wrong in your dress or manner. Whatever it was, I don't wish to know ...'

Alone, Kate shed tears of loathing as well as melan-

132

choly. Anything was welcome that turned her thoughts away from herself or the Leggatt household.

Word came of Sophy's release from quarantine; and Kate heard besides that they could soon look forward to going back to Cannings Fitzpayne. There at least she would sometimes be allowed to visit her mother and sister, and escape being shut up – Leggatt now being negligent about showing her in company – in the attics of their lodging in hateful Bath.

But she was far less glad, and all the more anxious to be home, when she heard of Rawley Fitzpayne's gift. Sophy had written:

... Dearest Kate, what should I do? I try to ask myself, how would you act? The more I think about it, the plainer my course appears. Of course I should keep Mr Fitzpayne's gift, whatever mama might say. For – only consider – might it not be perverse not to keep it? I mean, might he not mistake its return for a calculated provocation? As a deliberate cruelty? After all, I should hate him to think I was trifling with him or trying to be coquettish ...

Sophy's next letter, the following day, made Kate no easier.

... And now – only three days after I received the earrings, who should ride up to me in Parsonage Lane, but – Mr Rawley Fitzpayne!

What happened was this: I was on my way to Mrs Beddowes' to see a length of jaconet that she'd purchased for a summer gown; and I heard a pair of saddle horses coming up the lane – and there he was! And then, instead of just nodding and reining in his horse, he dismounted, so that he could properly engage me in conversation. 'Hey-day, Miss Sophia,' he said to me, as he dismounted and gave his horse to the groom. And just at that moment, who should come up our lane but Parson Beddowes and his son – and I believe Mr Fraser rode by, where it joins the high road, too. I was so pleased to be addressed by Mr Fitzpayne – I have to confess it — that I had to turn my head lest any of them should see me blush and smile so.

Oh, but Kate! There is more yet! No sooner had he — Mr Fitzpayne — greeted me — you know, in the way I have just described — than he actually had the man take back both horses to the Hall! Mr Rawley Fitzpayne actually volunteered to walk back to the Hall, all the way across the park, just so that he could stop at length to speak to me! Indeed, he said to me himself, 'You see, Miss Sophia, how highly I rate your company. There are not many people for whom I should walk a half-a-mile.'

And then, 'Are you about an errand of pleasure?' Mr Fitzpayne inquired, the two of us looking each other in the eye all the while, as straight as you please; and, before I could answer, 'Do you have much time to spend at liberty?'

Something made me tell him 'Yes' — I cannot tell what.

But can you guess what he said next? 'I was a fool,' he said, 'to part with eighty guineas each for such short-winded nags. But on the twenty-fourth I go to Upstowe to take delivery of a new pair of bays for the curricle. I may drive you there if you wish.'

And now, Kate, do you not see my dilemma? I cannot fail to accept this offer. Yet I may not even think of such a thing. Of course I care not a fig that anyone should think me compromised by driving out with him alone. In any case they should be wrong. How could anybody's respectability be lessened by association with someone as well born as he? Please, please, dear Kate, advise me by return. Yet of one thing I am absolutely sure. I shall go. But how? I must go. Even though, for aught I can tell, I may survive another eighty years, how can I know this may not be the last exciting thing ever to happen to me . . .

Kate was exasperated at her own helplessness. What could she say to dissuade Sophy from keeping company with such a man? She had overheard one or two vile rumours of him even from Leggatt, who usually fawned indiscriminately on his social superiors whether they were present or not. Before she could write, however, one of George's letters was forwarded to her. It included, she thought, the very information she needed to influence Sophy.

Old Fitzpayne had done famously ill for himself when I saw him in the Strand the other week. He wouldn't even speak to anyone of how he came by blacked eyes and a split lip; but Nordaby said the fight was altogether of his own making – so serve him d--ned well right, he said. Nordaby said he got them arguing the bill for drink in a house of ill-fame. I could not tell you such things if you were back at home, but no one else excepting you will see this. I would not argue with the owner of such a place, even if I were as rich as Fitzpayne. He would have gone up and struck the great blancmangey madame herself, said Nordaby, but that the women in the place screamed for the house oafs to throw them both out. Myself, though I daresay they are both perfectly good fellows, I see no reason why they should not pay the penalty in such a case, and find themselves barred from the establishment. I would that I could write such scurrilous things to Sophy, too, without mama reading them. It would make me laugh to think how cross she'd be, to hear of her idol fallen on such sordid circumstances. I mean flung out, unsatisfied, into a dungheap in a state of drunkenness ...

Cannings Fitzpayne 15 April

Dearest Kate,
I'm sure you intend well, but pray don't write me such things. I knew what your letter was really about, even if mama did not.
You need not have cautioned me in any case about driving out with Mr Fitzpayne. That has come to naught – I met him in the village yesterday, and when I mentioned it he said he had decided not to buy the ponies after all. And now he has gone to Salisbury to the Assizes with his uncle, and thence to London – so heaven knows when I shall meet him again.
An idea has occurred to me. I could write a letter to Mr Fitzpayne, could I not? Perhaps his going so many miles off is not such bad luck after all – for the greater the distance,

the better my reason to write to him. The more I consider it, the more I am convinced that I should write to him. And that I can do so with complete propriety ...

All this made Kate more thankful than ever that she and her employers should soon leave Bath. The wait for the packing up – Leggatt had insisted on bringing all their best linen and five sets of plate – seemed endless. At last the family's carriage, with Kate, the children and Mrs Leggatt's maid in a chaise behind, was ready to depart. The streets of Bath, as they drove by, appeared like a parade of personal defeats. Out in the country, the tall hedgerows and crowded fields could surely not have passed more slowly if she were limping home barefoot. If she looked forward to seeing her mother and sister again it was not because she had anything to say to them. It would be enough simply to know that they, at least, were her friends and close at hand.

Amidst the to-do of arrival, once they had returned to Cannings Fitzpayne, Kate ventured into her employer's study to speak to Leggatt alone. As she entered, he looked at her with more of his former conspiratorial flirtatiousness than he had for some days. Since his goodwill toward her usually reflected how badly he got on with his wife, she guessed that they must have quarrelled again on the journey.

She had a favour to ask; being homesick for a sight of her own family, might she bring her half-day forward from Sunday next?

Leggatt however was clearly not on such bad terms with his wife that Kate should once more be utterly delightful. 'We'll see,' he said, with a roguish smile that promised nothing.

'Thank you, sir.' Kate in turn gave a soft, grateful smile of insincerity, and tried to leave the room with an air of irresistible carelessness.

It must have had some of the effect she wanted, for instead of turning back to his paperwork he exclaimed, 'Dammit, woman, you take your half-day or whatever it is.

136

Don't loiter around here to ask permission of me, for God's sake – just go and do it!'

She dimpled at him with what she hoped was a look of adoration, and fled, before his whim turned against her once more.

At the cottage her mother was not cheerful to see her, so much as overwrought.

'But, mama – I'm not the one who's been in danger, am I now? What's the matter? What is it?'

'Nothing, dear,' said Mrs Byford, with a show of valour. Though she was genuinely near to tears at Kate's return, she was also anxious that the fact shouldn't go unnoticed. 'Only I felt sure one daughter would return to me, as the other was taken away.'

'What's happened?' Kate too found it an effort to sound cheerful. She had been looking forward to her sister's comradeliness and understanding, after so many weeks shut up amid cold looks.

'Did you not receive Sophy's note? You should have, you know, dear.'

'Where? Was it sent to wait for me?'

'Oh dear. She delivered it to the Leggatts' house herself. It shouldn't have gone astray there, should it? Are you sure you never had it, dear?'

Kate strove not to show what was in her mind. It would not be the first time that Mrs Leggatt, from spite, had delayed correspondence addressed to her. 'Do you know what she said?'

They were interrupted by an unexpected sound. Someone on horseback had stopped in the lane outside. The cottage stood so close to the public byway that through the deep window up in the wall on one side of the kitchen they could hear the horse snort and shift about as he was being tethered. None of the penniless Byford females was used to having many calls any more – much less from a man, as by his footsteps he was. Through the other window Hannah, the maid, who'd been hanging out sheets in the garden, could be seen hurrying across to admit him – and Fraser was shown in.

'I had word the lessons couldn't go on,' he said. 'No,

thank you,' on being offered a chair by Kate, 'I don't intend a social call ... Something is amiss?'

'No – no; there's naught amiss here,' replied Mrs Byford, and waited, as if further courtesies were someone else's responsibility. With people of her own former rank she had become fluttery and full of anguished smirks; but she could still respond to Fraser's dubious social standing by being truculent. Kate looked the same question at her, and she added, woodenly, 'My daughter's gone to London. I expect that was why she thought you should find instruction elsewhere.'

'Mama,' Kate murmured, distressed that her mother's diffidence should show as ill-breeding, 'I should like to know what has happened, as well as Mr Fraser. Has she gone for a position, after all?'

'Sophia has gone to be approved for a position.' Though Mrs Byford spoke for Kate's benefit, it was Fraser, as the outsider, whom she addressed. She sounded like a servant repeating a message. 'By the wife of one of her uncle's trading contacts. In an establishment in Wimpole Street.'

'Then she'll not be returning.'

'I think that would be most unlikely,' said Mrs Byford, in the tone of a housekeeper discouraging an unsuitable follower from lurking after one of the maids.

Only someone who knew him well, as a hasty, not to say indiscreet, man, would have noticed how Fraser hesitated, looking into the corners of the room as if in search of something to say. 'I thought so,' he remarked, and took his leave with as few fine words as he'd been offered.

Charity lay in the sun and shivered. She had no idea where she was.

Her first day's travel had brought her, toward sunset, to an area of woodland. She had never seen such a place before; in the Vale there had only been farmland set with little coppices. Great oaks, their new foliage still yellowish, reached across the unfenced road; and here and there a clearing could be seen through the trees, choked up with the wreck of last year's bracken. Charity had been following a forest ride, when the dark had come down. It rose and fell in a straight line beneath a great avenue of beeches as far as one could see – bound, so a shepherd had told her, for the drovers' road to London, along the downs.

Twilight had found her still with no house in sight. But in the last glimmering of dusk, a hovel, if it could be dignified with such a name, had come into view; a rough lean-to of brushwood and turves, not quite as high as a man. It stood in a dip close by the road; and Charity would have passed it unnoticing, but for the piles of turf and kindling and the large patch of ashes that its last inhabitant, a charcoal-burner, had left. He had not been long gone; for inside the shelter, and still no more than damp, there remained a bed of dead bracken.

The cold of the spring night had kept her awake until she despaired almost of closing her eyes. At last, toward noon next day, she woke from what must have been a deep sleep. White stabs of sunlight pierced the sides of the shelter. As she lay on the pile of bracken a bumblebee blundered in, sounding noisy enough to be bigger than she was.

She made her way outside and lay down in the warm grass. It was hunger now, rather than cold, that caused her to tremble. She had to have food ... if she was to get the strength to find food ... She must not move, if she was to save her strength ... The cooing of a wood pigeon sounded from far above, with unnatural suddenness – and she realized she had been asleep again. Whatever she'd been thinking had been urgent ... perhaps one minute more of drowsiness ... The wood pigeon purred on; and the shadows in the grass shortened a little and began to grow again as they changed shape around her sleeping form.

This time, when Charity awoke, it was late afternoon. She felt as thirsty as if she'd been poisoned. No longer could she afford to care if the sun was sinking, or that she was lost in the forest and as weak as ever. She had to find food and drink, even if it meant spending the night under the naked sky.

139

She climbed the bank that led up onto the road. There must be water, she thought, walking down the long avenue – or at least something she could eat. It was in vain, though, that she looked for a stream, much less an unmuddied spring. To fend off her hunger, she sat down beneath a beech tree and gathered some nuts. She had often seen pigs eat beech mast; so she reckoned it could do her no harm. The nuts tasted better than she expected, but wresting them from their tiny shells took too long for anyone as hungry as she was.

She walked on for an hour or so; and at last she could see sunlight at ground level through the trees. Soon, beyond the avenue lay open scrub, thick with dead bracken and the uncurling shafts of another year's growth. This area gave way in turn to pasture; and there she saw one of the things she had been looking for.

In a field set about with quickset hedges a herd of Shorthorn cattle was grazing. Charity waited to see which of them, having a calf to suckle, stood patiently instead of raising her hind leg to kick. Choosing the most peaceable-looking animal, she threw herself on the ground, seized one of the big leathery teats, and began to drink.

Charity hadn't imagined how thirsty she was. She gulped the warm, sweetish milk as desperately as a stranded fish gasping for the water, not even noticing the slurps and steamy breath of the calf drinking from the other side of the udder. Only when she stopped, panting, and sat back on her heels, did she see someone watching. His eyes were almost level with her own; he was barefoot and even more ragged than herself; and he was dragging a bundle of brushwood kindling far too big for him.

A little boy. Charity's fear of being caught stealing subsided. He went on staring, unembarrassed. It was obvious he rarely saw a stranger close to.

'Where be you from?' she asked. He pointed, without speaking. Charity looked, but could see nothing. 'Be that far?' But the child only looked confused.

Charity knew she couldn't choose where she asked for food or shelter. So, helping to drag his bundle, she set off in the direction he had indicated.

140

Within a quarter of a mile they came to a cottage, in a rough clearing of pasture among stumpy hawthorn trees. It was a semi-derelict place, with inside and outdoors mingled, as so often at this season. A bench and rough working table stood outside, and chickens and a litter of piglets roamed across the brick floor of the interior. A woman was winching up water from the well; and a very old man with a stick was sitting, expressionless, in the late sun against the cottage wall.

From her small store of money, Charity offered to buy a meal and a night's lodging.

'I'll not be taking money from you for a bed,' said the young woman – she looked young, close to. 'We ain't got nothing here that's worth the paying for. You can have some straw. But you best be out of here two hours past sunrise. My husband's back from market, then.'

Charity accepted this gratefully, together with a share in their evening meal of boiled potatoes in a cracked bowl of hot milk, and a piece of goat's cheese. The chimney was apt to fill up the cottage with smoke; so the cooking was done outside, over a fire of dead branches on a patch of bare ground littered with piles of kindling, wash-lines, goat and chicken droppings, and tarpaulin shelters for this and that. The woman indicated to Charity that she was to sit, facing the wall of the house, on a log to windward of the fire; and in order to avoid the smoke the four of them ate lined up together, like a group of friends watching an entertainment.

Charity knew better than to speak to such poor people while they were eating. Soon, though, the blackened pot on its crane over the fire was emptied, signalling the time of day when labouring folk might be at their most talkative. 'Know you the way to London?' she asked.

'I do not,' said the woman, and got up to go on with her work. But the old man, who had said nothing till now, started working his toothless mouth about and tried to point with his stick across the heath and fields behind them. 'Them drovers know,' he managed to say.

'Up on those downs?'

He went on moving his jaws about desperately. Charity

141

found it hard to tell whether he meant to answer her or not. 'Can you see to London from there?' she asked.

'Them drovers, they know them things.'

She knew there was no point in asking further. It was not stupidity, nor even isolation, that withered the knack of speech among these folk; it was simply their life of unceasing labour. A city-dweller might have been at a loss to hear them. But Charity, before rising in the world by going into service, had not only known such people but imagined, in her ignorance, that they were all there was.

To lie down at dusk that evening on clean straw beneath a roof seemed to Charity the most wonderful thing she had ever known. For the first moment since setting out she let herself look forward to seeing George and securing his help. How would it be when once they'd met again? She pondered no further, but fell as deeply asleep as if the world could have been struck from under her unnoticed.

She was awakened ten hours later by the woman shaking her. ''Tis time you left here.' She gave Charity a thick slice of bread to take with her. 'You best drink your fill, afore you go. If you be going up yonder,' indicating the direction of the downs, 'there b'ain't no water as you can find up there.'

Charity went to the well to wash herself and do as the woman advised. Leaving some money and her thanks, she set out again, and walked a couple of miles before sitting down beneath a hedge to eat her breakfast.

A little further on she came to a sight both familiar and surprising. The path crossed a field marked with two parallel lines of stakes, just like the site of the new canal beyond Cannings Fitzpayne. Another waterway? Surely the same one would never reach so far? To the right the rows of stakes ascended a rise. A deep pit was being dug out by a gang of men whose overseer was talking to a fair-haired young man on a grey horse. Seeing her, the workmen jeered appreciatively, and Charity, hurrying out of earshot, wondered, not for the first time, if it might not be a relief to be elderly and ignored.

Her youthfulness and beauty, however, gave her reason

142

to be grateful to the next person she met. Soon she came to a village; and seeing a shop, went in to buy food. The shop itself was in the front room of a cottage, and still looked like a private room. There were two upholstered chairs beside the fireplace, and ornaments along the mantelpiece, as well as the usual shelves of jars and ranges of opened sacks. Its owner was a dainty old lady with an out-of-fashion frilled cap and a clean apron down to her toes. Seeing Charity's stained clothes, pale delicate face and gentle manner, she made her sit down and drink a cup of milk.

In leaving, Charity asked the way to the drovers' road, and the shopkeeper came to the door with her.

'That's the road you must take, my dear. You can't mistake it for any other, on account of it runs so straight. The parson, now he says that's because the great Julius Caesar, it was he had it built – oh, ever so many years ago, that's for sure. It must have been before the old king's grandfather – if you stop to think about it, now, mustn't it – or he wouldn't be the third King George as we have with us now.'

It was noon when Charity reached the trackway along the summit of the downs. She sat down to look about her. Northward lay the forest she had left the day before. This side of it, there lay a countryside of farmland and woods, with here and there a wisp of woodsmoke going up from a farmhouse chimney or small village. Round many of the fields, newly enclosed, a pattern of young hedges made what the country people called 'poppling', where every few yards a sapling had been left to grow. Behind, to the south, the downs fell away more gradually, in a series of bare horizons.

When she had rested Charity walked on, remembering that at this time of day her shadow should fall to the left if she was to go in the direction she wanted. It was not hard to follow the drovers' road even though there was no more to see than two white ruts in the turf. On the bare hilltop the track could be seen for miles, rising and falling as it linked the summits of the ridge. The only features in this landscape were the occasional beech coppice, rising unfenced from a patch of naked ground, and at the highest points, the smooth grassy mound of a prehistoric tumulus.

Coming at length to one of these, Charity sat down out of the wind to rest again and eat. Even in such an open place the sun was warm on the grass; and once she had fed, it was more than she could resist to lie down and steal some sleep, lulled by the noisy rustling of the grass and the bleating, far and near, from thousands of sheep.

It was a not a noise that shook her awake. Instead, there was rush of shadows across her unconscious face, as a little flock of wheatears was flushed into the air by someone or something coming up the track. In a few moments a mongrel dog appeared, nosing hither and thither with his tail aloft. Where there was a dog there was likely to be people. Could they be the drovers she'd heard spoken of?

Soon, shouts and whistles became audible. Charity stood up on the mound and waited, while the dog, either hostile or in greeting, barked at her with idiotic persistence. She had no idea whether she should be afraid of these people. Back in the Vale, there had often been drovers passing within the parish bounds, as they herded their sheep and cattle eastward over the Beacon and Cannings Hill toward far, mysterious destinations. The villagers had avoided them, seeing them both as a low form of life, since they were vagrants, and, being bound for distant populous places, as city-dwellers.

After a minute or so a herd of cattle came over the hill. About a hundred head of Devon Reds were being driven along by a man and a boy of thirteen or so, both of them on foot. Behind came a painted wooden van, rather like a henhouse on wheels, drawn by a pair of tough little Exmoor ponies with dark brown coats and pale muzzles. Two younger boys rode on the front of the van, which a woman was driving just as slowly as the ponies would go without stopping to graze. Despite their leisurely pace, the cattle were thin and their coats were dull and all on end. It was clear they had been on the road for many days.

Charity waited for the van, to ask if she might walk with them.

'Nay, you may ride with us,' the woman said. At first sight she looked a grim-faced creature, but as soon as she spoke it was obvious she was merely concentrating, as she directed the ponies round the bumps and ruts of the track.

From politeness, Charity climbed into the dim little mobile cupboard – for that was what it was, rather than a home – and lay down on the narrow bed along one side. The van was unsprung, and lurched about violently enough to be excruciating for anyone unused to it. In this way, eventually dozing, and later walking alongside for several miles, she found they were out of sight of any country she had travelled earlier. To their left a town had come into view some seven or eight miles off, the smoke from its houses growing thicker as evening drew on. She looked down anxiously across the woods and fields, now laid with giant shadows. London, everybody knew, was a big town. Was it so big, then, that this might not be it?

The drovers must be able to tell her ... But shame at her ignorance made her reluctant to ask outright. At length, walking beside the woman, who had got down to lead the ponies by the bridle for a change, she said, 'Where be you bound, then?'

'Up London way. And you?'

'Aye, I'm bound for London, too.'

The woman looked at Charity, and said nothing for a minute or more. 'You've not been that way before.' It was a statement, not a question.

'No,' said Charity, a little confused at her tone.

'You shouldn't keep them boots on all that way. They'll get worn out, they will.' She herself, like all her family, was barefoot.

Charity strove to hide her dismay. So it was true what she'd heard below stairs at the Hall; it must be at least a hundred miles. She tried to picture such a distance, and decided it was as well she couldn't. Then another, more distressing, thought occurred: would her money last? 'When will you get there, think you?' she asked.

'I don't know about that. These'll be held up at

145

Guildford,' indicating the herd, 'while we pasture them.' Again she glanced at Charity, this time as if to confirm her perception of the girl's big belly. 'You mustn't think we ain't ready to have you come along with us someway. But you best leave us long afore we get to Guildford.' She had her own reasons for wanting Charity not to keep them company too long. It was evident her time could not be many weeks away.

She was not unkindly, however; besides she missed the company of other females. Hesitating, she inquired, 'Be you due to meet with kin?'

'I ain't got no kin ... I'm going up to London to meet there with a friend.'

The drover's wife paused again, and said, 'I hope then they're a good friend to you.' She thought it might not be tactful to take it openly for granted that the friend must be some young unsuspecting man.

Half-child though Charity might still be, she realized that from now on the woman looked at her differently. Her good intentions didn't lessen – she was if anything more openly kind. But thereafter she treated the girl as if there were nothing more to ask. To Charity it seemed that, while she herself made her way toward London as blindly as if feeling a stretched thread in the dark, to her companions her future was no mystery at all. Even here, on these spacious hills whose profiles vanished eastward clean out of sight, and beneath a sky bigger yet than down among the peaceful fields and lanes – even here they seemed to know how she would fare in the streets of London, when she should finally get there to ask people if they knew George, and where his lodgings were.

At sunset they stopped, above a long shallow combe. On the skyline stood a group of beeches beside a grass-grown mound, or barrow. A few yards below lay a dew-pond, dug out and lined several centuries before, by other herdsmen at some unknown date. Its water was of course too stagnant for humans to drink. Instead the drovers had their own supply, slung beneath the van in a three-gallon

146

pot, beside hay for the horses and a store of fuel for the fire.

After a solid, unappetizing meal of salt beef, biscuits and two pints of ale apiece, the children put themselves to bed in the van. The man settled to watch through the first part of the night beneath it, wrapped in sacking with a truss of hay wedged to keep off the wind. The woman meanwhile told Charity to bring some sacks and a blanket over to the mound.

A little bewildered, Charity did so. Only close to, did she realize what they were about.

In the side of the mound away from the track stood a rock-framed entrance. The whole structure was a stone-built chamber on which its architects, four thousand years before, had had gangs of slaves pile several tons of soil. Though few passed by who even guessed its origin, it had been the burial place of an Iron Age king. It had long since been plundered, so thoroughly that by now not a fragment of skull or broken pot remained. Except at the entrance, where in recent months some herdsman had made a fire, the floor was smooth and bare. The drover's wife, as matter-of-fact as if she were in a cottage attic rather than a pagan tomb, wrapped herself in some impoverished bedding and lay down to sleep. Charity, by now too tired to stand or, sitting, to stay awake, followed her example and fell unconscious as if from a blow.

'You best leave us tomorrow,' she was told next morning, as they followed the herd south and east above a vista drowned in early fog. The drover's wife spoke neutrally, without hostility or polite regret. 'You be going all that way, you best get you a ride. What you best do, you best go north to that canal. They got barges there, some of them go right down to London.' And she explained how, in addition to the regular packet-boats from one town to the next, for a few shillings poor people might find transport on a cargo boat.

Meanwhile the place of embarkation she described was still two days away; and as they made their way along the lonely hills it seemed to Charity that instead of growing

147

nearer it receded. The trackway rose and fell with no landmark in sight but the flat summit of a prehistoric earthwork or the head of an empty combe; and to avoid any steep ascent, it looped about as freely as a river on a plain. From thousands of acres of sheep-run came the random sound of bleating; the ponies' harness clinked and jingled; the van creaked like a frigate in a gale; and beyond these noises there was only the fierce outpourings of the skylarks and the endless wind in the grass.

Toward its end the day darkened prematurely. At the hour when sunset would have been they came to a saddle in the hills, and turned south. Half a mile on, they reached a flint-built cottage standing alone in the valley bottom by a vast yew tree. There was bread to be had here, purchased not one day old from the cottager's wife, and as much fresh well-water as one could desire.

Squatting by the roadside fire, Charity shared the drovers' meal of yet more salt beef; and for a few pence she bought a night's shelter in the cottage, on a real straw mattress up beneath the cobwebbed ties of the eaves.

She would have slept till noon next day, had not the cottager's wife awoken her. 'You don't want to go with your friends, now?'

Under a fiery sunrise the damp ashes of the drovers' fire were the only evidence that they had passed that way. Charity felt a pang of loneliness at seeing even such casual fellow-wayfarers pass out of her life. After paying for some breakfast she set out for the canal in the direction the drover's wife had indicated, all the more in haste for fear of travelling alone and unprotected.

As she walked, the sun, whose light so far that morning had been lurid rather than strong, went in for good; and rags of cloud began to hide the hilltops. Charity laboured as quickly as she could toward the bare horizon to see how far it was to any shelter. Before she got there, however, the cloud had already changed to fog. By the time she came back down into daylight proper, she was almost at the bottom of the hill, in the broad valley she had to cross to reach the canal.

This was a different country to the unpeopled swells of

grassland she was leaving behind. Compared to the Vale it was still not very fertile, being partly heaths and commons of bracken and silver birch. But what fields she passed were neatly hedged; the lanes were deep and muddy from frequent local traffic; and ahead she could see threads of woodsmoke climbing above the odd village.

About noon, as the road rose toward a tract of birch trees and furze, the weather finally turned foul. The light grew dingy; the trees and bushes leaned away from a wind that carried the last cutting blast of winter; and the countryside behind was hidden by drizzle.

Across a field newly cut out from the surrounding waste, Charity saw a barn and hurried toward it. A scatter of rats loped away squeaking as she entered. Sinking down out of breath, she piled loose hay up to her chin, like a child playing at bedtime, to muffle any draughts and stop her shivering.

The rain was set to go on for some hours. It was obvious she couldn't travel any further before the evening. She untied the handkerchief holding her supply of food and ate some bread and cold bacon. Soon she dozed; and woke; and fell asleep; and woke once more, to hear the rain still falling. As she was drowsing yet again, at dusk, it ceased; and when she woke again, roused to full awareness by the cold, it was already dark.

There was no way she could guess what hour it was. But for the wind flapping the trees outside, the silence would have been as seamless as if she lay deep underground and the doors of the barn opened onto a blind face of rock. She feared the night was at its earliest. In farmhouse kitchens full of talk, or by firelit cottage hearths, maybe even the youngest children would only just have supped; and in the village alehouses not a man was drunk enough to have passed beyond good cheer.

But it was too late to walk alone through strange country in darkness unrelieved even by broken starlight. Charity settled to wait out the night. After what must have been several hours, while the dawn still showed no reason why she should ever hope for it, she slept ... and yet,

when she woke, the night remained as dark as ever –
What was that!

Her heart leaped up to choke her, even as she realized
this was the one sight to be expected.

As soundless as if seen through a closed window, a
white, mothlike shape glided through the open door and
folded itself into the darkness of the roof. It was a barn
owl. Cross with fright, Charity waited for the creature to
start hooting while she was trying to sleep.

But she heard nothing; and the next sound she noticed
was the voices of sparrows. It was late, if not bright, and
the morning was half gone. Across the fields she heard a
dog bark. She scrambled to her feet in sudden anxiety, lest
someone in authority should find her trespassing.

Out on the road, however, there was no one to be seen.
The day was mild, and as she walked her limbs grew
warmer and her senses less punished by her wakeful night.
After so many despondent hours the ordinariness of
daylight – a yellowhammer singing on a gatepost and
workers stooping in a distant field – seemed almost too
good to bear; and at the top of a rise, dawdling to get her
breath, Charity paused and leaked a tear of gratitude just
to be alive and capable of hope.

'Who is he, then?' a voice said. 'Nay, don't look
surprised. No girl as pretty as what you are would cry her
eyes out over anything except a fine young man.'

It was a stooped man in leggings, who had just joined
the road from a path across the heath. His hair and beard
made a uniform grey stubble. He carried a sickle, and
gloves as thick as if he wore them on his feet.

'It ain't no young man,' said Charity. She didn't realize
how ludicrous this would sound to anyone seeing past the
folds of her cloak to her belly. 'But I be fearful hungry,' as
if offering an adequate explanation of how she, clearly
from some other parish, came to be weeping in the
highway, with hayseeds in her ragged hair and her petticoat and boots stiff with every kind of dirt.

The man, approaching, looked more closely at her.
'Well, you must come along with us, then.' His manner

became more serious as he took in the details of her appearance, and Charity guessed he had seen through her secret already.

She followed him across the heath until they reached an area of alders and osier thickets by a peaty stream. On a hummock beside a little ford stood a shelter of branches and turf, open on two sides. An old man, bent and tough-looking as a tree-root, tended a cooking fire in front of it. Stacked head-high around the shelter were dead bundles of osier stems and furze.

The man told her to sit by the fire. His father, as the old man appeared to be, gave her a meal of stale bread and rabbit stew. When she'd eaten everything they offered, as urgently as if she'd had to fight for it, she offered to pay. However, her money was refused, almost with contempt.

'I suppose I can ask if there's anywhere particular you think you're going?' the younger man said.

'Aye,' said Charity, defensive. 'Up to London.'

She got no reply though the man looked keenly at her once more. To break his silence she said, 'I be going up there by the waterway,' and in response to questioning repeated the instructions the drover's wife had given her.

'That ain't no way for you to travel all alone,' said the man, spitting into the fire. He paused, and with another glance he asked, 'How far you reckon you can walk?'

She hung her head and blushed. A little less harshly he said, 'Can you go seven miles by nightfall, now?'

'Aye ... Of course I can!'

'Then you listen. You don't take no fool short cut to that towing path. You go round by the high road to where you'll find the wharf, and houses where you can lodge. And you hear you, now; you don't take a ride just on any boat as comes along. There was a woman there, not two months past – a respectable woman, mind – and when they was done with her, they beat her to death. So just you mark what I say.' And forcing Charity to repeat the names, he made her memorize several boats, and their masters, with which she might travel.

When, a little sulky at his insistence, she finally had it right, he said, 'Have you money?'

'Aye – I've plenty of money.'

'How much is that?'

'I've got more'n a guinea.'

'Oh aye ... Be off with ye, then. If you can walk that far you can't stay here.'

By late afternoon she came to the wharf. It was a paved area by some houses where a winding, alder-fringed river and the canal itself were bridged by a turnpike road. Around the warehouses – large low timber buildings like the barn where she had slept – there was much activity. Several boats were moored alongside, as under the eye of the wharfinger a number of warehousemen, porters and barge crews loaded or disembarked cargoes of flour, timber, grain, barrel-hoops, osiers, and birch bark for tanning. None of the boats, however, bore any of the names she was looking for. Rather than brave any jeers or propositions from the men on the wharf, Charity made her way to a nearby lock, and questioned the elderly keeper at his cottage door.

'If it's one of them you want, this week I reckon as the *Nancy Drew*'s your only chance. She went up Hungerford way not two days since. So you bide here, she'll pass through by noon tomorrow.'

Squalid as Charity's appearance was, her beauty clearly touched the man, who responded with a kind of half-embarrassed deference. He invited her in to sit and eat, while on her behalf he made inquiries of a passing barge.

Within a short while he was back in haste. 'Miss! Miss! You come with me, now!'

The *Nancy Drew* was returned already. It stood, its horse unharnessed, waiting to go down through the lock. At the tiller, aproned, booted and shawled, with sleeves rolled up round arms that looked like thighs, stood the widow Drew herself.

'Missus Drew! Missus Drew! Can you take this young girl with ye? You know, in return for treating and such-like. She can pay her way.'

The woman looked Charity over for a moment. 'Aye. She can come with us, if she will.'

'How far be you bound this time, Missus Drew?' the lock-keeper asked.

'Queenhithe, come Sunday.'

'In London?' feigning ignorance purely for Charity's benefit.

'Aye, in London, that's what I said.'

The barge, crewed by the widow's two grown sons, was navigated through the lock; the horse was led down and harnessed; and the great oak gates at the bottom of the lock were closed again behind them. It felt almost too good to be believable. Charity, seated on the deck, looked up at the clearing sky, brilliant even as it faded, and watched the meadows and nearby hills slip past. She had a triumphant sense of her journey having almost ended. It was no matter that she would have to sleep three nights on deck, wrapped in whatever came to hand. Nor that she would wake each morning shrivelled to the bowels from cold, as they embarked at an hour almost dark enough for the world to have ended. She was happy just to know that all the while, the sky was growing larger and the valleys were broadening as they were borne down toward London.

On the second day, in a little town whose streets turned mysteriously out of sight behind the waterfront, they stopped. The horse was led away to be leased to another carrier, and the mast was raised. As they sailed on, suddenly the canal was there no longer, and they were out on the Thames itself. Under a square sail, the barge spun like a top before the breeze, almost twice as fast as a man could walk. The river, unremarkable to people who knew it, looked to Charity like a great water whose horizon was half the breadth of the sky.

'Be we there afore our time?' she asked at sunrise next day. It seemed impossible that this should not be London. The streets reached beyond the summit of a hill where a great castle stood; and there were even some houses on the opposite bank.

'This ain't Queenhithe,' the widow said. 'You see that flag,' pointing up at the castle keep. 'That's to show that's where the king lives. Sometimes they don't have no flag, and that's for when the king's gone away journeying. It weren't there last time we went by. No, this is Windsor, this place here.'

At moonrise that evening, as, becalmed, they idled, hull-deep in mist, past the fields below Hampton Court, the widow called to Charity, '*Now* you may see how close we be to London.'

Charity saw only the shapes of elm trees and a group of cattle by the water's edge. Then, in the shadows ahead, she heard, first music, then what sounded like a great creature in conversation with itself. As the barge crept nearer, the noise could be distinguished as hundreds of human voices.

'Up yonder, see, now there's your great lords and ladies and that, all at play for the night. Come sunrise, they'll be driven back to town in their carriages, just as honest folk are rising. T'ain't that far by road. By river, now –'

There was a popping sound, followed by a hiss. Suddenly the whole riverside ricocheted with light. A glittering curtain of fire, patterned to look like water, swayed in the sky. The firework burst heavenward again – and still again – and held still in blinding mid-exclamation – and lapsed again – and yet again shattered upward. Out on the river in the dark, Charity and her companions watched while a series of explosions revealed a Palladian villa set before a stately backdrop of cedars. Their light flared above a sweep of lawn and, further removed, dozens of carriages. They flashed every hue of brilliance on the upturned faces and shimmering attire of the great folk on the bank, as rapidly as if their audience were being drawn at speed past a series of illuminated windows. Soon, she thought. At last. God be thanked; at last.

The same lights had also been seen by another group, to all appearances as festive, a few miles to the east.

Unlike some present, George felt no horror at what they were assembled to do. He sensed nothing more than uneasy curiosity, and a feeling that after all this was what

154

everyone did when they had to. He had agreed to act as Dobson's second in a duel against Kilpatrick.

The reason for the challenge had been forgotten by most onlookers almost as soon as it was made. Dobson and Kilpatrick, awash in claret fortified with whisky one evening at their club, had fallen out over a seeming triviality. In fact the cause was just a dislike that had gone unspoken for too long. Dobson, more drunk than anybody there, later had difficulty remembering anything. He dimly recollected that their differences had concerned not a female next-of-kin, even, but a horse.

Of course, not knowing quite why the duel had been arranged made it doubly impossible for Dobson to offer or accept an apology. Kilpatrick, for his part, had shown a lawyer's tenacity in sticking by his case and resolving still to fight. It was evident that behind his quiet, neat motions and careful self-control he hid a feeling for violence that even his fellow-debauchees had not suspected.

It had been agreed that the duel should take place on Putney Heath at sunrise. The night was spent, by Dobson's party, drinking in an upstairs room at the Coach and Horses on the Guildford road. They included Nordaby and Underwood, with a couple of doxies they'd brought along while they waited for the show.

For Dobson, whether or not at the cost of his life, was to furnish a spectacle. Of that there seemed no doubt – at least, while the night lasted. He himself appeared to take this for granted, and applied himself like a man to their sodden frenzy of hard drinking. It was also clear that he was afraid. When at daybreak the surgeon's carriage arrived, he accompanied the others to the appointed place as haggard and sober as if that night had never happened. They too were brisk and solemn – likewise Kilpatrick and his second, waiting at a clearing in the bracken.

George had not expected things to be so swift and casual. If a man risked dying, it was owed to his dignity to let him savour the fact, even if he disgraced himself with a show of cowardice. But this – why – George was still expecting further preliminaries when – no, wait! he thought – the order to fire was shouted.

There was a dull clear thump, as if a stone had dropped into still water. Both men stood, Dobson with his pistol discharged.

No one who knew him was surprised that he'd chosen to do no injury. Though an oaf on occasion, he was gentleman enough not to wing his man once he'd called him out.

Kilpatrick held his arm aloft and aimed, as self-absorbed as if he were alone. Almost immediately there was the same feeble plop; and Dobson arched backward and fell slowly where he stood, his head hitting the ground an instant before his body.

They ran up and loitered helplessly while he thrashed at their feet, fighting against what had been done to him. The shot had parted his upper lip and lodged in the back of his skull.

After a while he lay wide-eyed and still, making a snoring noise, and was carried away to be driven home.

George left them to their own courses, and set out to cover the six miles back to town on foot. He wanted to make his way alone, and take as much time as he could before the sky above him shrank to the width of a crowded street once more.

It did not occur to him to think of the rights and wrongs of what he'd seen. He was not reflective, much less the brains of his family – but he was a sensitive man, for all that. As he dawdled eastward, past willows and flat meadows, and ditches whose banks bloomed with meadowsweet, his first sight of violent death crushed him beneath a sadness that felt fit to sit upon him all his life.

Crossing Westminster Bridge he glanced up, as any thinking creature would, over the water to where the city began. The low horizon of roofs spread away out of sight under the endless morning sky. Above a brimming tide the palaces along the Strand rode like galleons at anchor. Beyond, a hundred spires and more each flashed a gilded vane or summit in the first sunlight, pricking the mass of the city as thickly as the masts of a fantastical fleet. George had never guessed he could feel so homesick. So poignant was his memory of home at that moment, he could only just bear to comfort himself with it. He recalled the Vale, the village, and the people who lived thereabouts. And he thought of Charity, with the feelings of a dumb beast that yearns for the warmth of another of its kind within the same pen. But he was too miserable to think very closely of his own home or his family. To dwell on them, while he looked wretchedly down the river to where the sun was coming up, would have made their absence too much to endure.

And what did Charity think, as the barge bore her under the bridge into the same infinity of light? Whatever her expectations, surely this must be the moment when they were realized? To George the view before them both might appear like a place of imprisonment as endless as the hereafter. But what of Charity, to whom it stood for the sum of all her hopes?

She thought nothing; nor did she notice one brick of the city as it began to stir about her. While the river carried her on, she lay bundled on the deck asleep, too deeply unconscious even for waking dreams.

Charity drifted on, seeing nothing. Soon she was to suffer the last parting of her long journey; soon, too, her time was due when she should be brought to childbed. Meanwhile she slept, for the moment oblivious of her fearful lot – and of its banality; and its pity.

Chapter Eight

In a part of London very different from Queenhithe, Rawley Fitzpayne was cursing his ill luck.

He was at breakfast in the house in St James's Square. On the table lay the remnants of three meat courses. At the other end of the room, the season notwithstanding, a cocker spaniel and two wolfhounds snoozed or scratched themselves before a fire lit six hours earlier in readiness for Rawley's appearance. The sashes in the window at the back of the room had been thrown up to admit the fresh warmth of a May morning. Beyond the becalmed region of the square the town rumbled and murmured like the depths of a seashell. In the square itself and the garden behind the house, the great trees stood in a light edged, even at noon, with mistiness.

Various fragrances – from the garden, the glowing mass of logs in the grate, from toast, coffee and a good cigar – might normally mingle with his convalescent stage of hangover to make life quite acceptable to Rawley. Now, however, as he sat, one leg over the arm of his dining chair, re-reading a piece of correspondence, his face bore a scowl.

Here was that damned girl writing to him! And here – in town – from a lodging not one mile off, in Fleet Street!

It was one thing to spend time doodling after the Byford girl when exiled to Wiltshire. There, it was something to do, especially in the closed season for other sorts of game. And even afterward, avoiding her relatives would probably give life in the country some extra interest.

But he was damned if he had any use for her here. He rang for his valet.

'Answer this,' he said, holding out the letter without looking up.

'You wish the correspondence closed?' said the man, identifying Sophy's signature.

Rawley's frown deepened. 'No,' he said, twitching the letter back. It would be less trouble to hold her off with humouring than to start at the beginning again when they were both out of town. The valet, sensing himself dismissed, disappeared as if whisked away by a puppet-master.

In the library, kicking back the dogs from the door as they tried to follow him, Rawley sat himself down to write. He looked again at the letter, with disdain.

Dear Mr Fitzpayne,
  I know you will smile to see a second letter from me – but I do not care, for I have such a piece of news to seal up and send. I would say, that it is a surprise and you must

guess it, but that you will have discovered all on seeing my address!

Did you think I could be so churlish in receiving your present last month that I should be in town and not write you? If you were – well, then you must resign yourself to being sorely disillusioned, even if in replying, that is the only account of yourself that you can give ...

Who ever am,

Rawley wrote:

My dear Miss Sophia,
You are the most amazing creature alive. Who could have known but that I might expect you to rise from the stones of Piccadilly like a genie.
To the devil with genies. Like a mortal Venus, born again from nowhere.
Now, Sophia, no smirks or blushes, even though the good goddess did come upon the world as naked as the rest of us. If a tolerable-looking woman like you hasn't spirit enough to meet a just comparison full in the face – why, do you think I'd trouble with writing to her? Much less with sitting here as I do now, flailing at my brain lest I sound like some d--ed pitiful brute who can't write to one like you just as he should.
Meet me, Sophia. And no 'buts'. You needn't think me such a fool that I'd let you slip out of town, and lose a chance like this. Six o'clock, outside St Paul's in Covent Garden. You will be there. I know it.

The letter was handed to a servant, with instructions for its delivery. Meanwhile Rawley set about scribbling another note.

Dear Sophia,
This is the d--dest piece of ill luck that ever befell either of us. At a moment like this, to be called upon to tag along to his lordship – upon some confounded whim, you may be sure. The devil take all uncles, especially those who can dictate the expectations of a poor dog like me.
So now I must exchange your company for his. You may

159

*forgive him, but I'm d--ned if I shall. Who can tell how soon
I shall be free to meet you again.*

In disgruntled haste ...

George was listless from reluctance as, later that day, he
made his way to Sophy's lodgings. Of course, he was glad
of her company – even a little vain. Few young men in his
position got to be seen with any girl as pretty – even if
she was just his sister. The only decent-looking females
George knew of were either impossibly chaperoned, or too
expensive.

But he still felt dismay at the evening ahead. He was to
accompany Sophy to Wimpole Street for her inspection as
a possible governess. 'She should have been best accompanied by her aunt,' Charles Norton had told him. 'Or by
me, had I time to spare in town. Mrs Whitman did say she
should have preferred to see your mother, too. So I think
it would look better – your aunt and I are both agreed on
this – if Sophy were not to present herself alone, without
respectable connexions of any kind. And ... I did think
it well, as a matter of fact, to mention the circumstances in
which the last governess left Mr and Mrs Whitman's
employment. Mrs Whitman is a pious woman – a very
good woman, according to her way of seeing things – and
she did take exception to the girl reading a novel on a
Sunday. I thought your sister should know, before she's
introduced.'

Just as well, George thought, that if he must be racked
with boredom among his elders, it was for Sophy, whom
he liked, and whom strangers stared at as she walked by
with him.

But she was not there.

'Oh dear,' said the landlady, when George had been
admitted to her parlour. 'Oh dear. Only I thought it
mightn't be your note that came, because the maid heard
Miss Byford ask the cabman to take her to Covent
Garden. I remember thinking – mentally, I thought –
now why should she do that? That's not the likeliest place
for a young lady from the country, is it?'

160

It was quickest to run there. Already it was impossible they should be in Wimpole Street by half past six.

On the pavement opposite the market square, beneath the portico of St Paul's Church, there swarmed the usual mass of humanity. George, with muddied shins and a bad temper, paused. The only respectable women he could see were vegetable sellers, and a fierce old dame by the church door with a tray of glass eyes and elixirs.

Could that be her? There was a girl standing with her back to him, demurely dressed and carrying a parasol. From beneath the nape of her bonnet there curled a few tendrils of fair hair. She seemed to be looking, with unlikely interest, at a cage of geese. George noticed how despondent she looked – and only then that it was Sophy. As he made his way through the stalls a scruffy-looking man, who had been watching her, came up and took her by the elbow. Furious, she tried to punch him away. 'Now – now, that's not the way,' the man was saying. At the look on George's face he fled, as promptly as if he'd never existed.

'Whatever happened? It's nearly seven o'clock! We can't go and see those people now. Can we?'

'No, of course we can't go and see that woman! I never wanted us to anyway. *I* was supposed to have had better things to do!'

Timidity, not tact, silenced George. He gave Sophy his arm, and they picked their way across the square without speaking. By the time they were looking for a crossing-sweeper to clear a way over the Strand, the truth had begun to dawn on him. Mindful of something Kate had written, he ventured: 'Is that the real reason you came to London?'

'Why – what do you mean?' Sophy was beginning to be ashamed of having forgotten poor old George and left him no message.

'You know – to see someone.'

Sophy blushed and scowled. They walked on through a scatter of fowls scratching around the entrance to an alleyway. 'I still think papa was wrong,' she said, confirming George's suspicions. 'Why shouldn't we look

161

above our own station? I mean – if we don't – well, then what *will* happen to us?'

George said nothing, privately reckoning the outcome of what she'd done. The less he knew, at least the fewer explanations he himself would owe their uncle and aunt. Meanwhile – generous soul that he was – he felt truly sorry for his sister, and offered to take her that night to the theatre. But in vain. Sophy longed to go – and nothing would persuade her. She was determined to do penance for having caused so much muddle, by staying indoors and being gloomy. Besides, another letter might yet come from Rawley Fitzpayne. There were still two days before she had to leave. In that time, he was bound to explain himself.

The rest of Sophy's visit passed as slowly as if she were waiting in her little room to die of old age. It made her even wilder with impatience, to spend time thus at the centre of the whole world – in London! Everything she wanted must be out there, just waiting to be found and tasted. And while no word came, she had to set herself to turn her back on all of it!

For Rawley's excuses, though written out in such good time, never arrived. He had simply forgotten to pass them to the servant. The morning of Sophy's departure saw her looking as sad to go as if she had had the most wonderful excursion of her life. George, like a good fellow, had come along at seven in the morning to see her off at the Bull and Mouth. As they waited in the yard alongside the coach – it tipped about so if you got in before the other passengers – he felt he had to brace himself and mumble something encouraging, however feeble. 'I expect you won't always live at home,' he said.

'Of course I won't,' replied Sophy, with a resolute smile. 'Even with no money there must be ever so many things I *can* do.'

She believed it, too. And thought about it all the way in to Piccadilly.

But there it was that she beheld a shocking sight.

The coach had stopped, surrounded by a flock of sheep.

Sophy, gazing into the throng of scurrying people and steaming, filth-caked animals, was wondering, against her better sense, how near at that moment Rawley Fitzpayne might be.

Oh, but there – there *was* someone she knew! Half a score of heartbeats, though, had passed before Sophy realized who it was. Michaelmas – Charity Michaelmas, the undercook from the Hall. She looked, doubted, looked again, and tried in vain to disbelieve what she saw.

Charity was dirty in the way that makes a beggar's rags seem like a disease of his own flesh. Her eyes were rimmed with pallor amid the grime, and her hair looked like a tattered headdress. Some of the other inside passengers were watching too, as she faltered to and fro, leaning backward against the weight of her belly. There was nothing out of the ordinary in such a sight; but while the coach was held fast in the traffic, they had little else to look at.

'Do you see that young girl?' one traveller remarked to his wife. 'Shocked half stupid, from the look of her. She won't do well to go on long in that way.'

Truly, Charity looked as astonished by her circumstances as if she were new-born. She had blundered, though, on one regular beggar's trick. A young woman was approaching. She was dressed well enough, but unaccompanied even by a footman; and her clothes were more appropriate to a ball-room than the hazards of the street. Sophy was not too ignorant to see that she must be a prostitute. As she came near, Charity went up to her. But she neither spoke to the woman, nor made any gesture of appeal. Instead, she fell in behind her, at two paces' distance, and followed up and down as the plumed young harlot strolled the length of her territory. The woman turned, and, seeming not to notice Charity, cast a coin into the mud. Obviously she expected to make such payment quite often, to keep such people from frightening off her customers.

The coach became free to move at walking pace. Charity had kept level with them, and was going up to another painted creature, with a swansdown tippet and a gown of figured silks. This girl, however, did have an attendant, whom Charity had failed to see.

'You go on standing there, and I'll have your fucking face off!'

The old woman mounting guard on the girl's hired finery was only pretending to be angry. But it was obvious she meant whatever she threatened. For a moment more, Charity could be seen, too stunned to flee. Then the coach rumbled on, and the tableau on the pavement, one of thousands like it, and as anonymous as a snowflake in a drift, vanished from sight.

Until that moment London had been nothing but what Sophy had desired. It was only now that she was overcome by the knowledge that the city had another aspect. The smoke of its fires towered in a cloud of murk above the whole eastern horizon as they were being driven away through the hayfields and orchards of Kensington parish. She felt as if they could never get it out of sight.

She felt no pity for what she had seen. She was too crushed by an emotion she had not known before. Apprehension possessed her as she dwelt on that little spectacle in Piccadilly. How little good fortune stood between Kate or herself and the condition of that unlucky girl! Only the kindness of relatives and neighbours and the whim of employers who paid Kate just enough for her not to burden her family. And Sophy herself had even been mistaken for Charity Michaelmas! By someone who knew her – by Rawley Fitzpayne!

How foolish she'd been in looking out for ... something ... from Rawley when their paths were so uncertain to meet. And how she ached with remorse at having frittered others' money and good wishes. Henceforward she would be sensible, and expect as little as she could. She would try to be more like Kate, and struggle to beat down every hope.

A night, and another day, and here was the road down to Upstowe and the last change of horse. At the New Inn Sophy had to wait, in a little wainscoted parlour like a furnished half-landing, while a chaise was made ready to take her directly to Cannings Fitzpayne.

The New Inn was in fact ancient, with narrow dark passages and sloping floors that had grown piecemeal over the centuries. It held a warren of rooms that had been opened into each other and partitioned off again so often that you never quite knew where any nearby sound was coming from. Sophy, stiffly walking up and down and yawning like a cat, heard a log being cast onto a fire two walls away; and then, from the public dining room next door, a voice she recognized.

They were the tones, low but carrying, of Lord Fitzpayne. She pictured his entrance, the innkeeper bowing and the waiters hesitant as, without a motion of his features – like punctures in a great glazed ham, she thought – Lord Fitzpayne would have dismissed their attentions. No doubt the innkeeper would have reddened before his lordship's disdain; yet, she knew, he would still have forgotten to stop smiling.

And there were the voices of two other people she knew: Royal, the Secretary of the canal company; and Fraser.

'You may see,' Lord Fitzpayne was saying, 'how I am prepared to take you people seriously, from the fact that I have waited on you myself.'

'The reason we've decided to speak with you directly,' said Fraser, 'is that we have a duty to do so.'

'If I were to be dealt with directly, it would be by Sir Charles Dundas. I cannot comprehend what functions you people both have; but he is your Chairman, is he not?'

'He is, my lord,' said Royal, brisk as only a little man can be. 'But his other concerns –'

'Have left me to deal with a couple of intermediaries. Has either of you gentlemen, as no doubt you'd like me to call you, any reason why I should consider you anything more?'

Sophy, on the far side of the wall, guessed rightly. Lord Fitzpayne had no intention of sparing the rest of the room from their conversation. It was in the hope of giving embarrassment that he had chosen a public place.

To call his bluff, Fraser thrust back his chair and went to stand, hands in pockets, some distance off by the fire. 'We're here to meet you because we choose, not from necessity. It makes no odds who you think you've come to see.'

Royal, who saw himself as a manager of other men, sought to use reason. 'You'll find we are the men best qualified to discuss this matter, my lord. Sir Charles himself will vouch for us there.'

'Since you've troubled to come here,' Fraser interrupted down half the room, 'perhaps you'll tell us why you've no interest in hearing us out.'

'However distressing it may be to your lordship –' Royal began again –

'There will be no question of distress on my part, I assure you.'

'– the law –'

'The law, as any competent spokesman for your company would know, allows me to sell my land for whatever it is worth.' Having addressed Lord Fitzpayne like a rational man, Royal's penalty was to hear all this spoken very slowly, as to a child. 'Now,' his lordship continued, 'is there any individual on the responsible parliamentary committee to whose character you wish publicly to object? It was your organization, after all, who suggested one should be appointed to fix my price.'

For the sake of sounding decisive, Royal replied, 'Certainly not.'

'Lord Mowbray?'

'No.'

'Sir Jack Boone?'

'No –'

'Would you denounce my friend Lord Boddington as a knave or an incompetent?'

'No. But –'

'But what? Look you, sir – and you. I have made an inconvenient detour, exclusively to humour you. If you wish me merely to state the obvious, let me remind you it is as well there *are* men like these, to defend the rights of citizens against any damned employee who tells me I must make a sale of my own land. And if you want any other comment, I have none.'

'Before you leave,' said Fraser, as the nearest waiter rushed to move back his lordship's chair, 'there are two things you must hear.'

Lord Fitzpayne, not knowing what to expect, tried Fraser with a stare of intent indifference.

'In return for land, concession of further water rights is out of the question.'

'We shall lack water ourselves, otherwise,' said Royal, hastening to squeeze himself back into the conversation. 'But the land under discussion – I fear this must be said – the land in any case is not water meadows.'

'The nature of the land, sir, concerns no one but its owner. The other thing?' turning back to Fraser.

'It's proper to tell you that should your asking price be agreed by the committee, we shall still not be prepared to meet it.'

'But not for lack of influential interest,' Royal interrupted. 'Sir Charles has engaged the interest of His Majesty himself –'

'I care not what dotard your employers use to dress up their activities. Accept my price, or withdraw your thieving, pestilence-ridden rabble from this district.'

'Should the committee decide against the canal company,' Fraser continued, 'we shall –'

'And? And?'

'– appeal to an independent jury. They will be the ones to make a final decision.'

'I – God Almighty – now look here. My understanding is not too little to comprehend *that*. But what, for some reason, you cannot make clear, is what you think you're wheedling *me* to do.'

'Nothing. We are not making a request. As a favour' – a more wary man than Fraser would have said 'courtesy' – 'we are telling you of our intentions.'

Lord Fitzpayne stared, to cover his disadvantage, before sweeping from the room.

'We dealt well with him,' Royal said, in a firm voice.

To avoid answering, Fraser went to reach for his hat. As

167

he did so, Royal noticed him glance at the door. His own mind full of Lord Fitzpayne, he thought his lordship must still be present.

But that couldn't explain the shade of awkwardness that passed over the other's face. An arrogant young bastard like Fraser was the last man to respond like that to an adversary. Royal looked round, and understood. One of Lawyer Byford's girls. Seeing Fraser, on her way through the room, she too hesitated.

The man must be even more impatient to confound himself, Royal observed, than most folk thought already. It was common knowledge that the girl was destitute. What was more, any man half-witted enough to take her on would find himself lumbered with the mother and perhaps the sister as well. And expensive schooling was no substitute for a dowry – in the wife of an engine-wright, for God's sake, it would bring nothing but trouble. At best, Royal reckoned, a man never showed himself such a fool, even in the eyes of the women themselves, as at this stage of things. The protection of formal behaviour virtually thrown aside; but the bargain not yet struck.

'Is Lord Fitzpayne often like that?' Sophy asked Fraser a few days later. 'I'd never seen him close to, except in church.' Privately she had been as surprised as any villager that Fraser had spoken to him as an equal.

'Good God, yes. But I'm glad to see him thus. It shows he understands the advantage may not all be his.'

They were at the gate of Drove Cottage. Fraser had just ridden up leading a second horse, a small bay mare with her head stretched forward on the end of the rein; and Sophy was holding her while he tightened the girth.

'So breeding doesn't lift people above such behaviour?' Sophy had changed much in recent months; but even now the teachings of her elders could show themselves. As she spoke she eyed the bay's deep barrel and straight hocks. She really wanted to know why the mare was saddled for a lady.

'Oh, Fitzpayne disputing the price of his land is no different from a contractor who refuses to advance a

168

decent wage. Or one of the men arguing the cost of scrumpy.' Straightening up, he saw her look at the mare's side-saddle. 'I meant her for your use. As an extra payment.' The lessons were shortly to end; Fraser could read French and Italian easily enough now for his purpose. And to go on with them – as they both knew – would begin to look like paying court.

Sophy's face was brilliant with delight. Riding was something, in their poverty, that she had missed most of all. Scarcely before she could gasp out the smallest thank-you she had whirled round to run ahead and tell the others – and straightaway turned back, dismayed. 'Oh, but I cannot! We cannot possibly keep a horse. I know I've no business to tell you so – but we could never find enough money.'

'I know that.' Fraser's own years of going ill-shod had made him more considerate in his deeds than in his choice of words. 'She's meant for a loan, not for you to keep. I've told them at the Red Lion that you're to have her when-ever you want.' He watched her as she stroked the soft muzzle and looked the mare over admiringly. It did not occur to him that his own gaze wandered about the girl herself in much the same way. 'She is schooled for a lady – she's properly quiet,' he added, still looking at Sophy rather than the mare.

'Oh, I don't care about that!'

There was no question but that the bay should be put through her paces immediately. Sophy scurried to cast on her riding habit, squeaking out loud with impatience to find it at the very bottom of the box where her clothes were now kept. Back in the lane, Fraser helped her, a little confused at what he should do, to mount – and they were away, into a late spring afternoon so full of birdsong and soft breezes that it might have been made just to frame Sophy's own enjoyment.

It was like being restored to every pleasure of the life she'd known – and, she realized guiltily, had sometimes grumbled at. Of course things had never been so bad that, in being poor, she'd ceased to be pretty. However shabby she'd become, every soul who saw her still made some unthinking sign of homage to her beauty. But then, why *should* people be so foolish? Where was the triumph in being congratulated on her looks, when she couldn't help them anyway?

To sit a well-bred horse, though, and be admired for skill and courage – that did appeal to Sophy. On foot, her habit, despite its flowing skirts and its jacket cut tight as her own skin, looked nothing out of the ordinary. On horseback, however, its spare graceful lines showed to perfection how she could make her mount move beneath her as though she hardly noticed the creature. Her garments' sombreness, too, emphasized the warm silver-fairness of her long throat and smooth forehead, and let her heavy blonde hair make a contrast with the richness of the bay's beautiful coat.

Fraser, on the other hand, had never once ridden before he'd reached manhood. He kept his seat, Sophy noticed, not by balance but by physical strength – and certainly, no gentleman would hold his elbows out so.

He knew nonetheless how to appreciate horsemanship in others. Until now, Sophy hadn't been vain enough to notice how he sometimes looked at her. In her pleasure with her command of the mare, however, she couldn't fail to see the unselfconscious admiration with which he glanced aside at her.

Crossing Cannings Fitzpayne Common, to try her own nerve as much as the mare, Sophy put her over the bole of a fallen elm. Fraser, who himself took physical courage for granted, looked on more curious than appalled, even though the trunk lay trace-high. But as she cantered back beside him, shining with glee, he asked, 'Do you take every obstacle like that – so carefree?' If the mare had stumbled, Sophy would have been slung right beneath her belly.

'Oh, yes – like a fool,' she said, still breathless with triumph. 'I run at everything' – she guessed he didn't just mean her riding – 'without looking to see what might be on the other side.'

Fraser looked at her without speaking. She didn't appear foolish to him. For one thing, she was physical perfection; also what she described was his own way of facing things – and so far it had served *him* well enough.

'Kate says, with most difficulties you're most likely to succeed by going round, or under – if you're only a woman, she means. But I think, sometimes, if your life is impossible, you just have to risk everything. I suppose' – flinching away from the thought that she might be referring to Rawley Fitzpayne – 'there are times when all you *can* do is make a fool of yourself.'

He looked at her again. In his handsome face bewilderment was mixed with curiosity. Fraser wasn't an imaginative man; and since he didn't think of women themselves as lesser beings, it rarely occurred to him that their lives might sometimes be inferior.

Their way took them, at his suggestion, near the new embankment. To Fraser the notion of riding about at random seemed absurd. Besides, he wanted to inspect a sawpit beyond Park End Wood, where a quantity of timber was to be cut and seasoned on site.

As they came near the improvised woodyard, standing on its own in a churned-up field, they had to move aside for a team of horses bringing up more timber. Each of the four great Shires, a ton apiece and muddied all over, leaned into the harness and picked up its feet as precisely as a cat. Over the jingle of the bells on their harness and the creakings, as of a house being moved, from their wagon, Fraser indicated that Sophy should wait while he spoke to someone across the highway. The long wagon moved on, and from behind it, trudging as purposefully as the horses, a group of men came into sight. They included the ganger with whom Sophy had exchanged such hard words while looking for Dr Brown. She watched while, against the rapid to-and-fro sound of the sawyers at work in the nearby pit, Fraser questioned him about something. The man, his eyes flicking across to where she held the bay reined in, was clearly dismayed to recognize her as a respectable woman.

Fraser turned, waiting for Sophy to join him; and as they rode away, the man's surly nod in her direction showed how he resented having been misled by her former appearance.

They completed their expedition out from the village, and turned back past the new encampment growing up near Park End Wood. Another woman might have felt smug at causing such surprise. But Sophy merely became downcast, then angry, as the meaning of the encounter grew plain. Any man – of whatever rank – seeing her alone in a place where she was unknown, might be expected to treat her with insolence. And what now made her so esteemed in the eyes of strangers was not her genteel clothes or her sixty-guinea horse – it was the company of a man! Head up, and shoulders held as straight as ever, she was nonetheless so deep in thought on the way home that, more than once, her lack of attention made the bay nearly lose its footing. Reluctantly, as though peeping through her fingers, she forced herself to look at a whole parade of recent incidents. There were all the acquaintance who had so neglected her family – her mother in particular – since Thomas had died. In London – what terrible risks she'd taken, leaving her lodgings on her own – the man who'd tried to grab at her in Covent Garden square had been one of several. To be treated with disdain, as though compromised, one didn't have to look like that fearful last sight of Charity Michaelmas, in her flapping boots and beggar's deep-grained filth. It was not a woman's appearance that influenced the way she was treated – but whether she was with a man.

Chapter Nine

One dank evening toward the end of that May, a pale sky clearing in the west, a chaise was bringing Rawley Fitzpayne down to Wiltshire. It was a bitter, verdant day, the young wheat trembling in the wind, and the tossing roadside trees putting forth leaves as green as fire. In cottage gardens the fresh black earth was sprouting seedling vegetables, each row made up of something different, like lines of stitches across a child's first sampler. The only trees still bare were the walnuts in the farmhouse gardens; while in the orchard by the big thatched barns of each farmyard the cloud of apple blossom was already breaking up.

The chaise, bearing along from Upstowe, crested the last rise before the park. Rawley was surprised to see clouds of smoke beaten through the wet treetops ahead. Then he realized where they were coming from, and was astonished. How in damnation had it come to this? He'd known the canal had been advancing on Cannings Fitzpayne; but this was not what he'd expected.

It was the fires of the new encampment that produced the smoke, which twisted and swooped through the wreckage of two hundred acres of best arable. The tents and hutments extended to beneath the trees leaning over the deerpark wall itself; and in Park End Wood the undergrowth had been grubbed up for fuel and replaced by a clotted web of shelters and storage dumps. The fields and roadside were full of strange-looking men, with groups of brawny women and barefoot children. At this hour most of them were round their fires, looking as if a city had had its houses magicked into thin air.

They drove alongside the high park wall. Rawley felt more than usually morose at being down from town. Now that Lady Fitzpayne's illness was recognized as fatal, the dullness of the place would be worse than ever ... As the lodge gates were opened and they turned into the park, he caught a glimpse of the younger Byford girl. Under the tunnel of trees that framed the highway, she was standing, precariously, up on the roadside, to avoid a passing drove of bullocks.

There was always her, of course, if he cared to mend his chances ...

The damndest thing about his aunt dying, Rawley reflected, was not even the absence of company at the Hall. It was that she couldn't be counted on to be punctual about it. Here he was, posted down from town by his uncle to represent the family, whereupon not only her ladyship but the damned quacks themselves wouldn't give an honest answer as to when the great occasion would be.

At least nobody could say she would not be seen off in the grand manner. Lord Fitzpayne might be away in town, busy manoeuvring, in the House, and at his club, against the canal company. But Rawley had been sent to waste all summer in the country if need be. And the Hall was in preparation for the funeral as for the finest theatrical production. In the housekeeper's office Mrs Richards was assessing the cost of equipping every servant with a length of black ribbon or crepe to wear; the head gardener was calculating how he could release enough men from the kitchen gardens to scythe the grass in the approaches to the mausoleum; and the head groom was looking forward to the challenge of preparing the family hearse and its plumed harness, and having eight black carriage horses sound, shod and ready on the day.

The only hitch on the day she went, thought Rawley, was likely to be in the bedchamber itself. The impression he had of such occasions was that, for the women, this was likely to be the greatest day since getting married. Certainly there was no other time when one was expected to pay them so much attention. As a rule everybody would be there: the surviving grey-haired brothers and sisters; the grown-up children, travel-weary and glum; the upper servants, with a legacy in mind and full of respect; the crowd of grandchildren, quiet and cowed; the doctors, hired regardless of expense – and all of them ranged about the chamber like the reckoning of a life well spent.

No doubt his aunt fancied herself entitled to something like this, too. The fact was, though, that apart from social inferiors such as the doctors and the family lawyer, Rawley himself would have to bear the brunt of the occasion on his own. The prospect oppressed him even worse than the boredom of waiting. There was one household of cousins, on his aunt's side, whom one might expect to see at such a time. But Lord Fitzpayne had no intention of their retainers and horses eating for days at his expense. If his wife wanted someone of rank beside her deathbed to uphold the dignity of the occasion, she would have to make do with Rawley.

What a deuced bore it all was, thought Rawley, as he was driven under the gatehouse arch and up to the main entrance. In making his way up the great Elizabethan staircase and through the doors held open for him on the way to his own apartments, it was some relief to know that within the hour he should at least be able to drink himself insensible.

Of course Sophy had seen the chaise, as it turned off the highway into the park. She had seen Rawley looking at her, too; and if he thought his own life tedious, he would have been surprised at how many hours of boredom she spent brooding on that look. Sophy may not have been as idle as he, but she had far less to entertain her. For that very reason, however, the excitement she felt on glimpsing him soon turned to disappointment at being ignored. Then, since her self-esteem was strong even in the face of despondency, she grew to feel an angry disdain – for herself as well as for him.

Such a mood, one warm Sunday, was making it particularly difficult for her to behave as kindly as she meant toward poor mamá, and Kate, whose treasured afternoon off it was. The sisters were at work peeling vegetables from the garden plot Fraser had helped them to make. Aproned down to their ankles, they were sitting outside the kitchen door, to avoid the smell of fermenting thatch that seeped into all four rooms in hot weather.

Sophy had been riding again. On her return, Kate was working away beside her in silence. It was clear that there was something she expected Sophy to say.

At length Sophy remarked, 'You know, I think George is right to say James Fraser's horses are nearly the best-bred in the Vale.'

'Is that a comment on their owner?' Since their stay in Bath, Kate had been a shadow of her old firm-spoken self. But there were still moments when she, not Sophy, seemed the stronger of the two.

'I was only about to say, who else can you think of in

this neighbourhood – apart from Rawley Fitzpayne – but of course I don't include someone like him – who has travelled? Most of our acquaintance in Upstowe even speak of Salisbury as if it were the dark side of the moon.'

Kate stopped working. She was certain it was time to voice a thought that had been in her mind for some weeks. 'I hope James Fraser's not such an idiot that he'd think of falling in love with you.'

Sophy, head down, worked on faster than ever. 'What if he did – a little? It would never go beyond a small flirtation. And what harm would that do anybody in the long run?'

'But Sophy, *you're* not in love with *him!*'

'I don't understand you. What has that to do with it? I like him – that's enough. And how could I help it? Did you see how he looked at me today – as though his mind wasn't on what he said, but on me?'

'Since you must know, yes, I have seen how he looks at you. And if you don't discourage him, I shall think you very hard-hearted.'

'Oh, Kate, it won't come to him paying his addresses! How could it?' Sophy was certain she meant what she said. Besides . . . she didn't want the responsibility of this man falling in love with her. She certainly didn't want to choose between marrying him and staying here. A perverse impulse made her say, 'And what if someone like him did show me such attention? The sooner I can be provided for, the better. And it's not,' with a pang of anger at the thought of Rawley Fitzpayne, 'as if I'd be looking above my place in life, is it?'

Kate was too dismayed for tact. 'You mean you'd let it come to an offer of marriage? When there isn't a chance that you feel as you should?'

Both sisters were pink in the face by now, and far too ill at ease not to quarrel. Sophy had given up any pretence of gouging out the eyes of the potato she was holding. 'Nonsense,' she said, with a weak imitation of impatience. 'I've just told you it wouldn't come to that. And even if I were wrong' – poor Sophy grew pinker, knowing that she was shifting her ground – 'what harm would a refusal do to someone like him? To a man who can silence even Lord Fitzpayne? And if James himself isn't feeble, why do you think his judgement might be so weak, should he make me an offer?'

'You see! You start by saying he'll never propose – and finish by telling me that that's what he ought to do!'

Sophy was silent, astonished by her own blunder.

'And you can't just "like" him! Marry him for nothing more than that, and in the end you'll turn him against you. If you want a husband who resents you, make a half-hearted match with some pitiful creature like that curate at St Peter's, who's due to get himself unfrocked one day – not with James Fraser.'

It was not just that Sophy had ridden out with Fraser again that Sunday. They had begun to make a habit of such outings. Several times, as summer progressed, Fraser would rise while it was still dark, to ride, from whichever village he was lodged at, to Cannings Fitzpayne before starting a day's work. Once or twice, indeed, he had made the journey lightheaded from fatigue after an unbroken night of paperwork. The sense of unreality this produced was heightened by going from his work, where sometimes every man and clod of earth seemed set to resist him, into a world where Sophy's eager motions and sweet laughter now banished every other thing.

Professionally, he had more than enough to hold his attention. On top of problems thrown up by building the waterway itself, there was the need for his contractors to keep the peace by paying a decent wage. Their workforce brawled as readily as any that lived by its brawn, and was always willing to show a grievance by breaking windows or hanging up an unpopular tradesman by his heels. There was the question of appearances, too; the chief engineer, John Rennie, had written from London that the king himself was due to visit the work in progress.

But if in the meantime Fraser was becoming deep in love, it was not just with Sophy. His work was something that consumed him. Merely matching other men's wills to his own gave him no pleasure. But to turn everything his way – the men, their masters, the wartime uncertainties of the commercial world that funded him, the hidden stream beneath an earthwork that might break down a half-year's toil – to make all these work to one plan – now *there* was something that might fill a man with satisfaction.

So he was thinking one morning before first light, as he set out to ride the seven miles to Drove Cottage on an errand whose planning had kept him awake most of the night. In the still greyness before the dawn, when even the sparrows weren't yet stirring, he had saddled up and was making his way toward Cannings Fitzpayne along the line of the canal. As he rode past the shapes of uncompleted earthworks and wet fields still marked out with stakes, the dawn chorus began: two voices first, one near, one far; then growing till it was trilled and shouted everywhere in the early fog. The only other sounds were the snorts and dull hoofbeats of his horse as it brushed a dark trail through the soaking grass, or disturbed a sleeping cow and sent her striving to her feet and lumbering out of sight. The light, strengthening, gleamed white through the deep vistas of gateways overhung by hedgerow trees. Then came the surprise of meeting another wakeful creature, as the day's first labourer approached, followed by a trail of three score others. At this season they were mostly gangs of women going out to hoe, dressed more like men in their shapeless broad-brimmed hats and thick shabby coats. Soon, the air was clear enough for the first smoke to be seen coming from the chimneys of nearby hamlets. By the time Fraser rode down the green hollow of the lane leading to the village, it was into a brightening, busy day that looked as if its best hopes could only go on prospering.

At the same time that Fraser had been saddling his horse by lantern-light, Sophy too was awake. Even in summer there was scarcely time at Drove Cottage to finish the day's chores without the expense of working late by candlelight. For a couple of minutes after opening her eyes Sophy lay in bed looking at the patch on the ceiling where the plaster was dropping from the laths, and tried to bribe herself into getting up with thoughts of breakfast, two hours' work away.

Her toilette nowadays was simple enough. Ducking out from beneath the slope of the ceiling, she tiptoed barefoot over the splintered floorboards to the basin and ewer set down in a corner the night before. She cast her nightgown aside and washed herself, swinging her thick stream of hair first to one side, then the other. In winter this was done in fumbling haste, in water that had iced over. But in high summer it could be done leisurely, as a ritual.

There was little space in Sophy's room for furniture, apart from the bed. So for weeks on end all she might glimpse of herself was reflected in a little square mirror, nailed to the wall, that showed half her face at a time.

But if she couldn't look at herself, she could still tell by touch what she must be to behold. Stepping out of absolute darkness and under her little window, she felt her heart beat faster as she paused, naked beneath the bright stare of the moon. Gently – the thought of how she must look at this moment making even her breathing feel deliberate – she shook her hair looser. It moved about her body, as improbably long as Eve's in an old painting, a shining mass in whose depth a fanciful eye might see a stormy ocean or twilight-blooming skies. Would it be easier to be plain, in a life as restricted as hers...? She felt no desire that she knew of for the body of a man. What stirred her till she felt half-dead from yearning was her own body – the knowledge that her nakedness was something she wore with the splendour of a garment in its own right.

If she were less beautiful, then would she feel calm? She shook her head to and fro, feeling her warm hair stir heavily about her, as smooth to the senses as water. It seemed impossible that excellence like hers should not be matched...

The earliest household duties, once she was up and dressed, were those that could be done in the half-dark. Throwing her oldest shawl about her, Sophy went out into their narrow roadside strip of garden and down the ragged hedgerow where brambles tried to snag you in the face, to the well. There an underground stream, not many feet below, would in full daylight send up dull gleams as it slid past on its bed of greyish clay. The water had to be drawn many times a day, but always twenty-four hours in advance, so that it could then be ladled out free of sediment.

Then milk had to be fetched, from the steamy lamplit gloom of the nearby dairy at Preston's farm, where the heat from thirty cows, in their windowless byre, came at you like a hand thrust in your face. Sophy had come to be sorry that this expedition was made so early each morning; it was often the day's only chance of release into an outer world, cold and dark as that might be.

Back in the house, she had to help in the work of sweeping every floor, clearing the grates, and scrubbing the kitchen table, before coaxing a fire to life with a double fistful of wood chippings and dried bark. Wood for fuel was something they could least afford; but when there was a wash to be done, and the flatiron to be heated afterward for pressing, they just had to close their eyes to the expense.

Today there was a new problem. A plague of mice – in fact not many, but enough – had invaded the cottage. Droppings had been found in the big earthenware jar that held the flour; on both the straight-backed upholstered chairs saved from their last home; and across Mrs Byford's best black silk, kept folded away in the bleak hope that one day she would be justified again in wearing it regularly. The dress, however, had not taken kindly to one more wash. Sophy, going into the kitchen after breakfast, found her mother with reddened eyes, trying to look stoical at the sight of a frayed rent along the fold of the collar.

'Never mind, dear mama,' she said, taking away the garment and enfolding her mother in an embrace. 'Don't think about it for the present; I can find a way to mend it.' Sophy, as the one whose eyesight was still undamaged by close work, did most of the household's mending and seamstressing, often for nine hours a day.

Unlooked-for tears threatened to spring into her own

eyes, however, as she kissed her poor mama and tried to look encouraging. She knew well enough why such a small thing was important. The gown was not as needful as kindling or soap or dry bedding; but the loss of each garment marked their further descent into hardship and shabbiness.

'But how?' sniffed her mother. 'What can you use?'

'I can make a collar – and the frilling along the edge – from the top part of that old black dress of mine.'

'But Sophy – you can't! That's not an old dress.'

'Dearest mama, it's terribly old-fashioned' – a half-truth, since even the best of their clothes would soon be out of date – 'and besides, I've already got a better gown for half full-dress. Now sit down; and I'll go upstairs and fetch it.'

What she intended *was* a sacrifice, and not a small one. But Sophy was resolved to face her loss bravely; their circumstances seemed so much harder to bear when her mother was distressed than when they only affected herself.

It was while she was in her room that Fraser arrived. At the top of the stairs, carrying the dress to be cut up as indifferently as she could, Sophy was waylaid by her mother. It was not Fraser's usual time to call; but that alone did not explain why Mrs Byford looked wild-eyed and important. 'Sophy! Sophy!' she croaked, gesturing like a marionette run amok.

At the sight of her Sophy retreated a couple of steps into her room. 'Why are you whispering, mama?' She was solemn rather than curious, however. Already she guessed what might be happening.

Mrs Byford closed the door behind her. 'Oh, now Sophy – make haste, now; you must go downstairs immediately! It's only polite to him – to Mr Fraser.'

'Mama, I was about to,' she replied, standing in the middle of the room as if to make not a move.

'Yes, yes – but think of the circumstances!' pleaded her mother incoherently. 'And you can't go down like that,' eyeing Sophy's well-worn cotton print. 'Put on something else – yes, best wear that dress' – indicating the black silk draped over Sophy's arm. 'Nothing could serve as well as that.'

Sophy turned pale as her suspicions hardened. 'Has he asked to see only me – I mean in private?'

'Yes, yes – he has – yes. Oh dear!'

Sophy sat down on the bed. 'Oh. Oh dear.' She too spoke in a whisper; between them they sounded as if they'd just committed a murder without thinking how to dispose of the corpse. Neither felt the need to be forthright enough to say that Fraser had come with the object of offering marriage.

'But mama, you don't even approve of him!' Suddenly it seemed important to Sophy to pretend none of this was happening; or at least that any delay would serve for excuse.

'Oh – good heavens, no! When have I ever said that?' With characteristic feeble-mindedness, Mrs Byford might shy away from the fact of Fraser's lowly origins – yet saw any man ready with an actual proposal for her daughter as not to be displeased at any cost.

'Why, I do believe you'd like me to accept him,' said Sophy with an attempt at cheerfulness.

'I – really – I mean, that is to say – come now ...' Mrs Byford really had not thought things out that far.

Sophy herself was not much less confused. Her first impulse was to ask her mama to say she was unwell; but she put that behind her as cowardly. 'The sooner I can see him the better. But' – looking at her dress, with its soiled hem – 'he will have to take me as I am.' Some impulse murmured that she would be able to make light of the occasion if she devalued herself by looking shabby.

Though she feigned decisiveness, however, it seemed that every feeling was assailing her at once. There was the hard, sweet thrill of power, that she should be offered an escape from how she lived now – and, in the same instant, the gall of regret, that she should be shown this chance, only to destroy it. For she was certain she ought to reject Fraser. Kate had been right – as, for their own reasons, her aunt and uncle and all sorts of people would be, did they know what she had let things come to.

182

Then – to make rejection more melancholy, he was a man she liked, whatever others might say. She liked him very much indeed, now she came to dwell on it. Sophy didn't think any better of him that he should choose to court *her*. But the conviction that she was about to dismiss his offer – one, she knew, not to be lightly made – moved her to think more kindly of him than she had guessed possible. As she negotiated the narrow staircase, one hand gathering her skirts, the other against the wall to balance her, she was overcome by a gust of remorseful tenderness strong enough to make her catch her breath and feel her colour rise.

It was this look of warm solemnity, as she came to greet him, that Fraser saw; and misunderstood. And indeed, the sight of her, all infant-blonde softness and brilliant strong health, might have made a man of far less generous emotions think it meaningless not to be enslaved.

With more looks than words they hastened to leave the dark little parlour, whose air tasted of smoke from the kitchen fire; and after the manner of poor country people everywhere they walked out. As they made their way up the long flank of Cannings Hill, Fraser, seeing a new depth of kindness in Sophy's face, was at least half convinced his proposal would meet with success. That alone was enough to make him look down, and about, all unseeing, with a suppressed air of quick pleasure, as though, instead of riding for two hours through fields and lanes, he'd had to slay a dragon or two in order to arrive.

They reached the grassy summit of the Hill. There, every pair of lovers must have sat since the village began, imagining, as they overlooked the distances of the Vale, every kind of good prospect for their own lives. Marriage and hanging, it is said, are destiny. Fraser was committed: he had known that for days. Merely coming up here was enough to have every matron in the parish squeaking with anticipation. It was not just a place for courtship, either: every high summer at Lammas tide the villagers still celebrated here around a bonfire. Their festival was supposed to be Christian; in fact it was held in faintest remembrance of an ancient bloodstained goddess of fertility –

the same grotesquely sexual creature that made such a fearsome image down on the south doorway of the church.

Beside him, Sophy, dainty and sensually unawakened, knew little of such lewd associations. But Fraser had heard of the superstitions attached to the Hill, and it touched his fancy to imagine how apt they now seemed. He was in a mood only to picture the happy moments of the generations who had come this way. Of course he knew about the violence implied in any act of love. But his imagination was powerless to show him other things. He knew nothing of the shocking pain most of those long-dead lovers must have felt on finding that the man or girl they'd married had been a stranger all along.

They reached the prehistoric ramparts, at the highest point along the skyline. As every passing shepherd did without thinking, they turned into the prevailing breeze to face the Vale.

'I've never forgotten how you showed me a city from up here,' Sophy said. Her gaze darted to each horizon in turn, as if in the hazard of the moment she could reach out and seize everything in sight. She was not really attending to what either of them had been saying. All her thoughts dwelt on what she would have to answer him before they went back down the hill. She stared into the middle distance and asked, 'Does your work often take you beyond the Vale?'

'I have to dine sometimes with the principal committee at the Bath office and other places.'

At such a time, even the excitement of being courted by a fine-looking man was not agreeable. It was an annoyance – it distracted her, just when she knew she should be thinking more sensibly than at any other moment of her life . . .

'Is Bath where you're going to meet the king?'

'No; he's due to make a visit to the tunnel.'

'And you'll be introduced to him by name?'

'There'll be people there more important than I. But I expect so.'

Sophy nodded absently. She was trying to concentrate on nothing but what words she should use in rejecting him. But the harder she tried to do so, the more it served to melt her heart toward him even further. She felt tears of sorrowful goodwill starting into her eyes. It was all she could do to smile, and talk faster ... 'He didn't look very grand when we saw him. Will he wear the Garter for you, and a scarlet uniform?'

'Lord, no. I've seen him once or twice in London. He'll look like a bailiff, or Parson Hopewell from over yonder, who died falling drunk from his horse.'

If only it were over! If she could just force him to speak out as soon as possible, so that the question could be disposed of for ever.

'And when you meet him, will you bow, or will he shake your hand?'

'If he were Tsar of Russia, he might expect anything – but no; you just bow.'

'Almost like an ordinary acquaintance, as we did. Only ... I was thinking' – and she laughed and blushed – 'if you shook hands with the king, why, imagine how close even I might come to royalty if afterward I put my hand like this ... palm to palm with yours ... '

And putting out her exquisite little paw, with its pink, shell-like nails, she pressed it to his own calloused right hand.

She had meant to force the issue, certainly. But for the sake of retreating, not venturing an advance. Now that it was made, her gesture held them speechless, astonished to find themselves so suddenly in the pose of lovers making vows. For several seconds there was no sound but the wind ripping at Sophy's gown. She blushed again, thrilled and afraid. Her dismayed look of frailty was something Fraser had not seen before. He himself had never looked more vulnerable in his life. 'I can't say nothing,' he murmured, thick-voiced. 'Even if I'd wanted to.' He hesitated, feeling as though an invisible fist rained blows on his belly and throat. It was delight rather than apprehension that made him stumble in asking Sophy if she'd marry him. But in every other way he felt like a man making a gallows speech, whose concern is no longer life nor death so much as saying what he has to, loud and fearlessly, as a man should. 'If you would marry me, there's nothing I shouldn't do to make you as happy as I'd be.'

The moment she'd dreaded caught Sophy without a tatter of her usual confidence. Instead, a mob of other feelings – hope, curiosity, dismay, excitement, gratitude, conscience jostled with each other. She even cast about in vain for some notion of duty.

Yet she couldn't bear to prolong this crisis by hesitating. So it was that after all her response was the only one in keeping with her true character. There was nothing she could bear to say, meaning either yes or no; instead, she acted without a thought. On purest impulse, and with as little affectation as if they stood naked before each other, she put her arms around his neck and kissed him, pricked with tears whose cause bewildered her.

With a shudder of terrible exultation he embraced her, and kissed her fiercely.

What? she thought – what? – how? – me? She felt as if her heart had dissolved right down to her aching maidenhead, and left a singing void. But – is this how it ought to be? she inwardly exclaimed, looking up confused into his unspeakably happy face. She didn't dare describe to herself her body's unendurable pang of bliss. It was as if an unfriendly seraph had smitten her – there – just there (she hoped she was too modest to think the words themselves) – there – oh, no, please God, no – there – there.

So now it was over. Of course she knew he'd have to do the function on her that she'd seen performed so often, by pigs and sparrows, and Farmer Prescott's Shorthorn bull. Just the thought of the same farmer's grey stallion, looking as if it had another limb – did it really move her to nothing more than horror? And if so, why did she now feel she'd rather swoon into a martyr's slow death than slip from the knife-edge of pleasure where she was held by this man's mere embrace?

'Darling, before you say anything – no – before you say anything at all – we shouldn't have much money; maybe not for some years.'

'Oh, if you think I'd care about that –' Indeed, Sophy

was too shocked at what she'd just done to give such a thing more than a passing thought.

'You won't be marrying a rich man. But I'd do everything to see that you could live as freely as possible. I shouldn't want to make any woman wretched, least of all you, as my own wife. I can't think of any failure worse than not making sure you were happy.'

'Oh, I know you wouldn't like me to live with you in inns and lodging-houses,' said Sophy, her imagination delicately sidestepping a world of damp bedrooms and dirty tinplate cutlery.

'Of course I shouldn't ask you to do that. But you know we cannot hope to live for long in one place.'

Nothing could have given Sophy a greater thrill of reassurance than this promise of escape. 'Oh! If only you knew how happy I'd be to travel with you anywhere! ... How soon will your work here be finished?'

'I can't tell. Perhaps this year.'

'Surely it will be soon. I'm certain it must be,' said Sophy, fiercely happy just to hear this guarantee from herself.

'No – believe me – you cannot talk like that.'

His meaning was serious enough. But his look of pleasure contradicted it – at least in Sophy's eyes.

Fraser himself chose to read all his best and strongest hopes in her own looks rather than her words. Hand in hand they walked back over the down to the head of the long combe, through short grass starred with blue specks of milkwort and tender spires of black and purple orchids. Blue clouds of tiny chalkhill butterflies twinkled about them in a wind that gusted through their hair and clothes like a caress.

For all that Sophy could tell, not only he but she herself had climbed the hill meaning them to say and do just as they had. Certainly, as they came down from the lonely summit to the Vale, with its lanes and fields and busy farms, their self-absorbed look made them the image of every fine girl and tall young man who had walked together loaded with happiness, and resolved to hope that all might not yet turn out for the worst.

187

Chapter Ten

A month went by in which, at the Hall, nothing changed. The doctors and the family attorney and his clerk killed much time eating and drinking at the steward's table and generally being sociable with the upper servants. Mr Freeman, the steward, fretted meanwhile at the thought of showing his lordship the bill thus incurred by his wife's illness; and for thirty nights running Rawley was put to bed dead drunk by his valet, a former prizefighter who could cast an unconscious employer over one shoulder as easily as a labourer carrying a sack of wheat.

As the season neared its climax of perfection the wind still held from the mild quarter. In hayfields across the Vale the grass grew high enough to gleam in the breeze like water, and cock pheasants honked at each other from coppices deep in wood spurge and foxglove spires.

One such afternoon, when the indistinctness of the further woods and downs promised brilliant days to come, Rawley was riding to Marlborough to see a gunsmith. Approaching Cannings Fitzpayne he became aware that something out of the ordinary was going on. Around the churchyard and down the village street a number of people were gathered who had the air of onlookers ... But of course. Nothing so remarkable. A country wedding.

But wait. This was not just the preliminary to a coupling between two of his uncle's nameless and faceless peasantry. True, the bride and groom, just come into view, were walking to the church amid their relatives, with no ceremony at all. But they had the look of carriage folk, for all that. So if they walked it must be that they came from hard by the church. And the girl – he was damned if he wouldn't know her, without that veil. He stared – the sweetness promised by that little body! – and that other girl! – by God, he wouldn't mind if he could – either of them.

The Byford household. That was it. The younger Byford

188

girl! Marrying? ... Marrying, God damn her! Rawley felt unreasonably surprised, as if nothing could be more unlikely than one of the best-looking girls in the county finding a mate. That Byford girl! So that's who was due to have her maidenhead run through that night!

Rawley was irked. Chiefly by regret, with a colouring of hostility. He was envious, too. Who was the lucky son of a whore, anyway, who was going to take possession of *that* – of a creature who looked lively enough to pleasure a good man half to death?

Whoever the fellow was, he too was familiar. A smug-looking dog if ever there was ... *That* was the man. Their old housekeeper's grandson; that half-Scot from the canal company.

Passing them, Rawley stared several of the party in the face. The older women dropped their eyes, embarrassed. But that other girl – insolent shrew – looked straight back at him. And the Scot, too, merely nodded, as if he imagined he was confronted with an equal.

But the bride, now; her he stared at as passionately as a shallow man could. Seeing him look at her with undisguised lust, she blushed fiercely behind the veil of her bridal bonnet and glanced away. Oh, I know what's in your mind, thought Rawley, mid-way between resentment and satisfaction. And you know I know. I saw that look. You want it from me; I know that. In your imagination I've got on you already, and galloped away there for all you're worth.

If, as tradition says, no wedding is complete without someone gross enough for such thoughts, at least they merely came from a passer-by. Certainly no one else was there who wished to mar the day, as the bride and groom walked up the brick path beneath the churchyard yews. Soon Rawley Fitzpayne, spurring his horse out of the village, was lost not only to sight but to everybody's thoughts.

'Dearly beloved, we are gathered together here in the sight of God, and in the face of this congregation, to join this

189

Man and this Woman in holy Matrimony; which is an honourable estate, instituted of God ...'

Some things seem above circumstance or change, Kate thought, sitting beside her mother in the little cave-like chancel. Oh dear, she's starting to cry already. I hope Sophy doesn't notice; she'll be so cross, and no wonder. The same terrible, superbly wrought words are spoken in every church in the kingdom down the centuries, so that they seem as inevitable as the seasons of the year. Perhaps that's how they express more than you would ever find in the minds of the people speaking them.

Certainly Parson Beddowes didn't look dignified by what he recited. He was still just a small round man, red not only in the face but on top of his bald head. The words of the service meanwhile came winging down through him as though they had conceived themselves.

But James and Sophy; now they, thought Kate, didn't look like mouthpieces. Rather, the words they spoke made you look at each of them anew. Yet how different from each other in their manner! Fraser, his head high, gave the responses as though his very honour depended on speaking up. Beside him Sophy, gleaming in her white gown like a cloud of brightness amid the gloom of the ancient church, looked rapt, unapproachable. But what was she thinking? In the last month, Kate had found that for the first time in their lives she had no idea what could be in Sophy's mind. She recalled – all too well – her own warning against the match. Yet if Sophy were not as whole-hearted as Fraser, how could she endure to be there, the focus of so many expectations?

They stood, as if no one but they and the priest existed, their two fair heads almost touching as Fraser slipped the ring on Sophy's finger. 'With this ring I thee wed, with my body I thee worship, and with all my worldly goods I thee endow: In the Name of the Father, and of the Son, and of the Holy Ghost. Amen.'

He looked as happy as any man could. But, compared to his bride, more calm, as though unlike her he had already found the thing he wanted.

Should they be so unlike at a moment such as this?

190

Surely, though – if either doubted the wisdom of this marriage, could they hear the awful solemnity of what little Parson Beddowes was saying, and not be crushed by it? He was, Kate realized, not just binding them with a contract lasting until death. He was also casting a spell: it was by his incantations that he was meant to conjure all their future children into the prospect of life.

'God the Father, God the Son, God the Holy Ghost, bless, preserve, and keep you; the Lord mercifully with his favour look upon you ...'

It was over at last. With a smile about to break on every face, they lustily gave forth the last hymn. 'All people that on earth do dwell, Sing to the Lord with cheerful voice.' Then, as absurdly cheerful as if they'd all escaped a great calamity, they made their way under the big south doorway into the smiting sunlight and the clamour of a peal of bells.

As they left the church, laughing and talking like statues enchanted back to life, half the parish was loitering to watch them and murmur at the sight of the bride. Sophy was used to being looked at with surprise and admiration, even by people who had known her all her life. But no one was there that day who could remember her so light of foot and undaunted by attention, blest as if with the grace of a flowering tree. So many people were ready to wish her well, it was costing her blessedly little to change her secret fears at what she'd done into hope.

'Not every girl of seventeen must needs look her best in white,' confided the wife of the almshouse keeper to the curate's pale, child-burdened spouse. 'But this lass now ... I wonder how little those kid slippers are. Did you ever see such feet?'

'No indeed,' said the other woman, catching in Sophy's looks a memory of how it must have felt not to be pregnant all the time. 'And that shade of blonde hair is almost the same as her gown –'

'Aye, it is ... And I reckon there's several guineas' seamstressing there, at the least. Who'd have guessed, two

191

years back, that one of Lawyer Byford's girls'd be thought to better herself by marrying with an engine-wright?'

'Indeed . . . ' The curate's wife, not lavishly provided for by her own husband, felt it indelicate to dwell out loud on Sophy's sudden rescue from poverty. 'She may be very fair, as I say. Yet do you not think she has such health she makes white itself look like a living colour?'

'Aye, she does . . . aye . . . But will you look at him! Did you ever see a young fellow like him? Oh, if I had one like that at home to call my own!' chortling with lust. The curate's modest wife, tied to a man whose fertility was not matched by his looks, watched the couple and reflected that the ancient Greeks had identified the sun with a young man. Shocked at such pagan thoughts, she watched the bridal party go its way and hurried home to complete yet another hand-sewn shirt for her husband.

The first benefit of the marriage, for Sophy, had showed itself some days before. When they came to sit down to the wedding breakfast, it was not in Drove Cottage, but in a decent little house in Parsonage Lane, with two staircases, and a stable set behind evergreens.

It was remarkable that so few people – apart from the bride and groom, just Kate, her mother, the parson and his wife and two eldest sons – could make so much boisterous good cheer.

'We wanted a quiet wedding like this,' Mrs Byford said, raising her voice at Mrs Beddowes, 'because of my poor husband.'

'Oh yes?'

'Mama means,' said Kate, 'it is not a twelvemonth since papa was killed.'

'Why, yes,' said Mrs Byford, ignoring Kate. 'It is not a twelvemonth yet since my poor husband was taken from me.' Truth to tell, she was divided in her feelings today. Sophy, the object of all eyes, was the nearest thing in this life to a resurrection of Mrs Byford's younger self. On the other hand, she felt people should be made to recognize how recently she too had enjoyed the dignity of being a wife. It was in this mood that she had meant to wear her black silk, as a maudlin contrast with Sophy's wedding gown. But Kate's advice, and Sophy's outspoken opposition, had triumphed; and she now sat, less dramatically among the jollification, in a half-mourning of deep purple and dove grey.

The toasts were drunk and answered, and followed by speeches. As the company grew merrier, conversation lapsed into anecdote and gossip. Parson Beddowes had them weeping with laughter at an old story of a mishap suffered on the hunting field by Lord Fitzpayne, which by a miracle they'd never heard; Mrs Byford forgot not to talk and laugh with everyone else; and Kate found herself merely irked when Mrs Beddowes simperingly asked when her turn at marriage would be.

Throughout, Sophy could only pretend to be as cheerful as anyone else at table. But she was relieved beyond measure that so little was expected of her. The older people, in particular, took it for granted that she should fall silent as the time drew near when she must leave home. At length Mrs Byford nudged Sophy and, with a grotesque show of discretion, murmured that she should go upstairs and change. When Sophy replied, 'Oh, mama, do I have to go?' the others' shout of laughter could be heard right down the lane.

The chaise that was to take the couple away was drawn up at the gate; the trunks were lashed onto the roof; and the packages loaded inside for the next night and day of travelling. Kate started up the stairs with Sophy to keep her company while she changed.

'Kate! Kate!' exclaimed their mother, coming to the dining-room door.

'What is it, mama?' as Mrs Byford motioned her down with an inept display of secrecy.

'Now you will stay with Sophy while she changes her clothes, will you not? It is a rather important tradition, you know. And, Kate – how can you think to walk up the stairs in front of Sophy? Do you not know a bride has precedence?'

In this and other trivial ways Mrs Byford managed to show her own importance as next after the bride. And when the dreadful moment came for her poor nestling to be torn from her, she gave a performance worthy of the operatic stage. 'Mama, for heaven's sake find yourself another handkerchief or something,' said Sophy, embarrassed.

Fraser parted from his mother-in-law with invincible politeness. Even the most confident bridegroom could be pardoned for scrutinizing the mother of his bride for evidence of what his own wife might become. He handed Sophy into the chaise; the door was shut behind them; and to smiles, farewells, and slightly drunken attempts at solemnity from family and guests, they left for the road that was to take them west, then south, to Weymouth and Sophy's first sight of the sea.

She had no idea what to think or feel. The moment when the marriage started was not in church at all. Nor was it when, having been decked for half a day in white like a sacrificial victim, she put on ordinary clothes again. Vaguely she'd supposed it might begin some way through the honeymoon, when they came at length to unfamiliar places. But nothing she could fix her mind on would convince her that soon she *could* think of herself as married, and happy.

As they passed the end of the Fitzpayne deerpark and jolted past open country, she almost forgot where it was they were travelling. Instead she was dismayed by the suddenness with which all the festivity and public admiration and family support had stopped dead with the slamming of the post-chaise door. In place of all that, there was nothing to do but be blissful in the arms of the man of her choice. But how should bliss feel? Was there anything one should do to induce it? The raptures of heroines in novels were never something she'd understood; they were just a feeling to which she'd aspired.

She looked out of the window. They were passing Mill Farm, just below the Beacon. Like Park End Wood, it was still surrounded by the squalor of the canal workers' encampments. Its green fields, once bowered in deep hedgerows, had been scuffed as bare as the floor of a cave.

Close by, an unfinished stretch of embankment twice the height of the farmhouse had spilled thousands of tons of raw soil across a two-acre stand of foxgloves where a copse had stood. Sophy started, some way on, at a sound like a falling tree that would never reach the ground. Something above them cast a huge moving shadow; and then another. It was a windmill, built to draw up water to the canal's highest level so far; a whole crowd of them stood hard by, noisily flailing the air. Amid the strangeness of it all she almost thought, How did I come to be here with this man? For the first time she wondered if the violated landscape about them might not preoccupy Fraser even more than she did.

Sophy had never sought reassurance from another person in her life. At this moment, though, she was ready to take it gratefully from anyone. She hardly dared look up at her husband. What if his face, too, showed anticlimax and uncertainty?

He turned and smiled at her in acknowledgement of their discomfort as the chaise bumped them about. 'Even being abducted can't be worse than this.'

'Is it far to go?'

'I thought we should stop at Salisbury tonight. We'll be there by dusk.'

An instant of melancholy shadowed her face. She was going away, to a hotel with a man neither she nor her family had known a year ago; and there he would perform a carnal act upon her. Now that the consummation of the marriage was almost due, what too should she think of that?

'Are you tired?'

Crushed by her thoughts, she had not noticed Fraser looking at her. His concern could have provoked even her to tears. But there was something else about him, that she had never seen before. Astonished, she sensed that she was not in every way the weaker of them after all. He's frightened, she thought. But of what?

The dusk seemed to expand rather than fade as they journeyed. For the last few miles the roofs and spires of Salisbury appeared to come not a step nearer. At length, as Sophy was nearly asleep, they were off the high road, and clanging over the stones of a paved street, into the yard of the Bear.

Reaching down for Fraser's hand, she climbed from the chaise. The day's hopes and doubts had left her almost too tired to walk. She took his arm and was led across the yard. In a trance of fatigue she noticed nothing, beneath the azure sky whirling with swallows: neither travellers, porters, grooms, pedlars, idle onlookers, nor the racketing of the stage coach bound for London, with a shout of 'All right' from the guard as the horses' heads were let go and he raised his horn to blow a warning to the traffic in the street. Even the frank, lustful stares of the stable hands went unseen by her, as she strove to smile back at their host, and followed him to where the candles were being lit in the crowded dining room.

'Would you like to sleep?' All day Fraser had felt as though he had just been made happy by some heartless mistake. In the same way, sleeping, yet knowing he would wake, he had sometimes clung to a treasured object in a dream to take it back with him into consciousness. By the light of a pair of candles, Sophy lay with her yard of moon-blonde hair loose upon the pillow, and in a trousseau nightdress almost as exquisite as nakedness itself. She looked passive enough to be newly drowned.

If he touched her, what would happen? In the old stories, the princess was always restored to life by the kiss, so called, of her prince. But they never told you what he might have done with a princess who, on sitting down to unpack, shed tears of stress. Was it even humane to take possession of a creature who looked so frail?

'Dearest ...' He sat on the bed and leaned over her, not altogether happy. In his state of half-undress he looked, for once, as young as he was. Guiltily, his tenderness warred with more or less violent lust. '... would you prefer to sleep?'

'No – no,' she said, not looking quite straight at him.

196

It was what he was ready to surrender anything to hear; yet it was hard not to notice the resolution in her voice.

'Are you too tired? – too tired to sleep?'

'No – no, of course I'm not,' she said, with a sharpness that came oddly from a girl reclining on her bride-bed, fair as a drift of wild anemones. At a moment like this, what *were* the expectations of someone as politely brought up as she had been? The realization that she shared his own nervousness steadied him; how else were they to have enough sympathy for one another? He recalled something from a novel he had once tried to sample: 'It is cruelty to ask a modest woman for her consent.' Getting to his feet, he tore off the rest of his clothes as urgently as if undressing was the act itself.

From within the curtains of their old-fashioned bed, Sophy pretended not to look at him. She felt as cowed as a field mouse captured by a cat. Yet she would prefer to die of what he was about to do to her rather than delay it. Curiosity and fear made her as impatient as he was. She watched him hesitate before her as, unselfconscious, and unaware even of her own body, he strove a moment longer to understand what was in her mind.

Even Sophy knew his looks, of their kind, were fit to rival her own. But all she thought, as he got into the bed, was that she could have shouted out from sheer fright. Their silence was loud enough for the sheets to crackle like gunfire. Should she say something? she wondered. Should she even do something herself? Oh God, why did it have to be so matter-of-fact and terrifying? Why wasn't there a ceremony for this too, with her still hidden behind a veil, or with dozens of musicians dinning away outside so that they couldn't even hear each other?

'Are you frightened of me?' he asked hoarsely. His heart battered away as though it shouldn't be there.

'No,' she whispered, more intent on courage than truth. 'No – I mean yes. Yes! Please ...' Her urgency was touchingly absurd, as if she were about to suffer a stage death.

He laid his hand, over her nightdress, on her thigh, and she jumped like a shot rabbit. In an instinctive gesture of reassurance, much as one might stroke the head of a young child, he put his hand over her cunt. She blushed at his boldness, and parted her legs in gratitude at his gentleness. He hesitated. With a look of determination she sat up and clumsily pulled her endless tresses through her nightdress before casting it aside.

At the sight of her, tears of excitement stood in Fraser's eyes. 'I'm going to hurt you,' he murmured.

'What? How? Hurt *me*?'

'I'm going to hurt you,' was all he could answer. Now, he too wanted it over quickly.

'*You* would never hurt me,' she said. Her shyness smote him like an armoured fist.

They should have tried harder to understand each other. When, above her, he finally dealt her a blow with his whole body, she shrieked in anger as much as pain. His only impulse was to spare her from hurt; but without thinking he clapped his hand over her mouth.

Sophy twisted her head away. 'What have you done? Oh! What have you done?' she exclaimed, as they struggled apart.

'Darling – darling, I told you.'

'No you didn't!' she said, through tears of shock.

Fraser forbore to answer. It was not in his nature to make appeals, even to a woman from whom he had drawn blood. As one would an infant, he took her in his arms, and tried to soothe both her and himself. Sophy, face upward and open-eyed, felt bruised, as much as anything by her own incompetence. Even so, she couldn't bring herself to answer his endearments as she wanted. Both of them secretly wished she were just a little more unhappy, so that a proper storm of weeping might bring them sooner to a reconciliation. At last Fraser, watching the dim outline of her face, sensed her breathing change and felt free to sleep himself. The morning, he thought. By the light of day, not even couples out of love could feel as melancholy as this. And if she thought him a lout, surely she could be persuaded to say why, sooner rather than later.

Sophy had never woken so late, even though every night she fell as blithely from consciousness as any rosy two-year-old. She looked at Fraser, still asleep despite the noises from the street below, where a herd of cattle was blocking half the town.

Poor James, she thought ... But why poor James? If he were old or ugly she wouldn't feel so, just to see him unconscious. Watching him, she sensed her guilt deepen at her earlier crossness. She supposed he'd done nothing wrong, after all. Just what must have been expected of him on their wedding night. And today he was going to take her far away, right to the edge of the sea. The thought of such a journey didn't exactly make her happy – she was looking forward to it far too much for that ... Yes, she had been so unkind to James. She thrust the bedclothes out of the way and leaned closer to him. How warm to the touch he looked! She wanted to put out her hand and caress him, if only in the way one annoys a fine horse by patting it.

He stirred; opened his eyes; and showed confusion, surprise and helpless pleasure. And so should any man have looked, waking to the unfamiliar sight of Sophy soft and bright about the face, with a body for which the gods themselves might have jostled.

'You're shameless,' he mumbled, in a doped voice of pure happiness.

'What?' she said, not understanding.

'Naked as an immortal soul.'

'But James, improper people don't leave their clothes off either,' said Sophy, in all innocence.

He kissed her shoulder, and she blushed and laughed at such familiarity.

'Was that someone at the door?' she suddenly asked.

'I heard nothing.'

'Someone knocked.'

'No, I'm certain there's no one there.'

Samuel Pennyman, superintendent of masonry, waited in the grand club room of the Bear with unmixed feelings.

199

The news he brought oppressed him; so too did telling it in circumstances like these.

Fraser appeared, almost dressed, within a couple of minutes.

'Yes, Pennyman? Something bad?'

'The Mill Farm embankment, sir.'

Fraser knew it was worse than just a man-made landslip. 'There are men hurt?'

'Six dead. Three injured. A slip took one of the barrow-runs with it. We couldn't dig out all the men in time.'

'Is money needed, for the doctor and a funeral?'

'I don't know about that yet, sir. But one man won't work again this season.'

'Leave the money to the company and me. When –'

'Four hours back.'

'Which contractor's part of the embankment?'

'That sod O'Keefe, with due respect to my betters, sir.'

'The stretch banked up on just one side?'

'That's right. The other side's a cutting.'

'A spring, was it?'

'Yes, sir. Brought down three acres from the hill behind.'

'O'Keefe's successor – has he ever thought a culvert was needed there?'

'O'Keefe himself may not have known. That hill's a chalk outlier; the spring line's all over the place.'

'Are other parts of that section at risk?'

'Maybe the brickwork on the road bridge. He had a pane of glass fixed on as usual when we finished it –'

'And it's cracked?'

'Aye. Them bricks have shifted, all right.'

'Are the men angrier at the deaths than they might be?'

'Them foreigners O'Keefe left behind. You've seen them when they've been aggrieved. Pretending they don't speak a Christian language.'

'Yes. Nothing but Gaelic ... I'll be back this morning. How did you get here?'

'Post-chaise, sir. It's waiting for you in the yard.'

'I'll hire a saddle-horse, thank you. But take it yourself. Have you money for the journey?'

'No, sir.'

'Take this; it's not a loan. Thank you, Pennyman; I'll see you later in the day.'

And they went their ways; the older man relieved that Fraser had suffered his marriage tour stopped without a word of resentment; and Fraser to break the news to Sophy.

Chapter Eleven

It was the most deathly hour of all; the time when, in the woods, the nightjars had ceased their whirring, and there was neither rustling from small creatures in the undergrowth, nor even screechings from the tawny owls around the park. It was the hour before the dawn, when everything rests so silent it matters little what the season is. By day the meadows would be filled with shouts and talk among the year's first harvest hands, and on the downs there would be great gatherings of animals and men for late sheep-shearing. But in the timeless darkness of three o'clock the Vale was held as still as if beneath the iron frosts of January.

It was certainly the worst hour to lie even partly awake. Behind the east front of the Hall, Miss Hodgkiss, my lady's maid, was suffering a broken dream in which she was being forced to ride to church behind Mr Freeman, facing the horse's tail, and astride in her best gown. The church bells were pinging away in a strange monotone; and though they were late, however hard they rode they got no nearer. By degrees, Miss Hodgkiss struggled from her dream to realize she was being rung for.

The bell was being sounded by the maid who served as her ladyship's night-nurse. She had a summons for Master Rawley, of all things. A manservant was roused, protesting, to take a message via Rawley's valet, though Miss Hodgkiss privately doubted whether the young man would appear.

But either he, or his valet, had some sense that this was

urgent; for Lady Fitzpayne had not had her demand repeated more than once before he presented himself, more or less dressed. He even took pains, once inside the sickroom, to conceal his furious resentment at being got out of bed. Oh, you know what's good for you, don't you, thought Miss Hodgkiss. You have to run and jump when you're told, just like the rest of us.

Rawley approached the face beneath the canopy of the great bed. It looked almost as if its owner had been dead for several days already. For all that, Lady Fitzpayne had had herself propped upright, as if determined not to be seen, even by her Maker, lying down. Sensing Rawley approach, she opened her eyes, lizard-like within the folds of grey skin. Her decaying flesh, which already looked as though the bones might be about to break out through it, contrasted with the smoothness of the big goosefeather pillows and the snowflake delicacy of the lace around her nightcap. She indicated that Miss Hodgkiss and the nurse were to stay, and motioned Rawley closer.

'Don't worry,' she said, seeing his look. 'I shan't want you to touch me. I've sent for you,' she went on, in a voice whose weakness was contradicted by her dauntless eyes, 'because I know that that is what's expected of me. I shall not ask how many weeks you have been waiting here. Firstly I do not care. Secondly, to any man as worthless as you are, it shouldn't matter how he's forced to spend the time.'

Rawley, conscious of his inheritance, and of the two women kept behind as witnesses, looked at her with stony patience.

'Should I not die tonight, this is not an encounter I shall wish to repeat. I tell you this not for your reassurance, but for my own convenience, lest I see you here again.'

'Yes, Aunt Caroline,' said Rawley, trying to stare her down.

'If I see your face again, I trust it will only be as proof of the existence of God Almighty and my consequent damnation, along with you, in the fires of Hell.'

'I hope it won't come to that,' Rawley informed her. Faint noises of shock came from the other women. God damn her, he thought. She knows none of us can touch her now. But if she's confident she's going to her Day of Judgement, can't we see the woman cringe on account of *that*?

'You must not think I consider God unmerciful in letting me perish with little more than you for company.' Despite the endless plucking of her terrible hands at the bedclothes, her stare never faltered. 'You must not assume, either, that your likeness to your uncle displeases me. I regard it as a comfort,' pronouncing the last word with deliberate distinctness, 'that in you I can address both his former self and the future of his family.'

Rawley looked away in angry unease. He hadn't expected all this.

'If to die in anger is to guarantee perdition, then to be married to my husband is itself enough to put me in Hell – not only so long as we both live, but hereafter. No one but a fool would ask that I cease to hate him, merely for fear of my immortal soul. And how should I? How should I find the relief of indifference, when I am married to such a man as he? No; I was damned in the instant of my marriage vows, as surely as if the minister had chanted backwards, and had me give my hand and body to a goat or a baboon.'

She paused, seeking the strength to continue. 'If I must be damned, then let it not be merely for what I think or feel. At least I will be damned, as well, for speaking my thoughts aloud. I am glad to die, whatever may befall me – either because hereafter there is nothing; or because, if Heaven and Hell exist, in the inferno there is no passing of time, but only eternity; and there I shall not have to wait before I see my husband in everlasting torment beside me.'

Her eyelids fluttered; her breathing slowed; and Rawley thought she could say no more. Suddenly, however, she opened her eyes again and fixed her gaze on him. 'And you. To you, throughout your mortal existence, I wish one thing. I hope that you never shall share the thought that has sustained me all the declining years of my life. I want you to suffer misfortune such that you cannot even console yourself with the possibility that death may end all consciousness. I would deny you even the strength I have gained, as a woman and a wife, from the blessed chance of ultimate annihilation. For your own sake, and as my husband's heir, and as the source of all his heirs to come.'

She stopped; and closed her eyes, exhausted.

Without a word, Rawley got up and walked away. Back in his own apartment he shouted for candles and brandy to be brought. He had not forgotten his uncle's command to keep up appearances before the servants by showing deference toward his aunt. But even if she did have more to say, he didn't think he could listen. And if they expected him to sit up till the woman was gone, they could damn well look for him in his own chamber, where there could be light enough to touch every corner.

After a while he threw off the coat in which he had wrapped himself and got up from his chair to open the shutter at one of the windows. Down beyond the lake the horizon was at last more distinctly black beneath a paling sky. In a few minutes the nurse came to tell him his aunt was dead, doing so as briefly as propriety allowed and vanishing immediately. She knew it was more than her position was worth, to stand there, like a porter awaiting a tip, until he'd squeezed out some utterance of regret.

Rawley went back to the window and looked out for further signs of day. He felt relief in every way, as things near at hand grew outlines and then shadows. Not for him any vulgar superstition of unquiet souls stalking to catch at others' peace of mind. He watched the light strengthen, while the world thawed into life and the vapours rose from the earth as if all creation sighed in its hour of release.

The bell tolled on as if it would never cease. For miles about, the tenantry were converging on Cannings Fitzpayne church, walking, in gigs or on horseback. The carriages of the county families were present too, though, in keeping with aristocratic custom, most of them were empty. At the parlour window, Mrs Byford sat to watch them go by. 'Poor Lady Fitzpayne! Well, one thing I'm sure of,' she remarked to Sophy. 'Her ladyship would be so unhappy to know she was missing this. Still, we all have to accept disappointments. It is in the nature of life, after all.'

'The nature of death, in this case,' murmured Sophy.

'Of course, in a world that was just to all of us, your father would have had a grand funeral, too. I mean to say, how many people out there know it would have been a year ago today, but for five weeks come Tuesday next? Oh, now there goes another carriage – whose arms are those? They're Sir Jack Boone's – that's Sir Jack Boone's carriage; I'm certain it is. Oh, and here comes another – whose is this? I don't know whose carriage this is ... Ah, now here's one whose owners are riding in it. They must be tradespeople... Sophy, you're not looking.'

'I am looking, really, mama.'

'There! I knew I was right. It's Mr Leggatt and his wife, riding high – even though he is just a grocer. I suppose he thinks if they attend the funeral, he can get a contract to supply the Hall without bribing that Mr Freeman ... So the Leggatts have a new carriage and pair... Sophy, you're not listening! Some of the best families in the county are here, and all you can do is sit and look at the wall.'

Sophy excused herself and went upstairs. Alone in her room – she still thought of it, sometimes, as entirely hers – she sat at the window and looked out on the mourners. She found a kind of satisfaction in what she saw. The hushed populace, the sounding of the bell, the sombre pomp of the cortège itself – all these seemed to lend their dignity to her own glumness. For an interlude they almost lifted her disappointment above itself as she contemplated the truths of her marriage.

For she had not escaped after all. In marrying, she had bartered her lifetime's only asset – and still she had not escaped. It was not that things hadn't changed – but that they might yet alter, as she saw it, for the worse. During the weeks before marriage she had noticed only the possible advantages of Fraser's profession. From the very first month following their wedding, though, she began to be daunted by its insecurities.

As bad luck would have it, they were beginning to show themselves with a vengeance, as Fraser departed one morning to investigate work at his section's eastern end. Several things were causing delay; in particular one cutting where a layer of clay had been removed to show solid chalk and flint. The sub-soil could still be moved, of course, using extra gangs with pickaxes. But the share-holders' committee had pressed for a schedule that would mean this took too long. Gunpowder was the answer, but an expensive one. So much so that Fraser dared not think what other unforeseeable costs might occur before the next calls on the company's devalued shares.

As he rode he was overtaken by Samuel Pennyman. Together they made their way in silence along several miles of partly made canal, their shared preoccupation with what they saw taking the place of conversation. As they approached the cutting Fraser, full of his own thoughts, only half heard Pennyman exclaim.

'What ... who?' he asked.

'Dai One-Wing, that was.'

They had passed a man walking in the same direction. He was barefoot, with his boots hung around his neck; and he carried a bundle of possessions under his left arm. His right sleeve was sewn to his front, empty. 'I knew of him from a job I did up near Coventry. Caught his hand in a piece of winding gear.'

'Why should he be here?'

'That's how he lives, now. He travels round and brings the news. All the men know him, the country over. We'd best hope he's not been sent with tales of better money to be had elsewhere.'

'Better conditions, at any rate ... Confound it! Some of the men get too damn little in return for their wages, to hear comparisons from outside.'

'That Leggatt, now. He screws his gangs out of their due twice over. Pays them short –'

'In tokens, does he not?'

'Aye; mostly they can only be tendered at his own shops. Then he overcharges for food and drink.'

'The man's a fool. At the least he could reckon how many hands the harvest could take from us.'

'Damned if I know, sir, why we took him on. He's not a contractor in the usual way of things, is he?'

'No, worse luck. He's a grocer and a carrier – and that's most of the trouble. The company want his custom when the waterway's complete. Meanwhile I'm to bribe the man for them with tenders of work.'

Pennyman spat neatly over one shoulder, away from the wind. 'If you'll pardon me for saying, sir, them stupid sods should stay out of it. Instead of tittuping along cap in hand, offering serious work to shareholders, and businesses like Leggatt's.'

'Yes, dammit. Too many interests want to branch out like him, and take a chance at our expense.'

'Or your own, sir.' Pennyman understood the section's account books well enough to know that Fraser's own liabilities were enormous. Like most resident engineers Fraser himself might have to meet extra expenses beyond what the company were prepared to pay. And *they* had been short of working capital for years.

'God Almighty,' he said. 'Let's hope it won't come to that.'

The reach of canal they'd come to see had smashed a trail broad enough to make a landscape in itself. Along the edge of a wood newly broken into, the trees stood up tall and spindly. The skyline of the embankment above them was cluttered with the shapes of carts, barrows, piles of materials, and huge timber-built tripod cranes. They crossed a dell sprouting with weeds where the head of a valley had been cut off, and rode onto a new stone bridge to look down on the canal bed.

'Looks like Leggatt's working a bit short-handed here,' Pennyman was saying – and stopped as the site came into full view. He let out a whistle of dismay and glanced at Fraser. 'Eh ... he shouldn't ha' done that, now!'

'God damn the man to hell,' said Fraser in a steady voice. 'I told him not to start until the weather broke.'

It needed no professional to see what was wrong. The bed of the waterway, having got its seal of wet clay, should have been as solid as a beaten-earth floor. Instead, the heat of the sun had dried it full of cracks big enough to break a man's leg.

For several moments they looked down carefully at the work to be redone. Each knew it was pointless to comment. For twice as far as they could see, the canal would have to be re-excavated; a new clay-pit would need to be opened up nearby; and eighty more cartloads of gravel would be required. Pennyman, knowing how Fraser kept dismay or anger to himself, saw nonetheless that he'd turned pale. Almost to the last shilling he too could guess the arithmetic being calculated in the younger man's head. After a tactful silence he asked, 'You reckon the section committee can pay for this, sir?'

'Probably,' Fraser said, still tight-voiced, as he wheeled his horse about. 'They'll have to if they wish it done at all. Leggatt's not obliged to pay. And I can't.'

By the law of averages, that should have been the only bad news of the day. But in a nearby lane ... 'What's this, then?' said Pennyman sharply.

Ahead, where a crossroads alehouse and four cottages stood beside a patch of common, their way was barred. It was hard to tell if they had been expected. A couple of dozen workmen and some women, having seen them approach, were standing across the road. Fraser heard one or two of them murmur as if making a dare, and looked to see if anyone was armed. Beside him, Pennyman bristled as if faced with high treason. They rode up to them.

'Let's hear it,' said Fraser to the nearest man.

At the back of the group three boys of fifteen or so tried out a jeer, grinning at their own courage. The other navvies, more tense, ignored them. There were no weapons, but one of them held back a pair of dull-coated, desperate bulldogs on a leash.

The man hesitated.

'Yes?' said Fraser. The more these people's grievance, the less their readiness to tolerate soft words.

'You tell him!' said one of the others.

'Go on!' shrilled a barefoot woman on the edge of the crowd. 'You tell the buggers! They sit up there on those horses –' A clamour of angry voices drowned her out. The whole gathering having found their tongue, they seemed surprised by their own anger. One of the boys ran at Pennyman with the wild expression of someone proving himself, fist upraised to strike. Pennyman swung his horse around toward him, and the boy clumsily punched the animal on the neck and ran away.

'Williams!' Pennyman's voice thundered out over the broken curses of the crowd. 'Williams!'

A proper spokesman, known by name. Sensible man, registered Fraser, as the navvies made way for someone. 'What is it?' he demanded. He noticed he was addressing the crippled man they had passed earlier.

'It's their tack, you see,' said Williams. He looked less aggressive than the others. Several people repeated the sense of his words in lowered voices. Fraser guessed why the crowd was anxious for this man rather than one of themselves to be heard. Their distress made them see any outsider as privileged by comparison – even as a source of hope.

'The food, is it? Who do they work for – whose men are you?'

'Leggatt,' muttered several voices.

'It's that whore's son Leggatt,' one of the women shouted.

'Someone here'll sort the bugger out, iffen as you won't!'

'One of you write me what you want,' he said, raising his voice. 'I'll speak to the man. He'll have to see things can't go on like this.' And rode on, leaving them with a small anticlimax of astonishment at having got a hearing after all.

'How the devil will you do that, sir?' asked Pennyman.

'God knows. If I have to, I'll go over Leggatt's head, to Mr Rennie, or Sir Charles Dundas. Even then we may only get a temporary answer. But any fool should see where this could lead us.'

'Aye. Them riff-raff' – Pennyman spoke with the callousness common in men who have risen from the ranks – 'they'd be ganging up in a regular fighting force. And that damn-fool yeomanry 'ud let itself be panicked into shooting the Lord knows who.'

'James, how soon can we leave this place?'

Fraser had come home by the last gleam of the long summer dusk, to find Sophy already asleep, warm and languorous in their bed. Now, though, as he dragged off his clothes, aching as much from fatigue as desire, she sounded wide awake.

'Which place?'

'This village – the whole district – this county. Do we still have to wait for the waterway to be complete?'

'Why, yes.'

'How long will it take?'

'Forever, if we can't agree a price for Lord Fitzpayne's land.' He looked at her as she sat up in bed, his attention divided between what she was saying and how she looked. Her long hair was like a change of light on running water ... How he hoped she could still be spared from anxiety about their future!

'Poor James! How tired you look. Won't you come to bed?' There was a light in her smile, however. Already the fiasco of their wedding night was halfway forgotten. At another time Fraser might have allowed himself to feel smug. Twice, now, in the snatch of eternity between entering her and feeling as if his heart itself were about to explode out through his loins, he had seen her show – what? – yes – astonishment – at being pleasured so.

'The land,' she persisted. 'If you can agree a price?'

'I've not thought that far.'

'You've been too busy?' she asked, stretching.

'I suppose so ... Do you remember how I explained that I might be liable for some of the company's expenditure?'

'But only if something went wrong. It wouldn't really happen, would it?'

'Probably not. But while there was even a chance ... I couldn't let such a thing take you by surprise.'

She met his eyes as steadily as she could – even now she blushed whenever he looked her full in the face. 'But you said nothing like that was going to happen. And even if it did, surely you'd have enough money to pay for whatever it was?'

He looked down, casting for words. 'You remember the man who held my position before me?'

'Oh, everyone knows about Mr Benedict going bankrupt. But he was incompetent, wasn't he?'

'It wasn't his fault.'

'But isn't it always somebody's fault? Even poor papa –

'It was nothing to do with Benedict. Someone succeeded in a swindle and the company refused to meet the cost. He did lose everything, you know.'

'I know, I know,' Sophy answered, ashamed of having spoken lightly of someone else's misfortune. 'But how could anyone who works as hard as you do owe money they don't have? Why, you earn far more than papa ever did.' She tried to sound confident, but secretly she was frightened.

'My predecessor woke up one morning and found himself owing twenty-one years' salary.'

Sophy was too shocked to say anything. Her first response was embarrassment; she felt very small and foolish to have been so ignorant of such hazards. Another feeling overcame her almost as swiftly, as she tasted that exhilarating surrender to her own courage that she recognized from every time she'd risked her neck on horseback. Even now she didn't see hardship as something to be bravely endured. It was an obstacle to be run at, risking all with the rashness that – she knew – had been the main cause of her marriage.

Though she sat as still as a perfect reflection in a pool, her mind ran everywhere at once. She sensed the vibrant calm of someone aggressive enough to charge without a

211

care against any enemy. 'Then something *is* making you anxious?' She spoke with a tremor that he mistook for resignation.

'Don't think you should be afraid; I don't want that . . . There is one thing.'

'Tell me! What can *I* do?'

'I've had to meet some expenses from my own pocket – it's all right – the company has always paid in the past. The men who died in the landslip – they had to be given a proper burial and not just left to the parish. And there were medical expenses, too. And since then – there's a large piece of work that needs to be done again. Now I don't fear anything on account of this –'

'Unless –?'

'If we can't have Fitzpayne's land at a reasonable price, then – only then, you understand – the company may be unable to meet my expenses. And – darling, I have to tell you this – they would also have to make me liable for a much larger sum than I could meet.'

Sophy said nothing. Fraser, mistaking her silence for fear, was far sorrier for her than for himself. Exhausted, he finished labouring out of his clothes and stumbled into bed.

'And – what happened to Mr Benedict?'

'Mm?' With his head upon the pillow, all he could think of was sleep.

'After he went bankrupt.'

'What usually happens.' Fraser was too tired to feel anything but resignation. A moment of drowsiness touched him, as irresistible as if he were about to sleep for ever.

'What's that?'

'He went to prison. No one knows when he'll be freed.'

'I swear you even look like a schoolmistress now,' Sophy said. 'Dear Kate, how do you still bear it here?'

They were in the empty schoolroom of the Leggatts' house. Kate's time, when she wasn't teaching the two little girls, was not her own; instead, she had started to be employed by the household as a seamstress. Sophy, on

212

hearing that she was expected to do this work for nothing, had been angry enough to go to the Leggatts' behind her sister's back.

'You, Mrs Fraser?' Leggatt had said, eyeing her and putting himself out to be genial. 'Why, since you offer your own services too ... But you must be rewarded, you know. I shall certainly see to that.'

'So too must my sister,' smiling back at him with unspeakable deeds in her heart.

'Miss Byford's work is not good enough for payment,' Mrs Leggatt had put in.

'Then she shan't do it. I shall.'

The sum paid to each of them was paltry; but Sophy had still gained a victory. As much as anything, it was for the sake of each other's company, too, that the sisters now worked together for several hours a week. Today, a set of damask bed-hangings had to be re-seamed where they had been exposed to sunlight. The two girls were sitting with the fabric spread across a table, their fingers darting back and forth as swiftly as if they were musicians in performance.

Kate had come to treasure such times of tranquillity. With only a glance to make sure the door was closed behind them she said, 'I don't think too much of how I look. There's no one *here* whose good opinion I care about.' Her tone was passionless as, head bent, she worked nimbly on.

'I know, but ... how I wish you didn't look so ... stiff. I know you can't help being unhappy ...' Sophy trailed off, silenced by her own sympathy.

They worked on without speaking. At length Kate said in a low voice, 'Whatever my situation in this house, we can't be certain of not needing the money.' She paused in her sewing and looked up. 'Do you mind my asking ... Is James still likely to be in debt?'

'Perhaps, but ...'

'But what? Is it Lord Fitzpayne?'

'I suppose so.'

From Sophy's tone, Kate guessed she must be hiding something.

'Your plan of going to Mr Fitzpayne ... promise me –'

'Oh, Kate, do let it alone!'

'I know you wouldn't believe me before –'

'I said I didn't want to talk about it.'

'– but there are other stories. There's a particularly ugly tale about one of the kitchen maids –'

'Oh, for heaven's sake! Why must people always jump to conclusions about one? And why do you have to look so serious? It's almost like being nagged by mama. I swear I'm not sorry after all that I said you were like a school-mistress – I'm not, I promise you ...' Sophy tailed off into a mumble, and made a show of concentrating on her work.

'So you have been in communication with Mr Fitzpayne – you have!'

The warmth vanished from Sophy's naturally pale complexion. But she looked back at her sister without flinching. 'I will not just sit still and suffer whatever things other people care to do to us,' she said, in a small fierce voice. 'And if you think you can tell me otherwise, then I won't believe you even think of me as your friend!'

It was Kate's turn to blanch and pretend she hadn't heard. For a minute or so she went on working, dreading to say anything. Then with a motion of violence she got up and went to stand at the window. She trembled with frustration to find her eyes filling with tears.

'Oh, Kate! Oh, Kate! Oh! I didn't mean you to take it like that. I didn't mean it at all!' And Sophy ran to throw her arms from behind around her sister's waist and hide her face on Kate's shoulder.

'I don't care,' sniffed Kate through her handkerchief – there was no point now in pretending she wasn't crying – 'how like an elder sister I may sound. Only, please, *please* don't do anything to compromise yourself!'

'But, Kate – how could I compromise anyone, when all I want is to help my husband? Besides, you know I've never cared what our silly neighbours think!'

'It's not the neighbours. You can fall out with the whole parish for all I care. I wouldn't even mind what you thought of me. As long as – as long as – you didn't make an enemy of your own husband!' said Kate, fumbling for the words between sobs.

'Why –' exclaimed Sophy, stepping back to take a better look at her sister – 'how on earth should I do that?'

'Can't you picture him angry?'

'With me? How should I?'

'Not even with someone else, then? He came to see Mr Leggatt a few days back and you could hear their voices through two floors! I don't know if you're likely to be in love with him' – Sophy looked away, embarrassed at she knew not what – 'but if only he weren't a good man ... a good husband ... it wouldn't be so terrible to cross him. Just because I'm not married, too ... it doesn't mean I don't appreciate some of these things.'

'Oh, Kate!' Sophy said, embracing her again. 'I'm sorry you've been made so unhappy and you're still in love and everything – truly I am. But,' she added, as matter-of-fact as if she instead were the elder sister, 'I can't help it if you're jealous, can I?'

'Jealous of what?' asked Kate needlessly, in a wobbly voice.

'Why, you know.'

'I do not.'

'Yes you do. Anybody knows marriage is more than just the things it's proper to mention,' said Sophy with a maddening touch of complacency.

Kate wondered if she didn't want to slap her sister in the face. But the moment for answering back had already passed. They sat down and stitched on, as shaky, and as over-attentive to their work, as if both of them had been weeping.

After a while Sophy put her work in her lap and looked up. 'Would it make any difference,' she ventured to ask, 'if his wife' – neither ever mentioned Joseph by name – 'had been taken ill, too?' There had been an outbreak of yellow fever that summer in Richmond. A trading contact of Norton's, in writing to him of other matters there, had mentioned that the sickness had broken out in Joseph's own household.

'There's been worse news,' said Kate, biting through a piece of thread as if it were the limb of an enemy. 'aunt Norton wrote me last month that his wife had died.'

Sophy looked bewildered. Why had Kate held back such a thing?

'She's a fool,' Kate went on, with a look that dared her sister to murmur so much as a word. 'She thinks this gives me a second chance. To creep up and snatch at him, all smiles, I suppose. I wish to God the woman had lived. Or that he had died, too. What a cretin Aunt Norton is. Doesn't that stupid woman know how I'd dread to see him again? A man like that? What in heaven's name does she think I'd say or do? How does she think I could bear it?'

Kate was still smarting from her argument with Sophy when she found herself reminded of it. She was returning from an errand for Mrs Leggatt one evening, across a corner of the park. It was usually thought safe for any woman to walk there alone; but this time, seeing a man loitering under one of the avenues, she paused.

There had been rain earlier, and it was a sad, un-summertime light that fell on the wet grass and tossing trees. Shaded beneath a group of oaks, Kate felt confident of not being noticed. But should she be afraid anyway?

Looking more closely she decided maybe not. The man showed no sign of having seen her, and seemed in any case to be waiting for someone in particular. From his clothes it appeared he might be a gentleman ...

He idled, cigar in hand, out from the thicker gloom of the avenue – and Kate recognized Rawley Fitzpayne. Annoyance was her first response; at that moment she wasn't eager to be polite to anyone. She pondered whether avoiding the man was worth the trouble of going round by the highway. A couple of blackbirds nearby started plinking out their alarm call – and another figure appeared, walking fast, head down, as if uncertain whether to be seen. A woman; and no mistaking who. Kate stared, in a rage of dismay. It was Sophy.

A few feet from Rawley she stopped, as wary as a horse.

Their voices were inaudible; but it was clear he was the one with most to say. He circled her, trying to insist on something. Sophy appeared not to understand everything she heard. She hesitated between stepping closer to him, full of uneasy hope, and retreating. Her face, Kate knew, must be blushing as she looked up at him, frightened of somehow saying or doing the wrong thing. He moved nearer; looking hard in her eyes as he spoke, he put his hands on her shoulders. She made no move to avoid him. It was as if he could have used a weapon on her upturned face without destroying her anxiety to please.

He went on talking, demanding her agreement to something, over and over again. Eventually he did what could only have surprised Sophy herself. Still hectoring, regardless of anything she might answer, he pulled her against him. Perhaps she wavered – but in any case it would have made no difference. Sliding his arms around her, he locked her in what for want of other words could be called an embrace, and kissed her with the determination of wolfish indifference.

Chapter Twelve

Mr Leggat wee thought all of us Navvygators as how twas fitt to tell you now, Leggat, God damn you, that wee will meen you greevious ill for all that you have dun us rong. And you had not been gon from yor House, curse you, wee mite have dun it not won Day sinse now. But wee will do things to you and yors such as wee cannot say at this time, but wee will kill you you may not dowt us, and wot is more, wee will come after you with every sort of wepunn, and with pikaks handels and pistols too. So now you must be afeered, God curse you Leggat, for wee are resolved ther is nuthing now that you can do but to trembel at us all.

'Let me show you something,' said Leggatt, motioning Kate into his study off the big drawing room. 'You too, Mrs Fraser.'

217

What on earth was happening? As Sophy followed Kate into the room, Leggatt himself, a paper in his hand, was looking triumphant – while behind him his wife sat trying to conceal a fit of weeping.

He showed them the letter. 'You see what a rising man must contend with, if he is to achieve a certain style of living. And if I had failed to come up in the world, do you think the mob would still distinguish me with their hatred?'

His eyes sparkled; the prospect of conflict actually had him trembling with excitement.

'And I suppose the children and I are to linger here as blood sacrifices to these people of yours!' Mrs Leggatt exclaimed.

'Do you think my wife has any business to be afraid?' Leggatt asked Kate, with a quick look that was meant to show deference. He had not stayed disdainful toward her for long after Joseph's desertion; his own wife bored him too much for that.

'I think there's every reason to be frightened,' Sophy put in. 'The men who wrote this sound easily wretched enough to get themselves hanged.'

'Do you know, I always did wonder if you and your sister might not have Radical notions! – But don't worry,' squeezing her arm, 'in your cases I'm ready to make an exception. For you, I can pardon even that!'

'Mr Leggatt!' stormed his wife. 'You promised we could go away from here! Or did you only say so because you *didn't* mean it?'

'Upon my soul, I may have said something of the kind – but how should I know? What do you say, Miss Byford? Would it really be such a good scheme, to gad off to a watering place?'

'Why ever not?' Kate hoped neither of them could see that the thought of their absence made her rapturous.

'Why now, I do believe you could persuade me! But you must come too, if we are to go at all.'

'Oh no, sir, I had much rather not.'

'Nonsense! We couldn't leave you behind. You're

218

always too modest, you know. You're an asset. I mean that. One could be seen anywhere with a girl like you.'

Seeing Sophy glower, Kate checked her with a sharp look.

'She says she doesn't wish to go, Henry,' Mrs Leggatt said in a contained voice.

'Of course Miss Byford wishes to go – do you not?'

'No, thank you, sir.'

'You should like to go, truly; tell me you should.'

'No sir, I would rather stay near my family.'

'You wish to go; there can be no doubt of it.'

'No; I do not wish to go.'

'You wish to go with us to Cheltenham; I knew there could be no doubt of it.'

'Nothing, sir, could make me wish to go!'

'Very well; without you we do no such thing. It's settled: we stay.'

Mrs Leggatt stood up, pale about the lips, and pointed at Kate. 'I would not go in any case,' she said, shaking – she was so angry she could barely speak above a whisper – 'with your creature – she's your creature – I won't say what she is – I won't say what else she is –'

Kate made for the door. 'Shall we go?' she exclaimed, grasping Sophy's arm.

'No, by God, you will not leave!' exclaimed Leggatt. And seizing her he dragged her back. '*Now* you will see how I have to live!' All his self-satisfaction had been instantly displaced by ferocity. 'Now someone from outside this house' – gesturing at Sophy – 'as well as you can see how it is for me – manacled to *her* – to a woman whose only purpose is to destroy my self-esteem! Don't you dare touch her,' he snarled at his wife as she advanced to where Kate squirmed in his grasp. 'I dare you to come here and do her harm!'

The crash next door in the drawing room shook floors and windows throughout the house.

Even as they ran to see, half the servants were on hand as well, peering round various doors at the catastrophe. Mrs Leggatt hurried forward to examine what they were looking at – and started to shriek.

A splay of smashed glass lay across the carpet from the French windows to a deep new sofa with gilded griffin-head arms. Amid the sofa's striped rose-brocade cushions, almost as though nestling there, lay a dead dog with stiff sodden fur. It was weighted with bricks. Where its eyes had decomposed were two squeamish-making pits in the front of its head; and in the exploded flower-shape of its entrails a mass of maggots seethed.

Things had been better than Fraser had hoped.

He was making his way home one evening toward the very end of summer. At this season the shortening of the days was still at odds with the unbroken green of the elms overhanging the shaven cornfields; and brick walls facing west could give back the sun's heat a full hour after dark.

It was also the last of the day. Out in the lingering warmth the onset of night was hardly noticeable; but indoors it would already be dark. Somehow at this time, when all work had ceased, the countryside could seem more full of life than at any other hour. From half a mile outside Cannings Fitzpayne, now surrounded by new encampments of navvies and their families, several hundred voices sounded in the still air. Against their continuous murmur, it was the occasional raised voice of a woman that carried furthest; then groups of drunken men like fighting dogs; and here and there the flat, rather dismal eventide sound of an accordion and singing.

This was the hour, if any, for surveying one's achievements with relief. For Fraser, the question of Lord Fitzpayne's land still lay unresolved. But that was entirely in the hands of a jury – a body of men beyond his own power to influence. Otherwise, though, nothing threatened that he could not resolve by his own efforts. It was the first time for months, he realized, that he had ridden home with any feeling of satisfaction with his work.

Sophy was not there, to his disappointment. He still had to spend so much time away from the village, that they might go days apart from one another. In her absence Fraser consumed his supper of cold meats alone in the dining room by the light of a single candle. Then, still dwelling on details of good progress on the waterway, he went to finish some correspondence. His paperwork was done, when living at home, in the parlour, where a fire was lit for him most mornings at half past five. On his desk, Sophy's workbasket had been left on top of some books. In drawing out a paper from beneath them he spilt the whole pile, sending the little bobbins and pins and packets of whatever they could be, all over the desk-top and floor.

He stooped to pick up all his wife's mysterious bits and pieces – her silver thimble seemed scarcely big enough to catch a dewdrop – and carefully re-packed them in hopeless disorder.

Only then did he notice the Fitzpayne coat of arms.

It was on a piece of notepaper. The address was St James's Square; the date, not four days old.

Anybody watching Fraser as he read would at first have seen no change in him. His emotions ran too deep and were kept too much in check for that... The tone of Rawley Fitzpayne's letter was off-hand yet deeply intimate. Its subject was in places teasingly ambiguous; but the implications of what he read were so unbearable that to begin with Fraser merely understood the words without feeling anything at all. He forced himself to re-read the letter twice. Piecemeal all his protective numbness fell away, as a wounded soldier feels nothing more than strangeness at first, and discovers only by degrees that half his body has been blown away.

To begin with it seemed the worst thing was the references to himself. With what he recognized as a kind of tact, Sophy was being invited to share contempt for his own lowly origins. The everyday details of his scrambled, obsessive self-education were guessed at with a sureness he wouldn't have expected in someone so high-born ... But all this was forgotten as soon as he stopped to wonder what could be meant wherever his work itself was mentioned. What was all this? And – God in heaven! What could *she* have written, to provoke all these noises of clammy understanding, of lordly cajolery and flattering promises?

And worse than that – face it, now, like a man, he told

himself, almost aloud – what too could she have done? The possibility that she had been unfaithful – did it exist? – yes, yes, yes, of course it exists, you fool.

Wherever his mind dodged to avoid one source of pain, it collided with another. He felt as desperate as a man in a burning building who finds he can only flee the fire by jumping to his death.

He was still standing with the letter in his hand when Sophy came in. At first sight he looked shrivelled and ailing, as though facing his wrongs with the courage of a boy rather than the anger of a grown man. But Sophy, as he held the letter out, recognized the immovable hostility in his stare. Guessing at the rage about to break against her, she drew herself up in defiance. 'I did this for you!' was the first thing she could find to say.

'You did what? *What* did you do?'

She was panicked. Instead of trying to placate him, she met his freezing glare face-on. 'Everything I've done has been for you. Do you think I don't care what happens to us both, you stupid man?'

Even if she had pleaded, it might have been in vain. 'What I shan't forgive you,' he said in a level voice – the tides of outrage still had some way to rise in him – 'isn't that you've misjudged; nor that you've meddled; nor even that you've made yourself intimate –' Sophy started to protest; but he moved one step nearer as if to raise his fist, and she froze, ashen – 'made yourself intimate,' he repeated, 'with the scum of the earth. The reason I shall never forgive you is that you have acted behind my back. You have gone creeping after this man, to make him a present of my good name – yet I don't even care about that! – but you have run wheedling to make him an ally in destroying everything I've done. In secret! Because you think I'm not to be trusted with my own affairs. Because you think I'm an oaf whose company compromises you!'

It was impossible that Sophy should not feel every word. But as his voice rose, she grew more determined to justify herself. 'Someone had to do something!' she exclaimed. 'Somebody had to make themselves agreeable to the right people, before you just went bankrupt. And

222

even if it were true that you were too busy, it still had to be done by someone!'

Fraser couldn't bear to look at her. In the three days since he'd last been free to sleep at home, he had ridden more than a hundred miles. The suggestion that he had spared himself or courted failure left him unable to speak. He no longer cared if what he did now was unpardonable, nor even if he was in danger of hating her for ever. All he knew was that the harder he tried to spill out his growing rage, the less relief he got.

He strode from the room, pitching her aside with a movement of his arm.

'How dare you not answer me!' she cried. Her voice carried little conviction; she spoke really to persuade herself that she was angry, rather than dismayed. She ran after him. 'How dare you! If you weren't in the wrong, then you'd have an answer to give me!'

He turned on her, barely articulate. 'I could bear having a fool for a wife. But not a harlot!' And slamming the door he was gone from the house.

Alone in the parlour Sophy raged. Or so she told herself. Soon, though, with no thundering from her husband to contend against, she felt braced no longer. As yet she felt little remorse, for she could still not bear to look at any of her blunders that closely. But she was grieved beyond words that she and Fraser had wounded one another so. What though his suspicions of adultery were false? Even if she had betrayed him in that way, could things have been worse than they already were?

Her eyes lighted on the postscript of the hateful letter where her husband had thrown it on the floor. 'I yearn to see you again and play with your pretty little bubs.'

She shuddered, and ripped the paper across and across until it was in fragments no bigger than her own finger-nails. If only by destroying it she could ensure it had never been written! Not satisfied with tearing it up, she took a candle over to the fireplace and, with difficulty now the letter was in pieces, burned every scrap.

It was gone; yet with every minute she felt less relief, as

her mind ran over everything that had just happened. Sitting on the floor by the grate, stiff with misery, she ran her mind over every version of what might happen next. But try as she would, in none of them could she see herself wringing from Fraser one meagre symptom of love.

There was only one compensation; at least she had an idea where he might have gone. With Sophy, to think was to act; and within seconds she was running, bareheaded and in her indoor shoes, out of the garden into the lane. With the village now swollen to the size of a small town, there were few places left where anybody could be solitary. Sophy knew her way onto the down well enough to get there by night; and she was too stricken to have any fear of the dark.

Beneath a half-moonlit sky on whose horizons summer lightning flashed, she ran until she had to stop and fight for breath. But the nearer she came to finding her husband, the closer she must be to some worse, and final, rebuff. She hurried on to get it over with. As she scrambled up the long path beside Hychpen Bottom, tears broke from her. How much easier if strange men were to jump out of the shadows and do her to death after all. 'I'm sorry, I'm sorry,' she sobbed. If only she could stop living – just for a little while. It would be no more than she deserved. And then even if James did still hate her, at least she wouldn't have to know about it any more.

She was still thinking in this way as the path brought her to the prehistoric earthwork at the summit. The track passed at a bound over the old rampart – and Sophy, in the darkness almost cannoning into someone else, screamed with shock.

Fraser started too, though for all she could see with nothing more than unbearable irritation at finding her there. 'Yes?' His voice sounded with aggression – yet shakily, like someone else's.

'You didn't understand me,' she said faintly.

'No, God damn you! It is you who have failed to understand me!' He paused for breath. 'I will not go through my life carrying someone like you as a burden – as a makeweight that doesn't even think well of me!'

Sophy had run after him with no thought but reconciliation. She felt betrayed, now, that he didn't respond accordingly. Feelings of anger rose in her more readily than ever. 'If you can think so little of me so easily, why did you marry me?'

'God knows,' he answered, savouring his own cruelty.

'I've never been anything to you,' she shouted. 'All I've ever been to you is a pointless envelope to my – to the only part that interests you!'

He rounded on her and seized her by the arms, so that her feet almost left the ground. 'Now see you,' he breathed. 'When I married, I made over my whole life to you. You can take your precious cunt to Fitzpayne or any other cocksman you fancy. But don't you dare – don't you dare to tell me what I feel. I made over my life – I made a gift of a man's entire life to you, you stupid slut!' And he turned away as if he couldn't bear to speak another word.

How could Sophy fail to understand? How could she not have known it was despair rather than rage that had pulled his self-possession down around him in ruins? Alas, she had thought of him not just as a strong man but as one whose will nothing could shake. It never occurred to her that, thwarted by disaster, that very will-power might become a force that could break him.

As it was, all she could think of was to justify herself. In an anguished voice she cried, 'You wouldn't look away from me like that if –'

His body hunched, he spun round so suddenly she gasped. Now of all times she should have held her peace. But pride still made the words stumble out of her – pride, and the determination not to show herself afraid. 'You wouldn't look away from me now, if I meant anything at all to you.'

'Get away from me, before I break your neck, you fucking whore.'

Then it was, regretting the act even in the same moment, that Sophy did a dreadful thing. For no reason but to overcome her guilt, she hit him across the face.

His first blow brought the ground up to strike her

numb. She was too startled to cry out or even cower. Kneeling above her, feeble with rage, he hit her again and again across the head, until he scarcely had the strength to snarl or raise his hand.

He crouched, choking for breath. From around all the fires blinking in the dark down by the village, sounds of laughter and conflict could be heard. Leagues away, above the uplands of Salisbury Plain, the noiseless lightning darted to earth, more with a caress than a stroke. It lit him on all fours like a make-believe beast. Beside him, Sophy lay prostrate with shock.

He thought, at least there can be nothing worse than this. It seemed every drop of anger had been got from him, leaving nothing but hopelessness. Without a murmur, Sophy stirred, crawled clear of him, and staggered to her feet. If she leaves me now, he thought, and we never hear of each other again, would I care?

The answer was swift in coming. As, without a look, she turned to go, he raised a streaming face, and, against all the strength that he could find, the sobs tore themselves from him.

Sophy made an incoherent noise of protest and ran back. She too had thought there was nothing more to feel – but she had never seen a man weep before. The violence of it terrified her. 'Oh, God, no – please, please don't!' She bound her arms about him and groaned aloud in panic. 'Oh please – please, no! I never wronged you with that man – even if you don't care any more – I never did!' She clasped him tightly as if to root up all their grief by force. 'Let me do anything for you – I'll never see you again if you want – I promise – anything – only please don't!'

At length, with a sigh that sent a shudder through both of them, he mastered himself. He ceased weeping; but Sophy was beside herself in her anxiety to make amends. If only, despite the darkness, she could see his face! Was it possible that he should ever speak to her again? And if he had nothing but more words of hate, would she even mind, so long as he acknowledged her?

Under the lash of repentance, no one of Sophy's feel-

226

ings could care one jot whether she risked being ridiculous. She thought neither of her own pride, nor of his loathing, nor of anything he might do to make the memory of this moment even less endurable. Standing up, she made the only clumsy gesture of appeal that occurred to her. She seized her skirts and pulled them up above her waist. Beneath her petticoats she wore no more than any other woman in the land; so that now, trembling with hope and dread, she stood before him bare-arsed.

He should have been touched by her indignity. But there was still enough aggression in him to stop any pity no matter what she did. True, the unspeakable cruelty of rejection never suggested itself. What he did think to do, as he stumbled to his feet and seized her by the wrists, was to throw her down and fuck her in pure rage, as one might hurl oneself upon an unfeeling object until either it or oneself came to grief.

But he had failed to understand himself. Holding her down amid the plantains and sheep's droppings on the rampart's summit, what he felt as he went into her was not revenge but deliverance. She groaned, like someone suffering an excruciating release; and he paused, suddenly intent on her response. She moaned again, and strained against him in the dirt as he bent his head and rutted on her with fierce, swift, still-considered strokes, answering the frantic dinning of desire that boomed from her cunt right up into her throat. If she might only fuck more than just a man – if she could open her body to everything at once across the miles and miles of plain beneath them! If only it were all creation that strove and panted to rain blows into her while she sobbed and ground her teeth and shouted out at what was being done to her, again, and yet now, and again, in blinding explosions of darkness in her belly and beneath her feet! If she could perish, and not know that he would ever stop!

The ghostly axis of the globe, from leaning through her, heaved downward; and his business on her was nearly done.

They came down the hill without a word. It was the dead

227

middle of the night, with not a blindworm stirring and the moon setting like an expiring face. From a distance anyone seeing them, haggard to disfigurement, might think they'd shared some disaster, rather than catch any foolish look of triumph.

As the night lapsed toward first cockcrow, they crept to their room, each too used up to care if the bed had contained a stranger.

And slept, and nearly woke to the sound of all the village talking as it came out of church into a late bright Sunday morning, and slept again, and woke.

Not to dwell happily on their reconciliation. But to an urgent summons, several times repeated.

'What is it, mama?' Sophy asked round the door, trying to look serious.

'Oh, Sophy, you should have woken up, you know. There's a man in the kitchen from Mr Rennie being given breakfast now. But I'm to say he won't go until Mr Rennie's letter has been acknowledged.'

Closing the door, Sophy tossed the letter onto the bed and sidled back between the sheets. They took the chance of looking at each other for the first time that morning. More than anything, it was solemn relief that shone in their faces; catastrophe had come too close for them to feel complacent. Fraser opened the letter.

He read it, and almost invisibly recoiled. For several seconds he sat without moving. When at last he spoke his voice was expressionless. 'Have you much jewellery?'

'What you've given me. Why?'

'Make a present of it to your sister for safekeeping.' He paused, his mind working over she knew not what. 'You must give your clothes to her as well – all but what you choose to put on at the time – and wear them only on loan from her. You should also make an inventory today of all your other possessions – since legally every petticoat of what you have is mine – and make some arrangement for those ... I shall sell the horses and anything else I can think of, and your mother must invest the money on her own behalf. She will have to be the one, now, to provide for you if you're pregnant.'

'Oh, but I'm –'

'From last night,' he said, his thoughts elsewhere.

'But what's happening?'

'It may be some days before there are men in the house to list the things they'll take away. But I can't be certain how soon we'll be separated. So you must lose no time in saving what you can.' Seeing her face he stopped to explain. 'The appeal against Fitzpayne has failed. I'm bankrupt.'

Chapter Thirteen

Rawley Fitzpayne, lounging homeward one morning in the direction of St James's Square, looked preoccupied. There were lawyers in the house in town, and on terms that might leave any fellow, whose inheritance was insecure, feeling cursed ill at ease. Who could have foreseen the change that had taken place in his life? And what was worse, who could tell what might come of it?

Brooding thus, he turned a corner into a street where even at this hour the whores were numerous enough for respectable women to walk warily down one side only. From habit he eyed the day's offerings. Not a bad class of cunt round here. Expensive enough, some of them, to be almost plainly dressed. Not what you'd hope to get in any decent theatre, but a damn sight more worth poking than on the same pavement after sunset.

If his heart had been in anything, he reckoned, there would have been one or two he wouldn't have minded himself, even at twenty guineas or more. Prime veal cutlets, as good as untouched. He stared absently at one flower-faced girl aged sixteen or so who was crossing from a hackney coach to a well-known house, followed by a stooping man of distinguished appearance.

Rawley hadn't had her himself; that he knew. For one thing, her face didn't fit his knowledge of that part of town. So . . .

Three turnings on he had it. Charity Michaelmas! *That*

was who he'd just seen! The trollop dismissed from the Hall with a big belly from George Byford. God damn her eyes, he thought, but the cunning slut must have come up in the world, to be working in that particular street.

Did she look better for it, or worse? Rawley, having in mind her feathered bonnet and embroidered gloves, was in no doubt. The sly bitch had fallen on her feet in every way. Michaelmas! Well he was damned!

The scene of preparation outside the Fitzpayne mansion drove the girl, and anything else, out of his mind.

Lord Fitzpayne had ordered nearly half the household in readiness to leave that same morning for Wiltshire. He and Rawley were to stay in town; but over two days a whole train of vehicles had been assembled in the mews, to convey all the luggage and servants that were to go down to the country with young Lady Fitzpayne.

Rawley had been almost unable to believe his bad luck. That the old fart should marry again – and to a fecund-looking mare of twenty-two! His uncle might only have to heave himself onto her for one half-dead-and-alive encounter – and Rawley would be dished, his inheritance snatched from him and all his years of clambering up his lordship's arse gone for nothing.

God knows why being cuckolded is reckoned so damned hard to take, he thought, making his way upstairs. How could any fool grieve over losing exclusive access to some woman, when he himself might be expected to look cheerful at bidding farewell to a prospective rent-roll of fifteen thousand a year?

In the library his discontent reached a climax as he discovered his new aunt was there. Lady Augusta, dressed for travelling in a swansdown-trimmed pelisse, was seated by the further fireplace. One hand was held out to the warmth of the coals, while with the other she dallied through a novel. They managed an acknowledgement without actually looking at each other, and Rawley, having rung for strong coffee and a plate of eggs, loitered toward the big bay window at the back of the room.

His uncle had of course been particular in his choice. The woman was well-born and expensively educated. She had been suddenly penniless, too, which was doubtless expected to make her the more deferential toward her new lord and master. And physically she was more than passable. Rawley, who looked at any woman to fault her rather than admire, examined Lady Augusta's slender figure and heavy red-gold hair in a spirit of frustration. No doubt she was apt to get freckles if she went out in the sun – yet that wouldn't hinder the getting of an heir. And her body would surely grow ugly with a pregnancy or two – but wasn't that the one thing he wanted not to happen? For that matter the marriage couldn't succeed – the servants were already whispering that the woman had a temper. Yet how could that save his own prospects, if she'd given birth?

The footman came in bearing Rawley's breakfast.

'Can you tell me where his lordship is?' Rawley made a point of speaking loudly enough for Lady Augusta to hear and so mark that he had not asked *her*. Her frigid self-control notwithstanding, he saw her eyes narrow as she ceased to read.

Lord Fitzpayne was still with the gentlemen from the Temple, came the reply.

The mention of the lawyers made it Lady Augusta's turn to gloat. As the footman left the room she looked up at the man's back, her glance far too bright for any other meaning. Rawley suspected that the servant too was amused at his own discomfiture. God damn it, the whole household was diverting itself at his expense! Even now the lawyers might be drawing up some document that would disinherit him if the woman bore so much as a female brat. Or if she merely pulled off the master-stroke of an early widowhood!

She read, and he ate and drank. Each was acutely aware of the other, though determined not to show it. After some minutes the doors were thrust open and Lord Fitzpayne came in.

Rawley and Lady Augusta looked up, attentive. His lordship made as if to speak to Lady Augusta, then paused. He was clearly waiting for Rawley to cease intruding on them both.

Privately cursing his uncle for an oppressive old fool, Rawley hastened out of the room. Lady Augusta sat, meanwhile, with downcast eyes, a model of discretion. All right, you slut, thought Rawley, you needn't think he'll deal any better with *you*. He knew from experience that his lordship saw every personal relation in terms of power. Rawley was sharp enough, too, to guess that the hostility between himself and his new aunt was being used by Lord Fitzpayne – to play them off if possible one against the other.

The doors closed behind the young man, and Lady Augusta waited. Lord Fitzpayne paused for several seconds, to show the rightness of what he was about to say, before coming straight to the point. 'You will oblige me, when you are in Wiltshire, by bearing in mind that you are not in residence at Cannings Fitzpayne as just anyone of rank. You will be there not in your own right, but, as my wife, as someone of far greater consequence.'

She said nothing, but met his look without a tremor.

'You will be regarded by everyone there with whom you deal, as nothing less than my representative. In everything you do –' she had not contradicted him by so much as a look; yet he spoke as if she had – 'yes, in everything – you will behave according to others' expectations of *me*. You will not, as I believe you have done, entertain a notion of riding to hounds. That is for people's wives who cannot hope to maintain a public reputation. You will receive, and visit, only as I would: I expect to be reassured that you see no one I do not receive already. Otherwise I cannot think there is anyone with whom you need to continue an acquaintance.'

She flushed, possibly from anger, and said, 'Of course you do not include my own family. I know you have never been intimate with them –'

He answered her in a low voice, but with an intensity one might not expect in such a gross, frog-faced man. 'And should I have?' He paused, staring at her. 'Do you desire to tell me how I should have ordered my life?'

She looked back at him, hard-eyed as a bristling cat.

'I did not require a wife who would produce a dowry,'

he went on, shifting to a voice of strained reasonableness. 'I was prepared to think nothing of the fact that you could only bring with you a train of dependent aunts or what have you.' There had been a grandmother and a spinster sister, as well as Lady Augusta's widowed mother. 'But now that I have chosen to provide for these women, can you tell me how receiving an allowance entitles them to further claims? – To my hospitality, in fact?'

A footman came in, evidently to deliver a message. Lord Fitzpayne, staring his wife in the face without speaking, made a point of ignoring the man until he had started to go out again, his errand uncompleted. 'One other thing,' his lordship added – and then turned to where the door was closing behind the servant. 'Yes?' he bellowed, with a display of anger at not having been given the message.

The footman, who was resigned to the ways of the household, came back, and announced that the horses were ready. Lord Fitzpayne, having heard him, waved him away with a gesture of annoyance at having been disturbed.

'One other thing. You will do me the courtesy of dressing as I see fit. I am the person who supports you. And for that reason you owe it to me only to wear what I will pay your dressmaker to supply. When in public you will have no further use for your other things. And do, for God's sake, get rid of those damned yellow beads you were sporting yesterday. I can't have people imagine that I can't give you better than that.'

'The amber necklace was given me by papa,' she replied, in a hard unshaken voice.

He ignored her; yet she persisted. 'You never told me why I must go to the country ahead of you.'

Her question was futile, of course. Without a word he rang for his nephew; and together they waited, like a pair of dignified mutes, for Rawley to reappear and acknowledge his aunt's departure.

In fact Lady Augusta knew why she was being dismissed early to Cannings Fitzpayne. All through her chilly farewells – first with Rawley, then with her husband

– she sought some comment she could make on her unjust banishment. If her husband could only see his own absurdity! An old man, married to a girl; and too jealous even to let her go into company. A blubbery old man, with a body like a diseased bull seal, who turned nasty if anyone so much as spoke to her. Be damned to the old fool, she thought, as she followed the servant down to where the berline was waiting.

Outside the great house, the array of equipages drawn up for her would, a few weeks before, have given Lady Augusta a thrill of triumph in the wealth and power they represented. In addition to her own carriage the family coach and six was there, with two postilions and three outriders to go ahead and smooth their progress through turnpikes and coaching yards. So too was the barouche-landau, with four horses and a liveried escort, and a chaise-marine attended by two grooms and followed by a pair of stablemen armed with blunderbusses. All these vehicles were needed to carry the indoor servants, and the plate and linen, needed for the journey – not to mention the twelve trunks containing Lady Augusta's trousseau.

Before a crowd of onlookers the line of carriages clanged and clattered out of the square and through the half mile of streets that separated it from where the country began.

'That's a high-tempered one you've got there, and no mistake,' confided one of the footmen to Miss Hodgkiss where they sat up on the rumble of the big family coach.

'I couldn't say as to that.' For the sake of her own status, Miss Hodgkiss had transferred her fierce allegiance to their new mistress without a blush.

'I've heard stories of that one already, I have.'

'What stories?'

'Such as I wouldn't choose to repeat to a person of refinement like yourself.'

'My lady would never give cause for twaddle like that.'

'Maybe she would – and then maybe not. What I do say is, *he* needn't think he'll miss trouble by letting one like her out of his sight.'

South of Upstowe one autumn day the highway was an extraordinary sight. It was choked with groups of people, many of them families, making their way alongside a stream of wagons, carts and gigs. Most vehicles were bursting full, their passengers' heads waggling in unison every time the wheels hit a pothole. Among the water meadows and hedgerows of the Vale, there were knots of people joining the road from nearby field-paths. But once up on the downs, the mass of traffic rumbled across a landscape as empty as the sea. Any shepherd, seeing this crowd straggling from one horizon, might have thought a new invasion scare had put the whole county to flight.

A closer witness would have seen that these folk were on their way to a festival. Even the humblest wore their Sunday clothes; and there were sounds of drunkenness from several vehicles. Beside the country people to be seen about the lanes at any season there were others: a peep-show man and his ragamuffin helper; an itinerant fiddler; a print-seller; a party of gypsies; one or two soldiers; the odd pedlar; and even a travelling waxworks show.

Sophy was relieved to know that though travelling alone, she would be inconspicuous in such a mob. She was on her way to lodgings in Salisbury, where Fraser was being held in the house of the local bailiff's officer; for it might be some time before he was taken away, to London and a debtors' prison. There had been little money to spare, of course, for her fare. So now she sat, in her hardest-wearing outdoor clothes, up beside the driver of a carrier's van from Upstowe.

The man was as cheerful as anyone about them, and talked a great deal. 'Aye, well, mind we did have a whipping down Upstowe way once,' he was saying. 'It were for vagrancy or some such. 'E were tied up to a cart-tail, o' course, and our hangman – our old hangman, that was – whipped him all the way through the town and back again. And all us folk got together and gave the hangman extra to whip him harder, 'cause of how we didn't get many whippings. Besides, we knew the feller too, and knew as he was a rogue. Trouble was, we had such a damned rheumaticky old hangman, we might as well have saved our money.'

Sophy could guess why his talk ran on such subjects for miles at a time. All these people were, of course, out for the day to see a hanging.

Toward noon the road brought them down over the town bridge into the tight little streets of Salisbury. Though a city, whose cathedral bore the finest spire in England, the place was scarcely bigger than a prosperous village. The great inns around the main square were the size of palaces; but the downs looked over almost every roof, and from most corners you might see haystacks at the end of the street.

The crowds were out of all proportion to such a place. They were bound for the square, where, gathering fast, they formed a mob that roared and strained and swayed in a mass so dense that even a frightened horse might be held prisoner in it. There were faces bursting from every upstairs window, whether in public houses or dignified private dwellings. Toward the centre of the square was a circular rank of vehicles, including several splendid family coaches.

'And it's a creature as deserved it, if anyone did,' said the carrier to Sophy. 'A highwayman he were. You wouldn't credit it, not in times like these, you wouldn't. The two with him, they got themselves shot before this feller, he shot that Farmer Woodeson, as he was called, now – before this feller shot the farmer back. If you don't believe me, it's all in them pamphlets they're selling here today. I saw the man over there with them just now – over by the Golden Cross he was.'

His eagerness was something Sophy had never seen. The prospect of a death violent enough to climax all the other peepshows in the town had him as raffish as a boy of ten. 'If you got down now,' he said, 'you might get lost. And if I was a betting man I'd wager you'd never hope to get another view like this. I would now, believe me.'

On the parish church the clock struck the three-quarter hour. For a few seconds the noise of the crowd and the shouting of piemen and knick-knack vendors around the gallows foot was almost stilled. It was as though an introductory announcement had been made.

As the hour approached, the tumult in the square increased, until, mounting without any change of pitch or feeling, it heralded the execution party itself.

'Look you now,' bawled the man at Sophy above the racket. 'That's them! That's them! You can tell 'tis them – it must be – now I promise 'tis them now. You take care you look, mind; they be coming through the crowd this instant!'

A cart came into view, the crowd parting eagerly to let it through. A number of young lads, darting into the space, tried to make a self-important show of leading the horse, while the driver cursed them and laid about with his whip.

'I can't see him! I can't see him!' exclaimed the carrier above the roar of the mob. 'Why don't they stand him up? Ah, now there he is! Why, what an ordinary dull creature he looks, to be sure! He don't look as if he could even wave to us. I can't picture one like him doing anything so special as a murder, let alone him owning pistols and a saddle-horse like a gentleman would.'

The cart reached the gallows; and the condemned man was led up the scaffold steps, a clergyman following. A sudden silence rang through the square, except for one or two drunken cheers from the edges of the crowd where the gallows couldn't be seen. Sophy almost squeaked out loud as her arm was seized hard enough to turn her fingers white. Her companion was about to say something. His breath was in her face; but his eyes were on the centre of the square. The silence broke, to a riot of catcalls and booing; and he let go of her. 'No speech! He's not made a speech!' he exclaimed. 'I thought they always made a speech. Upon my soul, I did.'

The clergyman finished what he had to say to the condemned man, and the racket of execration and cheers died down again. Among the onlookers in the next cart two children were being supported by their parents so that they could stand on its rim for a better view. They watched with vacant-looking curiosity as the rope was put about the highwayman's neck to the sound of a blackbird singing two streets away.

'Now you watch,' whispered the carrier. 'He'll most likely go as quick as can be. But if he don't – *then* we'll see how little he thought to bribe them gaolers!'

The hangman stationed himself to release the trap.

Sophy sneezed, with a dainty catlike sound that could be heard from every attic window in the square. At the same instant the highwayman fell his own length into eternity with a bang, and a growl of released excitement broke from the crowd.

Almost as quickly, the gaolers were at work cutting down the body from beneath the trap. Everywhere the sound of talk grew louder. The couple next to Sophy were smiling and appealing to their children for approval of the scene. They looked as though they'd just run a victorious race.

Something more was due to happen. Not even the street urchins perched in the churchyard trees were ready to go just yet. Sure enough, the noise of the crowd fell to a whisper once it was clear another death was imminent. The gallows were made ready again; and as the highwayman's body was taken away, nearly ignored even by onlookers pushed aside to let it pass, another cart came into view.

This time few people cheered. There was a feeling that the serious business of the day was only beginning.

In the trees by the church one of the local small fry let rip a catcall. 'Shame on you!' responded a woman's voice.

'Be damned to the lot of you!' swore a man nearby. Somewhere in the crowd a woman could be heard sobbing. One of the urchins started to parody her in a joyous falsetto until shouted down by a chorus of angry voices.

Sophy stood on tiptoe to look at the hangman's cart. An unreasonable thought fastened on her imagination. *They've caught Charity Michaelmas.* It was only an absurd fancy, of course. There, being read at by the clergyman, sat some completely different girl of sixteen. There was something everyday about her swollen, tearstained face, as though she believed that if only she said sorry in the right way for whatever naughty thing she'd done, it could be forgotten. She looked as if she'd been neatened up for the occasion by someone else.

'Pa,' said one of the small boys next to Sophy.

'Quiet, you,' in a voice of concentration.

'Pa!'

'Be quiet!'

'Ma,' demanded the other boy.

'Be quiet. What's the matter with you?'

'What did *she* do?'

'Shush. Just watch, will you?'

'Did she shoot someone, too?'

'She killed her little baby, so now she must be punished. Just be quiet, now we've brought you all this way.'

Sophy seized her things and climbed down. She was filled with the frigid self-possession that sometimes goes with pure rage. Dizzy with anger, she thrust her way through the mob until she reached a side street. Only then did she begin to run, to get away before the roar of all those people should rise up and overwhelm her.

'Where be that young girl?' the carrier asked his neighbours a minute or so later. The crowd, its great moment past, was breaking up and trying to laugh itself back to normal.

'I don't know. Perhaps it was her first time. T'ain't everyone as thinks they can enjoy to watch them hang a wench.'

In her haste to run from such a shaming sight, Sophy had had no idea where she was bound. The streets vanished, and she found herself in the river meadows behind the cathedral. During she knew not how long she paced about a public walk beneath an avenue, unwilling to go back while the city hangman might be about his work.

What she had seen removed the last shred of fear or sadness for herself and her own ill luck. She was scourged by a sense of righteous fury that, as she walked up and down seeing nothing of where she was, settled to a feeling she had never known before. For the first time in her life the pity welling in her, at that one glimpse of a stranger, had nothing to do with the unfairness of things. Hitherto, Sophy had either not noticed other people's hardships, or they had made her sad and angry, as something that might befall her, too. Now, at last, she tasted a feeling that had nothing to do with herself. It was one thing to be frightened for her own future seeing someone she knew, like Charity Michaelmas, begging in the street. But not when faced with that girl in the hangman's cart, at the lowest ebb of wretchedness.

As the day declined and the crowds streamed, then dwindled, out of the city, Sophy made her way back. It occurred to her, expecting to see her husband for the first time since he became a prisoner, that even her sympathy for him had been lacking. His misfortunes, after all, were mostly hers too, so that she had had no choice but to face them. She had been ready to be stoical on her own account; but she had never once thought what it must be like for him, at twenty-one, to be shut away without even a convicted criminal's certainty of one day being freed. The thought filled her not with shame so much as a solemn eagerness to see him as soon as possible and start to make amends. She looked calm, if thoughtful, as she presented herself at the sponging-house where he had been taken.

'I don't know what good you think it'll do you, coming here,' said the woman in charge, holding the street door ajar. She clearly didn't mean to invite Sophy one step beyond the pavement.

'I've no intention of asking for lodging-room. Would you show me where my husband is, please?'

The woman looked her disbelief of Sophy being lawfully wed, even to a pauper. 'You won't find no husband of yours in here.'

Trying, for Fraser's sake, not to repay this show of scorn in kind, Sophy repeated his name. The woman indicated, with a motion of her head, that she should come in, if she must. She shuffled in front of Sophy along a passage narrow enough to brush both elbows at once. In silence she opened a door, casting a look at the girl to show that this was the room, and still without a word, shut it behind her and went away.

The place was lit by one candle. In the sudden draught, the shadow of Sophy's own head, monstrously big, leaped to and fro against the ceiling. Fraser turned swiftly as she went in. For some time he had been doing nothing but pace softly across the room and take three careful strides back again, all the while absently striking a clenched fist against his palm.

They looked at each other uncertainly. Fraser was especially unsure of what he should say or do. The thought that plagued him most at this moment was, how could he and his wife talk together amid so much noise? Through two of the walls, children could be heard crying, and in an echoing place below, there were shouts and clattering noises, as of women at work. A few feet over their heads, in an upstairs room, a man and woman were quarrelling ferociously.

To hide his unease, Fraser embraced Sophy, clasping her to him so hard that she half choked. Above them the woman's voice rose to a scream. 'You did say you would! You promised me! Damn you! Damn you!'

He released her, and they both began to talk at once – about any unimportant thing they could think of – just so that they could ignore where they were. How had Sophy's journey been? – How sorry she was not to have brought any letters! – What letters? – Why, any; none in particular ... And so on, their voices raised to match the surrounding noises of anger and toil.

Sophy didn't care to speak of what she'd witnessed in the town square. But the scene was still with her as vividly as if one of themselves stood condemned. She stepped back and looked up at her husband. 'James – tell me what I should do to help you. I know you can't guess how long you might be in prison; but *I'm* free. Just tell me, and I'll do it. I know you've thought – I mean recently – that I haven't had your own needs at heart. But – truly – I feel as sorry for you as you could yourself – indeed I do.'

She trembled with the sincerity of what she said. Tears

came into her eyes as she reached out to embrace him again.

'Don't touch me!' With a violent motion he turned aside from her, as though to get as far away, in that small space, as he could. She looked on, suddenly ashen-faced, but still not understanding, while he paced and dithered and exclaimed with rage, as if nerving himself to run straight out through the wall. At length, in a voice it cost him to keep low and steady, 'Of course there's nothing I want you to do! – No! I don't even want you to speak to me –' as, astonished, she started forward to say something. 'How the devil can you talk like such a fool? If there's nothing I can do to save myself, how in God's name do you think *you* can do anything?'

His fury left her dumb. They stood apart, avoiding each other's eyes, as the woman upstairs wept, lifting up her voice and pouring herself into one long roar after another.

After a while he turned wearily. At the sight of Sophy's pinched, unresponsive face he hesitated, then moved closer to her. 'Let me tell you,' he said, as quietly as the place allowed, 'how it is with me here.' Though they stood near enough for the hem of her dress to touch him, still they felt unable to look each other in the face. 'It's not just myself that I've got into trouble. I know I ought to say that I don't care too much on my own account – that if I'd brought only myself down to this, I could bear it. Well, I can't bear it, as it turns out – but that's not what matters most. The worst thing is that by being imprisoned I've got you into trouble, too. The truth is, I was weak when I took you for my wife. I did what I wanted, without thinking. I should never have married you. No –' as she made as if to disagree 'I'm not saying so on impulse. I've thought about little else since I was brought here.'

She was mute, searching for words. Seeing her softened look, he seized her hand. 'Forgive me,' he mumbled, bowing his head. Frowning, he held her clasped hand to his brow, his eyes shut. Sophy gazed at him in dismay. She would far rather be shouted at than see such a proud – an obstinate – man made too miserable to speak.

'You've done nothing you should ask me to forgive,' she

said. 'If you weren't in debt, then you wouldn't regret being married?'

'No.' He kissed her hand and looked at her. 'You do know I didn't come courting just because I desired you? More than once, you've said things that made me to wonder ...'

'Oh!' Sophy groaned aloud at the memory of their quarrel. 'Oh, no! No – no! I didn't mean ... anything I might have said. Truly I didn't. Only –'

'What?'

'I felt so guilty – Oh no, not because of that horrible man,' flinching at the thought of Rawley Fitzpayne. 'I mean, because I thought perhaps *I* shouldn't have married *you*. Tell me – you didn't choose me just because you felt sorry for me?'

'No. Why should I have?'

'We were so poor. And' – correcting herself hastily at the sight of the squalid room where they now stood – 'I thought that you imagined I couldn't bear it.'

He looked at her, not understanding. Sophy felt herself drowning in shame: even now, he hadn't guessed how desperate for escape she had been when she'd married him in order not to be poor. To hide her thoughts she added, with a grim little smile, 'And of course, you could hardly have wanted me because you were ambitious.'

'Ambitious?' still with a frank stare of incomprehension.

'Oh, good heavens!' with an unhappy laugh that showed only part of how deeply embarrassed she was. 'A joke – I meant that as a joke! I wanted to say, I couldn't have brought you a huge dowry, could I? And without that, what good is any woman who's been brought up to do nothing? But' – with a tremble of fervour in her voice – 'I will learn to be poor!'

He was still frowning as he gazed at her – but only from anxiety, to understand everything she might say. 'All I wanted was you,' he said. 'I would have wanted you no matter how you'd been brought up. I never stopped to think of anything else – until later.'

Sophy was silenced, overcome by humiliation and relief. That she should have gained a good man's love in return for so little – almost by accident! How could she have guessed that she had come here to be so happy?

'But,' he said, 'you haven't told me why you felt guilty. At marrying me.'

She drew a deep breath and looked away from him. 'I always knew – really – that you loved me. And somehow that made it worse ... No – no; that's not what I meant –'

'But you did want to marry me?' in a quickened voice. He looked aghast.

'Oh, yes! It seemed inevitable – no, I mean obvious – oh, no, I mean the natural thing to do. But so many people had told me how I ought to live – and I tried to listen to all of them. And all the time I was wondering if I was doing right. And though I know now that I was, all that time I was terrified. I'm so ashamed ... '

Fraser put his arms around her, to reassure both of them, and let slip a long sigh, like someone who has just escaped a fatal accident. They held each other in silence. At length he said, 'There is something else I'd like to ask you.'

She looked up at him. 'What?'

'Would you be willing to go on being my wife – would you agree to live with me? I mean in London, when they take me there ... I suppose I ought to say, for good. It could be done – if you could bear it.'

Her face was bright with certainty. 'Of course I would. I couldn't bear not to!'

'It may be worse than this. I don't mean the place where we'll live. But ... prison life ... If I'm vile-tempered now, who knows what sort of a husband you'll find in me ere long?'

'Don't say that; there's no question of us living apart. But when will they take you away from here?'

'They won't tell me. I shall write you, though, when I'm due to go.'

'Where will we be, in London?'

'In the King's Bench Prison. I don't much want to talk about it.'

He embraced her again, and they clung to each other.

244

They were too saddened to feel much desire, even in one another's arms. It was a moment to be treasured, for all that. Sophy couldn't help feeling the full truth of what her husband said – that they might find each other hard to live with – to like, even – over so many years of imprisonment. They had come to understand each other, and be happy together, at last. But could it always be so? As she shut her eyes against the shadows of the place where they stood, she willed herself to hold this house, and this room, in her memory for ever.

'I tell you as how things can't go on like this.'

In the kitchen at the Hall, this, from Mrs Beamish the chief undercook, met a mixed response.

'So how come her ladyship's not been called to heel already?' asked Mr Freeman. As steward he was much torn between economizing on the household and keeping up its dignity.

'Oh, you'll soon see her stopped from frittering, I'll be bound,' said Mrs Beamish. With her stubby arms and small fists she was going like a prizefighter at a pastry strip nearly five feet long. It was to top a pigeon pie. Tonight, for once, young Lady Fitzpayne was dining alone, her leavings destined, at the steward's table, to fill another half-dozen mouths.

'Frittering isn't in it,' said Mr Freeman. 'She's more like driving a coach and four through this establishment's accounts. That hunt dinner, now: you should know what that cost, what with a field of sixty at table for five hours.'

There was a chorus of grunts and sighs. Now day was dwindling, Miss Hodgkiss and Mr Johns the under-butler were there too, lurking by the kitchen's ale-barrel.

'But you can't begrudge her ladyship her day's sport,' said Miss Hodgkiss. 'And her so fine on horseback, too.'

'Oh, aye; the woman's got the nerve of the devil in the field, I don't deny.'

'If I had a horse break its neck right under me, I couldn't just up and gallop off again, I tell you,' Mrs Beamish said, her attention only half on the conversation. Out of the corner of her eye she was watching Sally Dace, who'd been given the job of dressing half-a-dozen wood pigeons. 'But I did hear, as that John Jakes come up with her spare horse, to find her standing by – all impatient, if you please – and the beast sobbing its life out like it was a mortal soul. He said, he helped her up on her new one, with all those skirts of hers and that, and he's blowed if she don't go off another fifteen miles, just –'

Her busy calmness vanished as she heard a dry spattering sound on the floor behind her. 'Lord's sake, girl! Be you an even greater fool than what you make out? Now, what have you done wrong? Just tell me that.'

'I cut its stomach, m'um.'

'Of course you have. And now you got a quarter pound of corn all on that floor. You ought to know them birds has got full crops this time of year.'

Dace, looking hangdog, went to fetch a broom, and the conversation resumed.

'It's not even the money her ladyship gets through,' Mr Freeman said. 'Leastways, if *I* was her husband that wouldn't be the first thing.'

'Do you say so?' said Mrs Beamish, neatly blobbing the pastry in rows with pork dripping.

'What would that be, then?' asked Mr Johns, who till now had been loitering nearby without speaking.

'She reckons on doing more theatricals.'

'Oh, is that all!' said Miss Hodgkiss. She gave a glance, however, in the direction of Mr Johns, whom she distrusted as a creature of Lord Fitzpayne.

'But look you,' insisted Mr Freeman. 'Last time's caperings was bad enough. And she needn't think his lordship won't hear of *them* any day now.'

'Aye,' said Mrs Beamish. 'And what a numskull going-on that was!' She paused to flour her hands again. 'Her ladyship should know she can't hate him out loud. Not in public, she can't. They say his first wife did that, to start with ...'

'But she must be daft,' Mr Freeman said, 'to try a mummery like that. Dressing up *that* one, in a costume made of old curtains –' motioning, voice lowered, to where Dace was coming back – 'and all those other stupid wenches, to dance round in the dark while she burns a likeness of her own husband.'

'Aye, that were sorry of her, right enough,' agreed Mrs Beamish. 'Fancy thinking as that lot wouldn't titter at her – not even behind her back – and then to run about striking at them and yelling!'

'If you ask me,' Mr Johns said, 'the best thing she can do for herself is to start showing a big belly from him. If she's got one in there, it can't be long ere we see something for it.'

With a deft unconscious movement, Mrs Beamish folded the pastry strip in on itself to make a block. 'No, she b'ain't expecting. If she were, she'd not be eating like she does, I tell you.'

'It's him, then,' smirked Sally Dace, looking up from sweeping the floor. 'He can't do it!'

'You be quiet and clean that up! You be behindhand as it is.'

'But ... just supposing she's not,' Miss Hodgkiss ventured. 'I'd be certain it's not her fault. Say what you will, he has lived three times as long as her; and they were saying in the London house how he was troubled with pains all down one side.'

' 'E wouldn't let that stop him,' Dace tittered. 'It don't take arms and legs and such, to do a job of work like that!'

Miss Hodgkiss and Mrs Beamish gave her a look, and she lapsed into solemnity. 'I'll wager, though, her ladyship'll have to present him with a boy before many months are out,' Mr Freeman said. 'Else, her play-acting follies or no, he'll make her feel the worst of him ...'

The October evening darkened, its hint of winter unfamiliar. The pigeon pie, with two other meat courses and an apricot tart, were served in order due in Lady Fitzpayne's apartment. Then, a corner missing from each, they were removed to the upper servants' table to be finished off. From nightfall to nine o'clock, below stairs was a scene of gossip and jollification. At length, in the rooms being lived in, log fires were doused; the head groom had made his round of the stables; and, from

247

outside, the great house seemed full of motion as the glow-worm light of candles was borne hither and thither toward bedchambers and attic rooms.

Two lights remained, after all the others were snuffed out. One shone in Lady Fitzpayne's apartment; the other, fifty yards of corridor and stairs away, was in the room where Mr Johns slept. Both these people were writing: Lady Fitzpayne with headlong speed, at a desk whose contents overflowed into a suburb of papers around her chair; and Mr Johns with frequent pauses while he scribbled a word or phrase on a separate sheet and frowned at it.

... as I appreciate your lordship knows, it can be no part of my intentions to displease your lordship. But yet I see it as my duty to bear in mind that nonetheless your lordship did expressly desire me to report to you – should the occasion arise – on domestic events here in your absence. I mean to say, among other things, of course, how my lady occupies her time.

Then I should like to inform your lordship, with all due regard, that in addition to the events heretofore described by me, my lady has indeed indulged in other – may I by your leave call them indiscretions?

Subsequent to the evening when she stayed up alone with the gentlemen of the party and was seen – with all due consideration for your feelings – smoking a cigar, there have been plans for another party. It is to be – I have to say this – a party of a theatrical kind. And I cannot feel it bodes well – not altogether well – that the preparations go forward in such secrecy. And indeed my informant – one of the maids, my lord, but a reliable source, I assure you – has seen the list of guests. What I mean to say, is that they are many of them not persons you yourself might think to receive.

There is, as I say, to be a theatrical production – a satire. My lady is writing it herself; and she is also to take at least one leading part. The main characters in this piece – this, you understand, according to my informant – are the fair Lady Disgusta, together with her husband Lord Littleprick and his disagreeable nephew Master Lordly Disdain. (My lord, I beg you to know, I do but repeat what I have been told.)

And further – with due respect to both your lordship's own feelings and to your desire to be informed – I would I could say this was all . . .

So often was Mr Johns' letter to be revised, anguished over, and rephrased, it might never have gone, but for the risk that his lordship might hear its news through someone else. With Lady Fitzpayne's party not one week away, and the estate carpenters at work converting the Long Gallery into a theatre, it left for London; and within two days it was being borne by the servant whose job this was, past Hyde Park Corner toward St James's Square.

The man had been in service in the Fitzpayne household for some years. So when, riding down Piccadilly, he found his attention suddenly caught, he should have known at once that the rouged and ostrich-feathered girl in the crowd was Charity. As it was, she was still lovely enough for her looks to show despite the way she was got up.

But even in the weeks since Rawley had been surprised at the sight of her, she had altered.

Had it been a change for the better? Certainly beneath her painted cheeks and mouth she looked healthier. Her clothes, too, though showy, were good. She could boast a muslin gown whose embroideries alone had taken a hundred and fifty hours of someone else's work. But she walked with purpose rather than grace; and where once she might have smiled, now she laughed out loud whether with reason or not.

Since she came to London, when had the worst moment been? Had it been in the fly-blown room where she'd given birth? Or seeking her initiation into harlotry? Could she have guessed that anyone would work her as hard as the Yankee madame in the well-known house in St James's Place?

Charity was thinking over her recent history now, as she hurried through the noisy, feebly lit dusk. She was on her way to her new lodging, in the top of a house off Piccadilly, to ask after her little girl. Afterward, she was due at a genteel place of assignation near Drury Lane. It was an establishment where only gentlemen of the first quality were admitted; and nothing but patient hard work had let her be employed there. Truly, she thought, there were times when dwelling on what she'd been through almost made her pleased with herself.

It was one thing to say so, however, and another to run full tilt into Rawley Fitzpayne.

With Frederick Nordaby and Walter Boone. he was about to get into a hackney coach. Seeing her, he turned. She ignored him and tried to hurry past. He seized her by the arm. 'By God, here's one now! Michaelmas –'

'Michaelmas!' Nordaby sniggered at Charity's quaint orphanage-given name. 'Michaelmas? *Michaelmas?*'

'Michaelmas,' said Rawley, taking up Nordaby's cue. 'These are flash togs, aren't they, Michaelmas? Dammit, Michaelmas, I don't know but what I wouldn't pay to fuck you this time, Michaelmas.'

In her best new London accent she replied, 'You may speak well of me, if you must. But no volunteer would care to touch a man with a prick like a wet thread.'

No slander could be less original; but it served its purpose. As if he'd just been stung, Rawley let her go, and while his companions transferred their cheers of derision to him, Charity fled.

Rawley was not used to being answered back. After half an evening of rum punch and fornication, at the Crown Street hop, off Drury Lane, he was still in an evil mood. The drink, too, had helped make him sullen and pugnacious. After Nordaby had taken a girl upstairs, Rawley impatiently awaited his reappearance, only to haul the child (as she happened to be) straight back to the room she and Nordaby had left. Then, as he returned, a milky-skinned Irish girl, fresh from being swived by Walter Boone, was seized on by him with the same petulance.

'Poxy cunt's not worth it,' was Rawley's comment on coming downstairs again.

Their gathering might have soon drifted apart, but for the chance arrival of more acquaintance; among them, Underwood and George Byford.

'Good God, it's Byford, from the City,' observed Rawley. 'How goes clerking, then – how's trade?' he mumbled under his breath. 'Byford – hey, Byford! You can't fuck them just by staring, you know ... How is it with pussy and you, Byford? Have you given the fair Lucy her due after all?'

In the heat and noise and gloom outside where the dancing couples were lined up, it was hard to attend to what anyone was saying. But Rawley was at the insistent stage of drunkenness. 'Damn these overpriced doxies,' he was saying. He fixed an unfocused stare on George. 'They're all poxed, anyway. There's only one way a sporting man can get his true deserts. You get them fresh. You don't get them here; you get them out of town. Here's a toast, now – here's a toast,' raising his voice. 'To village wenches – eh, Byford? To good, clean, bumpkin amateurs! Fill 'em up, now, God damn you all; and let's have a toast ... To village girls, especially Byford's sister!'

Despite the general hubbub the company about their table turned attentive.

'Fitzpayne, you don't mean it,' someone told him in an undertone.

'Sit down, Byford,' murmured somebody else, with the same urgency.

Rawley stood up and leaned forward, the better to look into George's furious, bewildered face. 'No, not them! I don't mean them – not miss and young madam! Not the overweening Miss Katherine, nor even the fair Mrs Fraser. I mean the house of Byford's by-blow. Their child of nature. Their winsome misbegotten. Their item of bastardy, complete with a bastard of her own.' Rawley's features shone with relish. He was beginning to enjoy the evening after all.

A waiter came up to them. There was a man in livery outside, wishing to speak with Mr Fitzpayne.

Rawley flicked a look at George and went out, in high good humour. Waiting for him was the servant who had earlier delivered Mr Johns' letter to his lordship. He had been sent straight out to find Master Rawley, on pain of instant dismissal without references.

'For God's sake, Byford,' said Underwood. Down in Wiltshire he heard much the same stableyard gossip as Rawley – Charity's alleged origins included. 'Don't drink with us if you're going to look so bloody maudlin. Everybody's father's got a bastard somewhere. And there can't be many where you come from who haven't opened their legs for Fitzpayne.'

'Maybe Byford's had her himself,' some wag remarked.

More drink was called for. No one noticed meanwhile how quiet and pale George had become.

'Here's a good 'un, Byford, come just for you,' someone said, just as Rawley was coming back down the room.

'Hey, Byford, you lucky sod, here's one come right after you!'

George looked despairingly at the splendid bosom half exposed for general inspection; then at the girl's face. He thought: a whore doesn't look at you like that –

I must look like him, thought Charity. She stared back into his face, unable to breathe. So, through everything she had done and suffered, there had been no worst moment after all. It had never happened. The worst thing that could befall her had been waiting for her, all along; here.

'Byford, you haven't!' murmured Underwood.

Nordaby and Walter Boone caught on immediately. 'He hasn't, has he?'

'The devil he hasn't had the pleasure!' Boone said in a low voice. His eyes glinted. The rest of the company, sensing there was more to the joke, grinned in anticipation, glancing hopefully between George and the others.

With a snap as sudden as the jaws of a dog, Charity, likewise not understanding, found herself seized and pinioned. 'Byford!' Rawley's voice sounded beside her, vibrant with revenge. 'Were you so short for it, that no one but family would oblige?'

A howl of pure joy broke all around them. One or two bystanders glanced aside at the group of high-spirited young gentlemen whose mirth had them pounding the table with their fists and embracing with tears of delight.

'Byford! You shouldn't have done that,' spluttered someone in mock reproof.

'Byford, you get monsters that way, you know.'

'Was it a little ape, then?' hissed Rawley from beside Charity's stricken face. 'Did you get a monkey on her, Byford? Did it have two heads? Was it one for the fairground? Was it an ape? Was it an ape, then? Was it a freak?' He wrenched at Charity to shield himself as George, frantic, exploded toward him.

'Hey, watch him,' warned someone. Nordaby and Boone, not wanting George to spoil such a capital caper, grabbed hold of him.

'I'll kill you! I'll kill you!' George's voice, half suffocated with rage, barely rose to a bleat.

'I doubt it,' Rawley said. 'Even if I chose to regard you as a gentleman, for the pleasure of blowing your face off. You can't expect a man to fight you over any damned slut.'

Around them, bright-eyed and open-mouthed, the rest of the party were as entranced as if they'd just paid to watch a beheading.

'I won't fight you just because she's become a whore,' Rawley went on. 'As a favour, though, I shall arrange to shoot you, if that's what you wish. But only because she's a whore *and* your sister. What do you say, Byford?'

Boone and Nordaby, sensing George hesitate, then show defeat, released him. They all waited, expecting him to trail out of sight without a word. For several moments he stood, head bent.

'He's blubbing,' someone whispered.

'No, he's not.'

'He is.'

He hurled himself at Rawley again, with a suddenness that took them all by surprise, pushing him in the face and grappling at Charity. Clutching at her by her clothes, he made her reel like a drunk as he wrested her clear of Fitzpayne. Several people, seeing him attempt a gesture of protectiveness toward her, tittered out loud.

What was there to say? Charity – even now – could have faced down any of them. But it was impossible that she could look at George. Unable to exchange one word with him, she hesitated, then walked away as slowly as she could bear, followed all the way to the door by a resounding cheer.

George turned to face Rawley. The others, either because there was no longer a woman present, or because someone might be shot after all, grew serious.

A few inches from Rawley's face, however, George found himself gaping like a stranded fish, lost for words. It was Rawley who spoke.

'Now, Byford, since you regard yourself as my equal, it follows that you must know the first quality of any gentleman. No matter what his circumstances, he will always know the right thing to say ... Are we to hear you, then?'

With a blow whose force surprised George more than anyone, he hit Rawley in the belly. Rawley made a sharp little choking sound and doubled up so promptly that the two of them nearly fell into an embrace. It was some moments before he could speak.

'Your second shall not be calling on mine tomorrow. Because I can't spare you the time. But that's not to say I won't trouble to put a bullet in some part of you when I'm next in town.'

At last young George found his voice. In offering to risk his life he sounded more embarrassed than angry. Even the back of his neck was blushing.

'You can kill me if you must. But I want satisfaction when it's due to me. I don't care where you're going, Fitzpayne; I'll follow you. And if you can't shoot me first, don't count on me to leave you even half alive!'

Chapter Fourteen

In one way, thought Rawley, their journey to Wiltshire couldn't have been worse. With four outriders for protection, they travelled through the night, stopping nowhere for more than three minutes' change of horse. On the flat stretch between Hounslow and Staines, despite the darkness, the coachman was instructed, God help them all, to take the road at a gallop. It was damned disagreeable, of course, enduring his uncle's company on such terms, as the price of his uncertain inheritance. But when Rawley thought of the turn events seemed about to take for his aunt, he couldn't but feel elated. Who would have thought the silly cow could be trusted to bring this much trouble on herself? In the devil's name, what could she have done?

At Hungerford, the sun coming up over the river and the town meadows, they were jolted from a doze more racking than any consciousness as they entered the yard of the Three Swans. They breakfasted and hastened on. By the time they were slithering through the perilous descent from the Marlborough Downs to the Vale itself the November morning was well advanced. There were clouds coming up from the north, the wind tasted of snow, and the hilltops were pale beneath a heavy sky.

In the last village before Upstowe, a lame carriage-horse made it worthwhile for the coach, with two of the outriders, to stop, while a fresh beast was led out in harness to be buckled to. It was market day in the town, and the roads were choked with cattle and sheep and every kind of traffic. Another carriage was due to edge onto the high road ahead of them, when they were greeted by its occupant, a beetroot-faced man in a grey wig. Rawley recognized Mr Charles Boone, a local magistrate and uncle to his crony Sir Jack.

'Would you credit it, Fitzpayne,' Boone exclaimed to his lordship, 'that I should be fool enough to answer for the king's peace in times like these! I can stand to see my tenants and their people get roaring drunk every market day. But now there's other things afoot. Your man here would do well to drive the long way round.'

'What things would those be?'

'God knows. The men are foreigners, from the waterway. They've ransacked the Golden Fleece, and now they're making mischief somewhere else in the town.'

At the mention of the waterway Lord Fitzpayne made a complacent noise of contempt. Boone was quick to hear the satisfaction in his lordship's voice. 'It may be very well for you, Fitzpayne, to enjoy a scrap over what you think is yours. But it would have been better for the rest of us if the work could have been done and the men dismissed. That fellow Fraser's the only man they'd hear out – and he's gone now. And I'll wager half the constables have crept away to ground.'

And Mr Boone was borne away at speed to the New Inn to join forces with the other magistrates.

'Should I drive the other way, m'lud?' asked the coachman.

'Do as you're damn well ordered!' he was told; and they drove on.

Most of the town wore its usual look of market-day. The two main streets were packed with hundreds of jostling, dirt-caked animals; and the bleating of sheep mingled with the shouts and handbells of street vendors and the sound of raised voices from every pavement and pot-house. There was no room here for mischief-making, beyond the usual 'prentice sport of unhitching immobilized carriage-horses as they snorted and jittered about. If there was trouble, it was nowhere near the market-place.

In the street leading out toward Cannings Fitzpayne, the press of traffic eased. But now, over the other voices in the town, they could hear something else: a sullen roar, at first hardly human. It was the sound of a crowd, with a common angry tone of its own.

And there, down the cobbled byway known as St Peter's Place, was the source of it. Maybe a hundred navvies, some clutching stones or clubs, were spilled out backward from the entrance leading to the Leggatt storehouse and office. The noise, close to, resolved into a howl. It came not from the street, but from the yard beyond. Out in the high road the tail end of the mob was swollen by men and grinning lads from the town, straining to see what was happening in the yard. Some, thwarted from joining the fun, turned to holler exhortations or insults at passers-by who caught their notice.

Suddenly, from the yard there was a grinding crash, as of a heavy door being splintered. Then a smash of breaking glass – and another. The coachman hesitated, reining in his horses.

'Yes?' shouted Lord Fitzpayne out of the carriage window.

'Shall I turn back, m'lud?'

'Good God, do they imagine we're not armed? And how the devil do you think they can overturn us, if you whip up the horses like you damn well should?'

The fringes of the crowd, seeing a gentleman's carriage at the end of the street, gleefully turned and ran across its path. With a yell more proper to a charioteer than a servant in a wig and braided coat, the coachman urged the horses into a hand-gallop. The carriage pitched like a rudderless boat, and sparks flew from the stones beneath the horses' hooves. Through a spatter of missiles and a cheer, part derision, part excitement, they burst past the mob, to be as quickly ignored as if they'd never existed.

A few minutes, and the town was left behind. They bowled under the arched lodge-house at the main entrance to the park, and up the avenue, with all the importance of a force of cavalry. Drugged as he was by lack of sleep, Rawley couldn't help feeling impatient to see what would happen when they arrived. Above all, the situation promised the appeal of the ridiculous. They were borne at last over the drawbridge of the Hall and drew up at the carriage entrance, where the earliest house guests for Lady Augusta's party had already been set down.

Within the Hall, Lord Fitzpayne's arrival had been heralded, but only just. The two outriders who'd gone ahead were the first sign that he'd left town. Covered with the filth of seventeen hours' travel, they made their way from the stableyard to the servants' hall. There, before an inquisitive audience of the guests' own retainers, they were questioned by Mr Freeman, together with Mrs Richards the housekeeper.

She was almost distraught at their appearance. 'Someone must tell her ladyship,' she said to Miss Hodgkiss. 'It can't wait; someone has to do it now, no matter what she says. *She's* the one who ought to take the blame if he doesn't like what he finds.'

'If!' exclaimed Miss Hodgkiss, shrinking from the certain anger of master and mistress alike.

'Well, do it, then!' exclaimed Mrs Richards, almost in tears.

With a sinking heart Miss Hodgkiss hurried off. Every part of the house seemed full of activity. Down a nearby passage Sir Jack Boone and several other young men were passing the hours until the dressing-bell by firing pistols at an improvised target. In the steward's parlour a party of actors was being entertained. Having been handsomely paid to support her ladyship's efforts on stage, they were trying to look more serious than they might about the theatrical efforts of the gentry. A band was practising in the main dining room, where a dinner-service of five hundred pieces odd was being laid out. And in the Long Gallery a stage had been carpentered into the ancient linenfold oak panelling and seating had been set out for an audience of three score.

In Lady Augusta's apartment, a last fitting was being made for her costume, which had the five housemaids recruited as seamstresses agog at its daring. The other fancy-dressed ladies there were not strictly speaking ladies at all, but a couple of actresses from the troupe downstairs.

'Oh, my lady! He's here! He's here!'

'Who, Hodgkiss? Whom do you mean? And pray don't run.'

'Oh, my lord! My lady – my lord!'

'My lord who, for goodness sake? Can't he be admitted in the usual way?'

'It's him! It's him!' shrilled Miss Hodgkiss, running back and forth between the window and her mistress like a fowl chased by a dog. 'Out there! Look – it's him!'

Lady Augusta hastened, frowning, to the window.

There was no mistaking even Hodgkiss' meaning. Though distant, the carriage advancing up the avenue could only be her husband's. She took on an angry look of

258

concentration as she stared unseeing through the dead
leaves gusting past the horses' hooves.

'Oh, my lady,' Hodgkiss moaned. 'Say what's to be
done!'

It was not true that Lady Augusta was untroubled. But
there were considerations apart from her husband's wrath.
At the cost of some thousands of pounds, half the county
would soon be there, keyed up to watch a superior
entertainment ...

There was just one thing she could do – And besides,
she thought, *he holds his precious reputation far too high
to contradict me – me – his own wife. Not in public.
Whatever I did!*

'You and you – quick! Come with me,' she said to the
two actresses. 'No – no; leave it, you fool,' to one of the
maids, who, goggle-eyed from holding a mouthful of pins,
was still on her knees trying to fasten a hem. 'Turn round
– quickly, turn round, now – yes, both costumes should
do. Now come with me. And for God's sake hurry!'

Rawley had never doubted why he had been dragged all
this way. His aunt had committed some indiscretion; and
as part of her punishment he would somehow be played
off against her.

What he hadn't known was how lavish or imminent
Lady Augusta's party was. He hadn't expected, for
example, that their carriage would be held up at the draw-
bridge while three others were driven out empty. But what
surprised him most was the look of the people waiting to
receive them.

Behind the butler were ranged the groom of chambers
and four footmen; so far all was as usual. The two upper
servants, however, seemed aware that their dignity was the
least they had to lose.

In the entrance hall, Lord Fitzpayne stopped dead.
Rawley saw what he was looking at, and almost howled
with blissful disbelief. Before them, the dozen servants
who could be found in time had been lined up; a number
of guests were also present, drawn by the commotion. At
the first turn of the staircase stood the two actresses in the

tinselled draperies made for them as her ladyship's stage attendants. To heighten her consequence, they were flanking Lady Augusta now. Despite their profession, they too looked self-conscious.

Rawley had to give his aunt due credit; she did know how to make people stare. He gazed past what he took to be some bungled classical reference in her dress, at her more intimate attractions, displayed with heroic frankness. What modesty she could claim came from a white chemise that clung beneath her breasts and then fell loose about her. Over it she wore an almost invisibly transparent ten yards of dampened white muslin. Her undergarment was so brief that in effect her knees and breasts were exposed for all to marvel at. Rawley gawped, anxious not to miss one pore. Gingerly, lest her train catch on anything, Lady Fitzpayne descended to greet her husband, with rouged cheeks, gilded nipples, and a fierce smile of unrepentance.

Lord Fitzpayne strode toward her without a word. She, given courage by not wanting to flinch before so many witnesses, hastened across the hall to meet him.

– And had to hop aside, staggering on her draperies. There was a snigger from some of the guests as his lordship swept past, seeming not to see a thing.

Lady Augusta had been braced – but not against any humiliation as unbearable as being cut. The array of servants looked as grave as before, but with a difference; and an undefinable vibration sounded through the guests. She motioned to the two actresses with the seriousness of someone who cannot imagine defeat, and, ignoring them all, marched back to her apartment.

The rest of the gathering dispersed. The ladies and gentlemen went off to tell each other what they'd just seen, and the upper servants to confer on what their orders might be, had anyone troubled to give any. Rawley made his way to his bedchamber, to fall dead asleep on the bed with the valet still removing his boots, and the shadow of a grin on his face ...

Waking, he was surprised to find the day had worn on hardly at all. The valet had tried to rouse him first with a cough, then with a murmur and finally with a cautious exclamation. Without moving, Rawley opened his eyes and stared at the man, as if to challenge the importance of his message.

'He wants to see me?'

'No, sir.'

'Has he sent for her yet?'

'Two minutes since, sir.'

Rawley pictured the entire house holding its breath. 'And is that all?'

'No, sir.' The valet held out a note. Rawley took it, cursing that he should be expected to find anything more important than his uncle's displeasure. As he read it, however, his expression enlivened.

'I need a list of her male guests. Have some hot water brought up. And ring for something to eat.'

The valet left, and Rawley studied the note again, with a mixture of contempt and satisfaction. In the circumstances it called for an instant response. The bearer was a messenger from the New Inn at Upstowe. It came on behalf of George Byford, from his second.

For George, the duel, once arrangements for it were in train, had already served its main purpose. Indeed, now it was so near, he could spare hardly a thought for the original quarrel. At first he'd thought, if only Rawley were annihilated, every unbearable thing he'd said might come untrue. All that had been made less important, now. Not just by the dawning of another day, but by the change of place. It had all happened in London, for God's sake. Whereas this was home, where such things were impossible.

He hadn't seen the place since leaving home last year. Compared with the changes in his own life its sameness was a shock. The identical tradesman was just out there, sweeping the pavement before his shop; and the same farmers were putting up their gigs in the yard for market day. Acquaintances of his father had greeted him, sizing him up as a fine-looking lad while asking after his prospects in London. It was as if George the happy half-grown boy, as much as George the young man down from town, was the one 'they' were out to shoot within an hour or so.

Loitering in the crowded coffee-room of the New Inn, George was suffering the tedium only met while waiting for something one feels will be unbearable. How long till Underwood, who was his second, returned? Should he write to his family? (No, of course he shouldn't. What could make the whole business more real than a letter to his mother and sisters, to be opened together with a will?)

Around him, local farmers and tradesmen were about their business, all their chat an interference with his attempt to think of nothing. Boone the magistrate, with several other gentlemen, was briefly there, before being called away in desperate haste. Meanwhile several people near the windows crowded to look at some commotion outside. Though incapable of interest, George realized the disturbance must be serious. There was no reason, otherwise, why everybody out there should be hurrying in one direction. They were moving, too, as if on impulse, like fragments sucked by a mighty draught.

Underwood returned; and with few words they got into a chaise that was to take them to the agreed place, in the park. George was reminded how, when Dobson had died, everything had seemed to go ahead of its own accord. He had the impression that everyone involved was acting neither of their own free will – nor yet against it. Am I the only person in the world who thinks all this absurd? he wondered.

Their route lay partway in the direction taken by the crowd. George, leaning back in the chaise with the apathy of a sick child, watched Underwood observing them all. Obviously these were the stragglers and would-be onlookers; the event itself was elsewhere. They passed the corpse of the Leggatt storehouses, disembowelled into the street in a mass of broken carts and smashed furnishings – there was even the remnant of a window-frame. The people hurried on; not in a compact mass, but like specks on the same stream. Breathlessly, they were craning like geese to see what was happening up ahead. It occurred to

George that at the least a capital offence must have been committed.

So someone's going to get himself hanged, he thought, as they turned off the high road toward the park. For arson, by all appearances; there was an unwonted amount of smoke in the air. But it was so beaten to and fro by the wind, and so obscured against the late afternoon sun that there was no telling where it came from.

They left the byroad, axle-deep in mire. A lodge-keeper's wife dropped a curtsey as they drove by her into the park and rolled onward over a smooth gravelled road. George looked out at the changing perspectives of the great trees, as they appeared to move past each other in a dance. He was no longer impatient to have anything over with. The weight bruising his chest and bladder would be nothing, if only they could drive, without arriving, for ever.

The chaise had pulled up. They couldn't have got there – not yet. Underwood, doubtless not understanding, was getting out. They were there.

The place appointed was by a little classical temple near the lake. It was part of a scene designed to look like the backdrop to one of those operas in which impossible-looking shepherdesses frolicked, garlanded with flowers. On the ruffled surface of the lake, and in the steep beech-woods tossing behind, there was not a blur nor gleam of colour. Rawley, looking nothing like a character in an opera, but neatly hatted and gloved, was there already. With him, hopping about beside their carriage in the cold, were Sir Jack Boone and two other men whom George knew only by sight. They gave the impression of being kept waiting.

The preliminaries were got through impersonally, with numbing speed. Someone formally asked George if he were sorry. He replied with something incoherent and a shake of the head, overcome by self-consciousness at the solemnity of passing final sentence on himself. Only some moments later, waiting to pace out his part of the distance between them, did it occur to him: that mumble, and that motion of a man with a fly on his nose, looked to be the last communication he might have with anyone.

Why hadn't they been told to start? If your heart was beating fast enough when you were wounded, might you feel less pain?

Someone called out the word and he started forward. Even while counting the strides he had to take, he was conscious of thinking any number of things – fast, faster; all of them hustling into his mind at once. They'd had to show him how the pistol worked. Well, imagine that. But what would he ever be likely to shoot, if not another man? Hadn't his uncle Norton told him, you qualified to sit on a hanging jury with a fiftieth of the property you needed by law to kill a partridge? Would his father have been capable of getting into a scrape like this? Yes, in all probability. How extraordinary. What would his mother, and Kate, and Sophy think, if they knew what he was doing at this moment? He reached his total, and turned.

In a panic, however. And fired, while still off balance. He was astonished that the device in his hand worked so promptly. One of the coachmen swore out loud, in disbelief that anyone could commit such a blunder.

It was Rawley's turn to fire. For a very long moment indeed. And then for more than that. 'By Christ, he'd better mind his cods,' murmured Underwood.

George could feel his eyes watering from the cold. Now that there was nothing worse to fear, he felt not terror, but self-pity. How had he come to anything so saddening as this? He was overcome by a compassion for himself so powerful that, from thinking of his own lot, he found his feelings spilling over to include everybody he could call to mind whom he'd ever loved. And now it was at last, no longer caring why he could see little more than a wash of tears, that for the first time that day he could bear to think of Charity.

Rawley fired.

'They never wear pattens in London, do they?' Mrs Byford was in Sophy's bedroom, helping her to pack.

'Oh yes; the streets will be just as bad as the lanes are

here. James says I should take anything I use very often at home.'

'But Sophy, what can you use in prison?'

'Poor mama! You mustn't make yourself unhappy by imagining things worse than they are. *I'm* not going to prison.'

'But you are going to live with James.' Mrs Byford's tone was meek rather than argumentative.

'Oh yes, but that's not as bad as it sounds. James may not be allowed outside the gates; but I can come and go as I wish, can't I? I shall just have lodgings inside the walls, like the warders.'

Mrs Byford said nothing. She had become rather deferential toward Sophy in the weeks since Fraser's bankruptcy.

'And I shall be perfectly comfortable,' Sophy said, holding up an Indian shawl to scrutinize it before casting it aside. 'It's all very decent, with shutters and a fireplace. So you mustn't be a foolish old mama, you know. Think how silly it would be, if my greatest worry was whether you were fretting over me!'

Mrs Byford tried to smile, and watched Sophy work on. 'I think, my love, you take this very well,' she ventured.

'Good heavens, no. Think how much worse, if there were nothing I could do – if I had to stay here in idleness, instead of living with James.'

'And how is he? ... I mean, in his last letter ...?'

'Dearest mama, I really couldn't tell you.' The truth was, since his imprisonment, Sophy had noticed changes in her husband that she couldn't bring herself to talk about.

The work of packing was nearly done. Sophy was preparing to walk across and see Kate before dark, to recover some of her things. Glancing out at the weather, she noticed something unusual. At the garden gate, Hannah, their maid, was striving to catch sight of something up the lane. Across the way their neighbours had come out to stare, and in the lane itself, several people stood transfixed.

Hannah came running up the path. 'M'um, there's

summat happening –' she panted at Mrs Byford in the hall – 'There's summat happening at the Red Lion! It looks like that road's so full it can't hold no more people.'

Out of doors there was a murmur that grew with every moment. The village in recent months had seen its share of drunken bottle-fights and ransacked orchards and chicken-runs. But this promised some new menace or excitement.

No one was too proud to go scampering after the best vantage-point they could find. In the Byford house this was up in the attic. Mrs Byford fumbled to open the window; and she and Sophy leaned out, while Hannah stood on tiptoe behind.

At first sight it looked like a scene of jollification. Above the crowd gathering outside the inn, there wavered the looted signboard of the Golden Fleece, borne all the way from Upstowe like an insignia. Several people really had joined in for a lark. There was a swarm of children, all curiosity and bravado; one or two women with babes in their arms; a shoemender from the town, still in his apron; a group of labourers with hedging-tools, who'd been overtaken on the road – even a pedlar from the market-place and a man who sold cage-birds. The ransacking of the Golden Fleece showed itself, too, in several men and women who were roaring drunk.

But it was at the centre of this crowd, now packing the lane for fifty yards each way and too dense for anyone to lift their hand to their face, that a different sound was heard. It flowed outward, swift as the shadow of a cloud, until people with no idea what was happening joined in too. Their voices rose to a noise between a cheer and the belling of hounds. The racket grew less – then swelled louder than ever in a roar that had people at doorways down the lane even more mystified.

A few minutes showed what had happened. The landlord of the Red Lion, seeing the sign of another hostelry paraded up to his door as a trophy of war, had no doubt of his own fate. Whatever might be said against him later in the village, his response was the only possible one. Without waiting to hear a word from anyone outside, he'd hurried two of his servants into opening the cellar and rolling the casks up into the street.

'Keep off, now; for the devil's sake, keep off now, will you?' A dozen or so nearly grown boys at the front of the mob were holding back their fellows to make room for the innkeeper, pop-eyed with solemnity at the importance of what they were doing. 'Are you sure it's all out, now?' one of them asked him, at length. 'We're warning you. We don't give people like you a second chance to answer us.'

Out in the road the last barrel was being rocked about with the others by raucous men and women jostling against it to fill their hats and shoes – anything – with free ale. Some were lying in the mud with their mouths open beneath the gushing taps. The innkeeper, grim-faced, gestured to his questioners to go in and put his good faith to the test. Accordingly a serious little group entered to examine the premises, as a token that their word, being law now, deserved respect.

From the attic window of the Byford house the scene was one of single-minded industry. Despite all the hollering and clawing and climbing across people bent over the taps, there was something workmanlike about the way the crowd set itself the task of drinking every drop. It might have been as an urgent duty that where puddles formed about the barrels, people lay on their bellies, elbows stuck up behind them, and tried to lap the drink from the ground.

'Oh Sophy, surely we should have locked the doors.' Mrs Byford spoke without moving her eyes from the confusion at the end of the lane.

'If it would make you happier, mama.' Sophy tried to sound assured; in fact she had no idea whether to feel flustered or downright terrified. 'Hannah and I' – turning to the maid with all the gravity of eighteen giving orders to its elders – 'can make everything secure downstairs for you.'

They did so. Almost as soon, it seemed unnecessary. The mob began to leave: first in groups, then in a mass; then as stragglers. By the time the chaise arrived bearing Mr Boone and the other magistrates, and accompanied by a score of special constables on horseback, there was nothing left but debris. Clubs, bricks, pickaxe handles and every sort of improvised weapon strewed the ground; there were shoes, hats, clogs, bits of clothing, discarded plunder including a smashed grandfather clock; and a lost mongrel dog running round and round in a figure-of-eight without picking up his master's scent. Like any battlefield, it had its moaning disabled – in this case throwing up rather than bleeding. And sure enough, in a short time doors were opened, and amid hasty silence some of the poorer villagers started to scavenge, stooping and pacing like gleaners in a field.

The crowd had streamed elsewhere, however, rather than dissolved. Its voices – or voice – still rose up in the distance. Mixed though the people were who made it up, the farther away it moved, the more distinctly its emotions could be heard. 'Oh, they do sound a baneful sort of body,' remarked Hannah.

'Let's shut the window and go downstairs,' said Sophy. 'You see,' turning to her mother, 'I knew they had no interest in harming us.'

'Oh dear. Oh dear, I do hope they don't mean to harass poor Kate, either. And her with no man in the house, this week.'

'There are always several men in Mr Leggatt's house, mama,' Sophy said, holding up her hem as they negotiated the most crooked part of the stairs.

'Oh yes, but having menservants about isn't the same, is it? I'm sure it's so much better if the master's known to be at home. Or failing that, to put just some small token of his presence – a hat and gloves, say – in the hall where they can be seen when the footman opens the door. To inspire a little extra respect.'

Sophy said nothing. Instead, she persuaded her mother to make herself comfortable by the parlour fire, putting up the folding screen behind her to keep out any draughts. Then, having supervised the getting of supper, she sat down with her, to continue reading aloud from – yet again – Mrs Beddowes' shiny old copy of *The Vicar of Wakefield*.

It was only toward dusk – shortly before a chaise drew up outside unexpectedly – that they began to smell smoke.

By noon, in the Leggatt household, it seemed they'd suffered the worst that would be done to them.

It was bad enough. In the front of the house, not a window had been left unbroken. The flowerbeds had been kicked to ruins; and on the ground floor the window-frames were smashed in, and the shutters were gashed and cracked.

None of it had been the mob's doing. A dozen passing louts was all it had taken, as they made a detour across the fields toward the main source of the fun.

Even from the time the canal had been dug to reach the village, no one in Cannings Fitzpayne had thought to lock their doors, day or night. And now there were stones and broken glass, and shattered clods of earth, all over the carpets in the front rooms of the house. In the kitchen, the boy who helped the gardener was looking enormously proud of the blood on his shirt, spilt from a cut across his scalp.

Kate hurried to the top of the house, to reassure young Alice and little Fanny that they could leave the school-room. It was hard to tell how badly they were frightened. Perhaps because their parents quarrelled so, they were quieter than most children anyway.

Throughout the house, as she came back downstairs, people were busy with mops and brooms, talking away whether they were listened to or not. In normal circum-stances Mrs Leggatt had been known to make housemaids weep with little more than a look. But now, in an atmos-phere of mingled aggression and relief, the servants were shouting from room to room, for all the world as if their mistress wasn't there.

Away in the village the mob was distant enough for their racket to sound like a continuous murmur from a single creature. Only toward dusk did it grow louder and fragmented. The crowds who'd ransacked the Red Lion were moving on, to justify the violence already done by some other show of grievance. Soon, across the fields and in the highway, groups of men and boys began to appear. Almost immediately the noise grew, with the approach of a mass of people several hundred strong.

They looked to be pouring toward the house from several directions, for the road was too narrow for more than four or five men abreast. In ragged files they were making their way along the sticky furrows of the fields, piling up in groups behind wherever a gate or stile was being kicked and battered down. There was no doubt of it; they were heading toward the house. As the first scatter of youths leaped over the rail fence at the end of the paddock they broke, with a yell, from a hasty walk to a run.

Kate was helping to clear up the debris, when the downstairs rooms suddenly echoed to a series of thuds against the front door. After a moment's lull, 'Leggatt!' howled one man's voice, in the gathering crowd. 'Leggatt!' others yelled all around him. The door could be heard shaking as it was kicked and pounded by whoever could get near. She started as a man's voice sounded through the hall itself. 'Leggatt! Leggatt!' it shouted, in a senseless chant. Someone outside, made idiotic from hatred, was standing on a window-sill to bawl over the top of a shutter.

Upstairs at one of the windows a woman's voice shrilled out. 'He's not here! He's not here! He isn't in the house at all! Oh please!' It was the housekeeper, nearly weeping from fright. 'Go away! Go away!' Kate pictured the poor woman flapping her arms to shoo them off.

In the passage by the kitchen she collided with Mrs Leggatt. The mistress of the house looked as overwrought as everyone else. Her hair, dangling pins, was half down about her ears. 'What are you doing? What are you doing?' she shouted. It was hard to tell if she was just hostile, or witless with fear. 'And where are the children?' she cried, before Kate could speak.

'I'm looking for them.'

'Then get on with it, you stupid trollop!'

There was a crash against the shutters of the morning-room window overlooking the drive. Almost immediately there was another, at the back of the house. Each one was followed by a roar from the swell of people outside. They were trying to batter their way in!

'Leggatt!' a voice shouted in at one of the half-breached windows. 'We'll burn you out!'

Kate opened the door at the foot of the narrow staircase used by the servants and ran up to the first floor. 'Alice! Fanny!' There was no reply. She went on, frantic by now, up to the schoolroom. If the house itself were in danger, she must take the children out through the closed yard where the main outbuildings were.

In the attics, wide-eyed from breathlessness, she wrenched open the door to the schoolroom. No one was there. 'Alice! Fanny! Alice!' Half to herself, 'Oh God, where are you?' she cried out. From downstairs the noise of shouting and breakage rose up more directly than before; some of the shutters had already been smashed in.

Suddenly, there was almost quiet outside, as if on the surging mass of faces turned up toward the house there was nothing but expectancy. A moment later, and on one side of the building a thunderous cheer rose up.

What could it be? What was it? Had they broken into the house? 'Where are you? Where are you? Oh, please! Where are you?' shouted Kate, as she hurtled from room to room, finding no one. Could the children be frightened enough to creep into a cupboard or under a bed?

There was nobody, though, even in hiding. Kate ran back toward the staircase, by now as frightened for herself as for them. From the landing window she thought she saw a group of servants looking up at the house from a doorway across the yard. Could the children be with them? What were they staring at anyway? ... And what was that gushing sound?

The illusion of hearing a waterfall lasted half a heartbeat. Then Kate understood. It was not the sound of a torrent, but the crackle of burning wood. The house was on fire!

With a sob of panic, she rushed down headlong to the door at the foot of the stairs. It was shut. She went at it to wrest it open. And found herself twisting and rattling the

271

knob in vain. Oh, in God's name, she couldn't be so scared she fancied it locked!

Could it be locked? Could it? For three or four seconds she stood paralysed, her forehead against the door. Lifting her face up, she shouted out loud in fear and rage.

Don't stand there howling – go back! She gathered her skirts about her knees and fled up the tunnel-like stairs, steep as a ladder. The air, still motionless, was every second nonetheless growing thicker, as though seen with failing eyes. She reached the landing where a low passage led to the main staircase. And stopped.

Was she surprised by what she saw? Not really – or she wouldn't have had the sense to pause, much less stand and calculate, even as the heat from the rooms below started glazing her face with sweat.

At the far end of the passage, facing her, was Mrs Leggatt. In her hand something glinted: the dainty two-inch blades of her embroidery scissors. Without taking her eyes off Kate she advanced toward her. Kate braced herself not to edge away. The fire, now louder than any human voice, was setting up a draught from every corner of the house. What amazed her was not the other woman's murderous intent, but her appearance. The suddenness of Mrs Leggatt's impulse had caught her looking almost matter-of-fact. She walked toward Kate, arms at her sides, as businesslike as a cricketer about to bowl. Her eyes smarting against the smoke, Kate watched her come close enough for Mrs Leggatt's face to be properly seen. She caught one glimpse of the trance-like, almost blank expression of purpose, and lunged forward.

Instantly, Mrs Leggatt's face became wizened by loathing. She raised her arm to strike. Pushed by fear, not courage, Kate closed with her and brought her own arm down hard on the point of her attacker's weapon. She let out a sexless bellow of pain as the shock of being wounded jolted through her. Mrs Leggatt, not expecting such a move, was momentarily confused. Kate gripped her by the wrist and dipped upward to bite her hand. She moaned soundlessly through the other woman's sinews at the effort of hanging on, her eyes turned up so that only the whites were visible.

Mrs Leggatt dropped the scissors and seized Kate by the hair with both hands. Behind, on the landing, lines of smoke were bending up toward them through the floorboards. Kate, pulled down by her head, blindly put out her hands to grab at Mrs Leggatt's gown. She kicked at her frenziedly, again and again, until released. Above the well of the main staircase, a chandelier the weight of a man was jumping about in the blast of scorching air sucked in by the fire. Mrs Leggatt ran at Kate again, her face so full of hate she hardly seemed to see her.

Above the racket of every surface in the rooms below being cracked and broken by the flames, there was a crash – felt, not heard – as some heavy structure leaned and fell. The two women, red-faced, sodden with sweat, and their hair in tatters, slapped and punched and tore at each other. Seizing Kate in both arms Mrs Leggatt tried to bite her on the cheek. Even as she struggled to hold her off, Kate noticed first one, then two, and then a third line of little flames sprout up from the direction of the servants' staircase, along the passage floor.

Suddenly, Kate saw rather than heard her assailant snarl at a fiercer pitch. Mrs Leggatt lessened her hold for a moment and tried to dodge something. With a lurch of rage that was really heightened terror, Kate realized what was happening. The floor beneath them was catching fire. A few moments more, and the madwoman trying to clutch at her with the futility of someone drowning would see to it that they both died.

Kate was almost beyond gasping in another breath. Only the knowledge that she wouldn't have to rally for a second chance – since there wouldn't be one – gave her strength to stamp on the other woman's feet, at the same moment pitching all her weight against her. Mrs Leggatt staggered. As she did so, Kate seized her by the hair and smacked her head sideways against the wall.

Though Mrs Leggatt didn't fall at the blow, she was stunned. Now would have been the moment for Kate to turn and run.

If, that is, escape had been the only thing she sought. But still she clung on, teeth bared to the gums. Twice more she slammed her would-be killer's head against the wall, each sweet dull thud reverberating through them both. Mrs Leggatt, from putting an arm up to protect herself, sank to her knees, her mouth slack and her face emptied. A line of fire had reached to her skirt. Kate started running for the main staircase, thirty yards away.

At the head of the stairs she paused, from instinct, and turned as if to ward off a shove. But Mrs Leggatt was not at her elbow. She stood, the floor about her seeded with an infernal crop of flames, some way down the passage, revolving this way and that.

But how had she grown so big? Kate, glimpsing her only as one among all the other spectres of light and blackness made by the fire, looked away; and only then knew what she'd seen. The flames, swift as falling water, had ascended Mrs Leggatt's clothes and hair so that now she stood veiled within a spout of fire seven feet tall, flattened at its head by the ceiling.

Over the boom and rattle of the blaze there was now another noise: a shrilling like the scream of a dismembered hare, repeated over and over. Kate understood that it was her own voice. Down in the hall the smoke was so thick that the doorways were only visible where they were shooting with flames. The only other way out she thought she could find led to a stone-flagged passage into the kitchen. At the foot of the stairs she took a breath that felt it must blister the pit of her lungs; and ran forward, eyes shut, into obscurity.

At twenty paces her heart seemed big enough to be beating against the roof of her mouth. Was she in the kitchen yet? She tried to turn, slamming into a wall hot as the inside of a half-kindled baking oven, and ran on. The din of the fire became duller as the blood boomed in her ears. For a second time she thought she heard running water: on one side of the house, where the wind bellied the flames like a mass of garments, the gutter-spouts were dribbling away into molten lead. She turned again. Had she reached the kitchen – or was this the passage leading to the cellar stairs? Her heartbeats felt as if her ribcage must be rising and falling like the wings of a sparrow. Something tripped her – a piece of furniture. Wherever she was, there shouldn't be any such thing. She changed direction again – she knew she shouldn't – and hit something else. Had either door to the yard been blocked? To hinder the mob, had they piled furniture against the kitchen door? Locked it from outside? By now not just her lungs and heart but her hands and feet felt swollen enough to explode in a spatter of bloody tissue.

There was a stench of melting flesh. It might be just a kitchen smell – the contents of the larder all charring and dissolving together. Otherwise someone must have died there already, and there was no hope for her. Another moment of not knowing where she was, and she was going to open her lungs and drown in smoke, so that she could put an end to her terror. She dared to open her eyes. But she was at the limit of her strength and knew she was fainting. Already blindness was so near, she could barely interpret the contortions of brilliance and darkness all about her. Around one arch of fire the flames appeared to gush inward, as if it were an opening. Kate ran toward it, into more darkness. She failed to recognize the place, and fell down senseless, blood trickling from her nose and her gown pitted with burns, onto the sharp damp cobbles of the yard.

After they had taken George Byford off to his mother's house, to live or die as may be, Rawley had himself driven back to the Hall.

As it chanced, he had never shot a man before. His reaction surprised him. At no time before the duel had he wondered if he himself might be injured. It was only afterward that such a possibility took hold of his imagination. Only at the sight of Byford being carried away, waxen-faced and unconscious, the blood chilling even as it soaked his clothes, had Rawley thought: suppose that were me?

It would be wrong to say his response was one of enjoyment. It was so far above that, it could hardly count as mere pleasure. Of course he'd seen men critically injured in the ring or the hunting field; he'd even known mortal danger at first hand. But to look straight at death as a condition of dealing it oneself! At that moment there was nothing he wouldn't have given, to go back and do it again. The sensation of daring and willing anything, of being omnipotent, had him as overmastered as a rat shaken to death by a dog. It seemed impossible he had ever known any other state of mind. So what if repeating the experience, so far from satisfying him, would make him just want to live the same hazard yet again – and again, for ever?

Rawley had forgotten the misgiving with which he'd kept the appointment. It was not physical fear that had made him hesitate, but the thought of his standing with Lord Fitzpayne, who'd been likely to send for him at any moment. Yet now, as he was driven home, nothing could have troubled him less than weighing his prospects as heir against his reputation in the face of a challenge to fight. His mind had room for one thing only. The fitness of things, that he – *he* – should be the one to survive, had him almost beside himself with satisfaction with his own boldness. He was a man who could do anything.

The carriage entered the main courtyard and drew up. In the hall the butler greeted him. As always when there was trouble in the house, the man looked as if someone had just fallen down dead. Rawley's fierce smile of elation grew brighter as he asked after his erring aunt.

'Where is her ladyship?'

'Why, with my lord. Sir –'

'Still?'

'She won't leave him, sir.'

'I beg your pardon?'

'The doctors were sent for half an hour ago. You might say, sir, his lordship is not sick, with respect, so much as worse than that.'

Rawley felt impatient. He had come back expecting high drama to match his own mood of trumpeting aggression. And now, just as he was sailing an ocean crest of invincibility, spoiling for something more, here was the place full of drawn curtains, embarrassed guests, and the need to talk in a low voice.

'Her ladyship particularly requested that you should attend my lord. If, she said, you were – ah – able, that is, sir.'

Rawley tried not to smirk at this discreet reference to the fact that he might have been dead by now. Going up the stairs three at a time he reminded himself that if the son of a bitch were as ill as the man implied, he, Rawley, might never have to look so serious again as long as he lived.

At the far end of the corridor to Lord Fitzpayne's bedchamber his lordship's valet was whispering with Mr Freeman and Mrs Richards as they awaited any summons. Watched by all of them, Rawley went in. It surprised him that the room looked so like a sickchamber. The curtains were open, letting in the last of the daylight together with the glare of whatever the devil it was burning down over near the village. And, true enough, no one was in attendance but Lady Augusta herself. She was still, for some reason, not properly clothed, but loosely robed as for her own dressing-room.

But the strangest thing was the sick man himself. No one perhaps had seen Lord Fitzpayne so apparently reposeful, yet so alert. On the counterpane his hands, corpulent enough to look smaller than they were, lay stiller than if he were fast asleep. His expression appeared both neutral and attentive. Rawley stood at his lordship's feet, not knowing what to do. He was accustomed to being kept waiting until spoken to. Yet what should he expect from a face like this, itself immobile for all that the eyes flickered everywhere at once? It was hard to believe it would ever speak again.

Lady Augusta advanced to his side, looking steadfastly at her husband. Rawley sensed rather than saw how tense she was. It was as if the least accidental contact would make her squeak out loud. He glanced at her face and thought: he must be dying. (But how, when he can look at us like that?) His aunt wore a bright ravening expression he wouldn't have imagined even in her. She looked, he

277

realized, just as he himself had felt from the moment of shooting his man. Part of him was utterly confused; it was hard for his imagination to separate the feeling corpse before him from Byford's semi-lifeless body. With an appearance of blandness, his lordship's eyes dwelled on Lady Augusta's animated face.

For Rawley the truth was slow to show itself. 'He can't move, can he?'

'No!' she replied.

'Can he not speak?' Rawley's voice, as he gazed back at Lord Fitzpayne, was measured and intent. But like her he was almost visibly trembling.

From between clenched teeth, Lady Augusta answered in a whisper, 'No!' She was breathing nearly hard enough to faint. She added, in a thick voice, 'Touch him! He won't move. No matter what you do! He could speak at first. He said he couldn't feel.' She leaned forward, the better to glare into the sick man's face. 'You could do anything. He'd just go on blinking at you if you gutted him!'

Rawley looked down at the figure regarding them from the bed. His throat felt constricted, and a vein throbbed in his temple. So this was how the man had been destined to end! Against the hellish light from the blaze beyond the park there was silence. The whiff of smoke, even in the Hall, clung everywhere. As good as dead! Under the sound of his uncle's breathing he could hear the scuttering of a mouse behind the skirting-board. No! – no! – better than dead!

And Lady Augusta – he could tell she was thinking the same thing. Even though they hadn't looked at each other since he entered the room. He was at least as much aware of her as of his uncle, gazing at them in that extraordinary way. So near was she, her mass of unbound hair brushed against his elbow. But, by God, she was a fool ... if she thought she could get away with teasing the old man by standing so warm and close as this ... if she wanted to torment her husband by nudging at his own cock ... like this. If she thought he'd just stand there ... as passive as the rabid mound of offal eyeing them from the bed. Damn

278

the bitch! If she thought he'd just stand still to let himself be used ... How could anyone sport a body like hers and still be so goddamned stupid?

Lord Fitzpayne looked on, with a passive expression that was due to serve him to the beginning of eternity. He watched, while Rawley seized his wife from behind, and fumbled desperately as though he'd never touched a girl before. With his free hand Rawley dragged the robe down from her shoulders. Her pert breasts bounded out.

She had eyes only for her husband. Had any woman suffered assault with such a look of rapt purpose? Rawley barged her, naked, forward over the bed – and still she stared back at Lord Fitzpayne.

Lips parted, powerless to speak or even cry out; eyes kindled in remembrance of every instant spent in raging subservience ... Had there ever been a face like hers?

Or two such faces? Two faces, yet upon them only one look.

With eyes half closed, the tendons straining in his neck, Rawley let slip a groan, part battle cry and in part a pang not to be endured. He parted his aunt's buttocks and thrust into her with all his strength, as rashly as if his cock could cleave her up to the very throat.

Chapter Fifteen

He was finding it hard to know who he was. Much of the time he didn't care. Except that whatever person he was had wronged ... someone? Something was wrong, anyway. And then all his sisters would have to come and stand over him like that. Someone was passing them off as spirits of light, there to wish him well. But he knew they were witches, from the way they changed from one to another. Charity was there most often. The brightness from her white gown sizzled, one time, and burnt his eyes. She kept pretending to be Sophy. Kate was there, too. Once, her hair being loose, it was lop-sided. Had it been shaved off, to show that he'd betrayed her into harlotry?

Singed by fire, someone or something told him. He was burning, and she touched him, and she'd been singed as a mark that something had been done wrong by him.

But these were not the worst times. Often he knew he was in a bed. It had been made up for him in a place that was his own room and yet was the bare earth, forever falling from under him into a bottomless cavern. There were other times, though, when instead he was the room itself, imprisoned in the rest of the house. It hurt, and he begged that he might be allowed to be something else. People sat down inside him, and whispered in terrifying voices; and he feared, in case being part of him might do them harm. While he was all broken up like this, to be made into a ceiling and walls, Sophy walked into him one day, and went to stand in a corner of him so that she could become a talking fountain.

And then he was a body again; but he was somehow the underneath of a great vault of darkness. It was the sky, and he had to hold it up by willing himself not to fall, even though the stars, which were pits of fire through to somewhere else, were scorching him. Then he was on the earth, which was moving about underneath him. It didn't want him; and while he himself couldn't move, it was twitching about like a horse's rump beneath a fly.

Someone told him, too, that a bullet had gone through him. It had hit him in the chest, to be turned through an angle inside him, all in less time than he had taken to fall. After that he was raving again; bound to the ground by his own weight while grass and trees grew up through him, so that the cracking of his bones deafened him as they broke. For George, there was neither night nor day, nor change nor rest. What fragments of reason he might have had had fallen away, as he tumbled down through an abyss, crying out against visions that terrified his hearers almost as much as they tormented him.

The Byford family's fortunes had the village divided in its opinions. On one thing it could agree: their business was its own, to be moralized upon at every opportunity. On two Sundays now, Parson Beddowes' flock had obediently sunk to their knees to pray for the life of that wild young man; and this in itself was enough to make the family's character public property. (And mentioned in the same breath as petitions for his lordship himself!)

The parson, whose habit of trying to please Lord Fitzpayne was too engrained to cease now, had preached yet another sermon against the canal. As forthright as if his patron were there, he described how 'a dweller in the tents of the ungodly' – meaning Leggatt – had got no less than his deserts. And how the innocent and the stranger within his gates – meaning Kate – had nearly perished in the flames of wrath ignited by his own greed and general association with the canal. (Or, in Parson Beddowes' discreetly Biblical terms, his 'whoring after strange gods'.) With no naming of names, but with all the lurid detail his listeners could desire, the parson drew the same moral from everything that had happened in the course of the riot; from the destruction of Leggatt's underinsured property and the death of Mrs Leggatt, to the yeomanry's arrest of fourteen rioters charged with offences that bid fair to hang some of them.

Afterward, 'There's nothing pleases a body more,' the almshouse-keeper's wife declared, 'than hearing folks' gossip swelled up into Holy Writ.' The other matrons of the village agreed, and felt free to let their tongues run all the wilder for that they'd had to look solemn while in church. Formerly, Fraser's imprisonment had seemed the most scandalous thing possible, showing as it did the penalties for Sophy of marrying the son of a foreigner. And now, the fate of the Byford family as a whole showed the unrespectability of finding one's place in the world not good enough, and gadding off to places honest folks had never seen.

Such was the opinion of the landlady at the Red Lion. She had no shortage of female sympathizers in her hospitable kitchen at the back of the inn. 'The parson, now, he said it was an omen when Lawyer Byford got blown away into nothing. And, there, he was another who tried to better himself by going off and mixing with people from Lord knows where, away down that waterway. And his

281

daughters – for all that one's married off and they've both been to foreign parts – they're still living as quiet and cheese-paring as ever. I'll wager you'll never see either of *them* rise high enough again to send their own sewing out.'

'Aye,' rejoined the almshouse-keeper's wife. 'But it's that young lad that makes one grieve. To think that such as he should presume to fight a duel, and call his betters out to do them mischief!'

At first George's disrespect in shooting at his lordship's heir caused more comment than his injuries. It was soon eclipsed, though, by the fascination of the quarrel itself ... Not just a painted woman, but one known to all the parish by name!

It was as well, Kate and Sophy agreed, that their mother was ignorant of the looks that would have been given her in the village. For while George could recognize none of them, but shouted and pleaded at the empty air, nothing he said counted beside the danger to his life.

Mrs Byford said nothing, showed nothing, but moved silently to and from the sickchamber with a look of dogged calm. Her daughters feared for her almost as much as for George. Through whole days or nights she would sit, bent forward in the wicker chair beside his bed, staring vacantly into his face. It was as if she willed every dram of strength she had into her son, until she lacked even the energy or will for grieving of her own.

To watch, and suffer, and do nothing was worse than any drudgery. Sophy, in particular, was tormented by their helplessness. 'Someone ought to make some sense of what poor George has said,' she told Kate one evening. They were speaking in low voices in Kate's room, where she was wrapping herself in a heavy shawl before taking her turn in the sickroom throughout the night.

'Why – how?' The word 'incest' was too much for either of them, no matter what they'd heard moaned or shouted out by George in his delirium.

'*I* don't know. In any way we can. I've thought about it so much. What can we do? There must be something. For George's sake. I can't bear to hear him reproach himself. Even if it's nonsense. Oh, Kate, what should we do?'

Kate could find nothing to say. They tiptoed into the darkness on the landing, the bare boards creaking underfoot like ship's timbers. Outside George's room Sophy paused. 'What I mean is, shouldn't one of us – I mean me, as soon as I can leave mama and you – shouldn't I, in London, see ... this girl?' Poor Sophy, for all her boldness, was still inexperienced enough to speak at times with the modesty of a little old lady.

'But how could that help?' The same thought had occurred to Kate; but she had dismissed it as wishful thinking.

'In any way. Oh, I don't know. But whatever we do, we can't do nothing.' Her hand on the latch, she hesitated. Even in the dark, Kate could picture her blushing. 'And anyway, why should George be the only one to know ... who she is ... I mean, what he's really done?'

The upshot was that Sophy's journey to London was brought forward again. Parson Beddowes, whose kind heart was at odds with his sermons, took it on him to drive to Upstowe to the coaching office at the New Inn and buy her ticket; and her half-unpacked trunk was filled and fastened once more.

But on the morning she was due to leave ... 'Oh, Kate, what am I to do?' she groaned angrily into her pillow. It was late, and she had overslept.

Kate looked at her. Her eyes were large with fatigue, but her rosy colour still spoke of invincible good health.

'Let me feel your forehead,' said Kate in her quiet firm voice.

'No, no, I don't feel hot. I just can't wake properly and sit up.'

'I'll ask Hannah to make you coffee and toast.'

'Oh no, please! My mouth feels as if coffee would taste like wetted dust. Please can I have some dry toast? Oh, Kate, I'm so sorry! What am I to do? All that money spent on the coach!'

Later that day it was Hannah's turn to sit with George. She found Mrs Byford noiselessly weeping.

'There, m'um,' she whispered, having glanced at

George's unconscious face. 'Why should you think he's worse, just because he's quiet now?'

Mrs Byford shook her head, the hot tears gushing down her wilted face.

'You cry if you want, m'um,' the maid said, trying to keep her voice lower than the clicking of the fire in the grate. 'But you've no call to do it from anything but thankfulness – truly you haven't. Now you go and rest yourself like a good creature; and I promise you that any news you hear will be good.' She was guessing, of course; just as she'd been uncertain whether Mrs Byford's tears had sprung from terror rather than hope.

But George's sleep did bode well. It was late afternoon when he awoke. He felt insubstantial, as though the least sound or movement might fracture him or blow him away. A delicious carelessness possessed him as he lay, nearly too weak to move even his eyes and filled with a sensation of floating. His body seemed far away, yet registered everything about him so finely he could imagine it a part of every object he could see or hear.

He watched the sunlight making the flames pale in the fireplace, and examined the miraculous detail of every knot in a humpy beam above his head. Outside there were sparrows chirping and everyday voices in the lane; and at the far end of the parish, on the down, a sheepdog barked. Beside the bed, Sophy was sleeping in a chair. Her breathing murmured almost as loud as the bleating of sheep two miles away. He dozed, waiting for her to wake.

Drifting into consciousness again, he found her looking at him. 'Sophy,' he told himself, pleased to know he was right. She gave him an unsteady, speechless smile.

'I'm hungry,' he said. 'Where is everybody?'

'Dear George, do you know where you are?'

'Of course I do,' he said faintly, as if up through a hole in the ground. His cheerfulness contrasted with his wasted face. 'Does mama know I'm here?'

'Oh, George! Oh, George, do you really not know how long you've been here?' exclaimed Sophy, sparkling with tears. 'She'll fuss, you know,' she added happily, 'once she sees you're getting better.'

'I'd like some hot buttered toast, cut thick,' said George. 'Is Kate at home? I thought I saw her.'

'Yes – oh yes – she was – I shall have to write to tell her now, shan't I?' Sophy paused to blow her nose. 'But she left this morning, on the London coach.'

A grey morning in London; yet, since this was London, not like morning at all. With no wind to scour away the smoke of a quarter million coal fires, the fog made it seem any time of day. In this weather the hours, like the long miry streets, had no beginning and no end. Even at noon the lamps were alight on carriages and behind private windows. The gloom was dirty enough to flavour every breath. Beyond a few yards' distance, people who were in sight a moment before might never have existed. The city's confused sounds, of voices and of horses' hooves and wheels grinding over cobblestones, were as unreal as noises off-stage around a vast theatre.

Outside the King's Bench Prison Kate paid off the hackney coach and got down. A crowd of prisoners' friends and relatives was gathering, ready to be let in. Even as silhouettes they were shabby and subdued. Some just stood, hunched before the high wall in an attitude of patience. Others, stamping about in the cold, turned aimlessly this way and that as they waited. Even the children were ghostlike and quiet.

Not knowing what the London streets would be like, Kate had dressed as inconspicuously as she could: a dark cloak covered her gown, and she was closely veiled. She was looked at all the same, as she joined the gathering outside the gaol. Even a hackney coach was impressive to such an out-at-elbows crowd. Besides, even Kate's confident motions and graceful walk hinted that she must be beautiful. 'They don't come here looking like that for long,' she heard one woman say.

The door in the high façade was opened. With the other spectres she made her way inside; and followed the turnkey to where Fraser was lodged.

It was less like a prison than one might expect. The main building, stretching away into the gloom, looked like another street with no ending. From its windows, horizontal poles were hung with dirtying washing. Just as outside the prison, there were traders' signs displayed – as if a bankrupt milliner or barber could find as much trade in these crowded echoing courts as in the world. There were shoals of ill-dressed children racketing about the place; and gossiping wives and loafing men outside a tavern. It was much as in some ordinary part of town where hard times might be taken for granted. The greatest difference was the occasional well-dressed prisoner who seemed to have wandered in from some fashionable thoroughfare only to be lost for months – or years – on end.

Fraser was in his room. It was a dingy little space furnished almost like a prison cell proper. Although he was wearing his greatcoat against the cold, there was an undressed look about him. He was lying on the bed with his hands behind his head. Not in repose; but with a face darkened by uneasy torpor. Hearing the rustle of a woman's clothes, he started to his feet.

'Where's Sophy?' he exclaimed, frowning.

Kate, knowing her appearance would disappoint him, had been ready not to look offended. Sophy's health, she explained, had temporarily suffered under looking after George. She felt bound to do no more than hint at business of her own in town. Instead she gave Fraser a hastily written letter from Sophy and pretended not to be there while he read it.

When he was finished he looked up. 'Is this all?' – though in fact he couldn't have said what it was he expected.

'I don't know what Sophy may have written you. But she can have no particular news.'

There was a silence. Kate could see Fraser wasn't feeling conversational. It occurred to her that the change from intense endeavour to idleness without end might have affected him more than anyone could guess. She had travelled for two days, however, to be in London; and politeness demanded they each say something more before she left.

'Have you had any visitors?'

286

'No; no visitors – do sit down,' offering the only chair. Fraser sat down on the bed. He looked crouched and patient, as though resigning himself to await her next question with due courtesy.

'Are there any errands I could do?'

'No, thank you.'

'Can't you be supplied with anything more – with some coals, or something?' The room was chilly enough for their breath to be visible.

'I prefer not. It could only be done at my wife's expense, one way and another. And she's suffered trouble enough by marrying me.'

Another silence, which Kate passed by examining the fit of her gloves. At length she said, 'Sophy never tells me what she's written you, of course ... But has she mentioned the people with an interest in seeing your debt redeemed? My uncle Norton, and Sir William Barrington – and Mr Rennie –'

'Don't talk to me of release,' said Fraser in a quiet voice, his eyes averted. 'I know I should be glad there might be business concerns on my side, as well as ordinary good intentions.' He paused. 'If I were due to be taken out and hanged – or even if they told me I was here for so many dozen years – I could make up my mind not to care. But being teased by thoughts of hope – that's more than I could bear. I'd prefer it if you didn't mention my employers. Or their clients.'

But beyond Fraser's work, and her own sister, Kate could think of little he might want to talk about. She gave him her address, at the George, up near London Bridge; asked his advice on cheaper lodgings; and decided it would be tactful to leave. 'Shall I tell you, when I expect to go home?' she asked, rising.

Fraser looked up as if startled from sleep. 'Yes – yes; please do,' he said, getting to his feet with sudden restlessness. 'I'd be grateful if you'd carry a letter to Sophy – if she's not in London by then.' He opened the door for her, and said, 'I hope you'll forgive me if I can't receive you as I should. The fact is, until I get used to living here, and

287

not being allowed outside the gate, I'm bound to be rather bearish.'

Kate understood well enough to smile as she gave him her hand. She promised to visit him once more before leaving, and made her way back; down corridors long enough to be tainted with fog; through the lost souls outside, anxious or resigned; and past the great gate, safely into the world of traffic, work, and normal life.

Back at the inn there were letters, and a message. A note from Underwood told her, 'A friend – though no discredit should be given him – could in fact help by supplying Miss Michaelmas' address. I dare hint,' the message continued, 'that Miss Michaelmas will perhaps be more helpful than at first – I cannot tell how I should write this – she might appear.' While Kate doubted the existence of the 'friend' she was all too moved by Underwood's readiness 'to do any service, no matter what, for poor Byford. Or failing that, for his family.' To overlook the hint of dreadful finality in such words, she opened the next letter as quickly as she could.

Her eyes had been pricked with tears of melancholy as she did so. A quick glance – and now they flowed as freely as could be. Not from sadness but, as she read Sophy's news of George, from every feeling that made up pure relief. For a while she could only walk up and down sobbing from gladness, lacking nothing but someone she could tell. What if George, recovering, had lapsed again, into deep depression? His life was safe and, for the moment, that was all that mattered.

In time she read on. The rest, typical of Sophy, was a postscript longer than the letter itself. She wrote: 'Yet another person is concerned that James should be "put back to work, where I need him". But whether his calling on us here is good or bad; why, that, dear Kate, is something only you can answer. Can you guess ...?'

Kate had no need to. Before she had even opened Sophy's letter the message in her hand, in the form of a visiting card, had told her. The caller at the house in Parsonage Lane would have been Joseph.

On the whole, she told herself, she was sorry. She could understand why it was in Joseph's business interests to concern himself with the progress of the waterway. But she wished he could do so without using her – since that must be his object – as some kind of go-between. There was nothing to do, she decided, but not think about him. To which end she sat down, her head and heart full of everything at once, and spent an absurdly long time writing to present her compliments at the address given her by Underwood.

Vine Cottage, in Prospect Place, stood in the rural suburb of Knightsbridge. This was one of those half-and-half areas where London proper was just visible across the fields, as a low horizon of roofs and trees – yet showed itself in smart new villas along every byway. The house where Charity now lived was nothing like the real cottages thereabouts, which were mostly cabins one storey high with uneven crinkly-tiled roofs. It was a comfortable stuccoed pretence of one, discreetly sheltered behind a high garden wall. The solid front door was graced by a fanlight; and there were two storeys of pretty bay windows on either side.

An iron bell-pull hung by the front gate. Kate rang, and listened for sounds from the other side. A maidservant appeared. Seeing Kate, she opened the gate wide enough for her to slip through, before reaching up to bolt it again. Kate followed her up a short path, into a quiet hallway and thence to a sitting room with a view over a recently made lawn. The place bristled with shiny new furniture, and cushions that defied you to leave a dent in them. Most of it looked unnecessary, as though the side-tables and what-not stands were the real inhabitants, and humans only lived there by accident.

After a minute or so Charity Michaelmas came in. The first thing about her that struck Kate was her face. Not the presence of a family likeness – though there was that – but just the transparent-seeming bloom and purity of line. Kate wondered where she'd seen the same quality of beauty before. Of course! she thought. In the mirror, you idiot.

Like the room, Charity was got up at some cost. Kate recalled that she had known her by sight for as long as she could remember. Yet she found it almost impossible to identify the self-possessed young courtesan before her with the little swineherd from Cannings Fitzpayne.

Charity acknowledged Kate without speaking, and sat facing her across the room. Kate felt painfully disadvantaged. Having invited herself here as a stranger, she had almost no idea what to say.

'My sister writes me that George is still recovering. He speaks of you – just as he did when his condition was serious – so ... I thought you might want news of him, too.'

'I'm glad he didn't die. It would have been stupid, over me, wouldn't it?'

Sidestepping Charity's unanswerable question, Kate said, 'I hope it's not inconvenient for me to visit here.'

'No, I'm allowed a day to myself every week.' She noticed Kate look at her overblown satin gown and added, 'My employer only likes me dressed like this. And besides, I don't have to do any work, do I?'

'Does he live here?' Kate was absurdly vague in her notion of a love-nest, so called.

'No; he keeps me here separately, the same way he keeps his hunters out at Croydon.' It was impossible to tell if this was said in bitterness or not.

'Is he an agreeable man?' said Kate, at a loss for something tactful. Beside Charity's calm worldliness she felt both patronizing and inexperienced.

'He only calls once or twice every week,' Charity said, as if this answer served. 'But he pays a thousand a year so he can tell his acquaintance he keeps me here. By the time he gets too used to me I shall be able ... ' She stopped, listening. A woman's voice could be heard upstairs; then the sound of a fretful child.

'So the baby lives with you?'

'I have her here once a week. Should you like to see her?'

The nursemaid was rung for and the little girl brought in. Charity took her on her knee, adjusting the exquisitely worked baby clothes with an indifferent look of efficiency. The child, who had been asleep, was just old enough to sit up on her own. She yawned, and rubbed her little fists around her eyes. In her embroidered cap she looked like a pretty animal taught to imitate human beings by a trick.

Watching her, they were silent. Both were thinking of George, whom already she resembled. At length Kate, cursing herself for not knowing how to come to the point, said, 'May I give George your love? He'd do the same by you. That is ... if he knew you wouldn't mind ...' She found herself blushing violently. Her gentility had never been such a handicap.

'He don't have to send his love out of duty to me,' said Charity, lapsing, with a note of fierceness, into her old Wiltshire voice. 'He ain't that close kin of mine.' Seeing Kate look questioning she said, 'He' – pointing at George's child – 'thinks this one was conceived in incest, doesn't he? Isn't that what you want to know?'

'Yes. He can't bear it! On top of everything he has to answer for. And if you'd heard the things he said – if you'd heard – in his delirium – you'd know why I can't bear it either. Because he thinks you're our sister –'

'And why should he think that?' Did Charity's voice hold amusement, indifference or scorn?

'The likeness? Between you and me?'

'Because he finds he's done me wrong, that's why! Because I'd be on his conscience anyway. But if he's anxious for the truth, there's no reason why I shouldn't look like them at the Hall, neither.'

'Who –?'

'Old Fart-Face himself, of course.'

'His lordship?'

'Him, yes. My mother was a bailiff's daughter. She's still alive, somewhere.'

'But ... we still resemble each other.'

'So we should. You think them Fitzpaynes haven't ploughed and sown on anyone of yours? Not your mother, I'll grant you. Nor hers. But your father's mother –'

291

'Grandma Byford? But she was such a pious woman –'
Kate stopped, and bit her lip from vexation with herself.

'I dare say she were – afterward. It takes a lot of
women that way, being caught with a bastard,' Charity
said, with a look that Kate found hard to meet. 'His
lordship's father, though, he had her, all right. Only once,
maybe. But that's all it takes, ain't it?'

'But I never knew any of this.'

'And whose business do you think it was to tell you?
Seeing as you were family.'

'Who told you who your own parents were?'

'All kinds of people. Once they'd got word of your
brother. Not all of them meant that well – why should
they? I dare say I disappointed some, when the man
who'd got me with a bastard couldn't be proved my own
kin.'

Kate recalled Underwood's letter, and its embarrassed
hint. 'Was Mr Underwood one of those people?'

'Him? Oh, yes. I heard he'd been asking questions, of all
sorts of folk.'

'I think *that* may have been kindly meant.'

'Oh, aye. He's a lout of course. But there are many
worse.' Charity hesitated. 'And it was *him* too.' She indicated the room and its contents, as if every expensive
knick-knack personified her employer. 'He'd known
already. It was his valet, see, who'd told him – who knew
about me, on account of having served his lordship
himself. *He*,' gesturing again at their surroundings, 'said to
me "I made a vow," he said, "that one day *I'd* have a man
who'd worked in a family of rank and title. And now I've
not just got Lord Fitzpayne's valet, but," ' her eyes
holding Kate's in a steady gaze, ' "I've fucked his
daughter, too!" He's new gentry, see; he made his own
fortune, in trade.'

Kate steeled herself, blush how she would, to return
Charity's look without a blink. 'Your employer?'

'That's right ... So now you know everything you
wanted to, don't you?' Frowning, Charity made another
absent-minded adjustment to the baby's clothes. The child
began to wriggle and whimper, and the nursemaid was

292

sent for again to take her away. It seemed the interview was at an end.

Kate stood up to go. 'But may I, after all, tell George you send your love? If only because he really is a relative of yours?'

'T'ain't no business of mine what you say. You can tell him what you like; I'll not mind.'

'At least let me say you don't hate him!'

'Very well. I don't hate him.'

Against reason, Kate still hesitated. Anything to break the frigid self-possession of this girl whose hardships had left her so unapproachable. 'Whatever kinds of men you've had to know, even you haven't the right to think ill of George. Good God, he nearly died for you! What more could you ask?'

Charity rose and advanced to within a few inches of where Kate stood. Her face was sombre and tense. 'When I was a street beggar, do you think I told myself I was unhappy? When I was the kind of whore who bargains in the public highway, do you think I hated what I did? If so, you'd be a fool. No one can live that way for long if they're reluctant,' pronouncing the last word with angry distinctness. 'Only now – since I gained the rank of a kept woman – only now can I afford not to like what I've done. And when I've earned enough to leave off living here, who knows if I won't feel dislike for every man I've ever had!'

'Then there's nothing else to say.' Kate turned to open the door.

But Charity was there before her. 'I'm not done yet – that's not everything I meant to tell you.'

'What, then?' said Kate, mistaking Charity's briskness for indifference.

'I don't hold anything against your brother. If you like, I can say better than that. You can tell him, if you wish, that I wouldn't dream of despising him. It's true I don't ever want to see him – but not for any reason you could guess ... You don't understand me, do you?'

'Indeed I do.'

'No you don't. I expect you think I'm just angry –

never mind with who or what. But that's not what I mean. I meant to say, when you live the way I do, you don't have different feelings for different men. If I were fool enough to like one man better than another – well, what's to stop me having dislikes, too? And then where would I look for business?'

'Yes. Yes, of course,' said Kate, now really anxious to leave. She dreaded hearing any more confidences. It would be unbearable, after all, to know that anyone as hard-tried and strong as this might yet break down and confess all. 'I can guess how you feel,' she said. 'Indeed I can.'

'Don't be so stupid. Of course you can't.' Charity reddened. But her voice was still as quick and firm as if she felt not a thing. 'Give him – give your brother – my ... greetings. Regards. Compliments. Whatever you like. But I don't want to see or hear from him as long as I live. Not on any terms. Because if I did, God knows which of us would get the worst of it.'

Chapter Sixteen

One by one, every familiar sight was sinking from view. The London Mail had rumbled and slithered to the summit of the road out of the Vale, and the near horizon was rising up, ready to blot them all out. Cannings Fitzpayne, from up here, was just a thicker group of elms amid the pattern of hedgerows, with only the square church tower still visible, and a curve of the lake below the Hall.

Inside the coach, Sophy was thinking of her wedding day. She remembered wondering, above all, when her marriage would properly begin. Now, at last, she thought she knew. It was here, going away from home for good. Today was the day that should be celebrated as an anniversary; not that morning so many months ago when she'd gone through the marriage ceremony in a trance of panic.

To be sure, *then* she'd hoped to be prosperous, whereas now she was a pauper. Even so, she felt more cheerful.

Gone were all the doubts of those frightening weeks just before and after she had so rashly tied James' life to hers. So too was her former bewildered sense of outrage, last time she'd found herself suddenly poor. Meanwhile she looked down at Upstowe's tight motley of roofs around the main square and the tall church spire, and caught the first inkling of how fondly – after all her discontents! – she was destined to remember all this. Swiftly the Vale fell away from sight, until even the white horse carved on the far downland had vanished, as thoroughly as if the coach were a ship falling off the edge of the world. When the last distant horizon had quite disappeared, Sophy ceased to look out of the window, and turned her thoughts away from home, toward the place she was bound for.

Not only had she no more doubts about her marriage; she was also free of regrets. In seeking freedom, she had ended by making *this* journey. Yet not a hint of her former desperate self remained. In travelling to be with her husband, she felt she was not going to prison so much as making a pilgrimage. It was with a kind of sombre pleasure that she now recalled how she had come to think of herself as really being James' wife. Not just according to the law, but in her own heart.

In that dreadful time between betrothal and marriage, when everything was going forward despite her own secret fears, how she had hoped that none of it was really happening! That *something* would prevent the wedding day. Liking James had only made it worse; part of her wretchedness, she now saw, had been because she was eaten up with guilt. What could be less forgivable, after all, than taking the love of a good man without knowing whether she could return it?

And all along, without her knowing, another feeling had been at work in her. Lust. Sophy could even say the word to herself, now that she properly understood its meaning. She shuddered inwardly – then gave a broad smile behind her veil – and as suddenly lapsed again into a frown. In her ignorance, it had so nearly led her astray – and yet, she realized, it had been one of the things that had brought her to marry James. How little she had deserved her good fortune in marriage! Why, he could have turned out to be any kind of man!

So she mused, as the winter sun rose before them, and passed them in the other direction as it climbed through its feeble zenith. The brook in whose valley they now drove grew, from a clear trout-stream along each village street, to a river set with marshy islets of alder trees and big enough to carry the odd reed-cutter in his punt; then, as its course joined and rejoined the canal, it became broad enough to bear barges going down to Newbury, en route for the distant Thames, and London. As the hours went by, Sophy sat, barely noticing when the signposts had ceased to point back at anywhere familiar. She only knew that with every mile that passed, she was taking another step away from childhood, and deeper into love and the hardships of marriage. Had it not been for George, she could even have thought of Rawley Fitzpayne without rancour. After all, it was only when she'd come close to losing her husband, on account of Fitzpayne, that she started to see her marriage for what it might be worth.

The first day's journey drew to an end, as they approached Newbury. The town itself was crowded, on account of the nearby races; and hundreds of vehicles, and thousands of people, packed its streets. Despite her anxiety to reach her destination, Sophy was dead tired. A hundred yards from the next change of horses, they were held up by the traffic for twenty full minutes, and the sound of the crowds roared about her like water about to close over a drowning man's head. It was more than she could face, to travel right on, all night and more. Accordingly, arrived at last within the yard of the White Hart, she had her luggage taken down, resolved to seek a bed.

To pay for a lodging was of course out of the question. Sophy knew however that she should have little trouble in working for one. Finding her way to the kitchen of the great inn, she sought out the landlady. 'Do you need a maid, ma'am? For one night's supper and a bed?'

The landlady, besieged with extra customers on account of the races, looked like a general directing a battle from the foremost rampart. Having glowered at Sophy for distracting her attention, she hired her immediately, too glad of more help to take much notice of the girl's genteel appearance and smooth hands.

Doing as bid, Sophy took off her outdoor things and got straight on with helping to set the long tables in the dining room. This, like every other part of the building, was crowded today. As she entered and set down her tray of utensils, more than a few glances came her way. It was what she expected, of course; even among people she knew it was impossible someone of her beauty should not move among admiring looks as if through air itself. She had changed inwardly, though, a great deal since the time when she could not endure to be seen going about Cannings Fitzpayne on humble domestic errands. So it hardly occurred to her that people were also staring because she looked so little like a chambermaid.

Parties of pleasure, from the racecourse, made up most of the evening's custom; and Sophy was not surprised to see, standing amid one such gathering, Rawley Fitzpayne.

She ignored him, all the while hoping her menial status would make him do the same to her. Only an unnecessary energy in her movements, as she worked her way up the room, showed how hateful she found the sight of him, now that he was actually before her again. Out of the corner of her eye she watched him. He looked both restive and morose, as if every horse he'd backed that day had led by a length only to break its neck at the final fence.

But though she was only a servant, so that the presence of ladies in his party should have made it impossible to acknowledge her, still he could not leave her be. Across a distance of some feet, 'The fair Mrs Fraser!' he exclaimed with mock surprise. 'So this is what they mean by being safely married. Mrs James Fraser. Well, God damn my soul to hell!'

'No doubt He will, Mr Fitzpayne,' Sophy said, moving away to finish her chore elsewhere.

Neither had raised their voices much; but people were looking at them from several parts of the room. She wondered if she should seek shelter at some other hostelry, in case he told the landlady she had been uncivil.

But outside in a passageway, he caught up with her. Barring her way, he seized at the empty tray she was carrying. 'Now then –' he said, as she tried in vain to hold onto it. Unable to go back to the kitchen empty-handed, she waited to hear him out.

Looking hard at her, to pretend seriousness, he said, 'You don't have to come to this.'

'Indeed?' without a trace of interest.

He groaned with what she was supposed to see as angry impatience. 'See here, woman, I'm trying to help you!'

'I doubt it.'

Rawley softened his voice and bent closer to her. 'You know you want me to.'

She was silent, filled with misgiving.

He tried a new line of persuasion. Looking past her, he sighed with exasperation, paused, turned his eyes on her again and said, in a low voice, 'Who knows but you underestimate me in more ways than one. *Mr* Fitzpayne, you said. How can you be so certain that his lordship – his *old* lordship – still lives?'

'If he might be dead, is that why you're on a voyage of pleasure?'

'Come now, Sophia! Would you mourn for such a man? ... I mean to perform a favour for you' – moving closer and lowering his voice to a murmur – 'whether you will or not. Only consider this. The minute my uncle is dead – *then* how closely do you think my affairs will be linked with your husband?'

The question was needless, as he knew it would be. Nonetheless he paused, to let her think on everything it implied. Sophy looked down, avoiding his eyes. But though her face was closed, her mind was darting every-where at once.

He spoke for her. 'A stroke of the pen – nothing more. It would take me no more than that, to return your husband to the world ... how many years earlier? Does even he know that?'

Again he waited. And watched, as she looked up at him, fighting to hide the hope that surged – oh, how painfully! – within her.

'Of course, I should need your help.'

'How?' was the exclamation that so nearly sprang to her lips. In the nick of time Sophy came to her senses, and cursed herself for a fool, that she hadn't understood at once what it was he was after. As swiftly as her heart had blossomed with thoughts of freedom, she felt it blasted by the cynicism of what, she knew, he had in mind.

Confidingly he said, 'You will come to my room to discuss it.' He squeezed her arm, and murmured, 'We both know you will.'

If she pretended she'd co-operate, would he let her pass? She braced herself to look him in the face again. 'When?'

He pointed up the stairwell to his door. 'At nine. Don't forget – I shall be doing this for you.'

It was only as the night drew on, and Sophy, having supped, retired to the attic room allotted to her, that she had time to stop and think.

She was not at all surprised that Rawley Fitzpayne still wanted to wheedle her into his bed. What if his family had helped to ruin her husband, and he himself had nearly murdered her brother? All the more reason for him to triumph, could he still succeed in compromising her.

The minutes passed, and her anger grew. She was not enraged so much by Fitzpayne himself; as a despicable man, he was only behaving as she would expect. But to think that the Fates themselves should be so cruel – that they should let anybody tempt her so!

It had cost her more than she had realized, to accept a life of hardship and imprisonment. While it seemed inevitable, she could have faced it without a thought. But now . . . Oh, how could she have let this happen to her? Why hadn't she just stayed on the coach?

James need never know. The thought leaped out at her before she could stop it. Anything could explain the change of heart that would have made Fitzpayne set him free. And suppose he did find out? No – no; oh, please God, don't let me think about that. But if he did? Say, if he suspected? She couldn't see him admitting what he thought – scorning to accept his release. What – deliberately choosing to return to prison? Never!

To secure a future for both of them – it might only take a few minutes. But if she did nothing: what then? Through every other moment of the wretched years that lay ahead, still she might find herself regretting the opportunity she'd lost.

How could anyone think of doing something so rash? Yet hadn't rashness served her well in the past? She had leaped into marriage without knowing what she did, and in the end she had not repented of that.

An hour went by; and still Sophy sat on the edge of her bed without moving. There was no knowing how long she might have stayed there, getting colder by the minute, but that a message was brought to her, 'to attend the gentleman in the front first-floor suite,' said the maid who delivered it, with a knowing look.

So, her dilemma was solved. If he was going to hound her, then, no matter what, she would rather die than oblige him. Only after some moments did she realize that the message was not from Fitzpayne at all, but from the set of rooms next to his. Another man, but clearly with the same intention. Whoever he was, she wished him, too, in hell.

But now that Sophy was stirred from her panic-stricken lethargy, she couldn't bear any longer to do nothing. Supposing she thought of something else on the way – if she hurried – she could still bear to go to Fitzpayne's room. She opened the door and stepped outside.

As she walked – more slowly than she'd meant – down the first flight of stairs toward her destination, another feeling took her by surprise. Only now, as she strove to keep all thought of her husband out of her mind, did her rage turn to sadness. She found herself murmuring his name, over and over again.

Why did she have to think of him with such tenderness now, of all times? Because it was for love of him that she was doing this. Every step seemed a league, but still she went on, out into the yard and across to the front part of the building. People ran to and fro outside – the mails would be passing through all night – but to Sophy it all seemed as remote as if behind a sheet of glass. Only thirty yards to go – and now the thought of her husband, so far from being a reproach, was all she could bear to hold in her mind. She went on repeating his name to herself, as the only thing that would give her courage to cuckold him. And came within sight of Fitzpayne's door.

Sophy stopped. She might have arrived. But did that mean she'd made up her mind, even now?

Any delay would serve – anything!

What did that other man want?

As if she need ask!

Fitzpayne wanted to be the first to debauch her.

Well, he wouldn't be! *And* she would tell him so.

Perhaps it was really a blessing, that another man had approached her, too. If she must become Fitzpayne's whore, she told herself, tapping at the stranger's door, it was easier this way. Better to be bedded, the first time in adultery, with a man you'd never seen, than with someone you knew and loathed.

There was a call to enter, and she went in. A middle-aged man got up from a desk deep in papers and advanced to shake her hand. Such formality, she remembered George whispering once, was indeed the rule in the better houses of ill-fame. Now that she had acted, however disastrously, she could actually feel a thrill at the peril she was in. Almost with perfect self-possession, she sat down, as straight-backed as she could, on the chair he offered, and waited to hear his proposition.

That same evening, as Kate, in her new lodging at a house in Oxford Street, was calculating the hours before Sophy's arrival, there was a knock at her sitting-room door. It was the landlady's parlourmaid, come to announce a visitor. Kate already had some idea who to expect. So she could look quite calm when in a few moments Joseph Lee walked in.

Even so, they were embarrassed to see each other. It was as well that in exchanging greetings they both had commonplaces to utter. They remained standing – it seemed the most natural thing – a little distance apart on either side of the fireplace.

'I'm grateful that you should see me.' Joseph threw his hat onto a chair with an unconvincing show of self-posses-sion. Thrusting his hands into his pockets, he turned to look at her as if bracing himself.

'I thought it might be important. You must have trav-elled some days to get here from Liverpool.' Even after all this time, Kate couldn't help sounding churlish.

'I have to be in the south of England in any case. But it may be important.'

'Oh? ... Please sit down,' recalling herself and taking a chair opposite him. He stayed where he was, frowning at her with an expression of which the strongest part was curiosity. Kate noticed he looked older, as well as more sombre. Had his widowhood, as rumoured, bruised him after all?

Steeling herself to say what she had to, she remarked, 'I hope my uncle Norton passed on my condolences. It seemed best not to write direct.'

'Yes. It was good of you.'

There was a silence. Glancing at Kate while he thought she was looking elsewhere, Joseph said, 'I wanted to see you on business. Since you hadn't objected to receiving me.'

'Is it to do with James?' Kate asked, anxious to turn the subject away from herself. 'I know you said you were a shareholder in the canal.'

'A customer, too. And an important one. Has your brother-in-law heard anything himself about his chances of release?'

'I think not. In any case he seems resolved not to hope. I doubt he's adaptable enough to make the best of things without a struggle.'

'Of course the fellow's in distress. Thwarted effort – a great project hindered – and then the pains of boredom itself ... The fact is, I called to know if he mightn't care to know what efforts were being made on his behalf.'

'That depends on their chance of success. Is there much hope?'

'I think so. Several voices have been raised for him on the executive committee – my holdings entitle me to attend a proportion of their meetings. There's been no end of trouble over the rioting during his absence. It's mostly agreed he's the man who could have stopped it. Also Rennie refuses to take another man as a replacement –'

'Why – to persuade the committee? Would such a gesture work?'

'Oh, you'd be surprised at the flutter among the shareholders, when their best chance of a return on investment was carried off to prison. I'd never have picked up so many cheap shares had there not been something of a panic.'

'But if it's true that James might be released, when would we hear?'

'I don't know. I posted into Berkshire yesterday, to attend one of the committee's meetings. It may not have been conclusive. But I'm damned if most of them won't see the advantage of cultivating custom like mine. And *that* can only be done by putting their best man back to work.'

'If you could help, my family would be more relieved than I could say.'

Try as she would, Kate couldn't avoid sounding ungracious – and yet she looked intensely aware of him. Joseph wondered if she was just embarrassed at having once fancied herself in love with him. 'Don't thank me,' he said. 'I'm only doing what my business dictates.'

What should he make of such neutrality? In resolving to see her again, his rather limited imagination had pictured only smiles of gladness, or fierce hostility. 'I don't care,' he went on, 'to continue importing all the way to London by sea. Even if the French allow me through the Channel, as an American, it still calls for a wind from three different quarters. And transport by road from Bristol is out of the question in wartime; the shortage of horses has increased the price of haulage to six guineas a ton.' Without noticing what he did, he had picked up a volume of poetry Kate had left face down on a table, and was flattening it open until the binding cracked. 'Of course, if the canal were

303

complete, I'd still have to use some part of the Thames –
and that's bound to be inferior to a man-made waterway.
But even so, my costs would be reduced by two-thirds.'

Kate knew he was talking simply to cover his own
unease. She felt a pang of wounded triumph that he
should risk an angry scene in order to see her once more.

'There is of course one man,' he said, 'who's able to do
far more for your brother-in-law than I ever could.'

'Who?'

'Why, your despotic local princeling, Lord Fitzpayne.'

'Him! How on earth should he do that?'

'By dying sooner. I fancy *that* might put a different
price on the land he's so keen to dispute.'

'Yes. That would be considerate of him – but only if he
had a different heir.'

'Different from whom? I thought the succession was in
doubt. Or so I heard in the village.'

'But even if he weren't dying – he can't produce an heir
now.'

'The rumour went that that might have been his final
deed.'

'Poor man!' said Kate, breaking into laughter despite
herself.

'Poor woman, surely?'

'For the chance of inheriting all that? Don't be absurd!'
she said, trying to smother her sudden cheerfulness. She
was angered to be smiling back at Joseph; it made her feel
untrue to herself. 'Anyway, one couldn't quote innyard
tattle at James as evidence that he could soon go free.'

'Good God, no. I've nothing to offer beyond good
intentions in any case. And as a stranger, I don't think
that justifies calling on the man in person ... I must go.'

'Whatever you say,' she told him when they were both
at the door, 'I'm sure it was kind of you to call.'

Her voice trembled. He gave her one more deeply
inquisitive look. There was no doubt he was a steadier, if
more troubled, man than when she'd first known him.
'Don't misunderstand me,' he said. 'I don't mean to ask
forgiveness for misleading you as I did. I'm sure it would

only try your patience – and humiliate me – for nothing. Do you see?'

She nodded, unable to meet his eyes. It had been a struggle not to be happy in his company. Yet it was also costing her cruelly not to look surly and bruised.

'Right,' he said. 'Goodbye.'

Kate had only arranged to spend a few days in London. Yet, between doing what she'd meant to, she hadn't guessed that time could pass so wearily. In town, it seemed, there were no amusements for an unaccompanied female apart from reading, sewing or going to church. Sunday was the worst day. Then, the miles of stony streets fell empty of everything but the tolling from hundreds of church bells. They rang out, plaintive or thunderous, from the east, across a five-mile dead forest of smoke-festooned chimneys; and from as far west as the built-up villages of Marylebone and Bayswater.

But it was also, as Kate hoped, nearly the last day of her visit. Two mornings after Joseph had called, as she was wondering what useful task could possibly pass the time till Sophy's arrival, there were noises outside the door – and Sophy herself burst in unannounced.

Kate sprang to her feet and looked in delight at her sister, who was laughing with pleasure at having finally arrived.

It would be ridiculous to ask if Sophy were better since Kate had seen her last. Her hair gleamed almost as bright as her eyes; and from the silvery-fair column of her throat to the smoothness of her brow, she was flushed with pleasure just to be alive. 'Oh, Kate!' she exclaimed, embracing her sister, 'how wonderful everything is! Here I am – and I have such news for you. Everything is going to be so splendid!'

'What –?' asked Kate, reflecting Sophy's brightness without knowing why.

'Oh, you couldn't guess the things that have happened since I set out from home! But I mustn't dither here – James must be the first to know!'

'But – is he to go free?'

305

'Oh, yes! But there's much more than that to tell. Dear Kate, please, please forgive me – but I mustn't stay another moment now my luggage is delivered. Just tell me the way over to Southwark from here.'

In the hackney coach carrying her down to the King's Bench Prison, Sophy was too full of glee to feel impatient. All through the acres of streets, swarming as thick as if a great calamity had driven people there, she could think of nothing but seeing Fraser again. To Sophy, the city, with its million striving souls, its vistas and its glittering river choked with craft, was there just as a background to her own elation.

At the prison itself, she scarcely saw the entrance, taller than the depressing streets of yellow-brick houses sprouting all around. The inner courtyards, vast yet mean, where hundreds lingered or scurried in a pretence of being alive – all this seemed, already, like something remembered, to give delight to the present because it was gone for ever. On the stairs her heart beat so, it was as though the pleasure of reaching her destination would be too sharp to be borne. How would her husband look? What could he possibly say?

The door was opened, and Sophy ran in, reaching out to where Fraser had turned to see who it was. In his face she glimpsed her own joy, made even stronger by surprise.

– And spoiled the moment, by tumbling down on the floor in a swoon.

'You're pregnant, aren't you?' Fraser asked, when she had recovered enough to open her eyes and pant for breath. He had untied her bonnet in fumbling haste, and knelt, cradling her in his arms. His first shock of delight was gone, banished by apprehension.

'Of course I am,' she croaked. She tried to move, but her head fell back. He held her closer, for fear she should look at him and guess how panic-stricken he was. It was several seconds before he could think what to say. 'Darling, you're not to be afraid.'

'Of what?'

'We'll find some way of providing for you.' He gathered resolution enough to look her in the face with a show of reassurance. 'I know you've married a useless bankrupt. But I promise I won't let you suffer for it. Neither you nor our child.'

'But, James –' Sophy tried again to move. But she had little more strength than a doll. She gave a feeble smile; then the tears broke from her. From gratitude, from love, from relief and tenderness – and from frustration at having failed to make herself understood. For a few moments she could do nothing but laugh and cry and let him dry her eyes.

At length she was recovered enough for him to help her sit up. 'My reticule ...'

'Smelling salts? Are there some of those in here?' he said, handling the little embroidered bag with a husband's unease at the female mysteries it held.

'No, silly. The letter!'

'For me?'

'Who else? From Mr Rennie. I called on him at Newbury. Oh, quick, quick – do open it, or I shall die. Or at the very least I'll have to tell you myself what it says.'

With an anxious glance of bewilderment at his wife, Fraser took the letter and opened it.

My dear Fraser,

It has been the damndest roundabout business you can conceive of. But justice and the welfare of your own concerns have prevailed. I could not have said, before today, how things might go. But, thank God, the Committee has been bludgeoned at last into knowing its own interests. The upshot being that the Company shall discharge its debts for itself, and your release must follow within hours.

My dear fellow, for the world I would not make light of your hardships; much less those of your wife. But I cannot doubt a fragment of them should have been worthwhile, could you have heard how you have been spoken of before the Committee. Let me not name the dolts among our employers; suffice it that the gentlemen in question might never have brought such trouble on you, had they listened sooner to Sir William Barrington's American, Joseph Lee. (I had told them that cultivating custom instead from Leggatt would not prove justified. It seems, bye the bye, that the fellow will be lucky not to change places with you ere long.)

May I be permitted, meanwhile, to rejoice for my own sake as well as for yours? I hope to make plain to you how highly your services are valued by the Company. But I should not presume to think you bear them *the same goodwill. What, then, can I say that will persuade you to remain in their employ? I do not wish to try your patience with more regrets. So may I venture a guarantee instead? The Fitzpayne land now looks set to come within our means. It may be that this very day his lordship passes on, to bluster at whatever lot his Maker intends for him. And it seems young sir may not inherit after all. The estate may go not to an heir, but to the prospect of one – since it is now certain that her ladyship grows, as they say, apace. And, as she is set fair to favour us at worst with her indifference, we can be hopeful of a proper price.*

Before sitting down to write this, good fortune gave me the chance, while at the White Hart, of seeking out an acquaintance with your wife. Nothing I might do for you has pleased me quite so much as being able to repair her fortunes at first hand. And as for the matter of your employment, I suspect I cannot do better than ask Mrs Fraser to petition you on my behalf.

Who would ever remain, etc.

Sitting beside him on the bed, Sophy watched Fraser as he read. His own thankfulness, she knew, must be greater, even, than hers. Yet as he finished, he showed no sign of it. He dropped the letter on the floor and turned to her. His expression, from being intent, seemed pained. At first she failed to understand. Then, putting his arms around her in a rush, he hid his face against her neck; and sobbed out loud at the relief of knowing both of them had had so many years of life restored.

Chapter Seventeen

'Kate,' said Sophy one evening later that week, 'shall you mind this dinner very much?'

They were in Kate's room in the Oxford Street lodgings, which they were all sharing for the few remaining days in town. Kate was dithering over what to wear. Sophy, already dressed for dinner, was sitting on the bed to wait for her, all tenderly wrought perfection in a new low-cut muslin gown with gold embroideries.

'I don't mind at all,' said Kate. 'Even without you and James, I shouldn't feel ill at ease.' At Fraser's invitation, Joseph was to spend the evening with them. 'Besides, if I didn't like the company you chose, I could always have left early for home... Which jewellery should I wear in my hair?'

'Oh, I think none. Here now, put on your silvery silk – I'm sure that suits you best of all.' In her newly restored prosperity, Sophy was far more the elder sister than Kate herself had ever been. 'And then I'll help you put up your hair.'

Kate submitted in silence – all that day she hadn't been very talkative. She sat down at the cheval-glass, and Sophy tied and hooked her gown for her and brushed her hair with long firm strokes. Both said nothing for a while, observing in the mirror the splendour of their combined beauty. 'How extraordinary,' Sophy remarked, when they were ready, 'that we should both be so good-looking. In most families with daughters, there's always supposed to be one in particular who's prettiest.'

'Mm,' agreed Kate, gazing past the candlelight at their likenesses. Certainly, seeing them there, like a melody varied within one masterpiece, it seemed a little absurd that Nature should make two versions of the same excellence.

Sophy, of course, was destined never to tell anybody one reason for her being in such splendid looks. All her

life, she thought, she would treasure that moment when
the chaise had carried her out of the yard at the White
Hart. Never, in the stupidest moment of infatuation, had
she been so pleased to see Rawley Fitzpayne. Hastening
out onto the gallery in his shirt-sleeves, he had looked so
foolish with astonishment that for an instant she thought
he might call out...

The little 'prentice parlourmaid came in, to announce
that Joseph was downstairs.

'Good heavens!' said Sophy to her sister, '– and James
isn't back. I know Mr Lee's not perfect – but he isn't
early, is he?'

'I think not,' Kate replied in a subdued voice, taking out
her watch. 'Shall we go down?'

'Oh no; don't let's do that. I mean – he won't want to
see both of us alone. I should feel silly sitting there with
you and him. Let just one of us go.'

'*I'm* not going to skulk up here on his account.'

'Then I shall. Tell him I'm not ready yet.'

On the stairs Kate was met with another message. 'I'm
to tell Mrs Fraser and you, miss, that Mr Fraser says he'll
be late by half an hour.' The little maid spoke as if
repeating a lesson learned at school. 'And I'm to say, miss,
that Mr Fraser's still at the Salopian coffee house with Mr
Rennie.'

Kate felt too restless to sit in the parlour and avoid
forbidden topics. 'Shall we walk about outside?' she asked
Joseph, when she had shaken hands with him and
explained the others' absence.

The nearest open ground was Portman Square. It was
early enough to walk there safely – the lamplighter had
scarcely begun his rounds – and quieter than on the main
streets. Joseph gave Kate his arm. For the sake of saying
nothing intimate he began to tell her about his planned
return, over several months, to Richmond. Seeing she had
little to say to this, he asked, 'Do you have plans?'

'I suppose I must look for another post. I can't just
loiter at home in the village. George will leave again as
soon as he's well – he's talking of going into the army.

And Sophy and James will go too, before long. Whatever happens, I don't mean to be the one left behind.'

They walked on among the leafless saplings in the square. Above, a cold bright sky was sheened with dusk. Joseph was uncertain what to say. Kate's politeness was the least thing he wanted to see – even anger would be better. Yet what if polite indifference were all she felt? After a while, 'I wish this dinner had been arranged differently,' he said.

'How so?'

'I feel like a creditor. And others have done just as much to get your brother-in-law released.'

'James didn't invite you out of obligation.'

'Yes; I understood as much when we met, the other day.'

'Sir William Barrington, for one, would have been invited, had he been in town.'

'Oh, yes; yes. Normally, nothing could be more fitting than that Fraser and I should sit down together and drink to his success.'

She paused before asking, 'Is it because I'm here?'

His silence told her yes. Weighing his words, he said, 'I failed to do what I wanted when I last called on you.' Seeing that she didn't understand, he added, 'I did wish to find out if you were prepared to forgive me. And I still don't know.'

Nothing could be more different than his businesslike tone, and the seriousness of what he said. She wanted to put him off with a trivial answer, but dared not.

'I still don't feel indifferent to the way you put me aside.' She let go of his arm. It was impossible to tell any truths while they were close enough to feel the warmth of each other's body.

They started to stroll round another circuit on the gravelled path. 'I'm glad of it,' he told her. 'What else can I say? If I were a man of conscience, of course I'd want you not to care. As it is, my own feelings – I'm sorry; I'd leave them out of this conversation if I could – make me pleased that at least you care enough to be angry.'

To hear him speak so gravely was almost unbearable to

311

her. Half of her yearned to respond in the same way. But the rest of her trembled for fear of her own resentment. Who could tell what she might say or do, should she give way to what she really felt?

She took refuge in flippancy. 'You've been a clod-hopper, Joseph.'

The lightness in her voice exasperated him. 'Look here,' stopping where they were on the path, 'I'm sorry; I don't mean to be short-tempered. But in God's name, woman! Surely you can tell me in plain English whether you'll always hate me or not?'

Kate whipped round to glare at him. The suddenness of her response astonished both of them. 'You fool! Of course I can't tell you.' She felt as if she might choke. 'I can't feel nothing but hate. I can't feel only love. So what should I say to you? Just tell me. What am I supposed to say?'

He looked at the ground without speaking. Even in the gathering darkness she could see he was trying to appear unmoved. In a low voice he asked, 'Would you like to go back?'

She shook her head. Now that she had spoken out, it was impossible to stop. 'I wish you'd never come back. Why couldn't you have waited? I was learning to think hardly at all of what you'd done.' The realization that she couldn't hold back her tears made her more furious than ever. 'And now you come back,' with a sob, 'and ask for a display ... of everything I feel. What use is that – to anyone but you? What should I care, if being shouted at eases your self-reproach? What could look more futile, anyway, than an angry woman?' She no longer cared who might overhear, no matter how distraught she sounded.

Joseph knew better than to offer comfort or excuses. If he touched her now, she would only push him aside or even strike him. He stood, not looking at her, for the longest minutes of his life. At last Kate was done with scrubbing her eyes dry with the back of her sleeve, and walked on. He followed, careful that she should be the first to speak. Her tears had ceased; but still she gave a dry sob with every other breath.

312

The church clocks of the district began to strike the half-hour. It was nearly time to return; yet still they dawdled on in silence. In the great houses the lamps were being lit – and one or two glances had been cast at them from area steps and passing carriages.

In time, Kate could speak in a steady voice. 'I'm sorry –' she said. Purged of months of unspoken anger, she was shocked at the violence of her outburst.

'Don't say that. I won't let you humble yourself, just because I've made you lose your temper.'

They were nearly back at the gate leading toward Oxford Street. Joseph waited for her to speak once more. If she said nothing by the time they reached it, there could be no reason for them to stay. At this hour it was no longer safe, even in the West End, to walk abroad.

Kate walked on round the square, quickening her pace. 'This is difficult for me.'

'I know it is.'

'At one moment I'm shouting at you like a draggletail. And then suddenly I'm ... oh, so sorry!'

'I said: enough of that.'

'Very well. But ... Joseph, how can I promise you anything?'

'Don't. Just let me promise you.'

'I shouldn't see you for some time, should I?'

'No.'

'Good. I'm sure I wouldn't be sorry to see you if you'd just been to America and back ... Why are you smiling? I don't see why you should be amused.'

'No?'

'No, I don't.' Kate stopped walking and looked exasperated. 'Oh, you are a stupid man! Haven't you any idea how badly I want not to quarrel with you?'

'Not until now,' he said, looking even more cheerful.

'Well then ... Well, I still think it's nothing to smirk about.'

'If you say so. But then you must look solemn as well.'

'Oh dear. Oh dear. We can't go back looking like this. At least, you can if you wish. But I shall feel so silly. The

313

others will guess. And they'll see I've been crying, too. What can we possibly say?'

'Let them guess. Besides, there's nothing we can say. At least – I hope you wouldn't agree right now that we should be married.'

'Of course not. I think it's a ridiculous idea.'

'That you should be my wife?'

'No, you imbecile. That you should ask me – No; no, I don't mean that, either. I mean, it's ridiculous that I should give you an answer now.'

He looked at her, serious again. 'Please would you take my arm?' She did so, and they walked on slowly, staring in silence at the ground. In a measured voice, at length he said, 'I am prepared, you know, to wait any time for you to answer me. No – no, don't say anything. My fear is this: that if you try – for any reason – to say you love me when you still feel anger ... why, then you may repent of loving me after all. I couldn't endure that.'

She was silent for a long moment. Despite the importance of what was being said, she was finding it hard not to be swayed merely by their bodies' closeness. Eventually she replied, 'I couldn't bear it, either.' Her voice rang with calm relief. Anything was possible, after all. 'Shall we go in?'

Rawley hadn't known it would be as bad as this. Six months ago, who would have foreseen him travelling on public transport? In God's name, on the London stage, among stock-jobbers and tenant farmers.

At his lordship's funeral, no one had looked more stricken than Master Rawley. Many an onlooker had been impressed to see how the young man – so dignified in his black mourning clothes – had appeared bowed under a weight of grief. But then the possible outcome of his uncle's death was something Rawley had anticipated. What, but his own non-inheritance, might he expect, once he'd glimpsed the unbearable likelihood that his aunt was pregnant after all?

By him.

He had been seduced. There was no other word to

describe the dastardly thing that had been done to him. He'd suffered seduction, to be followed almost on the instant by the terror of a suspected pregnancy. And then by the certainty that the worst would shortly come to pass.

Lord Fitzpayne's death had been a casual event. To the end the old man had appeared quite lucid. But he'd never once moved or spoken; and his actual passing had gone unnoticed for several hours. In the days that followed, before the reading of the will, Rawley knew his fears must surely come true. It was not possible to suffer such apprehension and then find it unfounded.

So here he was, with a trunkful of possessions, and the income on two thousand pounds, rattling along frozen half to death inside the Paragon mail coach. On the hill out of Marlborough the coachman turned them out to walk, to save the horses. It began to snow. By the time they passed the Grand Avenue that ran the length of the forest of Savernake, the trunk of every tree was plastered white all down one side. Shaking the snow from his hat-brim and eyelashes, Rawley took his place again in the coach and sat dripping over his fellow passengers.

Their pace dwindled as the blizzard blew stronger. The canal, running beside them a few fields away, and the downs, with the road the drovers used, were blurred out. Suddenly, from drudging along at two miles an hour, they were in violent motion. Snorting for breath, the horses thudded into a canter, then a gallop. The snow had started to drift; and they were having to charge at a hollow to gain the other side. They reached the bottom of the dip, the horses struggling like swimmers to pull them up again. All at once the coach lurched sideways, and smacked upright again with a blow that threw the passengers into each other's arms. They had stopped.

Cursing at their indignity, Rawley looked out to see what had happened. 'Here,' he exclaimed at the guard and coachman. 'What do you think you're doing?'

'What do you think it looks like we're doing?' said the coachman, unbuckling the nearside trace on one of his team's two leaders. 'We're taking the mails on ahead,

315

aren't we? You think we can get them through on a cracked axle-tree, you just tell us how.'

'And what the devil do you mean to do about us?'

'We ain't got no orders to get you through. You travel with the mails, you take your chance.'

And, each riding one horse and leading another, he and the guard shortly set off, leaving the coach half keeled over into a ditch with its empty shafts pointing at the sky.

There was no getting out to walk while the snow continued. Soon, though, it lessened. The colourless fields grew visible; then the sun broke through, and the last flakes of snow drifted out of a brilliant sky.

Behind them came the sound of several horses driven at a smartish pace. 'Do these sound like folk who'd stop for us?' Rawley's neighbour asked.

'Shut your mouth,' said Rawley, listening. Already he guessed who it would be.

As the twenty-two horses and four carriages of Lady Fitzpayne's entourage went by, Rawley looked down to hide his face. Why hadn't that fool George Byford shot him dead?

Only one person, however, had eyes for him. Lady Augusta had also anticipated their meeting. Despite the cold her carriage window was down, all the better for her to see and be seen as she drove past the abandoned mail coach. She wore her mourning like the trophy it was. The sun gleamed on her sables and on the Fitzpayne heirloom of black pearls in her hair and around her throat and wrist.

In the time it took for all her attendants and possessions to go by, Rawley had leisure to re-live every single thing that had brought him to this. The sound of hoof-beats died away; and he and his fellow passengers, huddled like sailors shipwrecked on a rock, were left alone in a world of snowbound silence.

In Cannings Fitzpayne, throughout that winter and the months that followed, the parish, and several lives within it, continued to change. The Hall remained uninhabited by its new owner. Its shutters went up, and most of the

316

servants were transferred to the house in town. In the deerpark, what had once been unthinkable now happened: the eight-foot wall, with its belt of oaks, was breached in two places, and the last part of the waterway was begun. Meanwhile at the growth of spring into summer Sophy gave birth to a boy, resolutely braving even the fuss with which Mrs Byford relished her grandmotherhood.

Soon after the christening came an event that caused no end of excitement in the village. A wealthy gentleman was coming all the way from America to marry Miss Byford. In the local imagination this was much as if Kate had been given by treaty to a foreign prince, and Joseph was to claim her with a guard of honour and speeches from the mayor and corporation of Upstowe. Otherwise, opinion in various kitchens and best parlours held that it was thoroughly wayward of a girl with her good looks to seek so far afield for a husband.

The wedding itself, in contrast to that of Fraser and Sophy just over a year before, was the noisiest, most crowded bout of jollification anyone could remember. Even casual lookers-on could swear to the evident happiness of the bride and groom; and the splendour of the occasion almost matched up to the rumours heard about it in advance. The landlady of the Red Lion vowed that Lawyer Byford's daughter, in her wedding bonnet and gown, looked every bit as magnificent as young Lady Fitzpayne herself, the day she'd come into the village to bury his lordship. And Mrs Beddowes, who'd wondered if being a republican meant being unbaptized, had to admit the bridegroom looked every bit a Christian gentleman, even though so sunburned from being weeks at sea.

It was somehow understood that Miss Byford being borne away by a foreigner, to a place as remote as Bristol, was all to do with the canal. From now on, it was felt, all sorts of unlikely things would become as normal as a wet washday. So the villagers looked forward to goodness knew what upheavals when the local newspaper, the *Clarion*, announced that the waterway would soon be declared open along its entire length. No matter that the great event would be a day's journey away, in Bath. As the

317

Clarion put it, henceforward the sons of toil inhabiting the Vale's rural fastnesses could consider themselves as citizens of every shire and borough along the entire length of this great trunk route. Not even the finest works of antiquity, it went on to say, could vie with the new canal in linking city with city. Moreover, it had helped gladden the wilderness with the face of humankind (a reference to young Mr Fraser's navvies that went down rather badly in Cannings Fitzpayne).

So the day came, one dank then golden autumn morning, when forty thousand people put on their best clothes and turned out to make the most of the festivities. In the meadows beyond the Abbey a fairground had sprung up, with flags and green branches decorating every booth, and vast crowds came to see two oxen being roasted whole. A dais had been built on Sydney Wharf, in the heart of the city, to seat the most important personages, and space had been roped off nearby for the firing of cannon. All day the church bells were to ring out, both to mark the waterway's official opening, and in honour of the canal company's royal guest. For the occasion was to be graced by no less than the gross, dandified form of His Royal Highness the Prince of Wales.

But, amid the speeches, flag-waving, ceremonial barges, band music, cannon-smoke, free ale, loud huzzas, fireworks, bonfires and public dinners, who could claim to be the proudest and happiest person there? Perhaps, if anybody present could be said to feel pure self-satisfaction, it was Mrs Byford, as she contemplated the latest fortunes of her children.

George, now recovered from his wound, had turned out as handsome as ever he'd promised. His months of illness had left his family so much accustomed to fussing over him, that no one remembered they now valued his life in proportion as he'd made a fool of himself.

Meanwhile Kate was soon due to leave with Joseph for America. At first this had grieved Mrs Byford almost more than she could express. It wasn't the distance, however, as much as the thought of Kate setting up home beside a forest clearing in a one-room hovel made of logs. 'But,

318

mama,' Sophy told her in vain, 'Kate's going to live in Richmond, not take ship all the way up into Ohio.' In the end it had taken Sir William Barrington himself to persuade her that, compared to Cannings Fitzpayne, Richmond had if anything rather more to offer of home comforts.

It was Sophy, however, who on this particular day gave Mrs Byford most cause for self-congratulation. Never had she suspected that this wayward daughter would find herself married so well. That Sophy should get herself a husband important enough to spend a whole day at the elbow of royalty! This alone was nearly too good to be true. Yet Mrs Byford's cup came even closer to overflowing, when Sophy, in the finest bonnet on the dais, took her turn to curtsey to the Prince of Wales, all the while peeping, slightly appalled, at the lecherous Heir Apparent's rouged and powdered cheeks.

Soon, though, there was to be a last and final leavetaking at the house in Parsonage Lane. After Kate, then George, had departed, Sophy, at long last, was to leave the Vale for the larger world she'd always coveted. Meanwhile it was dreadful, her mother said, to think that she and James – to say nothing of little Thomas – should live like gypsies, even on thousands a year. Sophy should rest assured, she said, that no one in the village need find out how the three of them would lack a proper home. Sophy pretended to look serious, of course – that much tact she had learned. But nothing in her future rootless, busy life, whether in Ireland or the North Country or London, could now daunt her hopes, either for herself or for the lives of everyone she loved the most.